Aru Shah

AND THE
CITY OF GOLD

Also by Roshani Chokshi

The Star-Touched Queen
A Crown of Wishes
The Gilded Wolves
The Silvered Serpents

The Pandava Series

Aru Shah and the End of Time
Aru Shah and the Song of Death
Aru Shah and the Tree of Wishes

Aru Shah

AND THE
CITY OF GOLD

A PANDAVA NOVEL
BOOK FOUR

ROSHANI CHOKSHI

RICK RIORDAN PRESENTS

𝔇𝒾𝓈𝓃𝑒𝓎 • HYPERION   LOS ANGELES   NEW YORK

First Edition, April 2021
1 3 5 7 9 10 8 6 4 2
FAC-020093-21050

Printed in the United States of America

This book is set in Andale Mono, Arial Rounded, Burbank Big Wide, Athenaeum Pro,
FCaslon Twelve ITC Std, Teethreedee Std. Front, Clairvaux LT Std/Monotype; Adorn
Roman, American Writer, Goudy Trajan Pro, Jenson Recut, Minion Pro/Fontspring

Designed by Tyler Nevins
Ornament illustration by Keith Robinson

Library of Congress Cataloging-in-Publication Data
Names: Chokshi, Roshani, author.
Title: Aru Shah and the city of gold / by Roshani Chokshi.
Description: First edition. • Los Angeles : Disney-Hyperion, 2021. • Series: Pandava
series ; book 4 • "Rick Riordan presents." • Audience: Ages 8–12. • Summary:
"Aru Shah and her sisters—including one who also claims to be the Sleeper's
daughter—must find their mentors Hanuman and Urvashi in Lanka, the city of gold,
before war breaks out between the devas and asuras"— Provided by publisher.
Identifiers: LCCN 2020040896 (print) • LCCN 2020040897 (ebook) •
ISBN 9781368013864 (hardcover) • ISBN 9781368057202 (ebook)
Subjects: CYAC: Supernatural—Fiction. • Demonology—Fiction. • Sisters—
Fiction. • Good and evil—Fiction. • Hindu mythology—Fiction.
Classification: LCC PZ7.1.C54 Arr 2021 (print) • LCC
PZ7.1.C54 (ebook) • DDC [Fic]—dc23
LC record available at https://lccn.loc.gov/2020040896
LC ebook record available at https://lccn.loc.gov/2020040897

Reinforced binding
Follow @ReadRiordan
www.DisneyBooks.com

For Cookie & Poggle & Rat—the most perfect, devious siblings one could ask for

CONTENTS

Dear Reader,

I have a confession. What you are holding in your hands (or your ears/talons, etc., etc.) is none other than a feral, hungry… story.

"What nonsense!" you say. "Obviously it's *just* a story!"

Harrumph.

Tomorrow, I'd make sure your book is in the same place where you left it yesterday—stories are living things, after all. They're quite sensitive. There's no such thing as "just" a story, which brings me to my next point.

Like so many of the stories I have written in the past, I consider this one a living thing and believe it is important for you to know that this story's roots come from a living, active religion: Hinduism. One of the most beautiful aspects about Hindu mythology is that it is deeply intertwined with the sacred. As a practicing Hindu, I wanted to let my imagination take flight but also do my best to make sure that it doesn't stamp its feet on hallowed grounds. For that reason, the majority of the deities you will meet in these pages are those who had more prominence in the Vedic Age, starting in roughly 1500 BCE. Many scholars consider Vedism a precursor to what we might now call classical Hinduism. Deities such as Durga-Maa, Vishnu, Brahma, and Shiva will not be characters in this series.

This story is not intended to serve as an introduction to Hinduism or Hindu mythology, which is beautifully nuanced and varies from region to region. Instead, I hope you see this story for what it is: a narrow, vivid window peering out into an even brighter ocean of tales and traditions. As storytellers, we respond to what we love, and one of the things I loved most growing up was listening to my Ba tell me stories about gods, heroes, and demons. To me, this series is one long love letter.

I hope it sparks your curiosity, tickles your imagination, and, if I am so fortunate, sneaks into a corner of your heart and stays there.

With love,
Roshani

ONE

I'm Your Long-Lost Family! (Insert Jazz Hands)

Aru Shah felt like she'd been struck by lightning.

Seriously.

And she knew all about that feeling, thanks to a terrible experiment. Once, when she was extremely bored, Aru had decided to find out what being struck by lightning would feel like by using Vajra, her lightning bolt and sometime Ping-Pong ball.

"Dude, are you serious?" Brynne had said.

"I can't watch this," Mini said. "You could—"

"I'm not going to *die!*" said Aru, rolling her eyes. "I'm a demigod!"

"That doesn't mean Indra is going to protect you," said Mini, crossing her arms.

Aru tossed up the Ping-Pong ball ("Trust me, nothing's going to happen."), then knocked it higher with her forehead.

Six hours later, Aru had woken up with a splitting headache, a twitch in her left eye, and a serious case of frizzy hair.

For a week straight, it had felt like someone had played soccer with her brain. Although this could also have been because Mini kept quizzing her about geography trivia to check her "neuro-logical state."

Aru had never wanted to feel that way again.

And yet here she was, chained to a rock in the Sleeper's cave lair, feeling like she'd been electrocuted. She stared at a girl named Kara, who was crouched on the ground across from her.

I'm *his daughter*, Kara had just said.

Aru blinked, her head buzzing. "You... You're the daughter of the Sleeper?"

Kara nodded. Earlier, she'd said it with pride, tilting her chin and looking down her nose at Aru. Now, something sad and unsure crept across the girl's face. "But you're his daughter, too.... Does that... Does that make us *sisters*?"

Sisters, thought Aru. She considered Brynne and Mini her sisters, even though they weren't related to her by blood. But her and Kara? This was different. For a moment, Aru wondered whether the girl was another reincarnated Pandava brother, but that was impossible. There were only five, and they'd hit that number when they met the twins, Sheela and Nikita.

Could *we be related?* Aru wondered. Kara looked about Aru's age.... Did that make them nonidentical twins? Aru searched the other girl's features, hunting for something shared in their faces, but she couldn't find it. Kara had a wide mouth, large honey-brown eyes, straight chocolatey-brown hair that fell to her shoulders, high cheekbones, and dark, glowing skin. Aru could brush her own hair for a century and it would never look that sleek. And the closest she ever got to glowing skin was standing under a lamp and spinning really fast.

Usually she tried not to let these things bother her, but Aru knew she looked nothing like her elegant, beautiful parents.

Whereas Kara... did. But if Kara was her sister, then why hadn't Aru seen her in the Pool of the Past?

"I know what you're thinking," said Kara.

"Doubt it," muttered Aru, but Kara didn't seem to hear her.

"He was worried you'd try to run, so he made my room look like an awful dungeon," Kara said. "But it's really not that bad."

Kara tapped a nearby stone with the shiny white-gold ring on her finger. When it touched the rock, the cave walls started to shift. The space transformed into a sumptuous library with shelves carved into the stone. Near the ceiling, an enchanted orb cast the illusion of warm sunlight, and all around Aru could see little niches piled high with pillows and stacked with dolls and other toys. In the back wall of one of the niches was a half-opened door, through which Aru could glimpse a neat bed with a bright-yellow quilt and a plush bunny on the pillow.

Aru was still chained to a rock, but she forgot all about it when she saw the huge built-in screen on the opposite wall, where a Netflix box read ARE YOU STILL WATCHING?

Aru stared. How did one even find an evil lair with Internet? For a bizarre second, she pictured a demonic real-estate agent patting the stone wall: *Comes fully equipped with a crocodile-infested moat* and *complimentary Wi-Fi!*

"I'm sure you're used to a lot nicer things in the human world," said Kara quickly. "But Dad did his best."

Dad.

An ache bloomed inside Aru's ribs as memories from the past day flew back to her. The only time she had ever called the Sleeper *Dad* was when she'd thought that she and her sisters didn't stand a chance against his army. She'd hoped calling him that had hurt him as much as it had hurt her.

She could still hear the sounds of clanging swords and battle cries as they'd fought in the magical grove that belonged to Aranyani, goddess of the forest and protector of Kalpavriksha, the wish-granting tree.

Aru remembered throwing her arms around the Sleeper's neck like she was hugging him. But it was never a hug. It was a reminder of the person he could have been, of all the memories he'd sacrificed in pursuit of the tree that he'd thought could change his destiny.

Aru even remembered finding the Tree of Wishes....

But she no longer remembered whether she'd made a wish on it. When she pushed herself, all her mind could conjure was a vision of snow.

It made no sense.

Aru shook her head. She could worry about it later. Right now, she needed to find out what happened to Brynne and Mini, Sheela and Nikita, Rudy and Aiden. Were they safe? Had they gotten away? Or had the Sleeper abducted them, too?

"What am I doing here?" demanded Aru.

"He wants you to be safe," said Kara, before adding nervously, "I hope you don't mind me prying, but I know lots about you, Aru. Dad told me your mom kept you away from him."

Your mom. So Aru and Kara weren't twins. Had the Sleeper cheated on Krithika? Aru wondered. It made her stomach turn. Was that the real reason Aru's mom had put him in the lamp?

"He brought you back here so we could be a family," continued Kara.

Family. Aru flinched at the word. If her father really wanted them to be a family, he wouldn't have become a monster. But even as she thought it, an oily voice in her head whispered, *But you saw how he was forced to give up his memories, Aru Shah. You know that perhaps he could not have helped becoming what he is....*

"Where is he?" asked Aru. "Where are the others?"

"He only brought you," said Kara quickly. "And then he left again. But...he made plans before he left. His army is planning to march on Lanka by the end of the week."

Lanka? Aru knew that name. It was the city of gold ruled over by Lord Kubera, the god of wealth and treasures. The words *march on* lit a panic inside her. An invasion? So soon? The devas weren't expecting that. She needed to warn the Otherworld. And her Pandava sisters. Her *real* sisters.

Aru glanced at her wrist. What she thought had been a chain connecting her to the rock turned out to be nothing more than an illusion on a thin ribbon. Aru jerked her hand and the ribbon tore, setting her free. On her other wrist, dangling from a braided string bracelet, was a glass sphere containing Vajra in Ping-Pong–ball form. Aru slammed the sphere on the ground, and the glass shattered.

Vajra bounced up and Aru caught it one-handed. A gentle, delicious electricity immediately laced up her arms, and Aru felt the familiar static energy lift her hair a little. She jumped to her feet, eyes scanning the room.

"You can't leave!" said Kara, panicked.

"Watch me," growled Aru, hurtling Vajra against the library shelves.

Electricity spangled across the hundred-foot-high wall of bookshelves. The air boomed with thunder, and a couple of volumes went up in flames. But the wall remained intact.

"It's reinforced with enchanted rubber," said Kara. "You could burn down the whole place, but that still wouldn't get you out. Only...Only *I* can do that."

Aru whirled around. She thought Kara would look haughty as she said those words, but instead she just seemed uncomfortable, as if she wasn't used to talking to anyone. She twisted the ring around her index finger.

"If...If you want to be free," said Kara, lifting her chin, "then...then you have to make me a promise."

"What do you want?"

Kara swallowed hard. "I want you to take me with you."

TWO

LOL No

Aru stared at the other girl. "Take you *with* me? Um... no? First off, I don't know you—"

"But... I'm your sister!" said Kara. "I know you grew up alone, and you're a reincarnated Pandava, and—"

"Look. We've never met! I know my *mailbox* better than you. Second, you'll probably turn us in. I heard what you called him, and it's not exactly like he's keeping *you* prisoner here," said Aru, gesturing angrily at all the toys and books.

"It's... It's not what you think," said Kara. "I've only been here for the past two years."

Aru frowned. "Where were you before that?"

"Somewhere... bad," said Kara. Her face looked pained. "All I know is that the people who were supposed to treat me like their daughter didn't. Dad told me that he'd been locked away for twelve years—otherwise he would've found me sooner and raised me himself."

"You don't remember where you were?" asked Aru, mentally calculating Kara's age. If she was fourteen, that meant she and

Aru must have been born to different mothers and the same father in the same year. It was possible—not to mention super gross—but it didn't seem believable. Aru had seen the Sleeper's memories. He had loved Krithika Shah. All he'd wanted was to come home to her...and Aru. It didn't make any sense.

"Dad said that he didn't want me to be in pain anymore, so he erased my memories of that life. He wanted me to be happy... and I *was* for a while." Kara took a deep breath. "But then I started wondering why he never lets me leave this place. And he was never home, either. I started snooping around, and I found where he keeps his memories. It's like this glowing library hidden in the caverns, totally different from this place, and the more I saw, the more I realized he was lying to me. When he brought you here, that's when I really knew. All those times he said he was on a trip, he was secretly gathering his armies and—"

"Literally trying to end Time?" added Aru. "And steal the nectar of immortality? Oh, and kill me?"

"I'm sorry," said Kara. Her eyes shone with tears. "I bet he even made up all that stuff about being locked away—"

"Actually, that part is true," said Aru quietly. "I know that for a fact."

Aru looked carefully at Kara. The girl didn't seem to be trying to trick her.... There wasn't anything sneaky about her. Just something *lonely*. Aru realized she pitied Kara, which only annoyed her more.

"How do you know that?" Kara asked.

Aru took a deep breath. "Because I'm the one who let him out. He was trapped in a lamp."

Aru waited for Kara to yell. Or sneer. But, instead, she nodded. "I'm grateful to you."

Grateful? No one had ever been grateful that Aru had freed the Sleeper. If anything, it was one of her biggest sources of guilt. And yet it was the reason she now had Brynne and Mini as her best friends and sisters, and Nikita and Sheela as the little sisters she hadn't realized she'd always wanted. It was the terrible event that had brought magic and the Otherworld into her life, and now Aru was learning it had led to Kara being taken out of a bad situation and given a better home.

Aru's mom always said *Everything happens for a reason,* but thinking that way only left Aru more confused. What was the reason for the Sleeper turning into a monster? Or Boo betraying them? But she couldn't afford to let her mind wander there. Right now, she needed to get back home and warn the others about the Sleeper's growing battle.

"Why do you even want to come with me?" asked Aru. "You're his . . . his daughter. He'd come looking for you, and then he'd find us."

"He wouldn't be able to find *me,*" said Kara. She turned around, lifting her long hair and revealing a white circle the size of a dime on the back of her neck. "To protect me, he gave me this enchantment, which works like both a ward and a beacon. It prevents me from being tracked by gods and demons. Even Dad can't trace me when I wear it. But when he's near, it lets me know, and I can call to him if I need to. I guess he figures he doesn't have to worry about losing me. . . . It's not like I've ever left."

Aru stared around the giant library, with its false sunshine and lack of doors.

"So, what, you just stay in here all day and night?" asked Aru.

Kara shrugged, gesturing at the screen on the wall. "Tutors

call every morning to give me lessons.... And, when he's here, Dad and I explore the caverns." Kara smiled. "Sometimes he'll create a forest illusion and come up with a scavenger hunt for me. It's fun...but, you know, quiet."

And even lonelier than Aru had first imagined. All locked up without the chance to go outside? *No thanks.*

"Look, I'm sorry, but I have to go, and I can't take you with me," said Aru. "It's just too big a risk—"

"Wait!" said Kara, grabbing Aru's wrist. "What if...What if I told you that it's even a bigger risk to leave me behind?"

"What's that supposed to mean?"

"Dad calls me his 'secret weapon,'" said Kara, her words coming out in a rush. "And lately, he keeps talking about how the right time is coming soon.... I'm scared, Aru. I don't know what it means."

"Secret weapon?" Aru nervously took a step back.

"I don't know what he's talking about," said Kara. "I can't do anything. Honest. I mean, he trained me to fight, but I don't really have any special powers."

Aru's mind snagged on the word *really*. That meant she probably had *something*, but what?

"Since you came, I've accessed even more of his memories. I saw his battles...all those ruined cities...all those scared people..." said Kara softly. "I don't want any part of that—it's wrong. But he's my family, and I don't want to hurt him. I just need to stop him. But I...I don't know what else to do."

Tears ran down Kara's cheeks, and Aru felt a sharp jab in her heart.

She understood what Kara was going through. It was the ugly, swooping sensation of missing the last step on a staircase, waiting for your foot to land...and falling flat on your face instead.

Aru had felt it when she realized how much her mom had kept hidden from her. She'd felt it when she learned that her teachers, Hanuman and Urvashi, had been part of the reason her mom had trapped the Sleeper in a lamp. She'd felt it when Boo—Aru's greatest mentor, the person who'd made her think he believed in the Pandavas the most—had turned them over to the Sleeper. She *still* felt like she was falling and her feet would never touch the ground.

"You *have* to take me with you," said Kara, scrubbing away her tears with a fist. "I know what he's looking for, Aru. I'll tell you what it is if you let me go with you." A fierceness spread across Kara's face, and she kind of looked like Brynne before a fight. On Kara's hand, her white-gold ring flashed like a sunbeam. Vajra sparked in response.

Aru was dying to find out what the Sleeper was after, but she hid her eagerness from Kara. *The moment someone knows what you want, it becomes a weapon in their hands,* Hanuman had taught them.

Aru made her expression go blank. "How do I know you're not gonna go berserk on me?"

"*Berserk?*" repeated Kara. Her gaze brightened. It was like glimpsing the person Kara must be when she wasn't scared and nervous. A curious person...It made Aru think of Mini.

"Did you know that word comes from Nordic legend?" Kara went on. "*Berserkers* were warriors who wore bearskin shirts and then went kinda crazy right before charging into battle! *Berserk* comes from *ber* for *bear* and *serk* for *shirt*! Isn't that cool?"

Privately, Aru thought, *Ooh, intriguing.* Out loud, she said, "How is *that* supposed to convince me?"

"It won't," Kara admitted with a sigh. "You don't have any reason to trust me. But...I'm your best hope of getting out of here, Aru Shah. So will you take a chance on that or not?"

Aru frowned.

"If it helps, I don't actually have a bear shirt?" said Kara.

Aru wanted to grin, but she forced it back. Part of her couldn't fight the instinct to *trust* Kara. There was something about her that really did remind Aru of her sisters.

What if she's lying? whispered another voice in Aru's head. *She wouldn't be the first to betray you.*

But what if she wasn't? What if, by leaving Kara behind, Aru ended up putting the Otherworld in even greater danger? No, she couldn't have that on her conscience. If Kara tried anything, she'd have Brynne, Mini, Aiden, Nikita, Sheela, and *Aru herself* to answer to. Besides, how else was she going to escape?

Aru took a deep breath. "All right, fine. You can come. Now get us out of here."

THREE

Every Breath You Take and Every Move You Maaake

Kara dragged her finger along one of her many bookshelves. Aru scanned the titles—some were familiar and some weren't. There was a collection of Grimms' fairy tales, three whole shelves dedicated to the Amar Chitra Katha comics that Aru loved to read, and nearby, she saw a novel she didn't recognize called *Sal and Gabi Break the Universe*.

"Is this one of those libraries where you pull out a book and a hidden passageway opens?" asked Aru, feeling mildly jealous. If she ever got to make her own villain lair, it would *definitely* have a secret book doorknob.

"Maybe?" said Kara.

"What do you mean 'maybe'?"

"Well, um, I haven't exactly done this before. In theory, the portal only opens for Dad, but lately I've been trying to watch how he does it.... It should work for us, too, if I can just find the right book. It's always the same one, but he never lets me see the title, and I think he puts it back in different places. When he grabs hold of it, a door opens, and he can step through to anywhere he wants to go in the world," said Kara. "Dad's really proud of the portal. Not even the *devas* know that it's here."

"But you don't know *which* book? So we could be stuck here! Which— Wait, where exactly is *here?*"

"I dunno," said Kara. "He's never told me. Every now and then he takes me out in the world, but he usually chooses remote places. Except a couple of months ago, he took me to a pastry shop in Paris for my birthday! It was so beautiful there. I ate the most amazing pink macaron—it was rose-flavored." Kara smiled to herself. "Dad likes the pistachio ones best."

Dad likes the pistachio ones best.

Aru felt those words like a knife slash. All she knew about the Sleeper were the memories he'd sacrificed. She didn't know anything about the kind of music he liked or books he read. He may have told Kara that Aru was his daughter, but he'd never been Aru's dad. It made her wonder what kind of father he would've been. Would he have taken her on trips, too? Would he have been the kind of dad who always snuck her ice cream, even when she was in trouble?

Aru almost asked for more details, but she stopped herself. What difference did it make? She pitied the Sleeper, but he was still her enemy. Imagining who he might've been was pointless and painful. Besides, if Kara was telling the truth, then he had betrayed Aru's mom, and so even the man he might've been wasn't that great.

"I'm sorry," said Kara. "I didn't mean to upset you."

Aru was jolted.

"I know you see him . . . differently," said Kara. "And, I mean, it's not like I know him as well as I thought, either. But—"

"It's fine," said Aru roughly. "Just tell me what to do."

Kara pointed at five shelves at the same level. "Mind going through these? The room will change when you pull out the right book."

"Yeah," muttered Aru. "Maybe I'll find a how-to on being a liar and a cheat."

Kara ignored the comment and they worked in silence. Together, they pulled out book after book and set them on top of a growing stack on the ground. Aru could stand silence . . . but curiosity? Way harder.

"So . . . what else do you know about me?" asked Aru.

"Oh, um . . ." Kara blushed. "Not a ton? Well, no, that's . . . That's a lie. When Dad brought you here, he showed me his memories of you . . . and also, some of what his army's surveillance had picked up?"

Aru's jaw dropped. "He's been spying on me?"

"Yes?" said Kara, grimacing. "But not to hurt you! He said he just wanted to watch you grow up. I saw the outside of the museum where you live—I like that red tree out front, by the way—and your school—the mascot is kinda weird, though—and I know you really like Swedish Fish, and I've seen you with the other Pandavas, and they seem really nice, and I hope they like me and—"

"Kara?"

"Oh. Yes?"

"This is really creepy."

"I know," said Kara, turning even more red. "So I shouldn't say all that when I meet everyone?"

Aru shuddered, trying to imagine exactly what she would

tell the others when she showed up with Kara. *HI, HONEY, I'M HOME! BTW, HAAAVE YOU MET THE DAUGHTER OF OUR ENEMY?* Hmm. She needed to work on that speech.

"Yeah, definitely not," said Aru.

Kara nodded. "Sorry. I was just excited to have a sibling, honestly."

Aru didn't know what to say to that. All her life she'd wanted a sister, and then, after Mini and Brynne came into her life, she'd no longer felt that ache for family. But sometimes Aru wanted a *different* connection, like what Nikita and Sheela had, with someone whose room was right across from hers and who could read all of Mom's moods, too.

Aru was still thinking about it when she mindlessly tugged another book off the shelf. The floor beneath her lurched and she stumbled, Vajra sparking as the throw rug rippled like the skin of an angry animal.

"You found the book!" said Kara excitedly. "Look! It's happening!"

The bookshelf in front of them began to shake. A seam of light shot down the middle, as if someone had cut it in half with a laser beam. With a loud *creak*, the shelves were magically wrenched apart.

"What book was it?" asked Kara.

Aru glanced at the cover. It was *Where the Wild Things Are* by Maurice Sendak. Her mom used to read that book to her when she was little. This copy looked old enough to be the same one, but that wasn't possible....

The jacket was yellowed and ripped, and when Aru flipped open the cover, she saw a note inscribed on the endpaper:

For my Arundhati.

This was the only book they had in the hospital gift shop, but I think it's perfect for my little girl, who is bound to be a wild thing indeed.

Love,

Dad

Aru felt an uncomfortable lump in her throat.

The message was a bit smeared, and part of it had bled onto the opposite page, as if he'd written it quickly and then closed the book before letting the ink dry. He must have been in a hurry.

To get back to me? she wondered. *Or to get back to his* other daughter... *Kara?*

How many days had he spent with Aru before her mother locked him in the lamp? Had he carried this book on his quest to find the Tree of Wishes?

A light tremor ran through the room. Books toppled off the shelves, thudding loudly on the floor. A cold shadow stretched over Aru.

"Uh-oh," squeaked Kara. "Tiny problem."

Aru snapped the book shut, her senses on high alert. She kept her eyes focused on the exit growing before them. It was barely a foot wide. At the moment, there was no way they could fight *and* run through it at the same time, but the opening expanded with each passing second.

"How tiny a problem?" asked Aru nervously.

"Well, um, I guess I forgot to mention that Dad said this whole place is protected by what he considers the most dangerous thing of all...."

Images of hissing crocodiles, hungry sharks, and irate baboons flashed through Aru's head.

"Books," finished Kara.

"Books?" repeated Aru, almost laughing. "But—"

WHUMPF.

Out of the corner of her eye, Aru spied something that looked like a heavy, multicolored tail whipping on the ground next to them. Only the tail wasn't made of scales, but dozens of angry *books*, their spines quivering as if they were alive. Aru spun around as more tomes dropped from the shelves.

The papers scuttled across the floor and fused together. A couple dictionaries formed a claw. A collection of old maps rolled into a tongue. Cookbooks jointed one atop the other, like vertebrae in a spine. The tail, cobbled out of fairy tales, wiggled forward to attach itself to the rest of the pieces. For a moment, the books rustled and flapped into a giant tentacled ball. Then they unfurled all at once, forming a massive creature that looked like a cross between a dinosaur and a dragon.

"Um, hi?" tried Aru, backing up slowly until she was against a shelf. "What are you, a Thesaurus rex? Ha! Get it? You know, I always thought a Thesaurus rex would be a really *friendly* dinosaur.... You seem friendly?"

The creature roared, ink and book-binding glue spewing from its mouth. Aru swiveled out of its aim.

"All right, never mind," she said, snapping her fingers.

Vajra shifted into a glittering spear.

"Look, monster! Go catch the shiny!" yelled Aru, hurling her weapon.

Vajra soared straight up in the air, raining sparks of electricity.

They dropped onto the tomes and erupted into tiny fires. The creature roared again, writhing and clawing at its body.

"Stop!" said Kara. "You'll hurt the books!"

"Better them than us!" said Aru.

She glanced over her shoulder. By now, the exit had widened to three feet.

"Let's go!" shouted Aru.

"I..." Kara hesitated, her eyes darting to a hardcover that lay nearby.

Slim and blue, it was one of the few books that hadn't joined to form the beast. Aru lifted her hand, and Vajra, who was still bouncing off the walls to distract the creature, zoomed back into Aru's grasp.

"Do you want to come with me or not?" demanded Aru, stepping foot inside the passage.

Kara steeled herself, then snatched the book off the ground.

"I do!" she said.

Aru and Kara ran headlong into the dark. Mirrors lined the passageway, so that it seemed as if they were running in infinite directions. A hundred feet away stood a door framed in light.

"That's it!" said Kara. "Just say where you want to go once you open it, and—"

CRASH!

Aru turned to see the book monster stick its snout and an arm through the corridor's entrance. It huffed at them. A cloud of ink seeped from its nostrils and spiderwebbed up the mirrors. The monster slammed a fist into the wall, and one by one the mirrors shattered, like a row of falling dominoes. At the end of the hall, the light around the door began to dim.

"It's trying to cut off our escape!" said Kara.

There was only one way to stop the portal from going dead. Aru prepared to hurl Vajra at the monster....

But Kara grabbed her arm. "No! We can't damage the books!"

"We've got to do something," Aru said with a sigh.

Kara took a deep breath, then tapped her ring. In a flash of white light, it shifted into a long trident that looked as if it had been wrought out of an actual sunbeam. It brightened the hall and turned Kara's eyes gold.

"My light doesn't electrocute things like yours does," said Kara.

Aru stared. "What the—?"

Kara aimed the trident at the book creature. The trident left a glowing trail before its three sharp-pointed ends sank into the monster's outstretched arm. The beast howled as ink burst through the air. Aru stood there frozen for a moment before Kara took her hand and yanked her forward.

"C'mon!" Kara yelled. "Sunny will catch up with me later!"

"Sunny?" asked Aru.

"That's what I named my trident!" said Kara breathlessly.

Aru's head was spinning. That trident looked like something that should be wielded by a *god*. So how did Kara get it?

The portal door was finally within reach. Aru lunged and pushed it. It felt cold against her skin. Her lungs pinched with hope. *Home*, she thought. She was going home!

Just then, something hot squeezed Aru's ankles. She looked down to see an inky coil wrapping itself around her. Before she could kick it off, the tendril yanked. Aru fell, her chin thudding on the mirrored floor. She watched herself being dragged back down the hallway toward the library.

Aru thrashed, reaching for Vajra to cut the inky rope, but she was being pulled too quickly, and every time her weapon sparked, the ink from the book monster ignited, making the passageway grow thick with smoke and smoldering flames.

This is how I'm gonna go? thought Aru miserably as she fought its hold. *A burned Aru casserole?*

Aru wrenched herself around, trying to catch sight of Kara, but the smoke in the air and the sparks glinting off the mirrors obscured her vision. Doubt struck Aru hard. Had Kara left her behind? What if this had all just been a ruse to let Kara escape?

Something whistled through the air.

Aru looked up just in time to see the trident slice through the inky tendril.

"C'mon, Aru!" yelled Kara.

Aru scrambled to her feet. She flattened her palm and Vajra transformed into a hoverboard. Aru jumped on, and Vajra zoomed down the corridor, casting a shower of electrical sparks as it went. All around her, Aru could hear the ink spitting and fizzing as it caught fire. The heat of the flames scorched her back. Up ahead, Kara whistled, and her trident flew back into her hand, shape-shifting into a ring the moment she caught it.

The portal door was within reach again.

Aru hopped off Vajra, who immediately transformed into a Ping-Pong ball and ducked into her pocket. She pushed the door with one hand, flinging it open. With her other hand, she caught Kara's wrist. Behind them the flames reared higher. Smoke burned her nostrils, but Aru squeezed her eyes shut and focused on the place she most wanted to be.

Home.

Aru pictured the front of the Museum of Ancient Indian Art

and Culture, where she and her mom had spent the last fourteen years. She saw the Japanese maple tree, as red as a sunset, and the peeling paint on the front door. She could smell the copper statues, the wooden crates, and her mother's neroli perfume.

Beyond the door was nothing but darkness, and Aru's stomach flipped as they fell through the void....

"AHHH!" screamed Kara.

Aru's eyes flew open just as the lawn outside her front door reared up to meet them. Frantically, she fumbled for Vajra, transforming it back into a hoverboard in time for them to end up stumbling across the grass instead of landing with a *splat*.

Kara righted herself gracefully. She looked around, her eyes wide and shining. But after one step forward, a strange expression fell across her face....

"Kara?" called Aru, going to her.

Kara's eyes fluttered shut and she fainted onto the grass.

Just then the front door slammed open and a stream of air burst out, hitting Aru square in the chest. She went flying backward.

"Ow!" she yelled as her head hit the ground.

A voice called out: "TAKE THAT, VAGABOND!"

"Brynne! How many times have we been through this? Look first, *then* attack!"

"Holy . . . Oh my god . . . it's *Aru*."

The sound of approaching footsteps echoed through Aru's skull. Blearily, she opened her eyes to see Mini.

"You're okay!" Mini said, bursting into tears. "We were *so* worried!"

"Shah!" said Brynne.

Instantly, they pulled her into a hug. Aru felt her heart

practically bursting with joy. Mini's hug was nice and warm, but Brynne's was starting to break her ribs.

"Need—air! Help!" managed Aru.

Her sisters released her, and Brynne hoisted her off the ground. Aru peered around, confused. The last time she was in Atlanta, it had been early spring, still chilly enough for her to need a sweater in the morning. But now it was warm...almost muggy. The sun glared down at them.

"Shah," said a familiar, velvety voice. "You're okay. I couldn't stop thinking about you. I mean, you know, thinking if you were okay and stuff..."

Aru looked up to see Aiden Acharya staring at her. As usual, his camera, Shadowfax, hung from his right shoulder. He wore a loose-fitting black tee and jeans. Even in the daylight, there was something about his eyes that reminded Aru of distant stars. For a second, it looked as if Aiden was going to hug her. Aru took a step forward.

But then Aiden's arms fell to his side.

Aru stepped back.

Whatever had *almost* happened fizzled and died on the spot when Aiden coughed and pointed to Kara, still passed out on the grass.

"Who is she?"

Aru took a deep breath, then looked at her friends. "So...as it turns out...I'm not the only daughter of the Sleeper?"

FOUR

TL; DR We're in Trouble

If there was one upside to certain doom, it was Brynne's cooking.

The moment Aru stepped into her apartment above the Museum of Ancient Indian Art and Culture, she smelled something baking. But not just any baking—it was Brynne's stress desserts: golden maladu, bright orange and creamy rava kesari, pistachio cake, and macarons sandwiched with honey and cardamom buttercream. Aru's mouth watered.

"Don't look so happy about the food, Shah," grumbled Brynne. "We've been worried about you for almost two months. It's been hard to find enough sugar lately!"

Aiden smirked. "Brynne, to be fair, you ran through a small kingdom's supply of ingredients."

Two months? It felt like she'd spent barely two hours in the Sleeper's lair. Aru glanced at the wall calendar hanging by the stairs, her heart sinking. When they'd started their search for the Tree of Wishes, it had been March. Now it was May.

Aru looked around the apartment she shared with her mom and frowned.

It was way too tidy and neat.

No half-empty coffee cups perched on chairs, no open books, no jasmine scent from the shampoo her mom used. At this time of year the museum should've been open for tours and summer camps, but it was completely empty downstairs.

Mini pinched her arm.

"Ow!" said Aru. "What was that for?"

"Checking your skin turgor for potential dehydration," said Mini. "What have you been eating? Have you been drinking enough water? Your skin looks—"

Aru raised an eyebrow. "Flushed and glowing from running back to you guys?"

"I was going to say 'dull.'"

"Thanks."

"How *did* you get back to us?" asked Brynne.

As Aru was steered to the dining table, she nodded toward Kara. Aiden had carried the unconscious girl up the stairs and laid her on the couch. "She's still out?"

"Your mom put an enchantment around the museum that makes any stranger temporarily fall asleep once they get too close," said Aiden. "Anyone with Otherworldly blood, that is."

"Pretty sneaky," said Brynne admiringly. "Kinda like you, Shah."

"Where is Mom?" asked Aru. "Is she out for groceries or something?"

Brynne and Mini exchanged a look.

"We've got *a lot* to talk about, Shah," said Brynne.

"If it's bad, tell me now," said Aru.

"It's not bad . . ." said Mini. "Just strange."

Aru wasn't sure what that meant, so she waited.

"First, why don't you eat and catch us up," said Brynne. "Starting with *why did you bring the Sleeper's daughter here?*"

Between bites of cake and gulps of milk, Aru repeated what Kara had told her—how Kara had been raised in the Sleeper's home for the past two years and her memories had been wiped, about the strange, glowing ward on the back of her neck and how the Sleeper called Kara his "secret weapon" even though she wasn't a Pandava. Aru even told them about Sunny the trident, now secure on Kara's finger as a shiny ring.

"I don't get it, though," said Aru. "She's my age, but I didn't see her in the Pool of the Past or in the Sleeper's memories. I don't know how that's possible—unless he was secretly a jerk of a husband to my mom...."

"Or...there could be another explanation," said Brynne, eyeing Kara. "It's rarely done, but sometimes rich Otherworld families can pay a timekeeper to take a baby and put it in stasis until the parents are ready to raise it. That happened with one of my aunts. She died in an accident right after my cousin was born. Her sister agreed to adopt him later, but she was super young—like eleven or something. So they magically froze the kid's development until my aunt's sister was old enough to take care of a baby. Which makes my cousin, who just had his fifteenth birthday, technically thirty. He tried to use that as an excuse when he threw a party and broke into my uncle's 'bad day' cabinet, but it didn't go so well."

"Timekeeper?" asked Mini, her eyes wide. "Wait. They can change time?"

"No," said Brynne. "That's impossible. But they can hold on to pockets of it. It's a whole other level of magic."

Aru frowned. So Kara *could* be her older half sister, from

before the Sleeper knew Aru's mom, but that still left a lot of questions unanswered. What had happened to Kara's mother? Did Aru's mom know about this? Had Krithika and Suyodhana planned to bring Kara into their family one day?

Mini still looked concerned. "Are there any health ramifications to freezing a baby's development? Does it affect their DNA? What about—"

"*Point is,*" Brynne said over her, "it's *possible,* but it still doesn't explain why you brought her along."

"Kara said she knows how to stop the Sleeper," said Aru, shoving a macaron into her mouth. "And also…you're not gonna believe this, but…apparently his army is marching on Lanka *right* now. They're planning to attack within a week."

Aru stared at her sisters, expecting them to look shocked. Instead, they looked resigned.

"We know," said Mini. "It's all over the Otherworld news. But Kubera, the ruler of Lanka and Lord of Wealth, says—"

Brynne held a finger to her lips, pointing at Kara, and dropped her voice to a whisper. "We'll get to that, but should we even be talking about this stuff with *her* around? I mean, how do you know we can trust her, Shah? All that stuff about stopping the Sleeper…Do you seriously believe her?"

Aru pictured Kara nervously fiddling with her ring and thought about that aura of loneliness that clung to her.

"Yeah, I do, actually," said Aru. "She's just found out that the person who promised to take care of her turned out to be lying. She's hurt. She just she wants to do what's right and doesn't know what that looks like. I can't fault her for that."

Aru's jaw clenched. She understood how Kara felt, even though her own feelings were complicated when it came to her father. She hadn't even had a chance to tell her sisters what she'd seen and learned about him from the goddess Aranyani.

Aru had known that the Sleeper had gone looking for the Tree of Wishes, but she hadn't understood that it was because he wanted to change his terrible destiny to bring destruction upon the world. All he'd hoped for was a quiet family life. But, in the end, trying to change his fate ended up sealing it.

Aru stared around the apartment. It was so clean and so quiet that it was honestly distracting. Where was her mom? And what happened to Sheela, Nikita, and Rudy? They'd all been together back in March, and Aru had half expected Rudy to storm in with a garishly colored outfit by now.

"Where is everyone?"

"Everyone is fine.... At least, we think so," said Mini.

"We know Sheela and Nikita are okay," said Brynne. "They're still annoyingly bad about crossing boundaries while we sleep, sometimes yanking us into the astral plane—which is *the worst*— but Mini and I have been able to train them in our shared dreams, so that's been kinda cool."

"Nikita recently informed me that my clothes are, and I quote, 'an abysmal representation of my dread powers and hopelessly one-note,'" Mini said, plucking at her black-and-purple tie-dyed sweatshirt. "She's going to send me a whole new wardrobe. She's calling it a 'deathly do-over.'"

Aru laughed, but her smile faded when she saw the grave look on Brynne's face.

"Aru...something happened the moment you went against the Sleeper," said Brynne. "It looked like you hugged him, and then there was this huge burst of light. After that, you guys were straight-up gone. His armies vanished, too."

"We looked for you for *hours*," added Mini. "We would've gone back to the garden, but—"

"But emergency alarms started blaring all over the place. We tried to call you through the Pandava mind link, but there was nothing but static," said Brynne. "We didn't know what else to do, so we went back to the Night Bazaar."

Aiden, who had been silently observing up to now, reached for Shadowfax. "It might be easier to show you what happened next."

"At first it was great!" said Mini. "Boo had tracked down the twins' parents, and he used his Council status to speed up their immigration paperwork. He brought them to the Night Bazaar so they could be reunited! Apparently, the twins' parents had been looking for them for years, but children under thirteen have all these protective spells surrounding them."

At the mention of Boo, Aru's chest squeezed tight. *You will hate him for his love*, Sheela had predicted. Aru wished she'd never heard that line of prophecy.

"Boo isn't who you—" she started, but a movement from Aiden interrupted her.

Aiden pinched Shadowfax's screen, pulling out an enchanted image. A holographic scene appeared over the dining table. Sheela and Nikita ran into the outstretched arms of their crying parents. Behind them, Boo hovered protectively. Rudy's lip trembled as he jammed a pair of sunglasses on his nose while Mini openly wept and Brynne looked somewhere else. Suddenly, gold rain fell from the sky, each droplet as big and round as a coin, hitting the rocky ground with a loud *plink!* And then, over the shower of gold, a loud voice announced:

"INTELLIGENCE FROM LANKA HAS FOUND TRAITORS IN OUR MIDST! BY ORDER OF ACTING

COUNCIL LEADER LORD KUBERA, RULER OF LANKA AND GOD OF WEALTH AND TREASURES, ALL TRAVEL TO AND FROM THE OTHERWORLD IS TERMINATED UNTIL FURTHER NOTICE! LORD KUBERA HAS ALSO HEREBY DISBANDED THE COUNCIL UNTIL INVESTIGATIONS HAVE BEEN COMPLETED."

The piles of coins started to quiver, and then the gold melted into pools that spread across the floor.

"RUN!" screamed someone in the Night Bazaar. "They're going to seal the exits!"

At that point, Aiden's images went shaky and blurred until they finally blipped out.

"Everyone found their families and vanished into their homes," said Aiden. "Rudy's parents appeared in a fountain and literally dragged him back to Naga-Loka. Haven't heard from him since."

"At all?" asked Aru.

Aiden shook his head.

"Hira has been staying with Gunky and Funky, so she's fine," said Brynne. There was the faintest hint of color on her cheeks. "Like, you know, she's okay, not 'fine' like..." She trailed off.

"I gave Rudy my number and thought maybe he'd text or something, but he hasn't." Mini sighed. "Anyway, we need to tell you about Kubera.... That announcement wasn't all he sent. Wifey?"

Aiden grimaced at the nickname but reached into his messenger bag and pulled out a gold coin. "Kubera is superpowerful but also kinda...eccentric," he explained.

"He's got command of the fiercest army in the world," said Brynne, gobbling down half a cake. "It's called the *Nairrata*, and all the soldiers are made of enchanted gold. They used to conquer *a lot* of territory."

Aiden nodded. "Centuries ago, the devas got concerned that his army was maybe *too* powerful, so Kubera agreed that he himself wouldn't use the Nairrata anymore. Instead, he agreed to grant control of the army to the Council's chosen heroes in times of need. The heroes can't be gods, but they must have the ability to wield godly weapons."

"You mean like . . . us?" said Aru.

"That's what we thought," said Brynne. "But then yesterday, we got a message from him."

Aiden flipped the coin onto the table. As it spun, it rapidly expanded and twisted into the molten form of a golden . . . weasel?

"That's a mongoose," said Aiden. "Kubera's favorite creature."

The mongoose shook its metallic fur and then scuttled around the table, examining them with its beady black eyes. It opened its mouth to reveal tiny sharp teeth. The apartment's walls faded away and were replaced with a street-wide view of an enormous city completely wrought of gold. The pavement shimmered like a hardened piece of sunshine. The buildings, rounded and stacked like thousands of coins, loomed over them. At the center of it all stood a magnificent palace that was so bright Aru had to squint just to look at it. A deep voice like that of a smooth-jazz DJ filled her head:

NAUGHTY GODLINGS! ARE YOU GOOD, OR ARE YOU BAD? WILL KNOWING MAKE ME LAUGH, OR WILL IT MAKE ME SAD? The voice paused to chuckle. *SO . . . AH . . . HERE'S THE THING. WHAT IS TRUST? I THINK WE NEED SOME TRIALS TO ESTABLISH IT, YOU KNOW? A LITTLE DEATH, A LITTLE DRAMA, ET CETERA, ET CETERA. IF*

YOU DON'T COME TO ME IN THREE DAYS' TIME, THAT WOULD BE A TERRIBLE CRIME. OOH YES, POETRY. I JUST... AH, WORDS. SO GOOD. OH, RIGHT, ANYWAY. IF YOU'RE A NO-SHOW, THEN THAT'S A NO-GO ON THE NAIRRATA ARMY, AND THAT'S MY FINAL SAY-SO! SEE YA SOON.

There was a jazz ditty, like something you'd hear in an elevator, and then the mongoose melted back into a golden coin. The image of what could only have been the shining city of Lanka faded away.

"What?" said Aru. "Why do we have to go through *trials* if he's supposed to give the army over to us anyway?"

Mini turned red. "After we didn't show up for the Holi party and you went missing, Opal's whole PR campaign around us failed.... People started blaming us and talking about that prophecy about the 'untrue sister.'"

"Lemme guess, *I'm* the traitor?" asked Aru.

Saying it didn't even hurt the way she'd thought it would.

Mini hung her head, which Aru took as a silent yes. "Aiden showed them images to prove that the Sleeper took you, but it didn't do any good. All they saw was that it looked like you hugged him and then disappeared...."

"People are scared, Shah," said Aiden. "They don't know what to believe."

"We tried talking to the Maruts, but they said this is a matter for Kubera. Hanuman and Urvashi went to Lanka to talk to him, and we think he's holding them captive there. We thought maybe Boo could help, but he's disappeared, too!" said Mini, tears gathering in her eyes. "And now people think he's a traitor again!"

Brynne's face softened as she moved to rub Mini's back. "We've defended Boo before, and we'll do it again. Right, Shah?"

Aru's mouth went dry as all eyes turned to her.

She had to tell them the truth.

"Boo *is* a traitor," said Aru, steadying her voice. "I saw it in the Tree of Wishes."

FIVE

Fun Fact: You're Cursed

All three of them stared at her.

"That's ridiculous, Aru!" said Brynne. "How could you say that?"

Aru flinched at her sharp tone but didn't back down. "I know what I saw. Aranyani showed it to me, along with the reason my...I mean, the Sleeper never made a wish. He'd had to sacrifice a lot of memories to get to the tree, but in the end he didn't want to give up his memories of my mom and me just to change his fate. So he turned around to come home, but by then the Council had convinced Mom to imprison him."

"The Council?" repeated Mini.

"They were just doing their duty," said Brynne, crossing her arms. "The Sleeper was always destined to fight a war that could destroy the Otherworld."

"Maybe he wouldn't have done that if he hadn't been locked up!" said Aru.

Brynne shook her head. "Listen, I get it. It's sad, but he's a monster, Aru—"

Vajra, who had turned back into a bracelet on Aru's wrist,

flashed angrily. "If you were forced to give up parts of your soul, you'd become a monster, too!"

Brynne's mouth clamped shut.

"Aru," said Mini gently, "we're just trying to understand what you're saying.... This is the first time we're hearing about this."

Aru set her jaw. Her ears were hot. She couldn't help feeling that she was being cornered right now.

"What about Boo?" asked Aiden. His expression looked carefully blank. "What happened with him?"

"Aranyani made me see all this stuff before I could get to the Tree of Wishes. She showed me that Boo made a deal with the Sleeper behind our backs," said Aru. "Boo used to be a sorcerer king before all this, and then he got cursed and turned into a pigeon. The only thing that can break his curse is something about how *a wish will free you from this earth* or whatever. And... And I guess Boo thought he couldn't protect us if he wasn't in his most powerful form. So, in exchange for being able to make his own wish when the Sleeper found the Tree of Wishes, he revealed the twins' location to the Sleeper's army. That's how they were able to kidnap them." Aru's face burned in anger. "Boo didn't think we'd succeed on the mission. Even after all his training and lectures and..."

Aru fell quiet. She didn't want to think about Boo perched on her head, shouting military drill instructions, lecturing the Pandavas about taking their vitamins, and always, *always*, reminding them that they would be great.

Because, as it turned out, he hadn't believed it himself.

Brynne was the first to find her voice. "But if you saw all this, then that means you got to make a wish, right?"

Aru nodded. "But"—she was so frustrated she felt like crying—"I can't remember what I wished for."

Brynne frowned. "If you can't remember that, then how do you know you saw all that other stuff?"

Aru went still. "It sounds like you don't believe me."

Brynne's gaze hardened. "I think you need to calm down, Shah."

"Calm *down?*" said Aru, shooting out of her chair. "Boo *did* betray us! And Hanuman and Urvashi messed up everything by convincing my mom to trap the Sleeper. Maybe they're trapped in Lanka, or maybe they just gave up on us, like Boo did!"

"You don't know that!" said Brynne.

And then too many things happened at once. Sparks flew off Vajra just as a gust of wind blew Aru back into her seat. Aiden dove forward, throwing out his hands like a referee. A huge burst of violet light shot across the room as Mini slammed Dee Dee into the ground.

"ENOUGH!" yelled Mini. "Aru, Brynne didn't say she doesn't believe you. And, Brynne, just because you don't like what you hear doesn't mean you have to sneer about it. Aru has clearly gone through a lot. All of us have!"

Aru stared at her sisters, feeling smaller and smaller by the second. Mini was gazing at her with pity. Brynne looked dubious. Why didn't anyone believe her? *Because they know you're a liar, Aru Shah,* whispered a voice in her head.

Aiden slowly lowered his arms. "Can we agree to start over? We're not going to find the answers we need until we get to Lanka, and we have to figure out how we're going to do that when all the portals are closed. Let's just focus on the next step for now, *okay?* Brynne, Aru, is there something you want to say to each other?"

Brynne and Aru glared at each other for about five more

seconds before Brynne grumbled, "Gods, Aiden, you're such an *ammamma*." Brynne looked up at Aru and sighed. "You're a mess, but you're still my sister."

There were a lot of things that Aru didn't know and didn't understand, but one thing hadn't changed. "Love you, hate you."

"Fair enough," said Brynne.

And that was that.

Mini and Aiden exchanged classic *tired-of-these-kids* faces before Mini said, "It is kinda weird that you can't remember the wish."

"I know," said Aru bitterly. "But every time I try, I see something else. Snow, and a bridge...I dunno."

Mini went pale. "Shukra's curse."

"Who?" asked Brynne.

Aru felt cold.

Shukra. The guardian of the Bridge of Forgetting in the Kingdom of Death.

While Mini explained who he was to the others, Aru felt dragged back into an old memory. Aru and Mini had been forced to fight their way out of that place, and in the process, Aru had hurt Shukra. Badly. In return, he had cursed her.

"In the moment when it matters most, you, too, shall forget," said Aru. "That's why I can't remember...."

Brynne threw up her hands. "But we *need* that wish! It's the only thing that proves whose side we're on! Without it, Kubera won't give us the Nairrata army. I bet he'll make a deal with the Sleeper. He'd do anything to keep Lanka—and himself—safe."

"Seriously?" asked Aru. "He would really do that to everyone else?"

"He's a god," said Aiden darkly. "It's different for them. Immortals don't care about stuff the same way humans do. They never grow old, and they can't die, so things like war don't mean much to them." He sighed, then added, "There's something else you need to know, Aru."

Aru frowned. "What? He expects us to compete in his trials as actual mongooses?"

"It's about your mom," said Mini quietly.

Aru went cold. "What about her?"

"She waited for you a long time," said Aiden. "And then, last week, she packed up and left. She said she needed to do some urgent research. . . . She found something that might give us a clue about the Sleeper's next move. He's still after the nectar of immortality, and he's getting closer to finding it again."

Aru thought back to the strange Ocean of Milk, and the great silver dome that held the *amrita* elixir. After the Pandavas had fought near it, the Council had supposedly devised a way to hide the nectar even from themselves. It was the only way to protect the powerful substance. So how did the Sleeper know where to find it?

"Where did she go, exactly?" asked Aru.

"I wish we knew more, dude," said Brynne sadly.

"She said she knew what she was doing, and she promised to stay out of harm's way," said Aiden. "She also gave me a message in case you got back before her."

"She did?"

Aiden looked deep into her eyes, and Aru felt prickly and warm all over. "I love you, Aru."

Aru's whole face went up in flames. *Uh, what?* "I meant the message?"

Aiden lifted an eyebrow. "That *was* the message."

"Oh my god, I was *joking*," said Aru, while quietly dying

inside. Honestly, now would not be a bad time to bounce Vajra off her forehead and electrocute herself again.

"We've been watching the place while she's gone," Brynne added quickly.

Through their Pandava link, Brynne added, *That was PAINFUL to witness.*

Mini winced. *Stop! I'm sure he didn't notice.*

Aru darted a glance at Aiden, who seemed extremely preoccupied with his camera. His face looked a touch red.

He definitely noticed.

Aiden frowned and crossed his arms, not looking at them. "So, uh, we've got two days left to get to Lanka and answer Kubera's summons, but there's literally no way to get there—"

A tiny *thud* made the four of them whip around to look at Kara. She had woken up, and in the process of sitting up, she'd let the book she'd carried from the Sleeper's lair fall to the floor. Kara immediately hunched her shoulders, looking around nervously.

"I, um, I think I can help you," said Kara in a small voice.

SIX

At Least There's Popcorn?

B rynne stood up.

The blue choker around her neck, which held Gogo, her camouflaged wind mace, glowed slightly. "Do you really think we'd take help from the daughter of the Sleeper?"

Really, Brynne, scolded Mini.

Kara turned to Aru, her eyes shining. Aru forced herself to stand still. She wanted to defend Kara, but she was afraid that if she did, it would make her look like the "untrue sister" from Sheela's prophecy. The rest of the Otherworld already thought she was bad news. She couldn't have her Pandava sisters thinking the same thing.

Kara looked down, hurt, and her hands curled into fists in her lap. "My name is Kara, and I'm not his only daughter, you know."

The whole room fell silent for a couple of moments. Aru felt her palms turning hot. She was about to go to Kara's side when there came the sound of a chair scraping back.

"This is ridiculous," grumbled Aiden.

He swiped a glass of water off the table and walked over to

give it to Kara. As she drank, Aiden bent down, picking up the book that had fallen off her lap. He turned it over, a soft smile growing on his face.

"A book of Emily Dickinson poems?" he asked, handing it back to her.

Kara flushed. "Her work has always made me feel...less alone."

Aiden's eyebrows shot up in surprise, and his gaze lingered on Kara. As Aru watched, something painful nudged at her heart.

"Okay, okay, this isn't book-club time," growled Brynne. "What do you really want?"

"I want to help—" Kara started.

"Why?" demanded Brynne.

Mini frowned. "Easy, Bee..."

"Why do you want to help us when Aru says that the Sleeper rescued you? You *owe* him, and he's your dad, so you probably—"

"Love him?" finished Kara quietly. "Yes, of course I love my dad." Kara looked at them, lifting her chin. "I believe he can be both a good dad and a bad person. I can want to stop the evil things he might do and still want to protect him. Maybe, by helping you guys, I can stop him before he makes a big mistake....I could give him a chance to change."

Kara's words knocked all the breath out of Aru's lungs. There was an ease and confidence in the way she spoke, and instead of pity, Aru felt...*envy.* Kara was at peace with an ugly situation. But Aru? Aru was angry.

Sometimes she felt so angry that she wondered if holding it in was the only thing that kept her pinned to the ground. Otherwise, the force of all the unknowns in her life might pull her apart.

Aru tried not to think about what she couldn't know, but the worries snapped at her anyway. Was her mom safe? Where was she? Why couldn't Aru stop missing Boo? Why couldn't she erase the memory of who the Sleeper had once been? Why couldn't she un-see the smudged ink of his inscription in *Where the Wild Things Are* and un-know that it was proof he'd been racing to get back to her?

Mini sighed, and the sound of it shook Aru out of her thoughts.

"I think the only way to deal with this whole thing fairly is to put it to a vote," said Mini decisively. "So...do we accept Kara's help or no?"

"Leave me out of it," said Aiden, holding up his hands. "This is between you guys."

"I vote no," said Brynne, crossing her arms.

Mini looked thoughtfully at Kara. "I vote...yes. We can't choose our family, and we didn't hold it against Rudy when his grandfather Takshaka had it out for us and blamed us for stealing the god of love's arrow."

Brynne scowled, then turned to Aru. "Well, Shah?"

Aru noticed that Aiden was watching her curiously.

"I vote yes," said Aru. "I...I believe Kara."

The moment Aru said it, she realized she truly meant it. Kara smiled shyly at her, but the moment was broken once more by Brynne, who threw up her hands.

"Okay, *fine*, we'll accept your intel and help, but you can't come with us," said Brynne.

"I'm the one person outside my father's army who knows why he's marching on Lanka," said Kara. "He's after a specific weapon, and . . . and if you don't let me come with you, I won't tell you what it is. Then, even if you win Kubera's trials and get the Nairrata army, you might miss the one thing he came there for."

Aru realized Kara must have been awake for part of their earlier conversation. *Maybe sneaky* does *run in the family*, she thought.

"This weapon . . ." said Aiden. "It's not the Nairrata itself?"

Kara shook her head, remaining tight-lipped.

"Are you seriously trying to manipulate us?" demanded Brynne.

"No, but I . . . I *will* stand up for myself," said Kara. "I won't be bullied."

"No one is *bullying* you," grumbled Brynne. "At least Rudy was somewhat useful. As a prince, he could get us into different places. But what can *you* do? If you don't give us that information about the weapon, then bringing you with us is just going to get us killed. We need someone who can fight—"

"I *can* fight," said Kara, standing up straight.

"Oh yeah?" said Brynne. "Prove it."

A few minutes later, Kara and Brynne squared off in the wide museum lobby. Aiden had his camera ready. Mini kept tapping her fingers along the edge of a first-aid kit. Aru leaned against Greg, the giant stone elephant statue that served as a portal to the Otherworld (that is, when the Otherworld wasn't in complete and total lockdown).

"Aru, you made *popcorn*?" scolded Mini. "That's terrible!"

"But delicious," said Aiden, helping himself to a buttery fistful.

"This shouldn't be a spectacle," grumbled Mini. "The vote

should've put the decision to rest. Now Kara will lose and we'll leave her behind, which will make things even *more* dangerous for everyone. If the Sleeper finds out that she's missing, then what?"

"You don't know that she's going to lose," said Aru.

"Against Brynne?" scoffed Mini. "*We* can barely hold our own against her."

Aru said nothing. She remembered Kara's escape from the Sleeper's lair—the way she'd darted quickly, and how her ring had instantly transformed into a brilliant trident. There was more to this girl than it seemed at first glance.

"Ready?" asked Brynne, twirling her wind mace.

Kara nodded.

Brynne blurred forward, spinning out her wind mace. A cyclone tore through the museum lobby. Papers and dust swirled into the air. Some of the papers folded themselves into birds with sharp beaks. As Brynne slammed down her weapon, the creatures rushed at her opponent.

Kara spun out of the way, then stretched out one hand. Her white-gold ring shattered apart, lengthening into the six-foot-tall trident. Brynne's eyes widened, and her jaw dropped as Kara waved her weapon. An arc of burning light followed the movement, incinerating the paper birds in mid-flight.

"You think you're the only one who knows how to play with fire?" asked Brynne. A red stripe appeared in her blue mace. She pointed the club downward and swung it so a line of flames raced across the lobby floor.

Kara aimed the trident and searing light exploded from its tips, meeting the fire in the middle of the room.

Beside Aru, Mini screamed, "Watch out!" She slammed her Death Danda, Dee Dee, on the ground and violet light ribboned around the room, sealing off the exhibit halls and staircases. Brynne's flames sloshed up the side of Mini's shield and then dripped down like lava, leaving Aiden, Mini, and Aru untouched.

"Quick thinking," breathed Aiden, who was crouched on the floor.

Aru groaned, looking down at the spilled popcorn. "But what a sacrifice..."

"It was either your popcorn or the entirety of your mother's museum, and I didn't want to risk the insurance plan," huffed Mini.

On the other side of the shield, Brynne's mace swept the flames into a great tornado. Smoke clouded the contained sphere of their makeshift arena. Brynne squinted, swiping at the air in front of her eyes, but Kara didn't blink or cough. Brynne stumbled out of the cyclone of smoke, gasping for oxygen.

Kara's trident zipped through the lobby, this time leaving a trail of light in its wake.

Brynne defensively swung up her mace, but Kara's weapon was too quick.

A second later, Brynne was pinned to the floor by her shirt. Her flames went out.

Aru, Aiden, and Mini stared in shock at Brynne's defeat. The moment the wind died down and cleared away the smoke, Mini dropped the protective shield and the three of them rushed over. Kara stood over Brynne and pulled up her trident. It shrank and swooped back into Kara's hand, where it transformed into her ring once more.

"Bee, you okay?" asked Mini anxiously.

"Ugh."

Kara looked nervous. "You're the one who wanted to fight."

Brynne scowled. "Where did you get that weapon?"

"It was a gift," said Kara defensively. "It's a drop of sunshine. Dad caught it for me and kept it in a bag made of night cloth. When I opened it, this is the form it took."

"That's a pretty violent gift," said Aru, ignoring the sudden pinch in her heart. The Sleeper had given his other daughter so much. Aside from the picture book he'd bought at the hospital, all Aru had ever gotten from her father was threats.

"Aru told us the Sleeper called you his secret weapon," said Mini, examining the trident. "Is this what he meant?"

"I don't think so," said Kara. "He said drops of light are uncommon, but they're not *that* rare.... I honestly don't know what he meant by that, but I *do* know Dad is looking for the nectar of immortality, and Sunny has nothing to do with that."

"Sunny?" asked Aiden.

"It's what I named my trident," said Kara quietly. "So ... can I come?"

Brynne exhaled loudly, still lying on the floor. "You're really not going to tell us about the weapon the Sleeper is looking for?"

Kara eyed them. "If you were in my position, would you?"

Welp. That was fair. Brynne looked like she wanted to push it, but Aiden toed her leg with the end of his shoe. She swatted at him.

"Okay, what's your idea for getting to Lanka?" she grumbled.

Kara beamed. "Well, it's easy, really. All gold roads lead to Lanka. We just need to find a place with some gold."

"A jewelry store?" asked Mini.

Aru perked up. "Or gold bars? Are we going to rob a bank?"

"Why are you like this, Shah?" Aiden sighed.

"What we really need," said Kara, "is a gold mine."

"A *gold mine?*" repeated Brynne, sitting up and staring up at them. "Sure, it's right next to Aru's corner deli—"

"Really?" asked Mini.

"Of course not!" said Brynne. "Who has a gold mine lying around?"

"Well, it's not around the corner," said Aru slowly. "It's about an hour away."

Brynne stared at her. "You're kidding."

"Nope," said Aru.

Augustus Day School had once taken the kids on a field trip to the Dahlonega Gold Mines. On the bus ride there, Aru had dreamed about finding a rare nugget of gold and triumphantly declaring, *I'm rich!* Would that make her an heiress, she had wondered? Aru had assumed that the gold mine would be paved in precious metal that shimmered like a tiny sun. But when they'd arrived, it was a lot more, well, nature-y. A giant dark tunnel where they got to pan for gold—Aru found nothing—and poke at the cave walls, which was somewhat more entertaining.

"It's near the mountains in northern Georgia," Aru told her friends.

Aiden tapped out something on his phone, frowning. "There's a bus heading that way in half an hour."

"What?" squeaked Mini. "I've got to pack! Brynne, you're on food duty—"

"Obviously," said Brynne.

"I'll figure out the logistics," said Aiden.

"I'll sulk and take up space," volunteered Aru.

"Or...you could clean up?" suggested Mini.

Aru scanned the museum lobby and grimaced. It was dusty, and a little bit scorched, too. If her mom were home, she'd be furious. Aru would much rather have her mom home yelling at her than not having her home at all.

"I really wish we had a robot," Aru said with a sigh.

"Did you know the word *robot* comes from the Czech word *robota*, which means *forced labor*?" said Kara. "A sci-fi author came up with it in the 1920s." She looked around at everyone brightly, as if expecting a response.

Mini gave her a pitying look. "I share all kinds of interesting facts like that with them, and they never seem impressed. Don't take it personally."

"That's pretty cool," said Aiden kindly.

Kara seemed shocked that he'd spoken to her directly. Aru was beginning to notice that whenever Kara was startled, her golden ring glowed a little bit brighter, which made Kara's complexion even prettier. Her luxurious dark hair fell to her shoulders, and her skin looked like it belonged in an advertisement. From the way Aiden looked at Kara, Aru knew she wasn't the only one who'd noticed.

Aru gave Vajra a mental nudge. *Can you make me glow-y, too?*

Vajra prickled with electricity, and Aru felt her hair shoot up around her head like porcupine quills.

"Whoa, Shah!" said Aiden, lurching backward. "You could poke someone's eye out."

Okay, knock it off, thought Aru.

Vajra sulkily returned to being a sleepy lightning-bolt bracelet.

By the time Aru had finished cleaning up the lobby, the group was nearly ready to go. The only person missing was Kara, who had gone up to Aru's room to borrow a change of clothes.

"I'll go get her," said Aru quickly.

Aru felt a little guilty as she climbed the stairs. She had missed her friends, but these days it sometimes felt like too much to be around other people. Ever since that last battle with the Sleeper, her world had tilted. She didn't understand how he could be both a monster and a victim, how Boo could be both family and foe, or how her own sisters could love and protect her but not fully believe her. She was starting to feel like a jigsaw-puzzle piece that had snuck into the wrong box. Even Kara seemed to fit in more naturally with Aru's friends. One of them might even like Kara way more than he liked Aru.

Tell me what to do. Tell me what's right, she begged silently.

But she didn't even know who she was asking.

Herself? The gods? Or maybe something even vaster… something that would calm this new restlessness that had sprung up in her soul and wouldn't leave her alone.

First, get to Lanka, she told herself as she walked into her room. *Then worry about the rest.*

Aru had expected to find Kara rifling in the dresser for a T-shirt and shorts. But the room was empty. She frowned, then turned around when she caught a flash of light across the hall. In her mom's bedroom.

For a moment, Aru's heart lifted. "Mom?"

Maybe it was stupid, but a small part of her hoped that her mom somehow *knew* Aru was home and had come back to her. But when she crossed the hall, she found Kara holding a bottle of Krithika Shah's neroli perfume to her nose.

"What do you think you're doing?" asked Aru harshly.

Kara jumped and hastily put back the bottle. "Nothing."

"I can see that," said Aru.

"I was just looking around," said Kara.

Aru could feel mean words rising in her throat....

But then Kara said, "I...I just wanted to know what a mom's room looked like. I'm sorry."

Oh, thought Aru. It felt like someone had stuck a needle in her anger. Aru had spent her whole life being curious about her own absent parent. It made sense that Kara would feel the same way.

"Actually, when I miss my mom, I do the same thing," said Aru.

Kara's gaze darted to a framed photo of Aru and her mom on the wall. "She's beautiful."

Aru nodded, unsure of what else to say.

"You're lucky to have her," said Kara, staring openly at the photo.

"What, um, what happened to your mom?"

Kara shrugged. "I don't know anything about her. Dad said she had to give me up but she always wanted to come back for me. She never has, though....Or maybe she did, and Dad hid it from me." Kara stepped toward the door, not looking at Aru. "We should go. Again, um, I'm sorry."

Without waiting for Aru to respond, Kara rushed out of the room.

The bus to Dahlonega was practically empty, so they could sit wherever they wanted. Aru grabbed a window seat in the back and immediately stuck in her earbuds. Aiden sat with Kara, who asked him about his camera. Mini cleaned her seat with an anti-bacterial wipe, and Brynne dove into the snack bag.

Aru had barely started listening to music before the rumble of the bus dragged her to sleep. Her dreams were a chaos of stars and planets. Her feet kicked wildly as she fell head over heels through the sky—

"Gotcha!" yelled a familiar voice.

In the dream, Aru opened her eyes and found herself lying on a bed of clouds. She recognized this place—it was the dream studio where Nikita liked to tailor elaborate gowns and outfits. When Aru sat up, two pairs of ice-blue eyes stared back at her. Within seconds, Sheela and Nikita piled onto her in an attack hug.

"We've been searching every dream for you!" said Sheela accusingly.

"Don't make us worry like that again," said Nikita imperiously.

The twins hadn't changed much in the past few months. Sheela was in a unicorn onesie, and the horned hood flopped over her head as she waved. Nikita was wearing a metallic pantsuit with a matching headband that held up her heavy braids.

"I hate panicking," said Nikita. "It makes me slouch and that ruins my clothes."

"I'm glad you guys are safe, too," said Aru, hugging them. "I was really worried...."

Knowing the twins were safe, sound, and still a little ridiculous felt like a much-needed gulp of air after being underwater too long.

Nikita's haughty look melted into a warm smile. "We're better now," she said. "We're back with our parents. But we spend some nights training with Brynne and Mini."

"I hate training," grumbled Sheela.

"I hate losing creative time to gross, sweaty *sparring*," said Nikita, examining her nails. "But all the Otherworld portals are shut down because of the Sleeper, so, not much of a choice."

"I've been seeing things," said Sheela dreamily. "Glimpses here and there..."

"Of what?" asked Aru.

Or who...? she wondered.

"Shiny things!" said Sheela in a singsong voice. "Scurrying stuff, and a man with a deep laugh."

Did she mean the Sleeper?

Sheela's eyes flashed silver as she recited:

> *You must remember to be polite*
> *Even to things far out of your sight.*
> *Not everything that glitters is gold....*
> *The truth will lead to the Lanka road.*
> *Choose poorly and you'll find that there's no way out,*
> *And you'll end up where no one can hear you shout.*

A tendril of cold fear curled through Aru's heart.

SEVEN

No One Said Anything about Demon Hamsters

Aru jolted awake when the bus slammed on its brakes.

"Almost there," said Mini from the seat in front of her.

Aru's shoulder felt damp.

Gross, she thought, *is the bus leaking?* She looked at her shirt. Nope. It was drool.

"Ugh," said Aru, pushing herself upright.

"Drooling *again*?" Mini sighed and started rummaging through her backpack. "Don't worry! I have wipes."

Aru looked beyond Mini to Kara and Aiden's row. Kara's book was open on her lap, and Aiden was reading it over her shoulder. The afternoon sunshine illuminated them so perfectly it was like they were *supposed* to be sitting together like that. Why didn't the light ever do that to *her*? wondered Aru. She gazed out the window. At that exact moment, a fly splatted into it.

Great.

"You know, you really can't trust any public surfaces," continued Mini. "It could be hiding a thin layer of E. Coli or staphylococcus. But I also pack these because Aru drools a lot in her sleep and—"

"Thanks for the PSA," said Aru, grabbing the wet cloth from her. "By the way, I saw the twins."

"Twins?" asked Kara, looking up from her book.

"Our other Pandava sisters," said Brynne.

Aru wondered if Kara could detect Brynne's unspoken next words: *Unlike you.*

"I've seen them before," said Kara. "How are they?"

Mini, Brynne, and Aru fell silent. Aru had told the group that the Sleeper had been spying on them, but to hear Kara confirm it so casually raised goose bumps on her arms.

Too late, Kara must have realized what she'd said, because she turned a violent red. "I'm so sorry, I didn't mean to—"

"They're fine, no thanks to your *dad*," said Brynne coldly before turning to Aru. "Did Sheela see anything?"

Aru shot a sympathetic glance at Kara, but she was staring down at her lap and didn't notice.

"It sounded like a prophecy . . . and not a happy one," said Aru. She recited it for them.

Mini paled.

Brynne frowned. "Well, that's cheerful."

"Could be worse?" said Aru. "Could've just been *Nice try, you're gonna die.*"

Aiden snorted out a laugh.

As the bus rolled to a stop outside the Dahlonega Gold Mines, Aru looked at Kara, whose expression was growing more and more concerned. She was probably scared. And why shouldn't she be? She hadn't gone through what the Pandavas had. They were pretty hard to frighten these days.

"You'll get used to the feeling of impending doom," said Aru brightly. "It's not so bad." She pulled up her sleeve a little to reveal Vajra glowing brightly on her arm. Aru hoped it said, *This lightning bolt has seen a lotta action.*

"Well, *I'm* not used to it," said Mini, rubbing her belly. "Ugh. Just hearing a prophecy makes my acid reflux act up."

"Acid reflux?" Brynne looked interested. "Is that a new weapon?"

"Only to my esophagus. It's being attacked by the hydrochloric acid that lives in my stomach."

Now Brynne looked horrified.

"To be clear, we're not *always* in peril," said Aiden to Kara.

"Much peril, very danger," contradicted Aru, stepping out of the bus and into the bright afternoon.

May in Georgia was a time of amiable sunshine before the muggy, awful, hair-sticking-to-your-forehead-heat of June, July, and August. Insects sang in the trees, and a gentle breeze ruffled the fragrant wisteria blossoms draping the brick walls. In the distance, Aru heard the sounds of kids laughing and splashing around in a nearby public pool. According to Aru's home calendar, school had been out for a week, which meant that Aru had not only missed out on all the fun end-of-year events, but also she was living out her mother's *worst excuse ever.* Apparently, Aru's mom had blamed her daughter's long absence on mono and promised that Aru would finish all her schoolwork over the summer, which was terrible for many reasons:

1) Mono was called "the kissing virus," and the closest Aru Shah had ever come to a kiss was when a bumblebee had stung her chin.

2) Now everyone was going to think she *had* kissed someone, and she'd have to make up a fake boyfriend in Canada.

3) She had never been to Canada.

4) She had to do homework over the summer on top of taking command of a giant golden army in, like, a week.

5) Last, and most important of all, Aru would have given anything to be able to point out these things to her mom in person, but she had no idea where Krithika Shah had gone.

Aru's spirits rose a little as a small museum came into view. Like her mom, she loved museums. Krithika had once said of them: *What we know of the world are blips and fragments. The only people who can truly speak of history are ghosts.*

There didn't seem to be any hint of ghosts here, though. The only sign was a small post with a brass plaque that read:

THE SIDEWALKS OF DAHLONEGA ARE HISTORIC
BE MINDFUL OF YOUR FOOTING!

"Dah-lah-nee-gah," pronounced Kara slowly. "I wonder what the name means."

"Does it matter?" asked Brynne. "It's not like that's gonna help us find the way to Lanka."

Kara primly squared her shoulders. "True, but it never hurts to understand a place a little better. That's why words are so important. They're like a soul and a story all in one."

A soul and a story, thought Aru. That was beautiful. Aru scolded her brain: *WHY DON'T YOU COME UP WITH STUFF LIKE THAT?* Her brain responded by unleashing the nightmarish KARS4KIDS jingle.

"Wait a minute..." said Aiden, glancing down at his phone. "We got off at the wrong stop. The gold mine is six minutes thataway." He pointed in another direction.

"So where are *we?*" asked Aru.

"We're at the Dahlonega Gold Mine *Museum.*"

"If we want to get to Lanka, we need the mine," said Kara. "Dad says there are golden guardians who watch over the Otherworld routes. Maybe we could find them? Is there any way to check for magic?"

"I highly doubt there's any magic here," said Brynne.

Mini brought out Dee Dee. In its compact-mirror form, it could detect disguised magic. When she opened it and spun around, the reflection glowed a soft violet. On Aru's wrist, Vajra began to spark. Brynne's choker flashed a brighter shade of blue, and when Kara raised her hand, her ring looked like sunshine bouncing off a windshield.

"Okay, scratch what I just said." Brynne swiveled her head left and right.

"But where is it coming from?" asked Aru.

She rotated slowly in place. Nothing seemed out of the ordinary, but when she turned around again, a bright shape loomed at the bottom of her vision. Aru caught a flash of golden fur and large teeth before yelling, "AHH! DEMON HAMSTER!"

Vajra instantly lengthened into a spear.

"Tourists!" squeaked the creature excitedly. "It's happening!"

"I am overwhelmed with joy," said another creature, who sounded decidedly joyless.

Mere inches from Aru's feet, the sidewalk had split down the middle to reveal a chasm. A bright marble staircase with veins of gold and silver spiraled down into it, and on the top step two tall rodents stood on their haunches. They came up to her knees and had golden fur, beaver-like noses, half-moon ears tucked close to their heads, and round black eyes.

If they were demon hamsters, they didn't look very demonic.

"You think we're hamsters!" said the first creature gleefully. It nudged the other one, who continued to stare blankly ahead. "I told you things were looking up!"

The second creature maintained its stony expression.

Beside Aru, Aiden moved closer to the animals. "What's happening?"

Kara shot a warning glance at Aru, her eyes flicking to Vajra. Aru twisted her wrist and Vajra shrank back into a bracelet.

"Greetings, guardians of the golden road," said Kara respectfully. She pressed her hands together and bowed.

Mini elbowed Aru, and the four of them copied Kara's movements.

"This is so exciting! Pleased to meet you. I am Sonu, your afternoon docent," said the first creature, bowing. "This is our illustrious curator, Kanak! Say hello, Kanak."

"No."

Sonu ignored that. "Might you be here for the twelve o'clock tour?"

"Say no," Kanak whispered to Kara.

"Stop that, Kanak!" scolded Sonu. "We haven't had tourists in almost a thousand years!"

"I'm . . . I'm sorry?" ventured Aru.

Sonu shook its head. "We had a miserable experience with the press. We did one interview—"

"I didn't want to do it," muttered Kanak.

"It wasn't too long ago, maybe fifth century, with Herodotus?"

"Yeah, super recent," said Aru.

Mini elbowed her again.

"But he mistranslated us and called us 'gold-digging ants'!" wept Sonu. "The Persians called us 'mountain ants,' you see, and, oh, it just became a PR debacle. Everyone running after anthills when we've been right here all along."

"So . . . you're not hamsters," said Aru.

"We're marmots!" said Kanak grumpily.

"*Marmota himalayana*, to be specific," said Sonu. "The Tibetans called us snow pigs!"

"Do not call us snow pigs," warned Kanak.

"It doesn't matter anymore," said Sonu, waving a paw. "Especially now that you've arrived. Here to see the famous gold roads, I take it?"

"Of course?" said Kara. She gave Aru a confused look. "I've heard so much about them. . . . But I'm so excited, I'm blanking on all their names."

"Ah yes. Well, we have the human-gold-mine road, which connects all known gold mines from the Cortez Gold Mine in Nevada to the Olimpiada in Russia and even the Kibali in the Congo," said Sonu. "Then there's our alchemical road, which controls the distribution of magical gold artifacts to Otherworld cities—"

"*Controlled*," corrected Kanak. "No one is trading anything these days with that state-of-emergency travel ban. Hmpf."

Sonu looked momentarily distressed but soon perked up. "And then there's the road for Otherworld cities of gold . . . El Dorado, Shambhala—"

"Lanka?" asked Aru eagerly.

"Yes, yes," said Sonu. "It's a treacherous, sneaky thing, quite off-limits to tourists ever since one of our sister museums misplaced a tour group back in the eighties. I believe they became mole people. Anyway. Do follow me! We'll go through our souvenir shop, where there's a lovely view of all three roads, then head to the galleries, and finish up at the café...."

Sonu scampered happily down the steps.

Kanak sauntered with utmost slowness, muttering about "the scourge of tourists."

"So, once we see the road to Lanka, we split?" whispered Brynne.

"That feels mean," said Mini. "Maybe we can buy a souvenir first so their feelings aren't too hurt?"

Aiden patted his camera and headed down the stairs. "Good work, Kara," he said.

Kara beamed, flipped her hair over her shoulder, and flashed a smile at Aru. "Come on, Aru," she said, winking. "No doom yet!"

Aru *knew* Kara was just being nice.... So why was it starting to annoy her?

No doom yet! mocked Aru through the Pandava link.

Brynne snickered.

I like that she has a good attitude, said Mini defensively. *It's refreshing!*

I have *a good attitude!* said Aru.

Brynne responded: *You have attitude, Shah. Big difference.*

Aru grumbled and followed them down the staircase.

The shining gold-and-marble staircase spiraled down into a dirt-floored cave.

It was cold and damp; the air was filled with the smell of rain-washed rocks and turned earth. In the half darkness, the marmots' fur gave off a soft glow, illuminating the rocky walls and high ceiling, which were adorned with roots and cloudy gem-stones, rusty license plates, and grimy pennies. A sound like a low moan echoed through the dark, and the hair on Aru's arms prickled. *What was that?*

Sonu scampered up to them, handing out brochures.

"Tourists!" it squeaked again. "So exciting! I hear you like things called *pamphlets*, so we have a multitude on hand for your entertainment and pleasure!"

Aru took one. Her mom's museum offered brochures with information about current and upcoming exhibitions, events, and a brief history of the collection. The marmots' pamphlet was a rectangular piece of paper that read:

this

is

a

pamphlet!

:)

Aru turned over the paper. There had to be more to it. . . .
Nope. Blank.

"Do you like it?" asked Sonu excitedly.

"Uh . . ." started Aru.

Mini shot her a look.

"It's really . . . efficient."

"Thank you!" said Sonu.

Kanak raised one side of its lip in disgust, tore up the pamphlet, and trotted toward a pair of ginormous glass doors. The glass seemed frosted, but Aru could still make out the blurry shapes of three glittering archways beyond it.

"The gold roads!" whispered Kara.

Now they needed to figure out which one would take them to Lanka. And fast. Time was running out. According to Kubera's invitation, they had only two more days to get there before they'd risk losing the powerful Nairrata army, not to mention the other weapon the Sleeper was looking for. If that happened, the Otherworld would be doomed.

A molten gold sign shimmered above the doors:

SOUVENIR SHOP!
WE KNOW HOW MUCH
YOU LOVE HUMAN WASTE!

"Human . . . *waste?*" Mini said, looking disgusted.

Sonu beamed, the fur on its cheeks glowing brightly. "We heard all about how humans love to waste time and money on frivolities, and that inspired our motto!"

"But the phrase doesn't mean what you think—" Mini started to say.

Aiden let out a cough. Its import was very clear: *You ain't gonna win this one.*

"It makes quite a . . . statement?" said Mini weakly.

"I am so very pleased!" said Sonu. "Well, that's quite enough about our humble operation. Let the tour begin! Kanak?"

The other marmot, who was waiting in front of the glass doors, glared at them, then reached into a pouch at its side for a party hat that it jammed onto its head. "Hooray."

Sonu coughed. "Aren't you forgetting something?"

Kanak rolled its eyes, reached into the pouch once more, and threw a tiny pawful of confetti into the air. "Yippee."

Sonu clapped excitedly, gesturing them to the souvenir shop. The doors swung open and a stream of bright light washed over Aru as the gold roads rose into view beyond the checkout counter. Kara, Brynne, Aiden, and Mini walked into the shop, but Aru stayed back and let the glass doors close in front of her again. Out of the corner of her eye, she thought she spied an uncanny white wisp moving across the door's panels. When the golden light from inside the shop hit them, Aru could just make out the shapes of groups of people trudging along a winding trail. They carried children and belongings on their backs. Some of them dropped to the ground, exhausted, and did not stir again. The low moan she had heard when they'd first stepped below ground now filled her ears. It was the sound of unimaginable pain and grief.

"You can see it, can't you?" asked a low voice at her side. "We call it a ghost window."

Aru turned around sharply. Kanak, the grumpy marmot, was also staring at the misty image. There was no hint of annoyance on its face now, only sorrow.

"Sonu doesn't like to mention the ghosts, but they are part of the history of the place, and they should be acknowledged," said Kanak. "Do you know what *Dahlonega* means?"

Aru shook her head.

"It came from the Cherokee word for gold, *adela dalonige'i*," said Kanak solemnly. "The First Nations people had known about the precious metal for hundreds of years. Then, in 1838, white men drove them out of this part of their ancestral lands so the settlers could have the gold for themselves. Of course, the Cherokee went on to flourish in the East and West, but the ghost window shows only one glimpse into their history. What you see happening before you, child, is the Trail of Tears."

Aru watched as the ghost window slowly faded out of sight, but not out of her memory.

"Gold is a beautiful but treacherous thing," said Kanak. "We keepers know all too well the lengths humans have gone to possess it." The marmot turned its dark eyes knowingly on her. "I don't know what it is that you want, but be forewarned: The gold road is intractable and unforgiving. It shall do no one's bidding but its own."

Aru swallowed hard. "I, um...I'd better catch up with my friends."

Kanak said nothing as Aru went through the glass doors. Her thoughts were a jumble of her mother's and Kara's words weaving together.

The only people who can truly speak of history are ghosts.

Words are like a soul and a story all in one.

The very name of the city was a ghost story. Even as Aru stepped into the bright light of the shop, she couldn't shake the feeling that no matter how shiny it was, the gold of this place was cursed.

EIGHT

I Ain't Sayin' She's a Gold Digger

As a general rule, Aru hated souvenir shops.

Every time she entered one, one of three terrible things usually happened:

1) There was a ginormous revolving personalized-keychain contraption, but no matter how many times she spun it and searched for herself, she never found her name.

2) She was *honestly, just looking!* at one of the shot glasses before it suddenly exploded in her hand and she had to pay for an ugly I WAS AT <ANNOYING CITY NAME> glass even though she didn't want one.

But Aru was not prepared for the gold roads souvenir shop.

It wasn't some dinky pile of bricks where snow globes were sold. At first, it didn't even look like a shop, but a large, empty courtyard in front of three huge arches. One led to the mouth of a cave. The second would have looked identical if it weren't for the tools floating in the middle of its opening, making perfect gold coins, sparkling gemstone slippers, and feathered hats. The last archway, however, was a mystery. Fog clouded the entrance. It looked like the smoke-filled mouth of a monster.

Aru pointed at the third arch. "I'm guessing *that's* the road to Lanka."

Some five feet away, everyone swiveled toward her.

"Oh!" said Kara. "You're here!"

"I'm surprised you noticed," said Aru.

Kara looked confused and darted a glance at Aiden. "Did I say something wrong?"

"No, Shah's just being grumpy," said Aiden. He patted his messenger bag and asked Aru, "Are you hangry? I know how much you like Swedish Fish, so I packed—"

"Spare me the pity food," said Aru, turning from Aiden sharply, but not fast enough to miss the flash of hurt across his face.

Why are you throwing a tantrum? came Brynne's mind-link message.

No one's throwing anything, shot back Aru.

Mini didn't respond, but she looked disappointed.

Aru pointed at the archway. "So now what?"

"Do we make a run for it?" asked Brynne.

Mini frowned. "Didn't Sheela say something about remembering to be polite?"

"Polite to a souvenir shop?" scoffed Aru. "That, by the way, has *no* souvenirs?"

Sonu, who had left the group to find Kanak, now scampered back to them. It rose up on its haunches and clapped its paws. A low tremor ran through the ground, and Aru stumbled backward as little mounds started bubbling up in the floor.

The mounds sprouted and shelves grew up. The shelves were

stocked with snow globes filled with gold flakes, candy molded into lifelike golden nuggets, bobble heads of miners, and shiny magnets. A flock of T-shirts with the silhouette of two marmots on the front flew past, chased by T-shirts with questionable logos like I VISITED THE GOLD ROADS AND ALL I GOT WAS THIS ENCHANTED, SELF-WASHING T-SHIRT (AND HEY, THAT'S ACTUALLY AWESOME!). Next, a six-foot-tall revolving rack of personalized keychains shot out of the ground less than a foot away from Aru.

She glared at it. "I've been wronged by you before," she muttered.

"Who are you talking to, Shah?" asked Aiden.

"No one," said Aru quickly.

Sonu tented its paws and exclaimed, "You're the first customers to visit this shop! I planned and organized all the merchandise myself!"

"Our marketing person quit," said Kanak.

Sonu's smile looked a little brittle. "Anyway! There's no need, of course, to buy anything—"

The enchanted merchandise, which Aru realized had formed a slightly predatory circle around them, inched closer.

"It would be nice, though," said Sonu sadly.

The souvenirs bobbed up and down in agreement.

"And once you've purchased something, you're free to wander through the arches and visit the human-gold-mine and alchemical roads—"

"What about the Otherworld-cities one?" asked Aru.

"Closed," said Kanak. "No visitors."

"I'm afraid that's true," said Sonu. "Too many security issues. The Otherworld-cities road is rather unpredictable."

Kanak nodded. "It has eaten people—"

"*But,*" said Sonu with a pointed glance at Kanak, "should anything unexpected happen, we can close up shop and evacuate within minutes! So do not fear! But also, maybe, don't get too close to the third archway."

Aru's mind started to race. Maybe the polite thing to do *would* be to buy a souvenir. After that, they could cause a commotion and make a run for the third archway.

Aru was on the verge of making an excuse to the marmots when Kara cleared her throat. "Would you mind giving us a moment to discuss our purchases privately?"

"Of course, of course!" said the marmot. "So many exquisite things to choose from, I know." After a nod and a smile and several bows, Sonu darted back to Kanak's side. Then they scurried into a hole in the floor.

"You, too," Aru said to the merchandise. The shelves and racks immediately withdrew a few feet.

Kara beamed at the group. "I think I have an idea! What if a couple of us purchased souvenirs and the others caused a distraction? Then we could make a run for the third archway."

That was my *idea!* thought Aru.

"Gogo—that's my wind mace—does like making tiny tornadoes," said Brynne with a vicious smile as she touched her choker.

"I can block them with my scimitars until you get through," said Aiden, showing Kara his wrists bands.

"I can blast them back with Dee Dee," said Mini, lifting her Death Danda. "Gently, of course."

"My trident's pretty good at catching stuff," said Kara. "Is that everything?"

Aru raised her hand. "Um..."

Kara looked embarrassed. "Oh, Aru! I'm sorry. Um, maybe you could buy the souvenirs? Maybe one of those personalized things for each of us?"

Aru's face felt hot. Was she that forgettable? Just because Kara's weapon was made of sunlight didn't mean Aru's was some used-up battery. Vajra sparked with anger on Aru's wrist, and electricity clambered up and down her arm.

"I'll go find the keychains for you?" tried Kara helpfully. "Aiden, could you help me?"

Aiden looked between Kara and Aru. "I—"

Kara glanced at the floor. "I'm just not sure how everyone's name is spelled."

"Oh...okay," he said, and followed Kara to the side of the shop, where the keychain tower loomed.

Brynne and Mini hung back, flanking Aru.

"You okay, Aru?" asked Mini. "I don't think she meant anything."

Brynne shrugged. "Maybe you guys should just battle it out."

Mini stared at her. "That's a terrible idea. Aru, maybe Kara's trying to be, I dunno, overly helpful? Don't take it personally. She might feel threatened by you."

"*Threatened* by Aru?" Brynne said with a laugh. Then she caught the look on Aru's face. "I mean, uh, yes. Definitely that."

"Forget it. Let's just get this over with," said Aru, stalking to the keychains.

Up ahead, Kara spun the rack and fished out another trinket. Two already dangled from her left hand.

"Kai...Kamari...*Kara!*" she said with genuine excitement. "I've never had a keychain before!"

The keychains chimed like annoying bells, thought Aru as she started rifling through the *A*'s.

"Mina... Mindy... *Mini*," said Mini. "I never find my name!"

"What about you, Aru?" asked Kara. "Any luck?"

Aru shook her head.

"Let me help," said Kara. She spun the top tier, frowning. "I think I found— Oh. Never mind. It says *Andrew*."

"Great. I'll never notice the difference."

Kara looked stung. "I was only trying—"

"To help," finished Aru, annoyed despite herself. "I'm going to call over the marmots and pay for these things. You guys start heading to the third archway. I'll meet you there. When I say *go*, that means start a commotion. Okay?"

"Got it," said Brynne.

"Yup," said Mini.

Aiden nodded.

Kara turned to Aru. "Can I stay with you?"

"Sure, I guess," said Aru, somewhat confused. "You're already here, aren't you?" Then she grabbed the keychains and dangled them above her head. "Okay, I'm ready to buy these!"

Digging and cracking sounds filled the air. Moments later, Sonu and Kanak popped out of a new hole in the marble floor about ten feet away from them.

"That will be approximately one thousand!" said Sonu happily.

"A thousand dollars for two keychains?!" asked Aru.

"Cash or credit?" asked Kanak.

Aru winced. Out of the corner of her eye, she could see the others heading toward the fog-covered archway.

"It doesn't have to be dollars," said Sonu thoughtfully. "A

thousand anything, really. Buttons, socks, rope knots... We couldn't decide on a standard currency, so instead we settled on a simple, fair number: a thousand."

"A thousand is *a lot*," said Aru.

Sonu gasped, covering its mouth with its paws. "It is?"

"Told you," said Kanak.

"Listen, all I've got is an emergency credit card from my mom," said Aru. "If you charge a thousand dollars to it, she'll kill me. Can't we agree on something else? I've got..."

Aru fished around in her backpack and found a half-empty packet of M&Ms, a bottle of hand sanitizer (probably stuck in there by Mini), a pair of dry socks (because she hated it when she stepped in a puddle and water sloshed over her sneakers), and... five packets of salt, courtesy of Brynne, because "certain sandwiches can go from good to great with just a pinch of salt." Aru had pointed out that sandwiches were elusive beasts rarely spotted on quests, and Brynne had responded by smacking her in the arm.

"Is that it?" asked Sonu, looking skeptically at Aru's meager offerings spread out on the checkout counter.

The room seemed to shift ever so slightly with the tone of Sonu's voice. Aru risked a glance at the archways behind her. Now all three of them looked foggy, as if they were shutting down because it was clear the tourists couldn't pay the entrance fee.

"Salt! Wow, Aru! I didn't realize you had so much white gold!"

Sonu tilted its head to the side. "White gold?"

"Well, of course," said Kara, winking at Aru as she plucked one of the packets from the counter. "Did you know the word *salary* comes from the Latin *salarium*, which means a payment in salt? In ancient Egypt and Rome, it was considered so valuable—for preserving food and stuff—that people were paid with bags of salt."

Aru jumped in. "And we've got *at least* a thousand particles in these five packets."

"Ooh, particles..." said Sonu, tapping its paws together. "We'll take it!"

Sonu dumped the keychains into Aru's backpack. Through her Pandava mind link, Aru asked, *Are you guys ready?*

Brynne: *Duh.*

Mini: *I hope the marmots won't be too offended....*

The moment the salt packets dropped into Sonu's paws, Aru yelled, "Time to GO!"

"Sorry!" Kara said to Sonu. "But thank you, and—"

"Now, Kara!"

Aru flicked her wrist and Vajra dropped to the ground, transforming into a hoverboard. Aru jumped on and pulled up Kara, and together they zoomed past the flock of T-shirts and towers of trinkets. Some fifty feet away, Brynne blasted a wind tunnel through the fog-filled third archway, clearing a path for them to the Lanka road.

"Come on, Shah!" yelled Aiden, as he gestured everyone through the opening.

Aru was about to holler a response when the souvenir shop sprang to life. The keychains flew out of their spinner rack, swarming like a cloud of bees. The T-shirts dove into the fray. A NOT A TOURIST smacked her across the face and an I ❤ GOLD caught her by the wrist. Aru tore them off her only to get attacked by an angry knot of BRADEN, BRADYN, BRAEDEN, and BRAYDON keychains.

"You have *four* versions of Braden, but not one Aru? Is this a joke?" shouted Aru, batting away the souvenirs.

Kara unleashed her trident, catching three of the keychains in the tines of her weapon, but the swarm had thickened into a tall wave.

"*CHARGE!*" yelled Aru.

She tilted Vajra forward. Using her trident like a shovel, Kara flung golden magnets, bobbleheads, and snow globes left and right.

"Get that gold digger!" hollered Sonu.

A rumbling sound chased them. Aru snuck a glance behind her shoulder and saw that something was tunneling toward them under the marble. The stone cracked, and Kanak shot up a few feet from the archway with one golden paw outstretched. "Halt, rude tourists!"

A message from Brynne blared through her head: *HURRY UP, SHAH!*

"I *am* hurrying!" said Aru, fighting her way through the flurry of knickknacks.

With a final burst, Vajra broke free of the cloud. Aru flapped one arm, shaking off the grip of a TRUST ME, I'M THE GOLD STANDARD T-shirt.

Aiden and Brynne stood under the archway. Brynne aimed her wind mace and blew back the fog and mist to reveal a cavern with faintly glimmering veins of gold stretching into the darkness. Mini already waited inside, her danda raised. Kara spun her light trident like a baton, and the resulting glare forced Kanak to cover its eyes and stumble back a few steps.

"Now, Mini!" yelled Aiden.

Kara jumped off the hoverboard, and Aru tried to do the same—but one of her feet snagged in the other foot's shoelace. Aiden caught her in his arms and spun her sideways just as a blast of violet light shot toward Kanak.

As the marmot tumbled back into the souvenir shop, Mini shouted, "Sorry! Thank you for your time?"

"You are *not* welcome!" huffed Sonu, scampering to Kanak's side.

"I'll leave a five-star Yelp review!" Mini shouted.

It was the last thing she said before Brynne redirected the force of her wind mace and pushed the camouflaging clouds back across the archway behind them. Aiden released Aru so fast she'd barely had time to realize that he'd had his arms around her.

"Sorry," he said quickly.

Vajra shot back up, transforming into a spear in Aru's grasp. Her head whirled with a thousand sensations. The violet glow from Mini's Death Danda, the ghost of warmth from Aiden's body. And now, the sudden cool darkness of the cavern ahead of them.

Aru quickly straightened her top and tucked her hair behind her ears, grateful for the cold air on her face. When she looked up, she realized Kara was staring at her. Aru felt the tiniest stab of guilt. She had no real reason to be annoyed with Kara. It wasn't Kara's fault she was nice and pretty and helpful.

Shamefaced, Aru cleared her throat. "What you did back there with the salt facts..." she said. "Thank you."

Kara beamed. "Sometimes I go overboard when it comes to history and words, but I'm really glad it helped."

"Um, Kara?" said Mini. "Could we get some light?"

"Oh, right!" said Kara.

She raised her trident, and the light ate up the surrounding dark. The Otherworld-cities road was in a long tunnel. For a moment, Aru thought she caught an eerie sheen nearby, like light skimming over saliva-glossed fangs. She heard the flap of wings and an animal cry in the dimness. Aru shivered, but it wasn't the dark that scared her.

Ever since that last fight with the Sleeper's minions, her thoughts had grown shadows. With every step Aru carried her worries for her mother, her fury at Boo, and her confusion about the Sleeper. Whenever she thought about the battles ahead, an oily voice whispered in her skull, *How can you fight when you don't know who to fight for?*

Aru pushed that voice aside for now. If she listened to it, she'd never find the strength to move forward. Besides, all that mattered was that the Otherworld was in serious trouble. Even if she didn't know who to trust, she could at least protect her home. But to do that, she needed the Nairrata army.

And she was determined to get it.

"You ready, Shah?" asked Aiden.

Aru twirled her lightning-bolt spear. "More than ready."

NINE

I'm Not Equipped for This Level of Decision-Making

Perhaps Aru was not actually ready.

At least, not ready to figure out how to get from one place to another.

It seemed that the golden road was tricking them. At first, their surroundings had seemed dark and eerie. But then, after they'd been walking for about five minutes, things changed. The shadows pulled back. The eerie animal cries vanished into silence. Aru had the distinct impression that the road was waiting and judging them somehow. For the next twenty minutes of their journey, she kept her lightning bolt raised and her senses sharp, but nothing happened.

Eventually, the tunnel opened into a pit where a sparkling mist surrounded a circle of tall statues. Aru saw what looked like an East Asian pagoda, an Aztec pyramid, a harp as tall as her body, and a pair of golden mongooses facing each other.

"I think all this is supposed to represent the interlinked Otherworld cities," said Mini, squinting. She pointed at the pagoda. "That must be for Shangri-La."

Brynne pointed at the Aztec pyramid. "And that must be El Dorado."

"There's only one place a mongoose could signify," said Aiden. "Lanka."

The moment he said the word, the air turned stifling hot. Carefully, the five of them approached the foot of the mongoose statues. Up close, the figures were at least twice Aru's height. Each mongoose had one palm up, with a sphere balanced in the center, and between the two statues levitated a basket. A strange glow reflected off the animals' metal teeth, making them look even sharper than they already were.

"I thought mongooses—wait, is it *mongeese?*—were supposed to be cute," said Aru. "These things look deadly."

"Makes sense," said Aiden. "They can kill cobras."

"*Cobras?*" Mini moved closer to Aru and scanned the ground. "No one said anything about Lanka having cobras."

"You got through Naga-Loka, and this whole time you've been afraid of them?" asked Brynne.

"Well, nagas are only *half* snake—"

"Is that actually better?" asked Aru. "Or is it like being scared of worms in apples and then biting into an apple and finding only half a worm?"

Mini gagged. "Ingesting insects through unwashed produce can lead to arsenic or lead poisoning, and if you do that, then—"

"You'll die?" said Aru and Brynne at the same time.

Mini huffed.

Aru looked up at the statues and studied the spheres in their paws. One ball appeared to be solid gold, the other solid lead. Beyond the ring of statues, shadows roiled around them. A smell that Aru couldn't identify seeped into the air. Like hot metal . . . or blood.

"Sheela's prophecy said that *Not everything that glitters is gold / The truth will lead to the Lanka road*," said Aru slowly. "My guess is we have to throw the real golden ball into the basket. Aiden said Lord Kubera is pretty tricky, though, so he's probably put an enchantment on them. Mini?"

Mini opened her compact, which could always see through illusions. She examined the statues' reflections in the mirror and then pointed at the golden sphere on the right.

"Looks like that one's the fake," she said. "Beneath the gold is lead, and inside the lead sphere is gold, so—"

Kara, who had been quiet, raised Sunny. When its light fell over the statues, her eyes took on a curious golden sheen. Brynne strolled forward and reached for the lead ball . . . but Kara blocked her with a thrust of the trident. "No!" she said sharply. "Don't!"

"Are you *seriously* pointing a weapon at me?" demanded Brynne, turning around.

"Don't touch that one!" said Kara. "The golden ball is the true one."

Mini looked annoyed. "My compact is never wrong—"

"But can it see through more than one layer of illusion?" asked Kara.

Brynne batted away the trident and reached once more for the lead ball.

Panic flitted across Kara's face. She bit her lip and swung out the trident again. "I'm serious!" she said.

Brynne whirled around, her wind mace up and aimed at Kara. "Who do you think you are?"

"I'm just trying to help!" said Kara.

The atmosphere between them felt charged. Mini's violet compact lengthened to a danda, and Vajra, still in spear form, was growing frantic.

"Let's take this down a notch," said Aiden, holding up his hands. "Kara, I really think—"

"I don't know how I know, but I know I'm right. Please believe me!" Kara turned to Aru. "You trust me, don't you?"

Trust.

The word needled Aru's heart. Ever since they'd met, Aru couldn't help but trust Kara, and she didn't understand why. Kara seemed like a truer daughter of the Sleeper than Aru was. There was so much about her half sister that Aru didn't know, so much that maybe Kara didn't even know herself. But Aru hated that Kara could tell she believed her.

Brynne stared at Aru, something wary sneaking into her gaze, and Aru's stomach knotted with guilt. Aru looked at Mini, who seemed confused, and then Aiden, whose face betrayed nothing. Her pulse started to race. Did all of them think she was the untrue sister from the prophecy? Had she confirmed their suspicions by bringing Kara along? A nightmare from long ago flashed across Aru's mind. She could see herself raising her weapon at her own sisters. She saw the hate in their eyes. . . .

All of Aru's carefully held down fury roared up inside her.

"*Trust* you?" spat Aru. "You do realize you're only here because you insisted on coming? You still haven't told us what weapon the Sleeper is after. I'm beginning to think you made it all up!"

Kara looked as if she'd been struck. "What?"

"I've had enough of this," said Aru.

She turned Vajra into a hoverboard and rose to haul the sphere out of the left mongoose's hand. The lead ball was at least fifteen pounds, and Aru's arms sagged under its weight as she zoomed forward and dunked it into the basket. Beyond the mongoose statues, the path of mist cleared, transforming into a walkway of golden bricks. Ancient banyan trees with twisty roots mottled with gold rose on either side. Through their ink-black branches, Aru could just make out the familiar split night-and-day sky of an Otherworld city.

"See?" snapped Brynne. "Told you."

"Let's go," said Aru.

But they'd barely taken one step onto the Lanka road when the ground beneath them shuddered.

A huge banyan branch swung toward them. Aiden leaped forward, his scimitars flashing brightly as he slashed it in half.

"What's happening?" shrieked Mini.

Aru's mind raced. *How did Kara know?* But then the bricks beneath their feet began to crumble, forming a glowing crater.

"The ground!" yelled Aru. "Move back!"

All at once, the road collapsed in on itself, plunging them all straight into a pit of churning gold coins.

TEN

Aru Shah Eats Humble Pie

You know that image of Scrooge McDuck diving into a pile of money?

Aru used to think: *THAT. That is 100 percent what I want for my life.*

What could be better than plunging into your riches, flailing your arms and making snow angels in piles of gold, while maniacally cackling, *MINE! IT'S ALL MINE!*

But in practice? Not so much.

Aru tried to claw her way out of the pit, but it was like quicksand, sucking her in up to her waist. More gold coins suddenly rained down thick and fast from the sky above. Aru struggled to gulp air as cold pieces of metal pelted her face.

Beside her, Brynne fought to lift her wind mace. Blue light flashed around her. For a moment, her form shifted, flickering back and forth between a giant bird and a long-tailed monkey, but the coins created a weird static and finally she gave up.

"I can't transform!" screamed Brynne.

Aru tried to clamber onto her Vajra hoverboard so she could haul everyone out of the money pit, but the torrent of coins only grew thicker, forcing Aru down until she was buried nearly up to her neck, her legs and torso immobilized in the swirl of gold.

Aru pried one arm free to block another onslaught of gold when purple light bloomed around them. Mini—buried up to her chin in coins—had thrust out her Death Danda. A shield bubbled over them.

Now the coins sounded like hailstones hitting a windshield. Within seconds, tiny cracks spiderwebbed across Mini's dome. With the downpour paused, Brynne managed to scramble up on top of the pile of gold. She hauled out Mini, who spat coins and gagged a little.

"We're"—*spit*—"going"—*spit*—"to—"

"Die?" offered Aiden as he wriggled his way free.

Beside him, Kara was struggling, so he extended his hand. Aru, meanwhile, was still stuck and panting like a dying wildebeest, and no one seemed to mind....

YANK.

"There ya go, Shah!" said Brynne, as Aru went sprawling on top of the coins.

"We're not going to die," said Aru, coughing and pushing the hair out of her face.

"The second the shield fails, those coins are going to trap us down here," said Brynne. "There's no way we can climb our way out—look how far away it is!"

Through the dome, Aru could just barely see the rim of the hole they'd tumbled down. It was at least a hundred or so feet away from them.

Brynne grumbled. "I can't transform, Mini's shield doesn't work, and Aiden—"

"Can document our final moments of terror and doom in the hope that future generations can learn from our mistakes?" suggested Aiden, patting his camera.

Mini whimpered.

"I have an idea," said Kara, looking at each of them in turn. "But this time...you have to trust me."

Aru's face burned a little. If she had listened to Kara in the first place, they wouldn't have ended up here. *Surprise, surprise, something else is your fault, Aru Shah,* whispered a nasty voice in her head.

"So, will you trust me or not?" asked Kara.

Mini, Brynne, and Aiden turned to Aru. She swallowed hard, then nodded. "Tell us what to do."

A minute later, Aru, Kara, Aiden, Brynne, and Mini were huddled under the slowly breaking violet shield.

"On my count," said Aru.

Kara twisted the ring on her finger, and it began to glow brightly.

"One..."

Brynne raised her wind mace.

"Two..."

Aiden threw up his hood.

"Three..."

Mini slammed down her Death Danda, and the shield shattered. Immediately, Kara aimed her light trident upward and let it loose in a deluge of gold. Aru thought it would get knocked down, but instead the trident flew straight, turning translucent in the places where the coins hit it, until it lodged in the wall of the pit about a foot below the opening.

"Now!" yelled Aru.

Mini created a small bubble around Brynne, who twisted her wind mace, gathering a cyclone around her. All the while, the coins piled higher and higher. Within seconds Aru was buried up to her hips again. Another minute and she'd be swallowed completely.

"Done!" said Brynne.

Mini retracted the shield, and a steady stream of air blew a path straight through the coins. A second later, Aru transformed Vajra into a hoverboard. Mini and Aru clambered on. They zoomed through the veil of gold until Mini could grab the handle of Kara's trident.

"Go!" said Aru.

Mini flipped herself up and over the handle. Once she was safely back on land, Mini blasted a new dome above her. Coins pinged and bounced off the hard violet shield as Aru zoomed down to grab Kara and Aiden. Brynne transformed into a blue osprey and together they flew up and out of the pit.

Aru gasped for breath, her hands braced on the warm dirt. Above her, the ancient banyan trees no longer looked menacing, but still and stately. The only sounds in the forest were the distant chittering of squirrels and an occasional birdcall.

She inhaled deeply, trying to center her thoughts. Her heart was still racing, and the smell of coins—like stale tears—clung to her skin. Aru turned the now weakly flickering Vajra into a Ping-Pong ball and tucked it gently into her pocket. Beside her, Kara heaved herself upright and stretched out her hands to summon her trident.

The moment Brynne caught her breath, she turned to Kara. "How did you know?"

Kara shook her head. "Sometimes I get this *hunch*. Like I can see the truth of a thing."

"I'm sorry we didn't believe you," said Mini. "It's just—"

"I get it," said Kara quietly. "You don't need to apologize."

Maybe the others don't need to apologize, thought Aru, *but I definitely do.*

Aiden stood off to the side, holding a bunch of small bags he'd rustled from his backpack. "Snack break?"

"Yes, please," said Brynne, stomping over.

"Who wants to eat after almost swallowing all those gold—" started Mini.

She must have seen Aiden look meaningfully at Aru and Kara, because she fell silent.

"I mean, wow, who knew coins were such an appetite stimulant? Coins are great. I should have kept some. Wait, I—"

"Why don't you stop while you're ahead, Mini," said Brynne, steering her toward Aiden, and leaving Aru and Kara alone together.

"Thank you," Kara said to Aru.

Aru's gaze jerked to hers. "What?"

"Thank you for getting us out of there. And I need to thank Brynne for transforming, and Mini for shielding us, and Aiden for, well—"

"Aiden was pretty useless," said Aru.

"I heard that!" shouted Aiden.

Aru grinned and shouted back, "For the most part, you're a great wifey!"

Aiden grumbled in the distance.

"Wifey?" asked Kara.

"Long story," said Aru before sighing loudly. "Listen, about what I said to you earlier ... That wasn't fair."

"But it was true," said Kara. She looked helpless. "When I look at it from your perspective, I get it—I really do. I thought maybe if I proved that I could be helpful, you guys would give me a chance, but I keep doing things wrong. I promise I'm trying—"

Aru groaned. She hated feeling guilty. It was like someone had held a lit match to her insides.

"You're not doing anything wrong," she said reluctantly. "If anything, you're doing everything *too* right. Like, *creepily* perfect. Not that you're creepy—"

"I used to watch you sleep," said Kara, twisting her golden ring.

"Welp, I take back what I said."

Kara laughed a little. "When Dad—I mean, the Sleeper, brought you to the cave, he kept you unconscious for almost two months."

She paused, staring down at her feet. "Every day he told me 'watch over your sister.' I loved that word... *sister*. The whole time, I couldn't wait for him to wake you up, Aru. I couldn't wait to be your sister. I know I'm not a Pandava, but I guess I just thought... I don't know... that it would be different or something. That's all."

Kara didn't look up. Aru stood there, shocked. Usually, she never ran out of things to say, but this time, she stayed quiet. Kara as a sister felt like something that could've been but never would be, like the Sleeper being her dad. But then again, maybe, like everything else in Aru's life, sisterhood didn't have a clear-cut definition....

"I know it's not how you thought it would be, but maybe we can figure out our own... version?" tried Aru.

Kara looked up. "Really?"

Aru nodded.

"I'd like that," said Kara. After a moment of silence, she sighed. "Do you ever wish you were someone else?"

"What, with this face and hair and while I'm clearly living my best life?" joked Aru, gesturing at her dirty strands, grime-streaked cheeks, and the dark forest around them. "Nope."

Kara laughed. "Looks like we've got something in common after all."

Not too far away from them, Aru heard Mini say, "*Finally.*" Brynne shook an empty chip bag and asked, "Are we out of food?" while the familiar *click* and *whir* of Aiden's camera merged with the sounds of the jungle.

"I'm sure we can eat once we get to Kubera's palace in Lanka," said Aiden, putting away Shadowfax. "Which way do we go?"

Brynne licked her finger and stuck it in the air before pointing straight ahead. "Thataway."

They'd only just started walking through the trees when a branch snapped loudly and tumbled to the ground by their feet. All five of them froze as laughter rang through the banyan forest.

Aru, Mini, and Brynne turned to one another and, without speaking, prepared to activate their weapons. Aru had only begun to adjust her grip on Vajra when the canopy above them shook.

"GOTCHA!" shouted a voice from on high.

"Heck no!" yelled Brynne, swinging her wind mace.

Aiden glanced up and brought out his scimitars. At the same moment, a huge sparkling net fell across all five of them. Aiden slashed at the mesh, but it was like he was hitting diamond-hard threads. His blades bounced backward once before they transformed back into bands around his wrists. He frowned and shook his hands, but the scimitars stayed dormant. Aru tried to activate Vajra, but it was useless. It was as if her lightning bolt had fallen asleep. Kara twisted her ring only for a lazy glow to bubble around her hand. Mini took out her compact and Brynne touched her choker, but nothing happened.

Kara looked stunned. "What's going on?"

Dirt sprayed across Aru's face as a huge figure landed on the ground in front of them. In the weak light from Kara's ring, it was impossible to make out the features of the being on the other side of the net. All Aru could see were broad shoulders and— Wait a minute.... Was that a *whip*?

"I think I'm suffocating," said Mini, panicking. "What if this net cuts off all our oxygen? We could get hypoxia! And if we get hypoxic, we'll *die!*"

"Then stop using up all the oxygen, Mini!" said Brynne.

Aiden grunted. "No—room—to—move—at—all—"

Aru wrinkled her nose. She felt uncomfortably hot and sweaty, and everyone smelled like metal and potato chips. Gross. "Okay, I swear if someone burps right now, I will lose it."

"SILENCE, TRESPASSERS!" shouted the person on the other side of the net.

"Are they really trespassers?" asked someone else in a higher voice. "Is this the part where we get to hit them over the head?"

"Please tell me it's not that part," muttered Mini.

"No, child, no . . . But I'm sure the queen will appreciate your eagerness in defending the Kingdom of Kishkinda from smelly vagrants," said the first voice.

Brynne sniffed herself and crossed her arms. "We're not smelly!"

"And we're not vagrants!" said Aru. "We're on our way to Lanka. We don't even want to stop in your Kingdom of Kitschy—"

"It's Kishkinda!"

"On your way to Lanka, eh?" repeated the first voice, laughing. "And how do you expect to get there?"

Aru frowned. What did that mean? This was the road to Lanka, wasn't it?

Kanak's voice floated through her thoughts: *The golden road is intractable and unforgiving. It shall do no one's bidding but its own.*

"Let us out, and we'll go on our way," pleaded Mini.

The second being cleared its throat. Through the netting, Aru thought she saw a long, furry brown tail. More animal guardians? But she couldn't identify what kind these were. The two creatures began talking to each other in low voices. Aru only heard bits and snatches:

"—be very angry, won't she?"

"No one here in thousands of years—"

"Fine, fine, but I get first swing!"

"Okay, what's going on out there?" demanded Aru.

"Well, if you're sure . . ." came the second being's timid voice.

The next instant, the net turned slick and translucent. All the dirt and leaves it had collected slid out of a small hole in the bottom, and then the opening sealed back up. Aru blinked wildly as her eyes adjusted to the light.

At first, she thought she saw a couple of monkeys.

But that wasn't possible. They were too big.

Aru rubbed her eyes and blinked again.

Okay, maybe it *was* possible.

Standing before her were two tall monkey-human hybrids. They didn't look like Hanuman, who had a simian head on a human body. These creatures had smaller faces and rounder eyes.

They wore military jackets on their wide shoulders and no pants, revealing their bowed legs and long, thin tails that curled in the air like question marks.

"You're . . . You're *vanaras,*" said Brynne.

"Vanaras?" asked Aru.

"Monkey-people," said Aiden.

Aru glared at him. "Yes. I can see *that* much."

"No one's seen your species in ages!" said Brynne. "I thought you were, like, extinct or something."

"And *whose* fault is that?" retorted the first soldier. "Cutting us off from the world! And for what?"

"That wasn't us!" said Mini.

"It was *your kind,*" said the first soldier, nodding at the vanara beside it.

The second soldier, who seemed younger and shyer, looked terrified. "Orders, sir?"

"Take them to the court," said the first soldier. "It's time to put these humans on trial for what they did."

ELEVEN

World's Worst Pokémon

Aru Shah did not like monkeys.

At all.

Okay, fine, their faces were a little cute, and she respected their ingenuity when it came to annoying everyone, but she'd stopped liking monkeys the day some had cornered her and stolen her corn on the cob during her one—and so far *only*—trip to India with her mom. And nobody else had seen them take it! Her mom had just thought Aru ate the whole thing really fast, and then she'd refused to buy her another one. Rude.

All that old resentment rushed up as the vanaras snapped their fingers, causing the net to rise up, as if the Potatoes were a bag full of laundry, and float down the dirt road.

"Brynne, stop shoving!" cried out Mini.

"Your elbow is digging into my stomach!" grumbled Brynne.

Aru had the great misfortune of having one side of her face squashed right up against the net. Kara was beside her, though her back was to the net, and Aiden had rolled up like an angry pill bug with his eyes squeezed shut.

"*Om . . .*" said Kara, humming.

"Are you seriously meditating right now?" asked Aru.

"I read somewhere that mindfulness helps in stressful situations...."

Aru heard the bigger vanara grumble, "Quiet, prisoners!"

Aru groaned. The net was enchanted against their weapons, and even if they managed to escape, where would they go? How far was Lanka from the kingdom of the monkeys, anyway?

"All this power, and we're trapped?" growled Brynne.

Aru sighed. "We're like the world's worst Pokémon."

"*Worst?* Speak for yourself," said Brynne. "I'd be a Charizard."

"What about me?" asked Mini.

They didn't have a chance to figure it out—although Aru secretly suspected Mini was a Shadow Psyduck—because the enchanted net landed and rolled against a ginormous pillar. Everyone tumbled forward, and Aru, hunched over with her face still pressed up against the net, caught her first glimpse of the ancient Kishkinda Kingdom.

The vanaras had brought them to the center of an amphitheater surrounded by a massive crumbling palace. The ground was studded with dull rubies and garnets, so that it looked eerily blood-spattered. Tiers of shabby throne-like seats surrounded them on all sides. In the middle stood a large podium and a tall structure Aru couldn't quite make out. Once, the amphitheater might have looked imposing, but now it was run-down. The elaborate stone carvings of solemn vanaras at the end of each tier were chipped and moss-covered, and the satin cushions on the seats looked threadbare. Overhead, the sky was no longer split between day and night, but was fully dusk. The bright, salty smell of the sea filled Aru's nostrils.

It was almost calming. . . .

Until the surrounding trees began to quiver and shake. From the branches, dozens of vanaras dressed in tattered uniforms, or just rags, leaped toward the agora, whooping and shrieking as they clambered to their stone chairs.

"Deceptive! Terrible!"

"—banishing us!"

"No right to return here—"

"SILENCE!" shouted the bigger vanara guard. "Humans have dared to trespass on our ancestral lands, and for the first time in thousands of years, they must finally answer for the crimes committed against us!"

The vanaras screeched and hooted. Some of them threw fruit, spattering the ground with pulp. The vanara soldier's lips pulled back into a grin, revealing shiny red gums and long yellow teeth. He tapped Aru's head, and the net's enchantment released her— and only her—forcing her to stumble forward. The moment Aru was free, the second vanara guard clamped a pair of enchanted ropes around her wrists. Aru nudged at Vajra in her pocket, but the ball only buzzed weakly.

"BEHOLD ITS GRUESOME VISAGE!" shouted a vanara in the audience.

Aru bristled, trying to shake out her hair. *It isn't that bad, is it?* Aru craned her neck to look back at her trapped friends. In her head, she'd imagined everyone wearing matching expressions of *LET'S GET 'EM.*

Alas, it was not to be.

Aiden's face had gotten squashed between Brynne's and Mini's shoulders, so he looked like an angry chipmunk. Mini's glasses had gone sideways and poked her in the eye, so she was tearing up. Kara's face had gotten stuck against her own arm. And Brynne had gotten so twisted, she was facing the other way.

When they took you out, a sharp rock bounced inside. I think I can open the net with it, said Brynne through their mind link.

YES, thought Aru.

Just keep them distracted.

By now, Aru had reached the podium. On one side of it was a rickety wooden chair, and on the other, a tall object concealed by tattered silk. She was forced into the chair, which faced a large throne where a vanara sat wearing a white wig and red robe. The creature glared at her.

"SILENCE!" it yelled, bashing a banana against the armrest of its throne. "ORDER! ORDER IN THE COURT!"

"Wait a minute..." Aru said.

"Where's the defendant's counsel?" asked the judge.

The younger vanara guard placed a rotten tomato beside Aru's foot and then stepped back, announcing, "Present, Your Honor."

"Hold on, you're giving me a *rotten tomato* for a lawyer?" demanded Aru. "It can't even speak! Don't I have a right to, I dunno, better counsel or something?"

She wasn't actually sure what she was saying, but she'd heard something like that in a movie, so it seemed close enough. Another vanara hopped down from the seats. He was dressed in an elaborate suit of banana leaves and wore a pair of sunglasses with one of the lenses punched out. He whispered to the judge, "Can she do that?"

The vanara judge shrugged and said, "Proceed with your questioning."

The prosecuting attorney puffed up his banana suit, then pointed a furry finger at Aru. "State your name for the court."

"Aru...Shah?"

"And what king do you fight for?"

"*King?*" repeated Aru. "None?"

"Nonsense! Which king enthralls your land?"

Aru considered this. "Uh...probably *Tiger King*, but I don't think—"

"YOU SEE, MY SISTERS AND BRETHREN?" said the vanara lawyer, rotating in a circle to address the crowd. "Once more, these kings and queens and gods and men drag us into their foolish wars. And who ends up paying for them? *Us!* Why do you seek to destroy us, oh Aru Shah, subject of the Tiger King?"

Okay, Aru was not going to be able to explain this one. It was time to be honest. She took a deep breath.

"So, I think there's been some kind of confusion?" tried Aru slowly. "You see, we're not trying to destroy anybody.... We're just trying to get to Lanka."

The moment she said *Lanka*, shrieks rolled through the amphitheater.

Uh-oh.

Brynne, how much longer?

It's going to take a bit! said Brynne.

"*Lanka*," seethed the prosecutor. "The city where our woes started...and you dared to utter its name in our presence?"

"Sorry—"

"AHA! Our official apology from the humans has come at long last!"

The vanaras cheered, throwing down cherry pits and banana peels.

"Read out the defendants' crimes against our people, counselor," said the judge, bored.

The lawyer puffed out his chest. "Thousands of years ago, you demanded our help! Do you remember that?"

"I'm fourteen!" said Aru. "I wasn't even there."

"The god king Rama, avatar of Lord Vishnu, *god* of preservation, demanded our help, and we gave it, did we not?"

The vanaras cheered.

"He wanted to cross the sea to Lanka, and what did we do?"

"BUILT! BUILT! BUILT!" shouted the vanaras from their seats.

Built? thought Aru. Oh, yeah...She knew the tale. Rama had needed to get to Lanka, where his wife, Sita, was being held prisoner by the ten-headed demon king Ravana.

"The sea would not answer to Rama," said the attorney, "so we threw rocks into the ocean and built the god king a bridge! But what did we receive for all of our efforts?"

The crowd went silent. A sea breeze blew through the amphitheater, rustling up dust and broken jewels. The lawyer turned slowly to Aru.

"When Lanka was set on fire, who did they blame? *Us.* When the prince of Lanka grew hungry, who did he devour? *Us.* When the world moved on, who was left behind and forgotten? *Us.*"

As one, the vanaras rose from their thrones. The only sound came from the drag of their tails over the stone tiers as they advanced toward Aru.

"You cut us off from the world, leaving us with nothing but scraps..." said the lawyer, jabbing a finger in Aru's face.

Aru tried to squirm out of her seat, but the guards on either side of her growled.

"Only broken things found our shores," the prosecutor hissed.

From the highest tier of the seats, someone shouted, "We want to know what happens after season three of *Law and Order*! Tell us, human!"

"Tell us! Tell us! Tell us!" the rest chanted.

Suddenly, the judge, the jury, and the lawyer made a lot more sense.

"How does the defendant plead?" asked the judge.

One of Aru's guards stepped forward and yanked the silk cloth off the object on the podium. Aru's jaw dropped. *Oh my gods . . . Is that a—?*

"VIVE LA FRANCE!" shouted a vanara in a wig and lipstick.

"What *is* France?" asked someone else.

Another nodded sagely. "You mean, *why* is France?"

"OFF WITH HER HEAD!" screamed a fourth.

BRYNNE, THERE IS AN ACTUAL GUILLOTINE HERE! HOW MUCH LONGER—?

Gimme . . . just . . . one . . . more . . . minute. . . .

The bigger guard shoved Aru toward the machine. Aru tried to shake the magical bindings off her wrists, but they only tightened. *Vajra! Vajra, wake up!* she thought. Her lightning-bolt ball seemed to get smaller, like a cat curling up for a nap. Something about the enchanted ropes was keeping its magic at bay.

Up close, the guillotine stood fifteen feet high. Tiny crabs scuttled up and down the wooden frame, and the whole thing leaned a little to the left. The blade, rusted by seawater and dinged up in places, still looked sharp.

"Any last words, human?" asked the judge.

Stall, Shah! And do NOT say "Let them eat cake!"

"Uh, don't eat cake?"

The judge frowned. Even the lawyer looked confused. Just then, Aru felt a release of pressure around her wrists. She glanced down and watched as her bindings slowly undid themselves. Some five feet away, Aru caught the faintest sparkle of violet. She grinned.

Don't worry, Aru . . . came Mini's gentle voice. *We're here! Had to get away from that net before our powers could work, but I've got the invisibility shield up and running. Waiting for your signal.*

"Strange choice of last words, human, but oh well!" said the lawyer.

Aru felt the last of her bindings slip off.

"Oh, right, I forgot one more thing," said Aru. She snapped her fingers, and Vajra shot ten feet up in the air before landing in Aru's hands as a ginormous agitated lightning bolt. Aru grinned. "I'm not *all* human."

NOW!

Mini threw off her invisible shield.

A gasp ran through the crowd of vanaras around them. For a second, it was like the whole amphitheater was holding its breath. Aru spun around, trying to find a clear exit, when a chorus of shrieks lit up the air. . . .

The vanaras charged.

Aru spun Vajra. The vanaras howled, tumbling backward. Aru had barely had a moment to grin when something pelted her. Fruit pulp exploded across the podium. A massive shape sailed toward her. Aiden's scimitars cut through the air, slicing an incoming basket of bananas clean out of the sky. Mangoes and giant papayas hurtled their way. Mini sprang forward, casting out a shield, and the fruit splatted across it.

ARU SHAH AND THE CITY OF GOLD

"What a waste of antioxidants," mourned Mini.

"I think I've found an exit!" said Brynne, pointing toward a break in the walls of the amphitheater.

Aru nodded. Now they just had to get there.

"All right, Potatoes," said Aru, "time to make like a banana and—"

Aiden's face darkened. "Aru, don't you dare—"

"SPLIT!" cackled Aru.

Everyone looked horrified except Kara, who let out a giggle. Mini turned off the shield when it seemed the last of the fruit had rained down on them. A knot of vanaras hopped forward, baring their teeth and raising sticks with dangerously sharp ends. In a flash of blue light, Brynne transformed into a giant baboon. She growled, curling her lips to reveal long, stained fangs.

The vanaras dropped their sticks.

Aru, Aiden, and Kara jumped off the podium and raced toward the break in the wall, Brynne and Mini close behind. The vanaras must have anticipated where they were going, because they leaped ahead and tried to surround them.

Aru transformed Vajra into a lightning net, spinning it out to catch a ball of vanaras, when a huge shadow fell over the amphitheater. She looked up to see a bare foot the size of a dining table slam into the middle of the space, nearly smashing the judge's podium. Aru tumbled backward, and Mini sprang in front of her and everyone else, preparing to cast a protective shield over them.

"Run!" Aru called as the giant's shadow loomed larger.

She turned to move only to collide with a giant soft brown palm.

"Shielding!" called Mini.

Once more, Mini surrounded them with a violet sphere, but

that just made it easier for all five to be scooped up together. Aru felt her stomach fall as the ground disappeared beneath them and they were pulled up and out of the amphitheater.

"Let me at 'em!" yelled Brynne. Her skin flickered blue as if she was on the verge of transforming.

"Don't!" shouted Aiden. "Mini's shield will break!"

Brynne growled.

"Get into fighting positions!" said Aru.

Even Kara, despite not being part of their group for very long, fell into place as they crowded into a tight circle, standing back-to-back in the center of the giant's cupped hands. Aru swiveled her head, trying to get better a visual on their foe. The giant's fingernails were neatly filed and... painted? Aru looked up. Not a giant... but a giantess. In the dusky light, her head was cloaked in shadow, but then she moved and Aru saw the ginormous face of a beautiful young apsara wearing a gold crown. She had large eyes and a small mouth, a piercing in each nostril, and her dark hair was shot through with red highlights and piled into a bun. She wore an expression Aru had often seen on her own mom. It said, *Very amusing. Now quit it!*

"Are you quite finished?" asked the giantess.

Far, far below, the vanaras shouted, "They started it, Queen Tara!"

Aru whipped around. *"Queen?"*

TWELVE

In Which the Pandavas Are Stranded, But, Hey, the Fruit Is Great!

"These are our new *friends*," said Queen Tara, holding the group aloft in her palm.

Aru felt a wave of dizziness when she looked down from so high up. Below them, the vanaras screeched and raced back and forth.

"Refreshments for our human guests!" Tara called out. "For we are celebrating!"

Slowly, she lowered Aiden, Aru, Kara, Mini, and Brynne back into the amphitheater. Then she straightened up and snapped her fingers—the sound of which reminded Aru of a distant clap of thunder—and shrank to the size of a human woman.

Albeit a very tall human woman.

"I need a moment to ready my quarters, and then you shall be summoned," said Tara kindly before strolling into the palace.

Brynne stared after her, a slight blush on her cheeks. "She's so regal...*and* she's so tall! Plus, she's pretty."

"Something about her seems familiar," said Mini. "I feel like I know that name...."

"Wow," said Kara, pointing at the amphitheater. "That's . . . certainly a makeover?" Several yards away, dozens of vanaras busily worked to transform the whole place. Now, marigold petals carpeted the ground. Someone had even strung the guillotine with garlands of pink and yellow carnations.

"Did you know that the guillotine was developed by a French physician who thought it was the most humane way of executing people?" said Kara brightly.

"Yeah, I had the exact same thought when I saw it over my head," said Aru.

Just then, a vanara wearing an elaborate turban ran toward Aiden, who was snapping photos of the kingdom. "We *love* celebrations almost as much as war!"

Aiden lowered his camera. "That's good?"

"Have you written your vows already?" he asked.

"Vows?" asked Aiden, darting a panicked glance at Aru.

Two more vanaras rushed forward. One of them leaped over to Aru, measuring her waist with red silk and holding up golden bracelets and earrings to her face. Another threw a garland around Aiden and began to comb his hair. Aiden batted them away, but the vanara only laughed.

"Okay, I'm confused," said Aru. "What's happening?"

"We're preparing for your wedding, obviously! The queen said there will be a celebration, which must mean a wedding! I love weddings! You're the blushing bride, right?"

Behind them, Brynne and Mini collapsed with laughter. Even Kara giggled.

"Wifey's bride?" Aru asked incredulously.

"Hmpf!" said the vanara in front of Aru. He tore off the red silk and snatched back the bangles.

Then he hopped over to Aiden, who put up his hands and took a step backward while looking very alarmed.

"So *you're* the bride!" the vanara said to Aiden. "We'll have to do this as a vow-renewal ceremony."

Aiden threw off the garland, grabbed the comb, and hurled it over the wall.

"No wedding, no vows, no thank you," he said, turning red in the face. "Been there, done that."

"Oh, I see," said the vanara, nodding sadly. "Separated?"

"Reincarnated," snapped Aiden.

He hefted Shadowfax and, without another look at Aru, stomped off in a different direction. The other two vanaras shrieked and bounced back to the amphitheater, cackling all the while.

"Hey!" grumbled Aru. "At least let me keep the bracelets!"

Brynne, Mini, and Kara burst out laughing. Even Aru thought it was funny. Obviously, Aiden had not.

Maybe if he'd just laughed it off she wouldn't have felt so embarrassed right then. It was one thing to say that it was silly. It was another to be so grossed out by the idea that he had to get as far away from them as possible.

Brynne squinted into the distance. "Oh, Ammamma. Let me go talk to him. He's been a little ... in his head lately."

"He has?"

"Ever since you got kidnapped, actually," said Mini.

"Why?" asked Aru.

But Brynne didn't have a chance to answer. The sound of trumpets echoed through the branches and a guard announced:

"Her Illustrious Majesty, Queen Tara of Kishkinda Kingdom, shall see you now!"

Two handsomely dressed vanaras sprang from a door in the courtyard wall and invited the Pandavas, Kara, and Aiden into the palace. The group was escorted through a passageway lit with floating lanterns. On the right, statues of former vanara kings with grim faces lined the walls. On the left stood a row of glowing silver pillars that broke up a view of the ocean. As Aru stared out at the water, a golden glimmer in the distance caught her eye. It looked like a star pinning the horizon into place.

"That must be Lanka," whispered Kara at her side.

"That's not so far, right?" said Mini. "I mean, maybe we could get there by boat in time for Kubera's deadline tomorrow...."

One day left, thought Aru, her stomach lurching. One day left to show up in Kubera's court, and less than a week before the Sleeper's army marched on Lanka. On top of that, they didn't even know if Kubera would give them the mighty Nairrata army to fight back with.

All that lay between them and Lanka was the sea....

But there was something strange about the water—it had an eerie, almost deliberate calmness to it that reminded Aru of a predator lying in wait.

Aru heard Aiden and Brynne whispering to each other behind her back. He hadn't said anything to Aru since the vanara's silly mistake. *Whatever,* thought Aru. *Just get over it already.*

Soon, the guards brought them to Queen Tara's private chambers.

Like everything else in Kishkinda, there was a faded beauty to the place. It looked as if it hadn't changed since ancient times. *Diyas* and gauzy swaths of silk floated down from the ceiling to give the room a peaceful air. In one corner, blindfolded vanara musicians struck up a tune. Rose petals were strewn across the floor, and a semicircle of satin cushions had been arranged around a low table piled high with gleaming fruits, steaming dishes, and crystal glasses of fruit-infused ice water.

Queen Tara eased herself onto one of the cushions. Even though she looked like a young woman, she moved as if she had grown weary of time. She wore a traditional sari of red-and-blue silk, heavy golden bangles about her wrist, and chiming anklets. On her forehead was a line of red powder that Aru recognized from her mom's art books as *sindhoor*, the sign of a married woman.

They all sat, unsure of what to do until Brynne—whose stomach was grumbling loudly—reached over, grabbed a plum, and gobbled it down. Aru grimaced. Watching Brynne eat was a lot like watching a human vacuum cleaner.

"I understand you wish to go to Lanka, but I'm afraid we cannot help you," said Queen Tara. "Lanka banned any contact with Kishkinda Kingdom after the war with the god king Rama. As you know, Rama was only able to reach Lanka because my people built him a bridge. We could not be forgiven for that. And after Hanuman set Lanka on fire, somehow we were the ones who took the blame."

"Hanuman did *what?*" asked Brynne, jaw gaping.

There was no mistaking the horrified look on her face. Hanuman, after all, was her half brother.

"Many people were harmed," said Queen Tara. "Some of Lanka's citizens ran across the bridge to us and found sanctuary among my people."

Brynne paused for a moment, shamefaced, but soon started eating again.

"The bridge remains in the human realm, but I destroyed it in the Otherworld," said Tara. "I have said it before, and I shall say it again: I want nothing to do with the games of gods and men."

Hey, that rhymed! thought Aru.

"What do you seek in Lanka anyway?" asked Queen Tara, waving her hand dismissively. "It is ruled by a king as hard and cold as his riches. He has nothing you could want."

"Except an army," said Aru.

Queen Tara eyed her shrewdly, then sighed. "So, it would seem there is another war brewing with the devas."

Brynne frowned. "It could destroy—"

"War always destroys. That is the nature of it."

Aru felt her cheeks turning hot again. She was tired of people refusing to listen. How many times did she have to hear someone tell her that what she cared about didn't matter? Vajra, now a bracelet on her wrist, picked up on her annoyance and sparked angrily. Aru was about to speak out, but Kara beat her to it.

"My father's army grows stronger by the day, and he's planning to march on Lanka in less than a week," she said quietly. "We have to do something."

"*I* don't have to do anything," Tara retorted. "I owe the world nothing after what it has stolen from me. I do enough already as queen. I have kept my people safe and well-fed. We do not *need* the Otherworld."

Kara straightened her shoulders. In the shadowy room, it looked as if she'd gathered all the light to her. "Someone once told me that just because you can't have the life you wanted, you shouldn't give up and fade out of existence. That's how we become living ghosts—by never moving on."

Tara frowned and looked longingly at the empty cushion beside her, as if she wanted to reach for someone who wasn't there anymore. The room fell silent as the vanara musicians finished their tune and prepared to strike up a new one. The queen glanced up, snapped her fingers, and the musicians leaped away, leaving her alone with Kara, Aiden, Brynne, Aru, and Mini.

"Who gave you that wisdom, child?" asked the queen.

Kara's gaze darted to Aru before she said, "My father."

A familiar knot of envy welled up inside Aru, but she shoved it aside.

"Even if I wished to help you, I cannot," said Queen Tara. "I will take you to the seaside to show you what I mean. But first, let me caution you." She scanned each of their faces in turn. "If you must fight someday, allow me to advise you about one thing: do not fight in anger."

As she said this, her eyes settled on Aru, who looked away. Queen Tara didn't know her. She didn't know how it felt not knowing where her mom was, or that someone who'd felt like family to her had let her down in the worst way possible.

"The gods ruined my life," said the queen. "So trust me when I say I know of anger. You see, the god king Rama killed my husband."

Mini looked shocked. *"What?"*

Tara raised her hand and then swept it down through the air. As her hand moved, a mirror materialized before them. But instead of seeing her own reflection in it, Aru saw Queen Tara in the past, standing beside a handsome vanara wearing a crown and a luxurious suit of royal blue.

"My love, Vali," the queen said sadly.

The image shifted, and Aru could see another vanara—one almost identical to King Vali—step into the picture.

"And my brother-in-law, Sugriva. They were twins, you see,

and very close.... But they had a falling-out. Years ago, there was a terrible attack on the kingdom, and we all believed Vali had died. To keep me safe from harm, Sugriva assumed the throne and married me," said Tara.

Aru made a face. *You married his brother? Awkward.*

Tara looked at her sharply. "Times were different then," she said. "When my husband returned, he was furious. He did not believe that Sugriva had done it to protect me. In a blind rage, he exiled Sugriva and kept both his wife and me as further punishment. I knew it was wrong, but Vali would not listen to *anyone*. Very few dared to cross my husband. He was fierce in combat, for he had won a boon from Lord Brahma himself that whoever fought him would lose half their strength."

In the mirror, the scene widened to show Sugriva walking through the forest with a small band of companions before coming upon three individuals. Aru recognized them immediately. There was Rama, the god king; his brother, Laxmana; and Hanuman.

Ravana has stolen my queen, Rama said to Sugriva. *Help me find my wife, and I will help you win back yours.*

The image shifted once more, showing Sugriva and Vali locked in combat.

Tears ran down Tara's cheeks. "I told Vali to make amends with his brother, to join Rama in his quest for Sita...but he did not listen. Anger over his brother taking sides against him clouded his heart. And for that he lost his crown...and his life."

As Sugriva and Vali battled each other, an arrow flew out from behind one of the trees, piercing Vali straight through his heart. He fell to the ground, and Tara, who had been watching from a distance, ran to his side. Rama stepped out from his hiding place, lowering his bow.

Tara pointed a trembling finger at Rama and said, *Just as you have separated me from my husband, I curse you, Rama, that soon after you find your Sita, you shall be separated from her, too.*

The mirror melted back into the air.

"Happiness destroyed only begets more destruction," said Tara.

Aru's chest felt heavy with sorrow. Why was everything so tangled? The Sleeper had tried to avoid his fate, only to end up making it come true. Aru had hurt Shukra long ago on that snowy bridge in the Kingdom of Death, and his curse had come true the moment when she'd needed the truth the most. So much of the world was out of her control that Aru felt dizzy even sitting there.

Beside Aru, Mini swiped at her cheeks, barely hiding a sniffle. Kara looked thoughtful, while Brynne was stony-faced, and Aiden stared down at his feet.

"I was angry for a long time," said Tara. "But my anger did nothing but cause another's pain. Remember my story before you rush into war. If you fight with poison in your heart, you will lose sight of what it is you are fighting for."

The queen rose to her feet and gestured to the door. "Now come with me. It is time for me to show you why you cannot cross our sea."

At night, the ocean looked like spilled ink. The soft white beach curved around the water in a crescent. Aru liked it here. The air smelled like salt and the citrus trees that grew out of the nearby cliffside.

Beside them, Queen Tara inhaled deeply. "After his city was burned to the ground, the Lord of Lanka declared that no one from our kingdom could ever again cross these waters," she said. "The sea knows his wishes and refuses to carry anyone from our shores. It even denied passage to Rama. The only reason the rocks we threw into the ocean were not rejected was because each one was inscribed with the name of Lord Vishnu himself. The sea would never insult the heavens by presuming to be above them."

"Can't we just try that again?" asked Aru.

Tara shook her head. "What was done once cannot be done again. The sea takes no counsel but its own."

Hmpf, thought Aru.

"Oh yeah?" Brynne rolled up her sleeves and stretched her neck from side to side. "Let's see about that. This ocean can't stop me."

THIRTEEN

The Ocean Stops Brynne

Brynne stretched out her arms. In a flash of blue light, she shape-shifted into a turquoise-colored seagull. She whooped, then soared off the beach and toward the water.

"Aiden, document my victory!" she cawed happily.

"Brynne, I don't think—" started Mini.

Aiden sighed, lifting his camera. Aru held her breath as Brynne skimmed over the first wave.

"She's doing it!" said Kara. "How—"

But then things changed pretty fast.

All of a sudden, the ocean seemed to contort. The water rippled and rose up, taking a strange shape, almost like a—

"Is it just me or does that wave look like a fist?" asked Mini.

The fist reared back and punched Brynne straight out of the sky. She went tumbling backward. Tara shot up in size so she could reach out and catch Brynne in her hand like she was a baseball.

When the queen shifted back into human size, Brynne was cradled in her arms, passed out. Mini rushed over to Brynne, snapping her fingers in front of her closed eyes and checking her pulse. Meanwhile, the sea smugly settled back into serene flatness. Aru imagined it was saying *Who, me? I did nothing.*

"Well," said Mini. "She's definitely out. I'm worried about a concussion.... Will she be okay?"

"She'll be fine," said Aiden. "I once saw her get knocked out by a skyscraper. She woke up a couple of hours later with a craving for pickles. That's about it."

"I regret to say that I told you it would be so," said Tara. "I shall take her inside. You all are welcome to rest in the palace until you are ready to return home."

Tara walked down the beach with Brynne dangling from her arms.

"What are we going to do?" asked Mini. "We have to get to Lanka by *tomorrow* to answer Kubera's summons!"

"I think we should go back to the gold roads," said Kara. "We can explain to the marmots that we need their help."

"I highly doubt they're going to want to deal with us after we trashed their souvenir shop," said Aru.

Kara wrapped her arms around herself. The wind tugged at her hair. "You don't understand.... We have less than a *week* before Dad marches with his army, and I've seen the plans. He won't stop until he's found the nectar of immortality, and he's getting closer every day. Going back is worth the risk—"

"But we're so close!" said Aru, flinging her hand at the ocean and the faraway lights of Lanka. "This may be the only way to get there in time! We have to try again."

Kara shot her a pitying look. "I know you're clever, but do you really think you're going to outsmart the ocean?"

"I didn't say that," said Aru, uncomfortable with the way everyone was staring at her. "I just don't think that Brynne turning into a bird and getting punched out of the sky was the *only* solution."

"Aru," said Kara gently. Once more the sun seemed to treat her differently, like she was always in a spotlight. "How many times are you going to try the same thing and expect a different result? Because that's the *definition* of insanity. At least that's what they think Albert Einstein said. And maybe it would make sense to try your way, but not when we only have one day left...."

"Maybe we should vote on it," said Aiden quietly.

"I vote that we leave," said Kara, raising her hand.

"Well, I vote that we stay and give it one more try," said Aru, crossing her arms. "Mini?"

"I...I think we should...leave," said Mini apologetically. Kara looked triumphant, and Mini turned the slightest shade of red. "To be clear, the person I'm agreeing with is the *queen*. If she's saying there's no way to get from here to Lanka, I believe her."

It was a tiny distinction, but it made Aru feel a little better. She believed that Queen Tara was telling the truth. Yet something seemed off. The queen looked deliberately untouched by time, and her kingdom—though safe—had turned strangely inward. Kara had recognized it on the spot and compared them to *living ghosts*. For all they knew, Tara wanted to stay a ghost. Maybe wanting to stay a ghost kept her from seeing a way out of here.

"I think Brynne would want to give it another shot, though," said Mini. "So I'll vote yes for her. That leaves you to break the tie, Wifey."

Aiden looked at the ocean as if he'd rather throw himself into the waves than have this conversation. "Count me out of this vote."

"Oh c'mon!" said Aru.

"I don't think you'll hurt anyone's feelings by choosing a side," Kara said to him, glancing pointedly at Aru.

Aiden looked from Aru to Kara, his eyes narrowing. "I don't pick sides. Let me know what you guys end up doing." He turned on his heel and started heading up the beach.

Aru, grumbling, ran after him. "Hey!" she called.

Aiden kept going.

"Why are you always walking away these days?" she yelled.

Aiden stopped in his tracks. He faced her slowly, the sea breeze tousling his hair. In the weeks she'd been gone, he'd gotten taller and broader, and he towered over her now. "What exactly do you think I'm walking away from, Shah?"

A thousand retorts flew through Aru's head: *From the monkeys joking about a wedding! From looking at me directly! From standing up for me!* But instead she just glared at him. What could she say? He wasn't walking away from anything except . . . her. If she pointed that out and he ended up telling her the truth—that she annoyed him or that he agreed with Kara—then what? She'd end up feeling even more miserable.

Aru decided to stay quiet.

"I'm not taking sides," he said firmly. "Especially not with you."

Stung, Aru stood there and watched him walk away. Again.

They ended up going back to the palace to sleep, and that night, Aru dreamed she was crossing a bridge made of snow, laced on either side with frost and icicles. She recognized it as the Bridge of Forgetting, although the guardian who had cursed her was nowhere in sight. Above Aru, the sky looked like the inside of an eggshell.

Dream perspective was strange. Even though she knew the bridge was dangerously high above the earth, she could see with perfect clarity the Tree of Wishes beneath her. She recognized its bright branches and the glow of its fruit, which looked like someone had decorated it with stars. Aru remembered what it was like to stand under that tree after learning the heartbreaking choice her father had made to free himself from his fate. She even recalled the *shape* of the wish she must have made. But what the heck had she asked for? In the dream, Aru opened her mouth, ready to hear herself utter the forgotten wish....

But instead of speaking, she sang.

And it wasn't the wish.

"LET IT GOOOO, LET IT GO! I AM ONE WITH THE WIND AND SKY—" Aru abruptly stopped, glowered, and stared at the dream sky. "Okay, *who* made me do that?"

Aru spun around and saw the twins, Sheela and Nikita, rolling on the bridge and laughing so hard they had tears in their eyes.

"Sorry...but...not...really..." Nikita said between gasps, kicking her feet in the air.

"I love you, but you can*not* sing," said Sheela, waving at Aru. The small clairvoyant was now floating upside down in the air like the Cheshire Cat.

"We caught you in the middle of what was going to be a nightmare, and we tried to fix it," said Nikita, standing up. "But then...it took a turn. If it helps, I changed your outfit?"

Aru looked down and saw that instead of her favorite Spider-Man pajamas, she was in a long ice-blue gown that looked a lot like...

"Do you want to build a snowman?" asked Nikita.

"No."

Ten minutes later—or who really knows because dream time is strange—Aru was building a snowman with Nikita and Sheela.

"We tried to get the others, but Mini is still awake, I think, and Brynne is dreaming about pickles," said Nikita. "She wouldn't come out of it."

"Yeah, well, Brynne got knocked out by the ocean pretty hard," said Aru, distracted. She was still thinking about Kara's plan to go back to the gold roads, Mini agreeing with it, and Aiden not siding with anyone at all.

Kara had been right about the sphere on the mongoose statue, and Aru hadn't listened, landing them all in trouble. What if Aru was doing the same thing now? What if Kara was just better at making decisions? Or, worst of all, what if everyone simply liked Kara more and would rather listen to her over Aru?

As if reading her thoughts, Sheela put her small brown hand over Aru's. "You're *my* favorite, Aru. You make me laugh."

Aru sighed. "Well, it's nice to be *someone's* favorite."

Nikita, who was now adorning the snowman with a bright white hat and a multitude of rainbow-colored feathers, tossed her braided hair over her shoulder. "I am always my *own* favorite. That works best for me. Maybe you should try it. Just be your own favorite person and then no one else's opinion really matters."

"That's not nice, Nikki…" said Sheela.

"I don't mean *you*," said Nikita, rolling her eyes. "We're practically reflections of each other."

Aru stopped.

"Reflections…" she whispered. "I think…I think I have an idea for how to get us across the ocean! Nikita, I think you might be a genius!"

"Duh," said Nikita imperiously. "And while you're thinking of a way to get across the ocean, ask yourself why you're always wearing Spider-Man pajamas."

"Because they're comfy!" said Aru hotly. "Why do you always wear ball gowns?"

Nikita raised an eyebrow. "Because they're fabulous."

FOURTEEN

That Big Demigod Energy

Aru jolted upright, nearly tumbling out of the hammock she'd been sleeping in.

The vanaras didn't like beds, so they snoozed in elaborate hammocks that hung from the ceiling, or, if they didn't want to stay indoors, tree branches.

It was early morning, and the light streaming through the windows of the chamber she shared with Brynne, Kara, and Mini looked blue and eerie.

Aru hopped to the ground, taking a step toward Mini's hammock to wake her. In the end, she stopped herself. All Aru had was an idea. She didn't know if it was actually going to work, and the last thing she wanted was to get everyone up only for them to see her fail.

Aru's chest tightened as she pulled on the hoodie she'd packed, and slipped out of the bedroom. In the past, she wouldn't have hesitated to show them her latest brainstorm, but things felt different now. These days, Aru couldn't lose the shadow of loneliness that had followed her ever since she'd been kidnapped by the Sleeper. Even in a crowded room, she felt alone.

Sure, she had the amazing company of her friends, but it didn't change the fact that she felt separated from everyone by a layer of ice.

Aru was alone in realizing that Boo had betrayed them. She was alone in knowing exactly what the Sleeper's lost memories had felt like. And she was alone in wanting to try one last time to cross the ocean.

Aru looked back at the sleeping shapes of her sisters and Kara. *I'll prove it to you,* she thought silently.

All she needed now was a mirror.

Aru remembered seeing a big one on the wall of the stairwell they'd climbed the night before. Maybe she could pry it off and return it before anyone noticed?

She raced down the steps and spotted the mirror...but someone was standing in front of it. Aru moved closer and saw that it was Queen Tara dressed in a pure-white sari.

Aru moved even closer. In the light of early dawn, Tara looked like a ghost. A *living ghost,* as Kara had said. That was the price of being unable to move on.

The queen didn't seem to notice Aru. She kept staring—not at the mirror, but at the wall next to it, almost as though she couldn't bear to look at her reflection.

"Hello?" called Aru softly.

Tara startled, turning around and clutching the folds of her dress. Her face was ashen, her lips pulled into a tight line. "Oh. It's you, child....Hello. Did you not sleep well?"

"Oh, no. I slept fine," said Aru, her eyes darting to the mirror behind Tara.

"Is there something you require? Provisions, perhaps, for your journey back?"

Aru nervously pointed at the mirror. "Actually, I was wondering if I could borrow that."

"The mirror?" said Tara curiously. She frowned. "My husband gave it to me."

Aru's face burned. "Oh, sorry. Maybe I could use a different one...?"

"No, no...please," said Tara. "I have no use for it."

The queen snapped her fingers and the mirror peeled off the wall and soared into her own hands. "I always thought the mirror was a strange gift," she said with a sad smile. "Would it not have been better to give me something useful, like silks...or valuable, like jewels? But I think my husband always suspected that he would meet a violent end and leave me to face the world alone. He told me that should there ever come a time when I needed answers, I would find them in this."

Tara still did not look down at the mirror's surface, but her fingers tightened around the frame.

"I tried looking into it a few times, but whenever I saw my reflection, I was reminded of who was no longer standing beside me."

She thrust the mirror into Aru's hands. For something so large—almost as tall as Aru—it was surprisingly light; it weighed about as much as her laptop.

"It's a lonely thing...to truly behold yourself," said the queen. "If you think the mirror might help you, please take it. It is enchanted and will readily obey your bidding."

"Thanks," said Aru. "I really—"

But Tara seemed lost in her thoughts, so Aru left the queen standing on the stairs and made her way to the beach.

The sun was just beginning to rise over the horizon. The

smell of brine and citrus hit Aru's nostrils as she stared out at the sea. It looked calm and smug, dimpled all over with sunshine.

"So, Ocean, you don't like anything except yourself," said Aru, adjusting the weight of the mirror. "Relatable."

Aru moved slowly toward the water, as if she was afraid of spooking the ocean. Tara had said the sea would reject anything that didn't belong to it, and Aru had seen that happen to Brynne. But would it be able to tell the difference between reality and a reflection?

Aru pictured the mirror floating parallel to the ocean's surface. She felt the mirror's enchantments making a connection to her, like a plant's fragile tendril reaching for the sunshine. Aru held on tight to that sensation, then let her hands drop. Instead of hitting the sand, the mirror hovered at Aru's waist. Aru flung out her hand, and the mirror smoothly soared forward, inching itself past the shoreline and over the sea.

Aru waited.

Any second now, she thought.

The ocean didn't react.

If anything, it seemed like a bored cat, its tiny waves curling gently in indifference. Aru waved her hands like an orchestra conductor, and the mirror followed her movements, swooping and spinning, rising high and dropping so low that its silvery surface skimmed the water. The ocean didn't care at all.

Aru grinned.

GET UP! she called through the Pandava mind link. *Time for us to get to Lanka, and I know the fastest route.*

Queen Tara and half the vanara kingdom showed up on the beach with Aiden, Kara, Brynne, and Mini. By then, Aru had called back the mirror. If her entire group was going to cross the ocean, they'd need something much, *much* larger.

Brynne lumbered over to Aru first, grimacing a little. "Why am I craving pickles? Also, I've decided I hate the beach."

"I'm sure the feeling's mutual," said Aru. She turned to Mini. "We're going to need your compact to grow into something large enough for all five of us to fit on."

Excitement flickered over Mini's face. "One mirror board coming up!" she said.

Mini waved the danda over her head, and a swirl of violet light shot out of it. It rose in the air and then fell back onto the sand, flattening into liquid silver that spread in a circle until it was roughly the size of a large dining table.

"Okay, who wants to try it first?" asked Aru as they watched the disk harden before their eyes.

Aiden's eyebrows shot up his forehead. "This seems like a Pandava decision, and as a Pandava *adjacent*, I'm bowing out."

"Um, me too," said Kara, raising her hand.

Brynne took a gigantic step back. "I already got punched by the ocean, I'm not playing guinea pig."

"*C'mon,*" said Aru. "I've already done an experiment, and it worked great."

"Nope."

"Maybe we should take a vote?" suggested Mini. "Or—"

"NOSE GOES!" hollered Aru.

Aru immediately smacked her hand to her nose. With a panicked squeak, Mini grabbed her nose so fast she knocked her glasses off her face. Which left Brynne ... who moved to cover her nose a *fraction* of a second too late.

"I hate you, Shah," she growled.

"I promise it's going to work," said Aru.

"And if it doesn't?"

"I'll be your taste-testing guinea pig in the kitchen," said Aru.

Brynne brightened. "Really? You can't fake it. I know your food allergies, and—"

"Yes, I promise," said Aru. "But if I'm right, you have to turn into an actual guinea pig."

"My body will reject that form," said Brynne, flexing.

"Just get onto the mirror?" pleaded Aru.

Brynne grunted, then stepped onto the disk. She created a blast of wind underneath the structure to propel it up and then forward. The reflective circle glided over the breakers, and Aru carefully scrutinized the water, holding her breath.

The ocean did not change.

At first, everyone was silent. But a moment later, they burst into thunderous screeching and shouts. Queen Tara clapped her hands over her mouth. Kara's jaw dropped. Aiden watched with his hands in his pockets, his mouth quirked in a small smile.

"WE'RE FREE!" yelled a vanara, flinging sand into the air.

Brynne sent the disk back to the shore and jumped off it with a huge grin on her face.

Mini ran forward and threw her arms around Aru. "You did it!" she squealed.

Aru hugged her back.

"Nice, Shah," said Brynne.

Aru crossed her arms. "I'm waiting."

"No..."

"Three, two—"

Brynne hissed something under her breath and then, in a flash of blue light, transformed into a blue guinea pig.

"Oh my god, you're so cute!" said Aru, reaching out to pet her.

Guinea Pig–Brynne nipped at her, then scuttled away.

For the next ten minutes, everything was a blur of activity. It took forever for the Pandavas, Aiden, and Kara to gather their things, because the vanaras kept grabbing the items and throwing them into the air, hooting gleefully all the while.

Aru picked up Tara's looking glass and walked over to the queen. "Thank you," she said, handing it back. "It had the answers after all."

Hesitantly, the queen accepted the mirror. She held it at a distance and kept her eyes averted from it at first, but then Tara finally met her own gaze in its reflection. Her expression looked a little stilted, as if she was out of practice. Slowly, her face cracked into a smile.

"One of the things I miss most about my Vali was his wit," she said, turning the mirror slightly. "I see now that he intended this to hold the answer both to my grief and to our isolation." She laughed a little.

"I've looked to the past to remember happiness for so many years that I'd forgotten how to look to the future to find happiness anew." Queen Tara bowed her head slightly. "You have given us a great blessing. Please accept our gifts in return, for your journey ahead."

She put down the mirror and waved both arms. Two vanaras burst through the crowd, leaping forward with baskets full of fruit.

"Ooh!" said Brynne. "Snacks for the road!"

Tara smiled. "I have one last gift to bestow upon you, Aru Shah, daughter of Indra. For your cleverness, I make you an honorary vanara."

"*Really?*" asked Aru. "What does that mean? Can I shape-shift into a monkey?" Take that, every monkey bar in the playground she'd ever fallen off. Ha!

"No."

"Oh."

"But whenever you have need of me or my people, we will honor your call," said Queen Tara, drawing herself up. "Kubera's Nairrata army may be mighty to behold, but do not forget that *we* once made Lanka cower."

Aru wasn't sure what to do . . . so she bowed. And that seemed to be the right thing, because the queen smiled warmly.

"Sneaky saves the day again," said Brynne, clapping Aru on the back.

Aru went sprawling on the sand. Brynne grabbed her by her hoodie and yanked her upright. "Ow!" said Aru. "Easy . . ."

Together, they started piling up the baskets. Mini stayed by the waterline, using her danda to mold something that looked like a canoe made of mirrors.

"Aru?"

She turned to find Kara standing beside her. The other girl looked a little guilty.

"I should've given you a chance yesterday," she said.

Aru shrugged. "Kinda like how I gave you a chance with the mongoose statues?"

Kara looked relieved. "Clean slate?"

"Sorta dented, a bit scuffed . . . but yeah, clean slate."

Kara smiled in relief and then headed toward Brynne and Mini.

"Hurry up, Ammamma!" hollered Brynne.

Aiden was the last to make his way over, ambling as if they

had plenty of time. Aru thought he would avoid her gaze, but when he got near, he stopped and stared right at her.

Aru glared at him. "And you thought I couldn't do it."

"I never said that." He still had his hands in his pockets. Aru crossed her arms, and Aiden sighed loudly. "I don't like picking sides. It's, um, not a happy memory for me."

Oh, thought Aru. She remembered all the times Aiden had snuck out of the house because his parents were fighting, and she felt a twinge of guilt.

"But for what it's worth, I'm always on your side, Shah."

Aru looked up at him. She hated the swoopy-elevator feeling she sometimes got when he stood too close. She moved back a step.

"Well...you could've told me that!" said Aru. "It would've been nice!"

"You don't function well under 'nice,' Shah," said Aiden, with a vague smirk. "You tend to do your thing when there are zero options left. I think panic brings out the best in you."

"Not true, and also rude—"

Click! Aiden snapped a photo of her so quickly that Aru barely registered it.

"See?" said Aiden, flipping Shadowfax around and showing her the picture of her expression. "It's a good look on you."

Aru studied the photo. Her eyes were dark and bright at the same time. There was a faint glow of electricity behind her that lifted her hair but didn't make it frizzy. She seemed...powerful.

Aiden was right.

It *was* a good look.

FIFTEEN

Rich-People Problems

At first, it was pretty fun to skim over the sea. They didn't have to worry about choppy waves, and the random sprays of salt water dried off quickly. Aru saw an occasional shark fin knifing through the water, and once a school of rainbow fish leaped out of the waves, their iridescent scales catching the sun and shining like jewels.

But then the hours melted together, and no matter how far they traveled, Lanka seemed the same distance away.

"Are we there yet?" asked Aru, who was now lying on her back, staring up at the sky.

How long had it been since morning? What day was it? What was *Time*?

"You asked that five minutes ago," grumbled Aiden.

"I thought we would be there by now!" said Aru. "From the beach, Lanka looked super close."

"But it's a magical city..." said Kara thoughtfully. "It's probably farther away than we thought. Or it could be a metaphor. Lanka is a place of temptation, and it's always said about greedy people that the more wealth they have, the farther away they think it is. I always thought that was strange, because the origin of the word *wealth* comes from the Germanic *weal*, or *health*. So really—"

"So we could be here for *centuries?*" interrupted Aru. She tossed Vajra up in the air and told it, "I'm going to have to start calling you Wilson."

"Who's Wilson?" asked Kara.

"Nope," said Brynne loudly. "Aru, if we're going to lose our minds out here on the ocean, you quoting some movie no one's ever seen is not going to help."

"*Castaway* is a classic, you heathens," said Aru.

"Hey, what happened to all the fruit?" asked Mini, rummaging through her rucksack. "I thought Queen Tara gave us a ton...."

Aru craned her head to see Brynne looking extremely guilty.

"I was hungry," she said.

"You ate *all* of it?" asked Mini. "How? When?"

Brynne shrugged.

"I told you we should lock away the snacks, but no one listens to me," said Aiden.

Mini started to rock back and forth, which Aru recognized as the beginnings of a MOMDPA, or Mini Obscure-Medical-Doom Panic Attack.

Aru sat up and held out her hands, as if calming a rabid beast. "Okay, Mini, let's think this through...."

"What if Kara's right and Lanka is farther that we thought?" asked Mini. "What if we really are stuck in the middle of the ocean? Do you know what will happen if we don't have enough fresh fruit? You can get a vitamin-C deficiency, and then your gums start bleeding, and you get weak, and then you get scurvy—"

Kara grew alarmed. "I'm sure that—"

"And then you *die!*" wailed Mini.

Kara looked wide-eyed between Aru and Mini. "I mean, I'm sure it's not *that* far away!" said Kara hurriedly. "Like, maybe another hour?"

"We thought that *two* hours ago!" said Mini, breathing fast.

"I did say we should go back..." muttered Kara.

"Really?" said Brynne. "You're bringing that up *now?*"

"Sorry!" Kara winced. "I take it back! I—"

But they never heard what she was going to say. Their makeshift raft slammed into something. Aru turned to see what it was, but sunlight glared off the mirrors and blinded her. Frigid ocean water sloshed over the sides, drenching them.

"Hold on!" yelled Brynne.

Aru's mind started racing. Was it a rock? A giant shark? She scrambled to grab hold of something as the raft tipped and they slid into the water. Dark waves closed over her head. Aru thrashed her arms and kicked wildly beneath her.

She broke the surface and yelled, "VAJRA!" and ended up gulping down brackish seawater. Then, as panic overtook her, "WILSON! WILSON?!"

Aru felt a strong pressure beneath both of her armpits. She fought back only to get hauled to her feet.

Wait. Feet? She could stand?

Aru blinked rapidly, rubbing water out of her eyes.

"I kept trying to tell you it was fine!" said Brynne, standing before her.

The four Potatoes plus Kara (Aru was still withholding judgment on whether or not she was an honorary Potato) were standing in the shallows of a golden dock that led to an archway studded with gemstones. There was no sign of a city beyond it—just shadows. It was like they'd stumbled onto some lonely pocket of the Otherworld.

Vajra, which had been hovering in the air, possibly waiting for Aru to stop thrashing around in the shallows, gracefully glided back to her hand.

"How long was I, uh, struggling?" asked Aru.

"Long enough," said Aiden, lowering his camera with a grin.

"Is that the entrance to Lanka?" asked Mini. "Why's it so . . . ?"

"Abandoned?" finished Kara, looking at it suspiciously.

"Maybe it's just the dock that looks that way," said Aiden. "Remember, Queen Tara said Kishkinda and Lanka haven't spoken to each other in, I dunno, centuries."

"Hope they'll talk to us," said Kara.

Brynne used her wind mace to dry them all off in seconds as they stood at the threshold of the archway. Aru peered through and thought she spied a glint of gold in the shadows. And was that laughter she heard on the wind?

Only one way to find out, she whispered to herself.

And with that, they stepped through.

Aru had expected Lanka and Kishkinda to look similar. They were both ancient kingdoms mentioned in the old myths . . . but that's where the similarities ended. The moment Aru left the archway behind, the landscape before her changed. She found herself staring up at a glittering city unlike anything she'd ever seen.

If the Night Bazaar was a place where magic came alive, then Lanka was the place where magic turned wild.

Huge glittering chariots raced across a street paved with gold. Giant pointed buildings jutted from the ground like golden fangs. Electronic billboards floated between the buildings or above shops, flashing so bright that Aru felt a headache coming on. From one screen, the image of an exquisite-looking buffet peeled off and floated toward her. Brynne whined and gripped her stomach. The illusion was so convincing that Aru could actually smell the spiced rice and naan slathered in rich ghee. From another screen, a beautiful green-skinned woman leaned out and beckoned to them. She blew them a kiss before pointing to the neon words now hovering in the sky:

PERFORMING FOR ONE NIGHT ONLY!
THE GORGEOUS VISHAKANYAS OF LANKA!
THESE POISON MAIDENS WILL KNOCK YOU DEAD!

But one billboard stood out from all the rest.

The image loomed over Lanka, like a blanket flung over the city. In it, a god lounged in a richly upholstered throne. He seemed to be staring straight at them as his booming voice declared, "WELCOME, VISITORS, TO THE CITY OF GOLD! THE ONLY PLACE IN THE MULTIVERSE WHERE MONEY CAN, LITERALLY, BUY YOU EVERYTHING." The god leaned forward and winked before settling back into his throne and turning as still as a photograph.

"So that's Kubera..." said Aiden, gawking at the screen.

The god of wealth didn't look at all like he sounded. His tone was so deep that Aru could've sworn she'd seen tiny nuggets of gold rattling on the streets. It was the kind of voice that seemed like it should belong to someone tall and imposing. But Kubera was a bald dwarf with a round belly, and stodgy fingers crowded with sparkling rings. He wore a golden tuxedo with a matching eye patch, and his uncovered eye seemed to change color every second.

"I don't understand," said Kara, looking around. "Everything seems...normal."

The citizens of Lanka wove in and out of the streets, disappearing into the giant buildings or emerging from bright storefronts with their arms loaded with shiny bags. They walked their pets—one of which was a slow-moving crocodile with emerald scales—and stared at their phones and laughed with their friends.

"But—" Mini stopped, shaking her head. "But what about the lockdown?"

"Or the *war*?" said Brynne, staring around her. "I thought they knew the Sleeper's army was coming!"

"They do," said Aiden. "But why should they care? Lanka is a rich city protected by a *god*. They're confident that if Kubera steps aside and gives him what he wants, the Sleeper won't attack them."

"But what about the rest of the Otherworld?" asked Aru, thinking about the images they'd seen in Aiden's camera. People running around the Night Bazaar, screaming in terror as they grabbed their kids and partners, hoping that in the end they'd get to stay together.

"Not their problem," Aiden said with a shrug. "Or so they think."

A wave of fury rose in Aru. She wanted to shake every person here. Didn't they know how much the Pandavas had gone through to get to Lanka? Aru's mom was somewhere on her own trying to help them, and Hanuman and Urvashi were probably trapped in this dazzling city. Didn't these people feel the constant threat of war, like a hand slowly closing around the throat? Or was it just Aru?

"It's not their fight," said Aiden, his lip curling in distaste.

Aru squared her shoulders, and Vajra sparked in solidarity. "Then let's *make* it their fight," she said coldly. "We're going to win Kubera's Nairrata army, and when the Sleeper shows up, he's gonna get the battle of his life."

Brynne snapped her fingers approvingly. Mini grinned, and Aiden flashed one of his closed-mouth smiles. Kara, however, wasn't as enthusiastic. She fidgeted with the golden ring on her finger and didn't look up.

"Now we just have to get to Kubera," said Aru, scanning the thin, sharp buildings around them. She thought his palace would be obvious, but it seemed hidden.

"I know how to get there," said Kara quietly. "I've seen the plans...and...and when we get to the palace, I'll give you the name of the weapon that Dad is looking for. As promised."

"Or you could tell us...*now?*" said Aru. "It's not going to change anything."

"I'm not going to be abandoned just like that," snapped Kara.

"Whoa. No one said anything about abandoning—" started Brynne, but Kara had already started walking ahead of them.

Aru's mind churned as she thought about what would happen next. In his message, Kubera had said he would put them through three trials before he gave them his army. But would he give them this weapon—whatever it was—too? Aru wanted to ask Kara, but the other girl prickled with unease.

"This way," said Kara stiffly.

They followed her as she wound her way through the glittering streets of Lanka.

As they walked, Aru couldn't help but overhear snatches of conversations around her. One guy covered in golden scales and wearing a pair of sunglasses on the back of his head started laughing into his phone. He wore an ID card around his neck: GRAYSON SURAPANENI, ANALYST.

"Bro, *now* is the time to invest in enchanted phone lines, I'm telling you. Everyone is like 'Oh no, are my loved ones okay?' and they'll pay *through the snout* to find out," he said.

Gross, thought Aru.

"Yo, I'm not worried. My dad can pay for all that stuff. I'd be *shocked* if I didn't get paid—"

Shocked, huh? thought Aru. As she walked past, she snapped her fingers, and a tendril of Vajra's electricity whipped into the air and smacked the analyst on the back of his head.

"WHAT WAS THAT?!" he yelped, jumping.

But by then, Aru and her friends had already turned a corner. Aru grinned to herself. Beside her, Aiden lowered Shadowfax. "I saw that, Shah."

"Saw what?" asked Aru innocently. "You didn't see me do anything."

Aiden raised an eyebrow. "I always see you, Shah."

Aru felt her heart beating a bit faster, but she scolded herself. Aiden didn't mean it like that. He only meant that he was super observant and whatnot. How many times had he reminded Aru that he only saw her as a friend? Even a simple misunderstanding about the two of them being together had grossed him out so much that he'd immediately walked away from her. Aru shoved her hands into her pockets and sped up.

Kara led them down a darkened alley. Here, the sounds of the city square faded to a distant growl. The golden walls looked dented and scorched in some places, and Aru remembered Queen Tara telling them how Hanuman had once set fire to the city.

In the middle of the dead end, a statue of a golden mongoose stood on a slender pedestal. It had a little silver bell tied around its neck. Aru's skin tingled from the rich sensation of magic flowing around this place. It reminded her of the thresholds to the Otherworld, but she felt a coil of misgiving all the same. Kubera liked playing tricks. Who was to say this wasn't one of them?

"This should be the entrance," said Kara.

"Maybe we have to ring the bell," said Brynne, taking a step toward the mongoose statue.

"Hold on..." said Mini. "I really don't like the look of the walls."

Aru followed her gaze and saw several large golden faces jutting out of the walls and staring down at them. They looked identical: male, mustached, lips pulled into a grimace under two short tusks.

Beside Aru, Mini wordlessly counted the faces. "Ten," she said, taking a step back. "Didn't *Ravana* have ten heads?"

Ravana was once the demon king of Lanka. Rama killed him after Ravana kidnapped Sita, the god king's wife.

"Yeah, but he's dead," said Aru.

"Lots of things that are supposed to be dead in the stories are still somehow alive," said Mini. "It's like their spirits go on."

"Fair, but look at this place!" said Aru, turning in the narrow alley. "There's no way Ravana could fit in here. Dude had ten heads. Can you imagine how big his hallways must have been? Or his bed? What if all your heads demanded Tempur-Pedic pillows?"

"Why did he have ten heads, anyway?" asked Brynne, rubbing the back of her neck as if trying to imagine the weight.

"In an act of penance to the god Brahma," said Aiden, "he

kept cutting off his head as a sacrifice. He did it ten times. And each time, Brahma replaced it with an additional new one. Ravana was really pious."

"He doesn't sound so bad for a demon king," said Brynne. "Stealing Sita was definitely wrong, but at least he didn't hurt her?"

Aru made a face. Her mom had always reminded her that sometimes heroes did bad things, and villains did good things, and you had to look at the shadow with the light. It was true Ravana wasn't all bad, but that didn't make him all good, either, which reminded Aru of a story her mother had told her about the demon king.

"The *only* reason he didn't touch Sita was because there was a curse on him that said that if he kept trying to touch women who didn't want him to, his heads would explode," said Aru.

Kara and Mini looked grossed out. Aiden was horrified.

Brynne gagged. "*What?* If he wasn't dead already, I'd totally chop off his heads."

"Same," said Mini, shuddering. "Let's just ring the bell and get out of this creepy alley. Kara?"

She seemed distracted. She kept twisting her ring, her shoulders bowed and her head bent.

"Kara?" asked Aru.

The other girl looked up suddenly. It was hard to see in the shadows, but were those tears in her eyes? Kara swiped at her cheeks, then rang the bell. A low peal echoed through the alley. The walls shifted around them, folding back and rearranging until it looked like they were in another place entirely on Lanka's map. Lights flashed, and Aru shielded her eyes as the golden mongoose statue began to spin, moving faster and faster until . . .

SLAM!

Aru was thrown to her knees inside a walled-in courtyard. Pomegranate and orange trees filled the neat grove, and the high walls were made not of gold but of intricately cut panes of topaz and amber, through which Aru could see the ocean crashing on the shore and the now faraway city lights of Lanka.

Aru shook her head as she stood up. Her friends were recovering from the translocation, too. "That wasn't so bad," she said. "I guess this is a different palace entrance—"

"Um, Aru?" said Kara.

"For a second, I kinda thought those heads were going to get us—"

"*Aru,*" said Mini.

"Which would have sucked, but at least—"

"Shah," said Brynne slowly. "You might want to turn around. Like, *now.*"

Aru stretched her neck from side to side and then spun around. "What is it? Oh."

On the plus side, they had found the palace. She could see jagged gold steps rising to a passage lined with tall mongoose statues. The golden structure loomed above them, its exterior covered with molded images of dancing yakshas and birds in mid-flight, their feathers studded with sapphires and emeralds.

The problem was, in order to walk up the steps of said palace, they had to get past . . .

"Ravana," said Aiden, his eyes going wide as he took in the giant demon king standing before them.

Ravana was at least a hundred feet tall, and his ten heads stretched over several pairs of broad shoulders. Each head sported a pointed golden helmet. Thick golden bands emphasized the muscles of his huge blue body. Ravana had twenty arms, and each arm brandished sharp and gleaming weapons as his eyes lasered in on the Pandavas.

Aru felt her mouth go dry with panic. With a shaking hand, she pulled out the golden coin Kubera had sent to them. She raised it slowly into the air.

"We . . . We have an invitation?"

Ravana stretched his arms to either side, his long swords glinting menacingly. "NO ADMITTANCE!" he roared.

"Except on party business?" tried Aru.

But Ravana didn't seem to care for her *Lord of the Rings* joke as he roared once more and then lunged at them.

SIXTEEN

Aim for the Head(s)

Ravana's gigantic blue hand swept toward them.

"Watch out!" yelled Mini.

She twirled her Death Danda over her head, and violet light shot into the air, heading straight for Ravana, but the demon king was too quick. Before the shield could even form, he'd snatched Mini off the ground.

"THIS IS VERY UNSANITARY!" hollered Mini as she thrashed in Ravana's grip and beat his fist with Dee Dee.

Ravana laughed.

"Let her go!" shouted Aru.

Ravana and his ten heads gazed down at them. A smug, bored look crept into all his eyes.

"Make me," he said.

Kara practically growled. She hurled her light trident. It spun out fast, hitting Ravana square in the chest and exploding across his armor. Ravana leaned backward, and for a second Aru thought he would topple, but then the demon king began to laugh.

"Is that all?" he asked.

Kara's trident bounded back to her arms.

"I've got a better idea," said Aiden. "Brynne?"

Aru didn't know what he meant by that, but clearly Brynne did. She and Aiden shared a vicious smile, and then Brynne swept out her wind mace in a wide arc. Gales blew forward, shaking the grass and the trees, and Aiden jumped into the air and started *running* on the wind. He clanked his wrists together and his two scimitars flew out. The sun angled behind him, winking on their blades. Ravana's main face scowled, and he raised his fist....

But if Ravana was fast, Aiden was faster.

His glowing scimitars formed a shining X, and then he swiped them at the place where Ravana's armor met one of his necks.

SCHWIP!

One moment, all ten of Ravana's heads faced Kara, Aiden, and the Pandavas.

The next, the leftmost head shimmered, turned to gold, and tumbled to the ground.

The remaining nine heads roared in fury. Ravana flexed his hands in anger, opening the fist around Mini. She dropped to the ground. Brynne wrapped a cyclone around Aiden, carrying him back to the grass, where he dropped gracefully, triumph shining on his face as the sun glowed behind him.

Ogle later, fight now, came Brynne's mind message.

I WAS NOT OGLING! Aru tried to say, but then Ravana let out a roar. He swiveled around and made another grab for Mini. She thrust out her shield, and Ravana's fist slammed into it, sending cracks spiderwebbing down the shield. A cold shadow fell over Aru. She looked up to see a giant boulder levitating overhead, thanks to Brynne's wind mace. Beads of sweat rolled down Brynne's face as she wound up and launched it straight at Ravana....

BOOM!

"Two heads down, eight to go!" she yelled.

"This isn't bowling!" shouted Aru as she looked around.

Ravana and his ten heads—well, eight now—were the only thing keeping them out of Kubera's palace.

"What do we do now?" asked Kara.

Ravana looked up from the ground and started crawling toward Aiden, which gave Mini just enough time to cast an invisibility charm on herself and run back to Kara, Brynne, and Aru.

"We've got to draw him away from the palace," said Aru. She snapped her fingers and Vajra transformed into a sparkling rope.

"Agreed," said Brynne.

"I can distract him with something shiny?" said Kara, holding up her trident.

Brynne smiled at the other girl approvingly. Aiden nodded at Aru, who gave him one end of her lightning rope. At once, they ran to the opposite sides of the courtyard as Mini's invisibility shield fell over them, concealing the lightning rope from view. It stretched taut in front of the demon king.

"HEY, YOU!" yelled Brynne at Ravana. "What's got eight heads and is still a loser?"

Ravana growled.

"If you look up the etymological history of *coward* in the *Oxford English Dictionary*, you'd find a mirror!" added Kara.

Aru winced. They were going to have to work on Kara's trash talk....

Ravana lumbered forward, and Aru crouched, her grip on Vajra tightening. The shadow of the demon king fell over them, and the ground trembled. Aru squeezed her eyes shut, all her strength focused on keeping the rope tense. Suddenly, Aru was nearly dragged forward. She signaled to Aiden to let go just as electricity zipped down the rope, delivering a paralyzing shock to Ravana.

"Now, Shah!" yelled Brynne, as Mini threw off the invisibility shield.

Aru gave Vajra a tug, and the rope coiled up like a rearing snake. By the time it was all back in her hand, the lightning had turned into a sharp, glinting javelin. Ravana fell over like a statue, the eyes in his eight heads rolling back as he thudded to the ground so loudly that the nearby trees trembled and roots jutted out of the dirt. Ravana started to move again, clawing the ground as he tried to push himself up to standing. At that exact moment Aru let loose her javelin. . . .

SWISH!

The weapon instantly skewered three heads, and they turned to gold as they rolled across the ground. Vajra returned to Aru as Ravana stumbled to his feet. His movements were shaky, his steps off-balance.

"Five to go!" yelled Aiden.

Brynne let out a savage whoop, and Kara tossed her trident into the air. It caught the light in such a way that it left Ravana momentarily blinded. He threw up his hands to protect his eyes, and . . .

TWANG! TWANG!

Two more golden heads fell to the ground around his feet as Aiden leaped back to the ground, breathing hard from his slashing maneuver. His scimitars dripped gold blood.

"Three left!" said Aiden.

"Two!" yelled Mini, as she flung out her Death Danda. Dee Dee whacked Ravana's remaining right skull just below the ear, and the head shimmered to gold and rolled off his shoulder.

"All you, Kara!" said Brynne.

Kara caught her trident one-handed, pulled her shoulder back, and let the weapon rip through the air....

"ONE!" yelled Kara.

Ravana swayed on his feet. Fury twisted his face, but when he tried to step forward, he tripped on his own heads, crashing to the ground once more.

His body disappeared in a cloud of golden smoke, leaving them standing in the now-silent courtyard. Kara's hair had gotten mussed in the fight, and her face was smudged with dirt. She leaned on Sunny and grinned at them.

"Victory!" shouted Brynne, swinging her wind mace.

Aru cheered. Aiden clapped. Mini lifted her Death Danda and shouted, "And with no risk of tetanus, because none of us got impaled!"

That was a somewhat strange way to say *We did it!* but then again, it was Mini. She looked around at their confused faces and sighed. "Tetanus is an infection caused by *Clostridium tetani*, which can be found on pieces of metal and transmitted into the bloodstream through breaks in the skin, and if that happens you could—"

"Die?" said Brynne and Aru.

Both of them fought back a laugh.

"Neuromuscular paralysis and possible mortality is not funny!" huffed Mini. "I'm just saying we should be happy it didn't happen!"

"I'm happy," said Kara, lifting her trident. "Hooray for a non-Pyrrhic victory!"

Now the confused faces turned to Kara. She blushed, lowering Sunny.

"Is Pyrrhic a disease?" asked Mini excitedly.

"It means 'a victory gained at too great a cost,'" Kara said enthusiastically. "The origin is from this battle in 279 BCE where Pyrrhus of Epirus won against the Romans but practically lost his whole army in the process. And all his friends. And I think some family, too."

No one but Kara and Mini was still smiling. Mini nodded approvingly. "That's depressing. I like it."

"Poor Pyrrhus," said Aru.

"Poor *Pandavas!*" said Brynne. "We lopped off all of Ravana's heads, and now what? Those golden steps don't lead anywhere, and we're trapped in this courtyard, and *all* the fruit on the trees is seriously underripe, so I can't eat it, *and—*"

Just then, Aru heard a soft squeak.

At the very top of the stairs, a golden-furred mongoose peered down at them. It tilted its head, squeaked again, then disappeared into a doorway that had not been there moments ago. Across the lintel, neon letters flashed:

WELCOME, PANDAVAS!

Aru stared at the entrance. It looked black as pitch inside. What if it was another trap? But what if it wasn't, and this was their last chance to get to Kubera? The deadline was today, and even if the citizens of Lanka didn't care that the Sleeper was moving closer and closer, Aru couldn't ignore that pulse of approaching war pounding in the back of her skull.

"Should we go in?" asked Brynne.

Aru shrugged. "Red pill or blue pill?"

"*What* pill?" asked Mini.

"It's from *The Matrix*."

Kara frowned. "It's from a rectangular array of quantities?"

"No, it's this movie where—"

"You're stalling, Shah," said Aiden. "What are we doing?"

Aru felt everyone's gaze on her. She spun Vajra around her fingers, then took a step forward.

"We're going in."

"Wait," said Kara loudly.

They turned to look at her.

"I can't," she said.

"Why not?" asked Aru, shocked. "Don't you want to come with us?"

Hurt flashed across Kara's face as she pointed at the sign. "It says *Welcome, Pandavas*. I'm not a Pandava."

Aiden frowned. "Well, neither am I, I'm technically—"

"A Pandava adjacent, I know. But I'm not even that," said Kara quietly. "I'm no one. I know it won't let me in. Watch."

Before anyone could stop her, Kara bounded up the steps. She turned sideways as if ready to bust down an invisible door, but the moment her foot met the threshold, a force threw her backward. Kara tried again . . . and was thrown out once more, this time all the way to the courtyard.

"See?" said Kara shakily. "I told you."

"Kara, we—"

"We had a deal," said Kara, not looking up at them. "I promised to give you the name of the weapon the Sleeper wants." She took a deep breath. "Ask Kubera for the *antima astra*."

Once Kara uttered the name, Aru heard a clap of thunder.

She looked up and saw a dark cloud intrude on the previously pure-blue skies of Lanka. On the horizon, the sun flared red for a second. In the courtyard, the fruit trees withered and then immediately sprang back to life. A gust of wind carrying snow blew past them, leaving a trail of quickly melting frost in its wake.

Brynne held her hand to the air, the wonder on her face turning quickly to wariness. "That was our...our..."

"Soul dads," breathed Aru, studying the patch of sky where she'd seen the thundercloud. There was no sign of it now.

Their soul fathers, Indra, Vayu, and Yama, never communicated with them. At least, not directly.

Mini looked at the trees, once brown and now a healthy green. "What does that mean?"

"It means they recognized the name of the weapon," said Aiden. "What is it?"

"It's a piece of the Brahmastra, the most destructive weapon in the world. It's like some sort of cosmic missile," said Kara. "After the last war, the gods destroyed it, but a sliver survived. Even that tiny piece is capable of destroying all godly weapons. And without your weapons—"

"We won't be able to fight back," finished Aru.

She held Vajra a little closer to her. Was it just her imagination or had her lightning bolt trembled a little at the word *Brahmastra*? Aru tried picturing what life would be like without Vajra and shuddered. Without her lightning bolt, she'd be so... ordinary.

And yet, as soon as Aru had that thought, she remembered Boo perching on her shoulder, affectionately nipping at her ear. *You are so much more than the weapons you fight with, child.*

Once, Aru had thought that was true.

But that was before Boo had betrayed them and gone to the Sleeper. Even *with* their weapons, Boo hadn't believed in them, and if the Sleeper destroyed Vajra and the rest, then nothing the Pandavas did would make a difference.

He would win.

And she would lose everything.

"Go," said Kara. "Don't keep Kubera waiting."

"What about you?" asked Aiden.

Kara tried to smile, but her face fell. "I don't know where to go now."

Aru was about to tell her that she didn't have to leave, but Brynne and Mini beat her to it.

"Stay put," said Brynne.

"You're not going anywhere," said Mini.

Kara looked up at them. "Really? You want me to stay?"

"Definitely," said Aiden.

Aru tried to ignore how warm his tone sounded. Honestly, she didn't blame him for liking Kara. She was kind and thoughtful. How could you *not* like someone like that?

"We'll find you after, Kara," said Brynne, heading to the steps.

Mini and Aiden looked back at Aru, but she motioned them forward. "You guys go ahead," she said. "I'll be right there. I just want to talk to Kara for a second."

While the others climbed the stairs, Kara eyed Aru nervously. "If you want me to leave, I will," she said. "I get why you might not trust me. I know that to you guys I'm still just the Sleeper's daughter."

Aru shoved her hands in her pockets. "Kara—"

"Before you say anything, just let me say this, okay?"

Aru nodded, unsure.

Kara took a deep breath. "I still get confused over who I really am," she said. "When I was with Dad, I always tried to be the perfect daughter, because I didn't want him to leave me behind. He spent a lot of time away, you know, and it was…hard. And now…Now I'm trying to act like he wasn't really my dad just so that *you guys* don't leave me behind. And honestly, all I want is…" Kara braced herself, and stood up straighter. "I don't want to be left behind anymore. That's all."

Aru knew exactly what Kara meant. She'd felt that way growing up, whenever her mom went on a business trip, or during those times when they were together and her mom seemed a thousand miles away. Aru sometimes even felt that way now with Brynne, Mini, and Aiden. In the Tree of Wishes, she'd seen things they'd never understand, and it had changed her.

For Aru, being related to the Sleeper made her believe that no matter what she did, she was always going to be blamed first. She used to try pretending that she wasn't his daughter or get defensive about it, but ever since Aru had met Kara, she'd had a new thought.

What if, instead, she said *So what?*

So what if he was her dad?

Kara had accepted the Sleeper as her father, but it didn't change the fact that she kept trying to help the Pandavas.

"You're not his only daughter, you know," said Aru. "And we're not going to leave you behind. We'll figure it out as we go, okay? After all, we're like—"

Aru caught herself right before she said the word *family*. It was too soon for that. Aru wondered if she'd hurt Kara's feelings, but Kara didn't seem sad or disappointed. She looked…*hopeful*.

"I gotta go," said Aru, taking a step toward the stairs. "Listen, it's going to be fine, okay?"

Kara shook her head but kept smiling. "I don't want it to be fine. *Fine* comes from the Latin *finis,* which means *end.* This feels a lot more like a beginning."

SEVENTEEN

You Get a Quest!
And *You* Get a Quest!

As soon as Aru walked through the doorway, a wave of magic hit her. One moment she was stepping into darkness, and the next she found herself in a grand theater with dim lanterns on the walls. Her friends were already seated in one of the several rows of red velvet seats that started about fifty feet in front of the huge golden stage. Theatrical spotlights swiveled over the closed saffron-colored curtains. Aru recognized the sound of classical Indian music—the humming of a sitar and the thudding cadence of a tabla—coming from the orchestra pit. Above her and to the sides were several golden balconies set beneath a ceiling painted to look like the night sky. Mongooses dressed in monocles and suits, ball gowns and feathered hats, chittered and chirped as they clambered up to their gallery seats.

"What is—" started Aru, when a golden mongoose wearing an usher's cap popped up in front of her.

It hissed, holding a tiny paw to its mouth to indicate *Silence!* Next, it hiccuped out a ginormous ruby. It considered the gem for a moment, then led Aru to a seat in the front row before scuttling to the stage and slipping under the heavy fabric.

Aru! When did you get here? said Mini through the mind link.

Like, a second ago, I think. She tried to look at Mini only to find that her neck was frozen in place, forcing her to face front. Her tailbone seemed glued to the chair, too. *Do you have any idea what's going on?*

No, came Brynne's message. *It's like he's forcing us to watch a show or—*

The curtains dramatically flew open with a loud rustle, revealing a large floating eye that looked like it was made of hammered sheets of gold. The eye blinked at them. Overhead, a voice boomed.

"YOU HAVE ANSWERED MY SUMMONS, O PANDAVAS! DO YOU KNOW WHAT THAT MEANS?"

We get to leave? wondered Aru, trying to pull her arm from the armrest. It didn't budge.

The eye on the stage quivered.

"YOU!"

The spotlight suddenly swiveled to Aru. She felt the slightest loosening in her neck muscles and realized she could now turn her head. Aru glanced at Mini and saw a violet light beam down on her next.

"GET!"

Brynne was bathed in blue light, while a hot-pink spot glared down at Aiden. He glared back.

"A!"

The eye burst into a thousand pieces, and golden confetti rained down on them.

"QUEST!"

Dozens of golden mongooses took to the stage wearing can-can dresses. Music blasted around them. *"You* get a quest! And *you* get a quest! And everybody gets a *quest*—HEY!"

In the balconies, formally dressed mongooses clapped politely. Beside Aru, Mini spat out bits of golden confetti.

The music died down as the voice of Kubera rang out through the theater once more:

"THREE TRIALS I GRANT YOU, ONE FOR EACH DAY!"

All at once, the spotlights swiveled away from the Potatoes and back onto the stage. The dancing mongooses were replaced with five in new costumes, complete with wigs this time. One of them had a camera, one wore a chef's hat, the third wore glasses, the fourth carried a book, and the fifth...the fifth carried a paper lightning bolt and was wearing what looked like...red-and-blue pajamas?

Aru's jaw dropped. "Is that supposed to be *me?*"

Overhead, Kubera's voice continued:

"TO START, THE LAND SHALL TEST YOUR HEART!"

A trapdoor opened in the stage near the Mongoose-Potatoes' feet, and they reared back and chittered in terror. The Brynne Mongoose swatted the Aru Mongoose.

"Accurate," admitted Aru.

"NEXT, THE SEA SHALL TRY YOUR MIGHT!"

A bucket of water was tossed up from the trapdoor, and the Mongoose-Potatoes pretended to sputter and drown. The eyeglasses flew off the Mini Mongoose's face.

"Oh no, its glasses!" said Mini.

"LAST, THE SKY SHALL JUDGE YOUR SIGHT!"

The Aiden Mongoose dropped his camera. It tumbled off the stage and exploded like a toy-car prop in an action movie.

"Really?" asked Aiden.

Aru jerked in her seat as firecrackers started going off onstage. The Mongoose-Potatoes squealed and swooned, running in circles and falling over one another. Gold smoke bombs went off around the actors, clearing quickly to reveal a line of paper-doll soldiers, each no taller than a pencil. Was that supposed to be the Nairrata army?

"ALL THREE THINGS YOU NEED TO WIELD SUCH POWER. WISDOM MUST PREVAIL FOR PEACE TO FLOWER!"

The little golden army rotated around the Mongoose-Pandavas to a trumpet march as a painted backdrop of dawn sprang up behind them.

"DO YOU ACCEPT?"

The spotlights swiveled back to the Pandavas. The glare was so bright that Aru immediately squinted and threw her arm over her eyes. "Ah!"

"GOOD ENOUGH!" boomed the voice. "And *fin!*"

The red curtains came down. The mongooses in the balconies stood and applauded.

Mini turned to Aru. "Why are you clapping?"

"What? It wasn't a *bad* performance."

"Were those supposed to be our trials?" asked Brynne. "We only have *three* days for all that?"

"What is it with everything having to be done in exactly three days?" asked Aiden.

Aru slowly lowered her hands. "Because the Sleeper is coming.

And if we haven't proven by then that we deserve the Nairrata army, we've failed."

Around them, the room started to change. The stage melted into the floor. The theater trappings—the balconies and painted ceiling, the curtains and chairs—disappeared. The Potatoes fell on their butts, and when Aru looked up, the room's transformation was complete.

Now it was a large chamber that looked strangely empty. There was no decoration aside from a few mongoose carvings on the walls. The floor was pure gold, but scratched and pitted. The "ceiling" was an expanse of open sky, and the only furniture in the room was a tall throne, on which Kubera sat and grinned at them expectantly.

Mini elbowed Aru sharply, whispering, *"Pranama!"*

Aru immediately touched the floor in front of her, then tapped her heart, keeping her eyes lowered as they all respectfully greeted the god. Only when they were done did Aru get a good look at Kubera. He was wearing a traditional *sherwani* and trousers, but the material was unusual. One moment, it looked as green as a dollar bill; another, it was silver, like a coin. As in the billboard they'd seen, he wore an eye patch, and his good eye seemed to shift in color the longer he stared at them, from the shiny bronze of a new penny to the green tinge of an old one.

"That was a *delight*," said Kubera in his smooth-jazz DJ voice. "I mean, the fight with Ravana? Brilliant. We just adored it, didn't we, Biju?"

A little head poked up through his armrest and nodded. It was the same golden mongoose that had hissed at Aru to be quiet.

Biju hiccuped. From its small mouth a bright diamond fell into Kubera's lap.

The god picked it up and scowled. "You're getting sloppy," he said with a sigh. "How many times have we been through the four *C*'s of diamonds? Cut, color, clarity, carats! I can see the inclusions on this one at first glance and, what is this, *four* carats? Peasant nonsense." Kubera dropped the diamond on the floor. "Take it away, Biju. Perhaps you could use it as a paperweight for the letters I have no wish to answer."

Aru was about to raise her hand. *I'll take it!* She'd be rich! But Mini shot her another warning glance, and Aru dropped her arm. Biju the mongoose huffed, retrieved the diamond, and disappeared.

"Now, where were we...?" asked Kubera. "Oh, right. *Loved* the fight. Very, uh, what's the word...?" Kubera snapped his fingers. "Cinematic!"

Aru frowned. "Thanks?"

"And I hope you enjoyed the mongooses' performance just as much. They worked very hard on it. It was quite possibly..." Kubera stifled a yawn. "Quite possibly the most fun I've had in two centuries. Too bad there were no games. I do like those, too. Oh well, can't win 'em all! Now off you trot—"

"Fun?" repeated Aiden.

Kubera, who had started to look bored, perked up.

"Respectfully," said Brynne in a tone that bordered on disrespectful, "it doesn't seem *fun* that there's an army heading your way. And if the Sleeper actually gets hold of the nectar of immortality, I doubt life is going to be *fun* for anyone else. The Otherworld might end up, I dunno...destroyed? And instead of enabling us to go find and fight him wherever he is, you're putting us through trials just to prove we're worthy of using your army!" A slight wind rose around Brynne, lifting the hair off her shoulders. "All this is said respectfully, of course," she said again when Mini glared at her.

"Speak freely," said Kubera nonchalantly. "Sass can be so refreshing. A little *zinger* here and there from blips of mortality is amusing."

Did he just call us "blips of mortality"? Aru asked via the Pandava link.

"Is none of this valuable to you?" asked Aiden, motioning all around with his arm. "Don't you care that it all could be lost?"

Kubera cocked his head to one side, studying Aiden. A wide grin spread across his face. "Ooh...I like you," he said, his eye glinting dangerously. "So earnest! So pretty! No, no, I don't mind a little destruction. If nothing is ever destroyed, you never find out what's worth protecting."

"What about Hanuman and Urvashi?" asked Brynne. "Are they worth protecting?"

"Of course!" said Kubera. "That's why they're in a comfy little jail cell under my palace! It's perfectly ventilated, and packed with *Friends* DVDs. What more could you want? Now, are we done? Don't you want to start your quest? Three days is all you get before the Sleeper's army arrives, you know. His ambassador showed me this wonderfully menacing depiction of the Sleeper's forces when he last visited."

He snapped his fingers, and a 3-D illusion of a sprawling army rose around them. Asuras and yakshas and beings with feathered arms and horned heads stormed past Aru with a flat, determined look in their eyes.

"Impressive, no?" said Kubera. "I take it the Sleeper's rallying cry has been quite inspiring. 'Change your fate! Remake the world!' Et cetera, et cetera."

At the front of the army, dressed in a dark robe that ended

in curling wisps of smoke, marched the Sleeper. His face looked gaunt, and his mismatched blue and brown eyes were fixed on some far-off destination. His collar was open just far enough to allow Aru to see that something glinted around his neck: the necklace holding all the memories he'd given up in an effort to change his destiny.

A lump rose in her throat. She remembered the picture book with its smudged inscription to her: *Love, Dad.*

Kara had said that he'd left the two of them behind to keep them safe. What would he do when he found out that Kara and Aru had left *him* behind? Had the necklace of memories changed anything for the Sleeper, or, when they were standing on opposite sides of the battlefield, would he still attack Aru? If the latter was the case, nothing they were trying to do mattered. She was, after all, just a "blip of mortality."

In that second, fury scorched Aru's veins. Vajra prickled on her wrist, sparking with electricity to match her anger.

Aru was tired. She was sick of always trying to prove herself to people who thought the worst of her. She wanted to stop avoiding battle and *fight* already. She wanted to fight Boo for not believing in them. She wanted to fight Kubera for mocking her. And, most of all, she wanted to fight the Sleeper for failing her in every way.

If she could, Aru Shah would take on the whole world.

"Ooh . . . *you've* got a feisty look in your eyes, little demigod!" said Kubera.

Through the mind link, Aru heard Brynne say, *Uh-oh . . . Did he just call Shah "feisty"?*

Mini warned, *Aru, I know you hate that word, but—*

"Do I look like a taco sauce to you?" Aru blurted, taking

a step toward Kubera. Ropes of lightning spiderwebbed up her arms.

Kubera clapped. "Is this a plot twist? Are you going to attack *me*? Fun!"

"We'll do your trials, and we'll earn your army, but you're going to give us more than that. We want Hanuman and Urvashi returned to us, and we want the antima astra, too."

At her mention of the weapon's name, the sky rippled with thunder, and a powerful wind gusted through the chamber, carrying with it the unmistakable whiff of rot and death.

The smile fell from Kubera's face. "Do not utter that weapon's name in my presence. You may call it *the astra* and nothing else." His voice was so powerful that the gold surface of the walls began to melt and drip down.

Then he relaxed into his throne with a deep chuckle. "You want more, Pandavas? You may have anything I control. How's that for generous?"

"What's the catch?" asked Aru.

"Shah..." said Aiden warningly.

Aru ignored him, and Kubera's smile widened.

"The catch is, well, *me*. My throne is the seat of my power. You want something that's in my power to give? Well, then you must reach my throne in three steps. That's all you get."

Kubera snapped his fingers and his throne zoomed backward. The golden chamber expanded so that it seemed as if Kubera and his throne were practically a mile away.

Brynne glared. "Even if I turned into a cheetah and took three giant leaps, I wouldn't be able to get to him."

Aru crossed her arms. "Yeah, but if you were a dinosaur—"

"We've been through this, Shah," said Brynne. "I can't turn into anything that's extinct! And Kubera is too far away!"

Aru scowled, staring at the ginormous room. She hated how she felt: small and powerless.

"Aru, are you okay?" asked Mini.

"No," said Aru. "I'm *annoyed*. Kubera doesn't care about the war, *no one* cares that we're trying to help, and honestly, I wish I could just stomp on this whole stupid palace and be done with it!"

Mini touched her arm. "We can't do that."

A thought tickled the back of Aru's brain....

"Actually," said Aru, "I can."

Aiden lifted an eyebrow, and from the look in his eyes, Aru could tell that he knew. He laughed. "I see you, Shah."

Aru, Mini, and Brynne lined up, careful to keep some distance between them.

"We're ready to take the steps," said Aru.

Kubera's laughter echoed through the halls.

"Silly, silly," he started to say, but Aru had stopped listening.

Instead, she concentrated on Tara's promise to answer if Aru was ever in need. It felt like something molten in the center of her heart. Aru mentally called upon the queen. *Your Majesty, mind if I use that power now?*

The transformation took place instantly. Aru felt as though a thousand needles swept over her skin, and there was the slightest stretching sensation in her arms and legs as her bones lengthened, her clothes sized up, and her stomach bulged. The floor pulled away from her in a matter of seconds, and the top of her head nearly poked out the open ceiling. From up here, Kubera's throne room looked like part of a glamorous dollhouse. Aru swayed, careful not to move her feet as she caught her balance.

"THAT IS SO COOL!" Brynne yelled up to her.

Aru knew it *had* to be a yell, but from where she stood, it sounded like a faraway squeak. She bent down and held out her palm so her sisters could step onto it. Mini, looking faintly queasy because she hated heights, clambered on first. Then Brynne. Off to the side, Aiden snapped some photos.

Close your ears, Aru said through the mind link.

Her sisters clamped their hands over their heads.

"First step!" said Aru, lifting her foot.

The golden floor blurred beneath her. In one step, Aru was fifteen feet away from Kubera's throne. He had stopped laughing, and his one eye was wide. Biju the mongoose had reappeared, and when its jaw dropped open in surprise, a chunky sapphire tumbled to the floor.

Brynne?

On Aru's palm, Brynne hunched down and Mini climbed onto her back as if she were about to take a piggyback ride. In a flash of blue light that looked from Aru's height like nothing more than a match catching fire, Brynne transformed into an elephant. Aru lowered her to the ground, and Brynne took one lumbering step forward.

"Second step!" Brynne trumpeted.

Now Kubera's throne was less than three feet away. Mini balanced on top of Brynne's back, swaying a bit.

"Step three!" she yelled, springing forward. Mini's fingers caught the edge of the god's throne and she pulled herself up to stand on the armrest. She raised her Death Danda high in the air.

"We took our three steps." Aru's voice boomed, shaking the

golden walls of the palace. "And in those three steps, we reached your throne. So we can claim whatever we want that you control," she said. "Here's what we want…"

"You'll return Hanuman to us," said Brynne.

"And Urvashi!" said Mini.

Aru leaned over to stare Kubera in the eye. His throne looked like something she could pinch into a coin.

"And when we finish your trials, you *will* give us the astra, along with your golden army."

EIGHTEEN

Sorrow with a Side of Cow

"That was . . . *delightful!*" said Kubera, clapping.

Delightful?

Aru deflated, both emotionally and physically. Within seconds, Tara's blessing melted away, and Aru felt as if someone were slowly reeling her in like a kite. Her bones shrank and the floor rose to meet her as she returned to her below-average height of five foot one.

"Handing over the multiverse's most powerful weapon to adolescents with undeveloped prefrontal cortices?" mused Kubera. "*Chaos.* I love it. Yes, yes, you can have it. . . . But only if you get through my trials, of course, so—"

Biju chirped loudly. A topaz fell to the ground, followed by an amethyst.

"Oh, right, right. Here." Kubera snapped his fingers.

A golden eye, roughly the size of a tennis ball, appeared in front of Aru. It blinked, and its pupil roved up and narrowed, as if it didn't care for what it saw.

"This will work like a portal and transport you to your next trial. Or maybe not, depending on how I feel," said Kubera. "Just know that, whatever happens, I'll be watching and judging. In each trial I give you, you must find and take my eye." He grinned and tapped his eye patch. "And if you don't, then"—the god shrugged—"I'll just continue my negotiations with the Sleeper. But I have to say, the *Ooh, I'm a giant now!* thing was *most* exciting. Subala was right—you are a clever little bunch."

Subala... That was *Boo.*

Aru froze.

"How did you talk to Boo?" demanded Brynne. "Did you trap him along with Hanuman and Urvashi?"

"Trap him?" asked Kubera, leaning out of his throne with a wide grin. "Why would I want to trap the Sleeper's ambassador?"

Aru's mouth went dry. *Ambassador?*

The god waved his hand through the air, and an image of Boo sitting on the armrest of Kubera's throne flickered before them. Aru didn't want to notice how thin his plumage looked or remember that he hated perching on metal because it was always too cold or too hot for his claws and that's why he preferred Aru's head.

"We have no quarrel with you, Lord of Wealth," said Boo. *"You cannot wield your army anyway, and we are not asking for it. We're merely asking you to step aside."*

"Perhaps I cannot wield it, but what of the little demigods?" Kubera mused. *"I must give them a chance, I suppose. It would be entertaining, at least. I do love a good show."*

Boo's feathers ruffled slightly. *"Don't bother with them!"* the pigeon said quickly. *"In fact, if you see them, lock them up! Don't be fooled by their cleverness. They're nothing more than weak children, not worthy of anyone's time or attention. Trust me, I tried educating them to no avail."*

Kubera waved his hand again, and the image faded. Aru tried to inhale and winced. It hurt to breathe.

Was this what it felt like to be heartbroken?

Aru had always thought "heartbreak" was something romantic and dramatic, like flinging herself against a balcony while wearing a gown.

No one had ever told her that heartbreak was a quiet unraveling inside, and so vast a feeling it was impossible to breathe through.

Ever since they'd found the true Tree of Wishes, Aru had known Boo had betrayed them. It was unforgivable, but at least... at least he had done it out of love. Or so she'd thought. Isn't that what Sheela had said? That she would hate him for his love?

Those words didn't mean anything now.

It was one thing for him to have betrayed them, but what she'd just seen in Kubera's memory was something else entirely.

"Three days, Pandavas," said the god, spinning a diamond over the tops of his fingers. "If I were you, I would go now."

Biju glared at them, then hiccuped out a chunk of aquamarine stone.

"Well said, Biju," said Kubera.

The next moment, Kubera, the mongoose, and the throne disappeared, leaving the Pandavas alone with the floating golden eye in the giant courtyard where they had first entered the palace. The sun was bright and warm, and it didn't fit with how any of them felt. They were as shell-shocked as if the god had set off a bomb in front of them.

"He really did betray us," said Brynne to Aru. "You were right."

It should have felt like victory to Aru. Instead, she was cold and numb all over.

"I wish I wasn't," said Aru.

"But he—" started Mini. Her shoulders fell. "I don't understand. How could he say those things about us? I can't believe it."

"*I* do," said Brynne, her voice rising. "He was a liar! He was on the Sleeper's side the whole time!"

That couldn't be true . . . could it?

"But Sheela said—" started Mini.

"*No,*" said Brynne viciously. She was shaking a little. "He was always lying to us. I hate him. And I hate the Sleeper, and I hate everyone who ever helped the Sleeper!" Then Aru heard Brynne mutter something else under her breath: "He's wrong. I'm *not* weak."

"I'm just as hurt as you are, Brynne, but maybe we shouldn't rush to judgment," said Mini.

Brynne acted as if she didn't hear her. "We have to lose Kara," she said. "She can't be trusted, either."

Aru looked around. Where *was* Kara, anyway? Aru had told her to stay here. . . .

"She's the Sleeper's daughter," continued Brynne.

"So am I," said Aru coldly. "Are you going to kick me out, too?"

"What? No!" said Brynne, turning red. "It's just—"

"Kara has done nothing but try to be nice and help us," said Mini firmly. "Without her, we wouldn't have found out what the Sleeper was really after."

"She could be a spy!" Brynne insisted. "She could find some other way to hurt us! She could—"

"Bee," said Aiden gently. He took a step toward her, but Brynne stepped backward sharply.

"Don't ammamma me!" growled Brynne. "It's either *us* or *them*! How am I supposed to keep you safe if you don't listen to me?"

She looked frantic. Her breath came in short, sharp rasps. Her wind mace, Gogo, created a warm breeze around her, as if trying to wrap her in a blanket.

"Brynne, I think you might be in shock, which is understandable, considering what we just saw," said Mini. "But you have to stay calm."

Brynne bent over and took a deep breath.

Just then, there was a little *pop!* as Kara appeared at the edge of the courtyard. She looked bright-eyed and excited, her arms full of neatly wrapped packages as she ran toward them.

"Hi, guys!" she said. "How'd it go?"

Aru frowned. "Um—"

"I figured out how to leave the palace, so I thought I'd surprise you with some stuff when you came back!" said Kara happily. She thrust a bag at Mini. "I noticed you were out of hand sanitizer, and this kind has gold flakes."

"Oh, thanks," said Mini quietly.

Kara handed Aiden a neatly wrapped package. "Aiden, I found this cool picture frame for you. I think the gold was melted down from some sunken pirate treasure," she said, beaming.

Aiden took it, muttered his thanks, and quickly tucked it into his messenger bag.

Kara gave Aru a bag no larger than her hand. "Aru...this is for you. I asked them to custom-make it."

Aru looked inside to find a golden keychain. When she pulled it out, she saw ARU SHAH engraved on it.

"Now you've finally got one of your own," said Kara, smiling.

Aru felt her chest tighten. "Kara—"

"Last one's for you, Brynne!" said Kara, holding out a box. "Figured you might be hungry, and this is a Lanka delicacy!"

Brynne didn't take it. Instead, she stared coldly at Kara until the girl's smile fell.

Kara looked around the group and slowly withdrew the present. "What happened?" she asked. "I didn't mean to offend anyone. . . . I was just trying—"

"To help?" snapped Brynne. "We've heard that before. A little too much, if you ask me. Thanks, but no thanks. You're only here because it'd be way too dangerous if your dad got ahold of you."

"That's out of line," said Aiden.

Kara's eyes went wide and she turned and fled across the courtyard. Aru felt torn. Part of her wanted to follow, but Brynne's comment was fresh in her mind: *She could be a spy.* If Aru went to Kara, would Brynne think *she* was the untrue sister from the prophecy? *It doesn't matter what Brynne thinks,* Aru told herself, but when she moved to go, she realized Kara wasn't alone.

Aiden was with her. He patted Kara's back and took the box of food, murmuring, "We just got some bad news, and Brynne is working through it. . . . She didn't mean that."

On the one hand, Aru was glad someone was comforting Kara. On the other hand, Aru felt a hot twinge of envy. It's not like Aiden had rushed to *her* when she'd returned from being kidnapped. He hadn't tried to pull her out of the pit of golden coins, either.

Aru, Brynne, and Mini stared silently at one another.

Dude, that was not a good look, said Aru through the mind link.

Neither is getting betrayed, said Brynne.

Brynne, maybe we should talk? pressed Mini.

But Brynne just held her hand out to the golden eye. "I don't want to waste any more time," she said. "Let's go—"

"Go where?" repeated Mini. "We should talk about what Kubera said."

"He said the first trial has to do with land: *To start, the land shall test your heart.* Seems clear enough to me," said Brynne, grabbing hold of the eye.

Through the gaps between Brynne's fingers, light streamed from the eye, forming a glowing portal.

"Whoa!" yelled Aiden. "We really need to talk about—"

Just then, golden light washed over Aru's vision. She felt her hair lifting off her back and the world whipping around her as if someone had stuck them all in a giant blender. Trees and buildings flashed through her mind, followed by a snippet of great crashing waves, and then...

Darkness.

Aru tumbled through the air, straight onto a field. She quickly tucked herself into a ball and rolled before she knocked against something soft and warm. The air had a weird funk to it, like sweet hay, wet dirt, and...

"HOLY COW!"

NINETEEN

At Least We're Not in a Parking Lot?

A milk-white cow with huge eyes stared down at Aru. She scrambled to sit up.

"Easy now," said the cow, taking a step back. "You took quite a fall! Come for some shopping, eh?"

Shopping?

They had ended up outside a little white barn. Over the door hung a large sign with big letters proclaiming THE BOUTIQUE AND BOUNTY OF KAMADHENU. The logo was a cow that had the face of a woman.

Aru recognized the name. Kamadhenu was the cow goddess of abundance. On the sign, a speech bubble next to her mouth declared: AH, THE SOUND OF MILKING. IT'S MOO-SIC TO MY EARS!

It appeared they were on the outskirts of dozens of meadows all knit together like a patchwork quilt, as if every cow pasture in the world met up here. One was red and dusty, and the cows in it had large bumps behind their necks and curving horns. Another field was tucked between rocky hills, and the shaggy cows had so much fur you could barely see their eyes.

Aiden, Brynne, Mini, and Kara looked just as confused as Aru felt.

"I'm sorry, where … Where are we?" Aru asked the cow.

"Goloka!" she announced. "The realm of cows! Inside the constellation you humans call Capricorn. This little boutique—or, as we like to call it, *moo-tique*—is a slice of heaven. Why don'cha come with and have a look-see? Haven't had too many visitors, what with the emergency state in the Otherworld realms." The cow shook her head, sighing with pity.

Normally, Aru would be a bit concerned. How, exactly, had they ended up in the middle of a constellation? But there were other things to consider, such as, how did this cow end up with a Midwestern accent?

Aru looked over her shoulder to where Mini, Aiden, Kara, and Brynne were crowded together. Kubera's eye was nowhere to be seen, but his voice floated back to her: *In each trial I give you, you must find and take my eye.* So where had it gone? On Aru's wrist, Vajra gave off a faint spark of electricity.

Brynne stomped over to the cow. "We want to see what's inside the barn," she demanded.

Aru frowned. Usually they made decisions *together*, but this was the second time in a few minutes that Brynne had taken charge without asking for anyone else's input.

What's up with you? asked Aru.

Brynne didn't answer.

"Of course! Follow me!" The cow trotted toward the barn, which was about a hundred feet away. Aru waited for the others and then followed, inhaling the sweet-smelling air. The farm felt calm and peaceful after the chaos of the vanara kingdom and the glittering sidewalks of Lanka. The only problem was that the ground was a bit soft, and Aru's shoes kept sinking into the mud.

She'd almost gotten the hang of it when the cow turned to look at them and said, "Ope, meant to tell you to watch your step!"

"Huh?" said Aru.

SPLAT.

Aru looked down at her foot and groaned.

"Smile!" said Aiden, snapping a picture.

There was one crappy drawback to the realm of cows, and now it was all over her shoe.

So much for treasure, thought Aru as she trudged toward the dark barn. Kubera probably meant for them to search for his eye like it was a needle in a bunch of haystacks.

"A bit strange your parents sent you to do shopping at this time of day," said the cow. "Don'cha know there's a curfew? Demons running about?" The cow shivered, and its flanks rippled.

Enchanted lights flickered on when they stepped inside. After the wonders of the Night Bazaar and even the Magical Plant Nursery at Home Depot, Aru was expecting something...else.

The moo-tique of Kamadhenu looked suspiciously like an ordinary convenience store. The ceiling was low, and the space was cramped. Products were lined up on a dozen peeling, rickety metal frames. A shiny cockroach scuttled across the floor, and the whole place had the cold-and-clammy feel of a neglected grocery-store aisle. Aru felt nauseated. Beside her, Mini fumbled for hand sanitizer, and Kara's nose was discreetly hidden in the folds of her sweatshirt.

"Ope, hold your horses there!" said the cow.

"I thought this was a kingdom of *cows*," muttered Brynne. "Do you even *have* horses?"

Aiden narrowed his eyes at her, but Brynne didn't look at him.

"Can I help you folks with finding anything?"

On one of the metal shelves, Aru caught a wink of gold. Her pulse kicked up. Kubera's eye! It was hiding somewhere in here.

"Maybe. We—" she started to say.

Brynne cut in loudly, "No, thanks. We'll look around ourselves."

The cow nodded. "You betcha!"

They passed a rusty, dented sign that said YOU BREAK IT, YOU BUY IT.

What if, when we're chasing the eye, we end up breaking something? asked Aru through their mind link.

"How would we, uh, go about making a purchase?" Mini asked the cow.

"I've got my mom's credit card," offered Aru.

"Oh boy. We don't take credit cards. Anyone who wishes to buy something from Kamadhenu's moo-tique must pay with a week's worth of service."

"A *week?*" echoed Brynne, gesturing at the store. "For *this?*"

A fly buzzed into one of the ugly lamps, got electrocuted, and fell to the floor. Dead.

The cow nodded. "Nothing too hard, I promise ya. Maybe use the sweeper a bit. Run some milk deliveries. If you can't do the work, well, tough tomatoes! No shopping for you."

"Right," said Brynne, rolling up her sleeves. "We can take it from here."

"Okeydoke," said the cow, wandering elsewhere. "Let me know if ya need anything!"

Aru headed down the aisle where she'd seen the golden glint of Kubera's eye. Along the shelves, the goods weren't magical at all, just stuff that was downright gross: moldy cheese and expired yogurt, bottles of yellowish cream, and even a cloudy vial of perfume labeled EAU DE COW.

"This is *nasty*," said Brynne. "I hope we don't end up having to shoplift just to get out of here with the eye."

"Shoplift?" said Mini. "Brynne, that wasn't part of the discussion."

"Do *you* want to work here for a week?" asked Brynne.

"Where'd the eye go?" asked Kara. She rose up onto her tiptoes, scanning an array of generic cereal boxes before pulling one of them down. "I don't see it anymore.... Uh-oh!"

Kara slipped and stumbled backward. Aru moved to break her fall, but Aiden got there first. He caught Kara in his arms, the movement causing him to dip her gracefully as if they were in the middle of an elaborate dance. Kara blushed as he helped her stand.

"Thanks," she said, tucking her hair behind her ear.

"No worries," said Aiden.

They looked...good together, thought Aru distantly. They both had this weird glow to them that Aru knew she'd never had.

The row next to her carried a bunch of cheap plastic mirrors with cow horns on the frames, and when Aru turned to catch a glimpse of herself, all she saw was...

A cow?

"AHH!" she screamed.

The milk-white cow had stuck her head through an opening

in the shelf and was staring at her. "Hiya!" she said. "Just checking in to see how you're getting along!"

"Fine?" said Aru.

"Okeydoke," said the cow, drawing back.

"Okay, *that* was terrifying," said Aru, turning back to the others.

"Let's try another aisle," said Mini.

They crossed into a row with expired milk from various decades. Something shiny winked brightly from one of the lower shelves. Aru rushed forward to snatch it, but it disappeared.

"Maybe it's behind the carton?" said Mini. She reached down to push one of the dusty gallons out of the way and then jumped back....

"AHH!"

"Hiya!" said the milk-white cow, trying to shove her muzzle through the space between the milk cartons. "Uff da!"

Again? Thought Aru. The cow should really start hollering SURPRISE!

"Don'cha know," said the cow, "I forgot about our little warning. Now, I don't think you kiddos would ever be up to any mischief, but do be warned that, in our store, shoplifters get a time-out!"

"A time-out?" scoffed Brynne.

The cow laughed its friendly Midwestern laugh. It was, Aru thought with a shiver, a little *too* friendly.

"Just a place to contemplate greed and the slow death of one's soul."

Everyone went quiet. The cow hummed to itself and slowly drew its head back out of the aisle.

"Okay, how is that cow moving around so quietly?" asked Aiden, shuddering.

"Who cares!" said Brynne, pointing at a different part of the aisle. "I see the eye!"

She pointed at a refrigerated case marked with a flopping paper sign: TRY OUR MOO-TIQUE'S EXOTIQUE DELIGHTS! It offered a tub of yak butter, a pint of water-buffalo gelato, packaged reindeer cheese, a quart of camel milk, and...

"Does that say 'human cheese'?" asked Mini, gagging.

Aru didn't want to know. All that mattered was that Kubera's golden eye blinked serenely at them just below the tub of yak butter. Before anyone else could react, Brynne sprinted over to it. The eye was stuck between two shelves, and when she pulled it out, the top one tilted, spilling all its contents. Camel milk splattered onto the floor.

"Let's go!" she yelled.

"Don't we have to pay for—?" started Aru, but Brynne had already flown past her.

The barn's exit was straight ahead.

"Ope!" said the cow, popping up to block their way. "Looks like ya made a little mess back there! Now, let's see, you could work for a week as—"

"Not a chance!" said Brynne. Aru recognized the look on her face. It was pure, cold determination.

I can fix this.

Brynne was talking to herself, but she said it so forcefully that it blasted across the Pandava mind link. It was like a scream unleashed in Aru's skull. She and Mini staggered backward at the same time.

"Don'cha know you gotta pay for that!" shouted the milk-white cow when Brynne sprinted past her.

Aru tried to follow, but she'd only managed a couple of steps when the convenience store transformed. Everything—the weird cheese, the rickety metal shelves, the dead fly on the stained linoleum floor—quivered and turned transparent. Beneath the illusion Aru could see what the moo-tique actually looked like: milk-and-honey waterfalls pouring down the walls, floating jars of gold coins, and rare nectar sitting in gleaming silver bowls.

Then, just as quickly as they had come into view, the riches flashed and disappeared, replaced once more with the ugly aisles.

Brynne was halfway out of the barn door when the shop sank.

Well, not sank, exactly.

It plummeted.

The walls blurred around Aru as she and her friends fell into a deep hole in the ground. Aru's hair flew around her face and her stomach swooped violently as they tumbled head over heels. High above, the barn ceiling ripped away, revealing close-up constellations and bright lunar mansions.

Aru kept trying to haul herself upright and turn Vajra into a hoverboard, but she couldn't get control of her lightning bolt. Eventually, they all slammed into the ground. Stars exploded behind Aru's eyes. When her vision finally cleared and she looked up, it was like she was staring out from the bottom of a deep pit. Hundreds of feet above them, the milk-white cow poked her head into the hole.

"Jeez, I hate to do this to ya," she called down. "But, ya know . . . tough tomatoes."

Aru tried again to go for her lightning bolt, but her arms were yanked backward. Heavy silver chains magically attached themselves to her wrists and dragged her down into a chair. The next second, a huge silver spoon appeared in her hand, the handle at least three feet long.

"What the—?"

Aru looked around, confusion turning swiftly to horror. All five of them had been shackled to a chair of their own, and each held a huge spoon. Their chairs were brusquely pushed up to a giant metal table, and a cauldron appeared in the middle.

Aru swiveled her neck to see *hundreds* of other "diners" in the same predicament. They thrashed in their seats, their jaws dripping black saliva, their faces so thin that their cheekbones and tendons stood out. The hair had fallen off their scalps. Some of them were screaming, a raspy sound of terror. The other tables also held cauldrons brimming with a shimmering liquid.

Vajra frantically threw off sparks of electricity, but the weapon was now encased in a little net dangling from an elastic loop around Aru's elbow.

They were trapped.

"How do we get out of here?" asked Brynne, struggling against her restraints.

"You shouldn't have stolen!" yelled Aru.

"I was trying to help!" retorted Brynne.

"Stop yelling!" said Mini. "We have to figure this out—" But the rest of Mini's words were cut off as she winced in pain.

Kara sighed, slumping forward. A slit appeared in the middle of her chest, leaking a silver liquid. It dripped onto the tabletop and formed a thin stream that ran up the side of the cauldron.

"What's happening to her?" asked Aiden, panicking. "Aru, Brynne—"

But whatever else he was going to say was choked off in a

scream as a slit materialized in his own chest. Aru looked at Mini and saw an identical line forming.

Across the table, Aru's eyes met Brynne's, and she said, "We'll figure it out, it's going to be—"

Then Aru groaned, crumpling forward. She would have grabbed the bottom of her neck if she weren't restrained. It felt like someone had taken a hot knife to her skin, and yet this pain was different... it seemed to go deeper. As if her soul had been covered in paper cuts.

"Aru!" cried Brynne.

She thrashed. Gogo glowed bright blue at her throat, but her wind mace could not save her.

A woman's voice echoed in the space around them.

My poor thief, you must pay the price for trying to steal from me. Your heart was not strong enough. Look at the cost of what you have done, daughter of the god of the wind.

"Help!" yelled Brynne. "Please!"

What shall you do?

Aru tried to respond, but she felt herself... dissolving. Being erased. Her very soul was flowing out of her in a thin stream of silver that hit the metal table. Her consciousness slipped away....
She was...

Huh.

That was strange.

She was seated at a table with people she did not know. There was a girl with chin-length black hair and glasses, her head lolling to the side. A slumped-over girl with polished curls. A boy with wavy hair, his dimples flashing even as he grimaced. And last, a girl with wide shoulders and a grim-set mouth that was roaring at someone.

Who was she?

It didn't seem to matter anymore.

Aru was the silver liquid on the table. She was in the cauldron, mixing with the silver soul-streams of the others. And then...

Darkness.

TWENTY

Souls by the Spoonful

Brynne Tvarika Lakshmi Balamuralikrishna Rao was a lot of things.

She was an amazing cook, and a fierce wrestler. She had an awful temper and once tried to crack a cinder block just by barreling into it headfirst. Granted, she got knocked out for an hour, but the cinder block *definitely* had a line through it, so that was pretty much a win. Brynne was even fairly decent at playing the harp, though she hated admitting that her uncles, Gunky and Funky, had signed her up for lessons on *that* instrument.

But if there was one thing she was known for, it was never giving up. She absolutely, flat-out refused.

It wasn't even a thought worth entertaining up until this very second. Because, for the first time, Brynne was completely alone.

Her arms were shackled to the armrests of her chair, and a spoon was stuck in her right hand. Her best friend couldn't raise his head. Her sisters were slumped over in their seats. Even Kara, whom Brynne had grudgingly started to like, was passed out, and it was all Brynne's fault.

Around her, the air was hot and cloying, steamed up by the shrieks and howls of the other thieves, chained to their own seats. Guilt filled Brynne like the worst kind of syrup—thick and sticky and suffocating.

Ever since their visit to Kubera, Brynne hadn't been able to stop thinking about Boo.

He had *left* them. He'd left them despite everything he'd promised.

Learning that had made the world tilt around Brynne. What if Aiden and her sisters left her, too?

She couldn't let that happen.

She *had* to prove she was strong enough to protect them, that she could get them through these trials faster than anyone. If only she could move her arms! She would overturn this stupid table, gather up the others, and climb a thousand steps to get them out of here.

But she couldn't.

Across from Brynne, the eerie cauldron bubbled with silver liquid. *Not just any liquid*, thought Brynne, her stomach turning as she stared at the glowing slits in her friends' chests, their souls slowly flowing into the cauldron. Brynne craned her neck around.

Something skeletal flew at her, screeching.

Don't avert your eyes, child! This is what it looks like to be without a soul. Our souls can easily turn rancid when bitterness and ugly words are left to fester in our hearts, making us act in ways both foolish and tragic.

Brynne whipped her head around as the speaker disappeared. "Who are you?"

A friend.

"Yeah, I can see that!" said Brynne, trying to shake her chained hands. The long silver spoon clattered on the metal table.

You are in need of friends.

"I *have* friends! They're just…" Brynne couldn't bring herself to say it. Hurt? Dying?

Or, rather, your friends are in need of you.

"Then let me help them!" screamed Brynne.

I am not stopping you.

"Are we seeing completely different things, lady?" asked Brynne. "I can't move! I can't even—"

Brynne sucked in a breath as a sharp pressure needled at her ribs. It felt like someone had slipped their fingers between them and was now slowly prying them apart.

Brynne looked down at her chest. A slit of silver met her eyes. Bits of her soul began to bead up in the slice, sliding down to the metal table like raindrops on a car window.

"No," she whispered. "*NO!* I have to save them! You can't do this to me!"

Can't I? I have given you more than enough.

Brynne growled. She wished she could take this stupid silver spoon and clobber it over the head of whoever was talking to her. Even as she imagined it, she could feel her thoughts growing cloudy. The stream of her soul was flowing out fast. Could she use the spoon? Maybe scoop up the liquid and pour it back inside her? Maybe then her strength would return and she could save the others.

But the spoon was too long to use on herself.

It was so long, it touched the other side of the table, where Aru…

Brynne paused.

She couldn't help herself. But the others? She could reach them.

Ah, now you see, don't you? said the voice. *But will you actually do it?*

"Of course I will! I can do anything!" growled Brynne.

She dropped the spoon to the stream of Aru's soul. The moment the ladle touched it, all the silvery liquid flowed into the utensil's hollow.

Ha! thought Brynne.

She raised her arm to dribble the liquid into Aru, then screamed in pain.

The movement had ripped something out of her.

A memory of Anila, Brynne's mom—although she hated being called that—rose in Brynne's mind. Anila was supposed to come over to Gunky and Funky's house for Brynne's birthday dinner. Brynne had been planning it for days. She'd brined the chicken for roasting, prepped the greens, cooked down the sauces, and even assembled her own multitiered birthday cake. As a surprise, Gunky had taken Brynne to the print shop so she could make the kind of fancy menus she saw in her favorite restaurants. The morning of her birthday hadn't started off so great, because Brynne's team had lost a soccer game, and all because *she'd* missed the winning shot. But it was only one game, Brynne told herself. She could make up for it next time. Maybe Anila could come to that game?

That thought kept Brynne excited for her birthday dinner.... But when the time rolled around, Anila hadn't arrived. Brynne waited an hour, and they called her three times, but no one picked up and the food started getting cold.

Let's just start this wonderful feast, okay? Gunky had said. *I'm sure she just got caught up at work.*

Brynne nervously spun one of her melted-down trophy bracelets. Anila always seemed happiest when Brynne won something. Sometimes she even said *That's my girl!* Had Anila somehow found out that Brynne lost the soccer game? Was that why she hadn't come?

Eventually, Gunky and Funky had convinced Brynne to eat, but the thought kept lurking in her brain.

When she was a winner, people showed up. When she was a loser, people left her behind.

In her head, she saw Anila's face twisting to meet hers: *Even if you manage to restore your friends' strength, they'll just leave you behind. You failed them.*

The spoon in Brynne's hand slipped a little, the soul liquid sloshing dangerously. Quickly, Brynne righted it, careful not to lose a single drop.

Do you have the strength to help them, thief? Anila's face was replaced with the mysterious skeletal one.

Strength.

It was what Brynne was known for. She could throw heavy weights long distances. She could command a cyclone and unleash it on an army. She could turn into a bear and pick up demons by the scruff of their necks.

You're my strongest Pandava, you know, Boo had said on the last day she'd seen him, after Aru had been kidnapped.

It wasn't the first time Boo had praised her. When it came to their physical drills, Brynne always outshone her sisters. But the way Boo had said it then was different. He was just as worried as the rest of them about what had happened to Aru.

You'll have to be even stronger now, Brynne, Boo had warned. *I hope you can do it.*

Brynne was confused. *Of course I can.*

She'd been so distracted, she didn't remember the moment he flew away.

When she thought of it now, angry tears pricked her eyes.

Aru had said that Boo went to the Sleeper thinking that if he could change back to his true form, he'd be powerful enough to protect the Pandavas.

Maybe if Brynne had been stronger, he never would've made a deal.

It made her hate him as much as she missed him. What was she supposed to do now? She had tried being strong, and it had only brought them here.

Brynne blinked, her eyes focusing on the metal table, her unconscious friends, the spoon in her outstretched arm. All she had to do was pour it into the gaping hole in Aru's chest.

Brynne could feel her strength—the very strength she had thought made her useful and special—leaving her. Her arms felt so heavy, her eyelids even heavier. Aru's face was already sunken-in. Mini's hair had turned gray. Aiden's skin had paled to a blood-less pallor. Kara looked thin and small.

Do it, she told herself.

But what if she got them out of here only to end up so weak that they left her behind?

So? whispered a voice in her head. *Then you saved them anyway.*

It was that thought that steadied her hand. Brynne felt the world screech to a halt around her. Maybe she couldn't fix herself, but she *knew* she could fix them.

After all, Brynne Tvarika Lakshmi Balamuralikrishna Rao knew lots of stuff.

She knew how to whip up a perfect soufflé, knew a dozen ways to knock someone unconscious, and (All right, fine!) she knew how to play the harp, and she was pretty great at it. Plus, it was very soothing. . . .

But she also knew something else in that second.

She knew she was strong enough to be weak.

She extended her arm as far as she could. The soul liquid in the silver spoon wobbled a bit, but Brynne kept her hand steady. She could feel something tearing at her heart. She flipped her wrist, and the liquid poured down, gathering once more in the seam in front of Aru's heart.

Brynne watched the seam close slowly. She saw Aru's face brighten as color returned to her cheeks. Then Brynne collected Mini's soul liquid, and her heart soared when her sister's gray strands shimmered to black. She raised the spoon to Kara next, and last, to Aiden, her best friend in the world.

What would he say if he could see her now?

Maybe joke about how much her hand was trembling. Would that make *her* the ammamma for a change?

Brynne laughed. Her eyes started to close. Sounds faded away. Before everything went dark, she thought she heard her sisters' voices calling her name.

TWENTY-ONE

Congrats, You're a Potato

Aru woke up to a world that could only exist in a dream. It was a cool, dark forest. All the trees were tall and silver. When the wind rustled through their shimmering leaves, it sounded like tinkling bells. The "sky" wasn't sky at all, but sunlight shining through water. It reminded Aru of the times she'd gone swimming outside, opened her eyes underwater, and looked up. Yes, it stung, but the view was like watching a crystal melt.

Beside Aru, one of the twins, Sheela, lay on her side, dragging her hand through a river thick with stars. She glanced at Aru and grinned happily. "Oh good! You're here!"

"Where am I supposed to be?" asked Aru.

Her memories felt a little hazy. She remembered the table. The weird cauldron. She recalled a strange sensation in her chest, like drinking a long, slow glug of perfectly cold water. She had woken up just as Brynne slumped into unconsciousness. Aru hadn't known what to do, but Aiden had. He'd poured Brynne's soul back into her chest with one scoop of his ladle.

And now Aru was here.

Which meant that, back in the real world, she was fast asleep.

Or maybe unconscious again?

"I took charge of your dream before you could turn it into Home Depot," said Nikita, stepping out from behind one of the trees. She was wearing a crown of tiny stars that winked and lazily circled her forehead.

"I don't *always* dream of Home Depot," grumbled Aru.

"Uh-huh," said Nikita.

There was a slight *pop!* beside Aru, and suddenly Brynne and Mini were standing on her left. Aru jumped to her feet. Mini looked unfazed. Brynne stumbled forward, heaving deep breaths. She looked between Aru and Mini, her eyes wide in shock. Aru was glad to see her, but to be honest, she was still grumpy that Brynne had gotten them into that mess *and* had been a massive grouch ever since they left Lanka, so if Brynne wasn't going to be nice, then—

"You're okay!" yelled Brynne, hug-tackling her Pandava sisters.

Aru was so stunned she almost fell over.

"Okay, that's *a lot* of contact," said Mini.

"There's no germs in dreams," said Brynne, hugging them tighter.

Mini relented.

"Plus, it looked like all of our souls were mixing together in that gross cosmic fondue thing, anyway, so it's probably too late," said Aru.

Brynne hugged the twins next. "Are you practicing those moves I taught you?" she asked when she let go.

"Yes," said Nikita.

"I *think* about practicing," said Sheela dreamily. "But I don't really like physical exertion...."

"If you don't practice, then you won't improve at fighting!" said Mini. "You do know there's a battle heading our way, don't you?"

"There are other ways to fight," said Sheela primly.

"Starting with a war on being basic," said Nikita, critically eyeing the others' clothes and rubbing her fingers and thumb together as if trying to wipe off something nasty. "No worries, I'll have different wardrobes sent to you after this."

"Practice," said Brynne, hands on her hips. *"Now."*

Nikita rolled her eyes but hauled Sheela to her feet. They moved some distance away and ran through the same sparring and defensive techniques that Boo had once taught the older girls.

While the twins were out of earshot, Mini turned to Brynne. "You are acting *super* strange. Did you hit your head? This might be a symptom of a concussion or—"

"I'm sorry about how I acted earlier," blurted Brynne.

Aru's eyebrows shot up her forehead. *Brynne* admitting she'd done something *wrong?* Maybe Mini's concussion theory wasn't that far off the mark. Brynne took a deep breath before turning to Aru.

"I really wanted you to be wrong about Subala, Aru," said Brynne. "I think...I think I *needed* you to be wrong. Now it's just...confusing. If the Sleeper isn't totally evil, and Boo isn't totally great, then what do we do? Whose side are we really on?"

Before Aru could answer, Mini chimed in.

"Our own," she said.

There was something so simple and *true* about it that Aru felt a weight lifting off her chest. Sometimes their enemies, like Lady M, had ended up being more like a person the Pandavas should help rather than a person they should hurt. Sometimes their allies, like Boo, had ended up hurting them when they should've helped. The only thing Aru could count on was her family.

"We will always be on the same side," said Aru.

"And we're all together, which is just as important," said Mini, smiling at Aru, Brynne, and the twins.

Sheela paused in the middle of her practice and tilted her head, a faraway look in her eyes. "Not all."

"I'm sure Wifey won't feel too left out," Mini said with a laugh.

The dream started to fade at the edges.

"Time to go back," said Nikita sadly.

"Keep up those drills," said Brynne. "Nikita, I want you to practice conjuring more thorns. Sheela, you need to work on *being* in the present. Your homework is to watch every Jason Statham movie."

Nikita scowled.

"Wait!" called out Sheela, even as the dream world turned pale and started to dissolve. "I see something!"

Her eyes glowed: *"Two trials before you; two friends will return. One you will welcome, the other you'll spurn."*

By then, the tall silver trees looked like no more than twigs. The river of stars had dried up. Nikita blew them a kiss and then winked away. Sheela stayed longer, her eyes, bright as frost, pinned to Aru. Her voice had that prophetic layer to it, so she sounded both ancient and young. It raised the hairs on the back of Aru's neck.

She awoke with Sheela's voice ringing in her head: *"Be careful what you wish for, Aru."*

"You weren't kidding. . . . She *really* drools when she's asleep."

Aru frowned as consciousness slowly returned. She threw an arm over her face. The light was so bright, she could feel it through her eyelids. Who was talking? Sounded like Kara.

"At least she's not snoring."

That was Mini.

"Wait a couple more minutes."

That was Aiden.

"But Kubera gave us three days, and we're on day two! We gotta keep it moving, team!"

Definitely Brynne.

An eerily *upbeat* Brynne.

A different voice said, "Come now, child. It is time to wake up."

The next second, Aru was hauled upright. She felt like there were cobwebs in her skull.

"That's it," said a soft, soothing voice. "You took quite a fall once you left the holding cell. More so than the others, I suspect."

Aru opened her eyes and found that she was staring into the face of a beautiful woman. She had large liquid-black eyes that reminded her of a cow's serene gaze. Her lips were wide, her nose long, and her skin a rich brown. There was an unusual scent to her—it reminded Aru of milk cakes and sweet hay.

When the woman pulled back, Aru scuttled away on her hands and feet and bumped into a low shelf. The woman's face was human, but the rest of her was a milk-white cow. Aru looked around her. The run-down convenience store was gone, replaced with a glittering Otherworld shop beneath a vaulted ceiling. It offered jars labeled WINNING LOTTERY NUMBERS and boxes of incense sticks for "cleansing rotten luck." She saw bowls full of gold coins, and tall crystal jars filled with milk. It was a place full of abundance and good fortune.

"You're . . . You're Kamadhenu," Aru said, bowing her head respectfully.

"I am," said the cow goddess. "And you have successfully completed your first trial."

Beside Kamadhenu stood Kara, Aiden, Mini, and Brynne. Kubera's golden eye, hovering nearby, blinked at her.

"We *did*?" asked Aru, surprised. "But we, I mean, Brynne, no offense—"

"Stole from me?" asked Kamadhenu. She laughed. "You will discover that when the Lord of Wealth is involved, he is testing how you handle loss as much as victory, for his Nairrata army is very dear to him."

What victory? thought Aru. She remembered the exact wording he'd used: *To start, the land shall test your heart. . . .*

At first, that didn't make sense, but Aru had a sneaking suspicion that Brynne had gotten them past the first trial, even if Aru didn't understand exactly how. She looked at Brynne and smiled at her with new appreciation. Her sister grinned back.

"For your strength, daughter of the god of the wind, I have a gift for you," said Kamadhenu. "When all other kinds of payment fail, never forget that a drop of kindness has far more weight more than gold."

On the marble floor before them appeared a small carton of milk, the kind of thing Aru would get in the school cafeteria. Brynne looked a little confused, but she still smiled when she picked it up. She bowed to the cow goddess, then handed the carton to Mini, who placed it in her backpack.

The cow goddess walked toward the open barn door, which glowed softly, the outside obscured completely by warm golden light. When she stepped over the threshold, she disappeared. Kubera's eye floated in the same direction, beckoning the rest of them.

As they followed it, Brynne cleared her throat. "I've decided that tables are not to be trusted," she declared.

"Or cows," added Aiden.

"Or mongooses," said Mini.

"Or mud," said Aru, wrinkling her nose as she narrowly avoided another cow patty.

Kara raised her hand, and they turned to look at her.

"Or spoons?" she added shyly.

"Look at you!" said Aru. "Now you're thinking like a real Potato."

Kara scowled. "A potato?"

"We needed a group name, so that's what we called ourselves. Potatoes."

Aiden groaned. "We could've had *any* group name, but no—"

"I want to be a potato," said Kara quietly.

Aru paused. Before, she'd stopped herself from calling Kara *family*. Now she felt a little guilty about that. Kara had faced monkey-people, a ten-headed demon king, and creepy tables. All Kara wanted was to belong, and the more Aru thought about it, the harder it was for her to imagine going on any adventure that *didn't* include Kara.

Brynne caught Aru's eye and nodded slightly. Beside her, Mini beamed.

"Are you sure you're ready to take on the solemn task of being a spud?" asked Brynne loftily.

Kara looked up, hope flitting across her face. "Yes."

Aru turned and addressed Kara in a formal tone. "Kara We-Don't-Know-Your-Last-Name-And-Neither-Do-You-So-It's-Fine, we ask you to . . ."

"Kneel," whispered Mini.

"Really?" asked Kara, caught between confusion and amusement.

"Really," said Brynne, smiling.

Aiden brought out his camera, finger poised over the button.

Kara knelt. On her wrist, her ring glowed brightly.

Aru extended Vajra into a sword and gently tapped each of Kara's shoulders. "I hereby declare you an official . . . Potato."

TWENTY-TWO

Begone, Worthless Rogue!

The moment they left the barn with Kubera's eye, they found themselves standing outside a decrepit, musty tunnel.

"Ugh, what is this place?" Aru asked, staring around her. "It looks abandoned."

"I think this used to be part of a train station in the Naga realm," said Mini. "I remember Rudy mentioning something like this."

"Oh yeah..." Aiden grimaced. "He once wanted to bring me here so we could take 'edgy' pictures for his album cover, *Rudy Rocks: The Genesis of Rock.*"

"He's in a band?" asked Kara.

"I mean, *he* thinks so," said Aiden.

Aru wanted to laugh, but something about this place felt *off*. On the far wall of the station, dim signage flickered over a single stone archway, the words ROUTE OUT OF SERVICE running in a continual loop. One moment, Kubera's eye hovered beside them...the next, it was all the way across the station, winking just below the arch.

Kubera's task for them was simple: get the eye.

The eye wasn't very far away—maybe the length of Aru's school gymnasium.

The real issue was that, between where the Pandavas stood and where the eye hovered, the train station was flooded.

The water looked like what would happen if you drowned weeds in soy sauce, and it had risen so high it practically lapped at their toes. A faintly rotting smell, like pond scum on a hot July day, hit Aru's nose, and she tried not to gag.

"So this is the second trial?" she asked. "Cross the icky pool?"

"Easy enough," said Brynne. She aimed Gogo downward, and her wind mace blew a powerful gust. The water split down the middle, sloshing up to form two liquid columns at least fifty feet high. "ONWARD!"

Brynne ran down the slippery steps, and everyone followed her. The once-shiny-now-grimy floor was covered in trash like half-dissolved receipts for Slitherbucks coffee and empty chip packets. Their shoes slid on the slimy tiles, forcing them to take each step slowly and carefully. In the walls of water on either side of them, Aru spotted two jellyfish pulsing away and the unmistakable silhouette of a shark.

"Is it just me, or is that shark stalking us?" asked Aru, lifting her foot.

Aiden glanced over his shoulder. "Definitely stalking."

"You're safe, Shah, don't worry!" said Brynne, puffing out her chest. "If it comes after us, you can sizzle it with Vajra and I can turn it into fukahire!"

"Which is ...?" asked Aru.

"Shark-fin soup! Mmm."

Kara piped up. "Did you know the word *shark* comes from the sixteenth-century German word *schurke* and means *worthless rogue?*"

"Really?" asked Aru, delighted. She turned back to the shark still weaving lazily after them. "Begone, worthless rogue!"

The shark remained indifferent.

At the front, Brynne swiveled around and started walking backward, careful to keep Gogo pointed in the same direction, so she could face them. "GOOD VIBES, PEOPLE! KEEP IT UP!" she said.

Ever since she'd been imprisoned in Kamadhenu's jail, Brynne had seemed different. Way less mean, which was nice, and also a lot more... energetic? She reminded Aru of that one coach who gave everybody a medal just for showing up to the game.

"All right," said Brynne cheerfully. "Let's run though our strategy again."

"We have no strategy!" said Mini. "All we have is what Kubera told us! *To start, the land shall test your heart...*"

"*Next, the sea shall try your might,*" said Brynne. "We've got plenty of might, team. Let me hear you say it! We are mighty!"

"No thanks, Coach," said Aiden.

Brynne scowled and looked ready to say something when Mini gasped.

"The eye!" she said. "It's gone!"

Only a few seconds earlier, Kubera's eye had glimmered like a bright beacon less than ten feet away. Now, it was nowhere to be seen. Kara snapped her fingers, and her trident filled the station with sunlight as the Potatoes entered the archway where it had last been lurking. The entrance led to a wide platform made of seashells. A glass ceiling towered hundreds of feet above them, and beyond it was the ocean. In the shadowy waters, moon jelly-fish stood by as silent sentinels.

"Where'd the eye go?" asked Mini, whirling around.

"Can we call to it?" asked Aru, panicking. "HEEEERE, DETACHED GOD-EYEBALL...THING...C'MERE!"

"Yeah, that'll definitely work," said Aiden.

"At least I'm trying!" said Aru. "I can't believe you didn't catch where it went on your camera!"

"Why would I do that?" asked Aiden.

"Because you're *always* taking pictures!"

"Am not!"

"Are too!"

"D2! Ugh, Shah—"

BOOM!

They were thrown backward as an inky-black cloud of smoke bloomed around them and a deep voice announced, "AT LAST, AN AUDIENCE TO WITNESS THE DEEDS OF THE MAGICIAN TANUTKA!"

"What the—?" started Aru, choking on the smoke.

"YOU HAVE SUMMONED ME!"

"Can we *un-summon* you?" asked Aru, waving her hand in front of her face.

"A magician?" asked Brynne. She twirled her wind mace, and a gust of air blew all the smoke away to reveal a short, pale-skinned man with a tuft of dandelion-white hair. His entire body was cloaked in a giant purple cape.

"TA-DA!" he said. "Tanutka can perform any trick you desire! And at a mostly reasonable price!"

TWENTY-THREE

Wanna See a Magic Trick?

Aru Shah *really* disliked magicians. She blamed this mostly on Corey Holmes's fourth-grade birthday party, where she somehow ended up trapped in a closet and the hired magician refused to let her out until he was done pulling a giant rabbit from a tiny hat. Which would have been okay, except the rabbit was extremely chubby and got stuck in the hat, so Aru was trapped in the spider-filled closet for twenty minutes.

But Tanutka didn't look like a party magician. He just looked like a short, sad man in an oversize cloak. And he also happened to refer to himself in third person, which was deeply unfortunate.

"Tanutka is one of the greatest *artists* of the crossroads, known far and wide for uncanny"—he paused to waggle his fingers—*"illusions."*

Just then, Aru noticed that there was an upside-down top hat on the ground, with a little cardboard sign leaning against it that read TIPS ARE WELCOME! She was beginning to understand who Tanutka really was. In Atlanta, there were lots of street musicians and artists. Aru found most of them pretty cool. Some of them, though, would follow her down the street insisting that she purchase their latest CD.

"You're in luck, fair travelers! Normally, Tanutka is surrounded by an admiring crowd, but the slow approach of a demon army has thinned our gathering to a rare intimate performance of *magique*." He grinned and blew smoke into the air.

Aiden carefully stepped around Tanutka. "Thanks, but we really have to be on our way."

"Very well. Tanutka can serve as your traveling court magician, then." He picked up his top hat. "But there shall be a per diem."

"What? No!" said Aiden. "We'll go alone!"

"Then, perhaps a fee to un-hinder you from Tanutka's highly sought-after company."

"You want us to *pay* you to leave us alone?"

Tanutka blinked as he considered this question, then nodded. "Yes."

"You're outta your mind," said Aiden.

"Well, *excuse* me for offering some help!" snapped the magician.

Kara raised her hand shyly. "Um, if you want to help us, did you happen to see"—behind Tanutka, Aru, Aiden, Mini, and Brynne all frantically waved their hands in a *STOP! DON'T DO IT!* gesture, but Kara didn't seem to notice—"where a golden eye went? Last time we saw it, it was under this archway, and— Whoa, what's wrong, guys?" asked Kara innocently.

Aru let her hands drop. Too late.

The moment Tanutka realized they needed something, a greedy glint entered his gaze. "An eye?" he repeated. "Oh... Oh, yes... Yes, Tanutka remembers it now. It was shaped like... an eye."

"I say we take our chances and go down this tunnel and see what happens," said Aru loudly.

"No, no, no!" called the magician. "Please! Tanutka can show you where the eye went. But first, just watch one magic performance! Tanutka shall serve up such a delight and wonder that you will continue upon your journey newly refreshed!"

"All right, fine," said Brynne. "Make it quick."

Mini elbowed her and added a polite *"Please."*

"Tanutka the Great can summon *any* kind of water you wish!" said the magician. "It is a rare thing in these parts."

Aru pointedly looked up at the ocean pressing against the ceiling of the underwater terminals. "Just so I'm understanding this," she said, "your power is summoning water...underwater?"

"WITNESSETH!" said Tanutka. He clapped his hands and a tiny rain cloud appeared. "Is it not amazing? Does it not *defy* your mortal senses?"

Kara smiled weakly. Mini forced a couple of claps. But Brynne, Aiden, and Aru were not impressed.

"Okay, now tell us, where did the eye go?" asked Aiden.

"Ah, but wait—there's more!" said Tanutka, sounding a little nervous. He threw open his cloak to reveal dozens of pockets in its lining, each holding a tiny vial of water. "Tanutka carries water from all over the world! Municipal water supply of Hoboken, New Jersey? Right here. Rain from a cloud shaped like a barking dog? Tanutka has it. Melted corner of a glacier from a fjord in Norway? Impossible to come by these days, but not for Tanutka!"

"Fascinating, but we have to go," said Aiden, moving past the magician. "Let's just try the tunnel."

Tanutka lunged and grabbed Aiden by his shirtsleeve. "Please!

Surely, you can spare something! That was an untold display of magique! Please!"

Perhaps Tanutka had used some of his magic on himself, thought Aru, because when he lunged after Aiden, his purple cloak no longer looked shiny and pristine, but dull and frayed. He was now barefoot, and his ragged pants had holes that revealed skin crusted over with scabs. His fingernails were long and yellow and packed with dirt. His hair, no longer like a tuft of dandelion fluff, was greasy and matted to his shiny scalp.

"Give me your camera, perhaps?" he pleaded. "That way Tanutka can record his marvelous magiques!"

Aru could see that some of his teeth were missing, and the remaining ones were black.

Aiden wrenched himself out of Tanutka's grasp, his face twisted more in embarrassment than anger. Aru felt the same hot pinch of humiliation. Tanutka wasn't a magician...he was a poor beggar. No wonder he hadn't gone home to hide like the rest of the Otherworld citizens. This terminal was probably the closest thing he had to a dwelling.

Aru was no stranger to homeless people. In the winter, she and her mom would leave coats and hats on the fence posts outside the museum so those in need could take them and stay warm at night. Sometimes hungry folks approached them for food or money, and Dr. Shah would always grab Aru and walk away quickly, her head down. Aru hated that, and didn't understand it. She knew her mom cared and gave to charity. Wouldn't it be better to acknowledge the people and say sorry instead of acting like they were invisible?

"I can't give you my camera," said Aiden, not looking Tanutka in the eye. "And I—I don't have anything else, honest."

Tanutka's head dropped sadly. "There have been no visitors and no audience for Tanutka, and he is quite hungry. Little girl, do you have anything for me?"

Kara lowered her eyes. "I wish I did. Truly."

"I believe you, child," said Tanutka, but he looked disappointed.

Before Tanutka could ask her, Aru held out her empty hands. "I don't have anything, either. . . . I'm sorry."

She wanted to meet his gaze, but she felt too embarrassed that she had nothing to give.

Aren't there any snacks in Aiden's bag? she asked through the mind link.

I ate them all, Brynne sent back sadly. Then she brightened. *But we've got the milk from Kamadhenu! We can give him that?*

Yes! thought Mini, swinging her backpack around and drawing the carton out of it.

It didn't look like much, thought Aru, and Tanutka had said he was hungry, not thirsty. But when he saw the milk carton, his eyes widened.

"Ah, such kindness for an old magician," he said, holding out a dirt-streaked hand. "Tanutka is most-est of gratefuls."

Out of all of them, only Mini looked the magician in the face, and when she saw that his hand trembled, she reached out to steady it before placing the carton of milk in his grasp.

"We packed pretty light and we have to be going, but is there anything else you need?" Mini gently asked him.

Aru recognized that tone. It was her *stay-calm,-I'm-basically-a-doctor* voice.

While Tanutka gulped down the milk, Mini discreetly used some hand sanitizer. The magician emptied the carton and sighed loudly. "Ah. Thank you, child. As for the eye of Kubera that you seek, I can show you the way and perhaps even open your own eyes a little more."

Aru blinked quickly as the magician started to change shape in front of her. His hunched back slowly straightened, and he grew taller before them. His wrinkled face became smooth, and his long nails shortened. Now he looked like a young man, except for his white hair, which hung around his ears like puffy clouds.

Aru peered closer.

They *were* clouds.

When he stretched his neck from side to side, droplets of rain fell down his collar. A tiny flash of lightning dangled from his left ear like an earring. His cloak, once frayed and purple, was now a majestic robe made of silver-laced storm clouds.

Kara found her voice first. "Who are you?"

The magician smiled and swept a bow. "I am called Uttanka," he said in a rich, deep voice. "Will you hear my tale?"

Aru felt the others' eyes turning to her. She lifted her chin, looked Uttanka in the eye, and said, "Yes."

TWENTY-FOUR

The Tale of Uttanka

A tuft of Uttanka's hair broke off and drifted toward them.

On the one hand, Aru was shocked. Who was Uttanka? Why did he show up as a beggar first? On the other hand, Aru was deeply intrigued by his cloud hair. Aru plucked at her braid. Her mom always told her to keep her hair tied up so she'd stop "shedding all over the house." Did Uttanka have the same problem? Or would his fallen hair just dissolve into cold puddles? If he tried to tie up his cloud hair, would a man bun even hold?

The tuft expanded, transforming into a screen so wide that it blocked their view of the tunnel. An image bloomed on it, showing Uttanka and someone else—a blue-skinned figure draped in light with a peacock feather behind his ear. Aru recognized him immediately as the god Krishna, an avatar of Lord Vishnu, the god of preservation. In the memory, Uttanka put his hands together and bowed in worship.

"In my time, I was a well-respected *rishi*, and the god Krishna once offered me a boon of my own choosing," Uttanka explained to them. "As I was often thirsty in my travels, I asked for the ability to find water whenever I needed it."

Aru's jaw dropped. *THAT'S IT?* she thought. *YOU COULD'VE HAD ANYTHING!*

Through their mind link, Mini scolded her with a sharp *Shhh!* and Aru closed her mouth.

"For a while, I did not need to call upon the boon," Uttanka went on. "Then, one day, that changed."

The image shifted to show Uttanka limping through the desert, his face raw with sunburn, his lips chapped. He held out his hands, begging: *Water.* Nothing happened. Uttanka raised both arms to the sky. Only hot air shimmered above the sand.

A figure came over the horizon, followed by a pack of dogs. Uttanka grimaced when he saw that it was a man covered in brown gunk. Aru desperately hoped that it was mud.

The stranger approached and asked, *"Are you thirsty, friend?"* He had a toothless smile, his eyes were bloodshot, and his hair hung in matted ropes.

"I . . ."

"Here, I do not mind sharing! Why, I share with my dogs all the time!" said the man. He untied a pouch of water that was around his waist. Flies circled the dirt-encrusted cap. One of the mangy dogs sniffed excitedly at the container, panting and wagging its tail.

Uttanka took a step back, clearly disgusted. *"One such as myself cannot accept water from you. Please be on your way."*

"Are you sure, friend?" insisted the man. *"If you are thirsty, you must drink."*

Uttanka shook his head, shuddering.

"Very well," the man said with a sigh.

The next moment, the man transformed. He had glowing dark skin and wore a crown that sparked with electricity. His eyes were the silver of storm clouds and he was bedecked in jewels that shone like miniature suns. On one palm he balanced a small golden pot. In the other hand he clutched a weapon that Aru recognized instantly:

A lightning bolt.

And not just any lightning bolt.

Vajra.

As Aru watched the screen, Vajra perked up. Tendrils of electricity snaked toward the image, like a dog curiously sniffing someone new at the park. *Huh.* Vajra dimmed and coiled back around Aru's wrist as if saying, *Meh. Looks fake.*

Aru knew exactly who she was looking at: Indra, king of the gods, deity of thunder... and her soul father. She felt a terrible longing in that second and wished she could reach into the story to get his attention. *Am I doing this right? Helloooo?*

But the vision was nothing more than a piece of the past, and Indra did not turn his gaze toward her. Instead, he spoke to Uttanka, his voice at once rumbling, like thunder, and gentle, like the soft rain that coaxes flowers to open.

"You received a boon from Lord Krishna to find water whenever you needed it," said Indra. *"But he wanted to offer you something greater."* Indra raised the golden pot. *"He wished to give you amrita, the nectar of the gods."*

Uttanka fell to his knees. *"Immortality? I would've been... immortal?"*

"I suggested that we first test you to determine whether you were worthy of such a gift. To find out whether you would choose to see beyond the forms that others show you, or whether superiority would blind you to another's godhood."

Uttanka looked shamefaced.

"You have failed, Uttanka."

Aru winced. *Failed* was a bit of an understatement. For example, she'd totally and completely bombed a Spanish final—it was hard juggling demigod duties with ordinary schoolwork—by writing *Donde esta la biblioteca?* instead of completing a chart of verb conjugations. *That* was a fail. Being scolded by a god and finding out you lost out on the nectar of immortality? NOT THE SAME.

"But you may still draw upon Krishna's boon," continued Indra. *"Wherever you go and whenever you wish, rain clouds shall follow you. They shall henceforth be known as Uttanka's Clouds."*

The images disappeared and the cloud screen fell onto the rocky ground and dissolved into mist.

Before them, Uttanka shook his head. "I was sent here by Lord Kubera to test whether you were worthy enough to skip his second trial completely. He was torn between amusement and displeasure during your first trial."

Aru's breath caught.

"He wanted to know how you saw the world. Had you behaved as he'd hoped, he would have spared you the ocean trial," said Uttanka. "But you were ashamed of my presence. You were embarrassed. You pitied me and showed me compassion, which was a good and true reaction, but you could not look me in the eye."

Kara turned red. Aiden's mouth was pressed into a tight line. Brynne averted her eyes even now. Aru forced herself to look at Uttanka, but shame coiled hot in her stomach.

"I say this not to humiliate you, for, as you saw, I made a

similar mistake," said Uttanka. "I wanted to teach you what I, too, had to learn the hard way."

Where's he going with this? Brynne asked via the mind link. *Are we excused from the trial or not?*

Aru was about to answer her when Uttanka continued.

"But there is one whom I must except from my observation." At this, his eyes slid to Mini, and he smiled.

"How fitting that it was the Daughter of Death, the great leveler of mortals rich and poor, fair and hideous, old and young, who met my gaze," said Uttanka. "You should be proud, daughter of the gods. It is only because of you that the Lord of Wealth did not call off your quest altogether. You possess true sight."

Aru felt a burst of pride for her sister even as she herself wanted to shrink into the ground.

"Oh..." Mini pushed her glasses up the bridge of her nose. She shifted from foot to foot. "Well, my ophthalmologist said minus three eyesight isn't very good, but—"

You're doing that thing again, warned Brynne. *It's a* compliment! *Not a* Mini,-please-list-all-your-faults-ASAP *request.*

What she said, added Aru.

Mini shot a glare at Aru and Brynne before taking a deep breath and looking at Uttanka. "Thank you?"

Brynne shook her head. *We're going to have to practice this later.*

"What lies ahead is a test of true vision," said Uttanka. "My gift to you is a warning: remember, we are all our own beginnings and our own ends."

A ripple of water overhead made Uttanka startle. A frown darkened his face. "They are coming closer..." he said.

Aru didn't have to ask who he meant by *they*. She pictured the army Kubera had shown them—dark, seething, and vast, and Boo flying over them, a fierce look in his pigeon eyes.

Uttanka shook his head, as if startled out of something, and then pointed down the archway lit by moon jellyfish. There, a dim flicker of gold caught their gaze. Kubera's eye.

"Hurry," he said. "For you are running out of time."

TWENTY-FIVE

Go Ahead, Make My Day

The Potatoes followed the eye down the ocean tunnel. Glowing anemones and fluorescent sea moss clung to the craggy walls and cast a stingy light around them. The whole place had the damp, mushroomy smell of a long-abandoned shower stall, and the cold air raised the hairs on Aru's arms. Kubera's eye bounced slowly in the air until they caught up and then it zoomed forward.

Aru shivered. "Dark, creepy tunnel? Check. Monsters?"

"TBD," said Brynne, transforming into a sleek wolf.

"I hate this part," said Mini. "When we don't know what's coming next."

"Brynne, which side do you want to guard?" Aru asked.

"I'll take the front," she said. "You with me, Ammamma?"

"Always," said Aiden, releasing his scimitars.

"Aru...?" said Mini nervously. She hated guarding the back.

"I got it," said Aru. Vajra crackled awake but didn't transform into a spear. "Kara?"

Kara, who had been distracted ever since Uttanka had vanished, looked startled. "Yes?"

"Why don't you stay with me," said Aru.

"Of course," said Kara.

"So..." said Aru, glancing at her. "What's wrong?"

Kara bit her lip. "I failed Uttanka's test."

"We *all* failed," said Aru.

"Not Mini."

"So?" asked Aru. "We thought we'd failed at Kamadhenu's boutique, but it turned out failing was the whole point. Brynne saved us that time."

Kara sighed. "It's not the same for me. You guys are *demigods....* If you mess up every now and then, you can do something even bigger to fix it...."

"Yeah, I wouldn't call that the pattern of my life so far," said Aru.

"I just...I want to belong to something...good," said Kara. "That sounds dumb, doesn't it?"

"In the words of the infinitely wise Galadriel, Lady of Lothlórien, 'even the smallest person can change the course of the future,'" said Aru.

"Galadriel?" asked Kara. "Is she a teacher?"

"Um...no. When all this stuff is over, you and I are going to sit down—" started Aru.

Just then, she heard Brynne's voice in her head:

We found something up ahead. Something...strange.

"Time to hustle," said Aru. She flicked her wrist, and Vajra finally lengthened into a spear.

Aru expected to find the ruins of a train station at the end of the tunnel: iron nails, rusty tracks, and plasticware from someone who had dropped their lunch during a commute.

Instead, she was met with...the ghost of an underwater garden.

Aru let Vajra slip a little in her hands.

Maybe calling the place a *garden* was a bit of a stretch. It was the size of her cramped bedroom. The floor was made of polished seashells and the walls were blocks of cement draped in glowing kelp and sea lichen the color of shining pearls. Far above, the ocean water looked like swirling ink. The only light came from the glowing anemone and fluorescent moss that bloomed in between the cracks of cement. Maybe it used to have tons of plants on display, but now there was just one: a blue lotus. It hovered, suspended in a thin column of light. Even though its pale roots weren't in soil or water, the flower looked perfectly healthy, with petals like slices of sapphire.

Yup. Definitely strange.

"This is the last place I saw Kubera's eye," said Brynne. "I think it disappeared into the lotus."

"Or maybe the lotus ate it," said Aru. "Are lotuses carnivorous?"

"Carnivorous plants tend to sprout in places that are low in nutrients, like bogs," said Aiden, snapping a picture of the flower. "This lotus doesn't even have *dirt*."

"Let me guess," said Aru. "You know this because of a nature documentary."

Aiden sighed. "Some of us prefer informative cinema."

Before Aru could mock him, Kara spoke.

"How do we know it's really a lotus?" she asked. "What if it's only enchanted to look like that?"

They crowded around the entrance of the not-a-garden, scanning the space. Aiden experimentally tossed a pebble into the room. Aru tensed, half expecting the lotus to sprout fangs and chase them, but the blue flower didn't move.

It was, honestly...

"*Creepy*," said Aru. "But it also low-key reminds me of the enchanted rose in *Beauty and the Beast*." Aru placed one hand on her heart.

Mini groaned. "Aru, no—"

"Really, Shah?" asked Aiden.

Aru ignored them. "'*If he could learn to love another, and earn her love in return by the time the last petal fell, then the spell would be broken.*'" She ended her speech by dramatically lifting Vajra in the air.

It was supposed to be a small, silly, useless movement. But it didn't stay that way.

Maybe Vajra got caught up in the performance and sparks of electricity shot off without Aru noticing. Or maybe Aru stepped over the threshold *just* far enough. Whatever the case, Aru heard the lotus flower sigh. It sounded like the first stirring of someone waking from a long nap.

Aru turned slowly. The once-dormant lotus flower had begun to open and close its petals like a hand slowly flexing its fingers. With a grinding sound, the cement blocks shifted. They slid backward and expanded. The floor stretched until the chamber was the size of an arena.

"Now would be a good time for an enchanted prince to show up?" squeaked Mini.

The lotus emitted a puff of blue smoke.

"Cover your mouth and nose!" yelled Brynne.

She spun her wind mace into action, trying to beat back the...pollen? Creepy flower mist?... *stuff* with a gust of air, but the blue fumes just snaked around it. Aru tugged the collar of her T-shirt up over her mouth and nose.

"Get back!" Mini yelled. Her violet shield blasted up, but the smoke wafted through it.

Aru spun around, ready to race back down the tunnel they'd come from, but it had disappeared. A new wall had sprung up in its place, locking them into the chamber.

Kara threw her trident against it, and a few fractures appeared in the cement, but the wall didn't budge.

"I can't get rid—" Brynne started to say.

But then her words cut off. She lowered her wind mace, her gaze losing focus as the blue smoke drifted into her face.

"Brynne!" shouted Aru, reaching for her sister.

The movement dislodged her T-shirt, and as Aru drew a breath, a strange odor invaded her nostrils. The fragrance of the blue lotus was unlike anything she'd ever smelled. It wasn't sweet or floral or rotten, but like an emotion distilled to a scent.

It was the smell of vengeance.

The aroma of every perfectly timed biting comeback; a whiff of rage simmering just beneath the surface of the skin. It made Aru's mouth water and her heart race.

It smelled . . . *great*.

The blue smoke wafted around them.

"It's not dangerous at all!" said Aru, laughing.

"I'm not allergic to it!" said Mini, twirling around on the spot. "I feel . . . stronger."

"Could this be a perfume?" asked Brynne, sniffing her wrists. "Because I'd definitely wear whatever this is every freaking day."

Aiden nodded to himself, his mouth a grim twist, his eyes fiery as he whispered: "I'll show them. . . ."

Kara wasn't as entranced as the others. As the blue smoke wafted back toward the lotus, she lowered the arm that had been blocking her nose and mouth.

"Something's wrong," she said. "Can't you feel it?"

"I feel *good*?" said Aru, spinning as though preparing to throw Vajra like a discus.

"But it's the smell of . . . revenge," said Kara. "That doesn't feel like a good thing. It feels, I dunno, self-destructive or something. Can't you tell?"

Self-destructive.

Aru used to joke about that word. On days when she woke up particularly hungry and discovered that they were out of cereal, she'd beep around the kitchen and say, *T-minus one minute until Aru self-destructs* in a robotic voice. It always made her mom laugh.

But she didn't know where her mom was anymore.

And when she thought of self-destruction now, Aru was pulled back into one of the last times she'd seen Boo. He had just finished a lecture on vengeance and was fluttering around the classroom, sometimes settling on the pieces of armor that hung from the ceiling and other times, on Aru's head.

"Not everyone fights fair in war," Boo had said. "You may be tempted to seek revenge, but I caution you against it. You have no idea what kind of grief you could bring down on yourself when you do such a thing."

Boo looked unhappy when he said this, and at the time, Aru had been clueless about his curse. She'd chalked up his grumpiness to the fact that Brynne had eaten the last of his Oreos before class.

Boo continued, puffing out his chest. "The great Chinese

philosopher Confucius once said that 'if you seek revenge, you should dig two graves.'"

Brynne scowled. "What if you have more than two enemies? Two graves isn't enough."

"You are misunderstanding!" said Boo.

"It's a metaphorical grave, right?" said Mini. "Sounds really unhygienic otherwise."

Aru raised her hand. "What if you set your enemies on fire and there's nothing left to bury?"

Aiden looked horrified. "Shah, for the billionth time, why are you like this?"

"GIRLS!" Boo yelled.

Aiden coughed.

"And Aiden," Boo amended. "You are missing the point! The point is that, should you try to destroy someone, you must acknowledge that in doing so, you are also destroying yourself. Hence two graves. It is a lesson that even the wisest of us some times forget."

Aru jolted back to the present as Kara waved a hand in front of her face. "Aru?" she asked. "You okay? Whoa, your eyes..."

Aru took a step back. "What? What's wrong with them?" She blinked and looked around the room, but nothing had changed since the blue smoke had seeped into them. The flower was still opening and closing its petals. The room was still empty.

Nothing had changed except for how Aru felt.

She kept thinking about her mom's smile, the feeling of Boo's feet on her head, the terrible look of pain in his eyes when he'd betrayed them and gone to the Sleeper. Sheela claimed he'd done it so he could protect them, but that didn't fit with the ugly tone of his voice when he'd told Kubera the Pandavas were *nothing more than weak children, not worthy of anyone's time or attention.*

Aru thought again of Sheela's sorrowful prophecy: *You will hate him for his love.*

But Sheela was wrong.

Aru didn't hate Boo. She hated herself. She hated that she missed Boo and pitied the Sleeper. She hated that she wanted to yell at her mom even though she longed for her so much it felt like a constant weight on her chest. She hated that even now—with the Otherworld counting on them, the Sleeper's army approaching, and Kubera dangling his army in front of them like a toy—she still couldn't muster the will to fight.

The good guys weren't so good. The bad guys weren't so bad. So where did that leave her?

Mini gasped. She held up her compact to Aru. "Our *eyes.*"

Aru glanced at her reflection.

Her eyes were *blue.* As blue as the heart of a flame. And the others had been affected, too. Aiden's night-sky eyes had lightened to the color of frost. Mini's milk-chocolate eyes had shifted to turquoise. Brynne's hazel eyes were a livid teal. Only Kara's remained the same—a warm, steady gold.

Kara's gaze flew to something behind Aru, and Aru lurched backward. Vajra transformed into a lightning-whip in her hand, its long coil tensing and sparking. "Oh no," she said.

Aru felt a storm gathering in her chest as all her fury and hate surged together. There was only one person she wanted to fight right now, and as she turned around, she saw that her wish had been granted.

Aru Shah was staring at herself.

TWENTY-SIX

One Aru Is Enough

One Brynne. One Mini. One Aiden. One Aru.

But weirdly, no Kara.

The doppelgängers were almost identical to them—their clothes were just as rumpled, their skin just as grimy. They even had the same weapons . . . only theirs were tinged the same shade of blue as the lotus petals.

The only difference was their eyes, which were the Pandavas' usual colors, whereas Aru could still see the sapphire sheen of her gaze reflected in Mini's shield.

It made her feel ill that the thing that wasn't her looked more like herself than she did.

This wasn't the first time Aru had been in this situation.

Almost two years ago, a rakshasi had shape-shifted to look just like her. Another time, their rakshasi friend Hira had impersonated Aru as a joke. But on those occasions, someone had just copied her face. Not her mannerisms.

This time was different.

The Other Mini gave the same twitch of her left shoulder that always preceded a fight. The Other Aiden cracked his neck in a familiar way while clenching his jaw and peering at them through the fall of his hair. The Other Brynne perfectly mimicked real Brynne's roll of the shoulders before settling into a wide stance.

When the Other Aru's mouth twisted, a shiver ran down Aru's spine. Her counterpart moved closer. There was hardly twenty feet between her friends and their foils, and the air around them felt burning hot to Aru, as if someone had placed her hand too close to a candle's flame.

"*You,*" said Other Aru.

Aru flinched at the sound of her voice.

"*You* did this to me," said Other Aru. "And now you're going to pay for it."

Behind the row of doppelgängers, the blue lotus was fully open. Kubera's eye hovered an inch above the petals, its eyelid peeled back as if it didn't want to miss a single moment of what was going to happen next.

"We have to fight *ourselves* to get to the eye?" asked Brynne.

In response, Brynne's counterpart aimed her wind mace straight at her. Brynne narrowly dodged the stream of air. Both girls growled at the same time.

"Okay, you wanna fight?" asked Brynne, her teal eyes glowing brighter.

Aru felt the too-hot quality of the space threading around her, straining tight, and then . . .

"Let's fight," said Brynne.

The thread snapped.

Aru focused all the anger she had inside her, and it exploded toward the line of replicas. "Fall in!" she shouted.

The Potatoes gathered into a knot and leaped shoulder to shoulder.

"They can't fight us if they can't see us," said Aru.

Brynne grinned savagely. She aimed her wind mace at the cement walls, and clouds of dust whipped up, obscuring the clones' view. Mini's violet shield snapped around them.

"Light 'em up, Shah," said Aiden.

Aru touched her lightning bolt to his scimitars, and Mini retracted the shield.

"Kara, keep them away from us!" hollered Brynne.

She nodded, fixing her stance and slashing out with her trident.

One of their enemies yelped—it sounded like Other Mini—and Aru grinned.

The duplicates swarmed forward only for a huge gust of air to shove them back. Other Mini formed her own shield, and the doppelgängers fanned out defensively around the blue lotus.

"CHARGE!" yelled Aru.

Both lines—doppelgängers and Potatoes—stormed forward.

Brynne and Other Brynne unleashed identical cyclones. Dust flew around them. Aru caught occasional flashes of blue light before the wind died down enough to reveal two blue wolves snarling and snapping at each other. Aru spun around, blocking a lightning javelin flung in her direction. As she turned, she caught sight of Mini and Other Mini. They were staring each other down, their Death Dandas raised to eye level as violet light shimmered around them. A sudden crash drew Aru's attention, and she turned to see Aiden and Other Aiden clanging their scimitars together. They parried each other's blows....

One jab at the throat, blocked.

One jab at the knees, blocked.

This was, Aru realized with a sinking sensation, pointless.

The doppelgängers knew their foes' every move and every weakness. How could either side win?

Beside her, Kara had focused all her concentration on Kubera's eye still floating above the blue lotus. Over and over, she cast out her weapon, as if she was trying to catch the eye in the tines of her trident. Aru spun around, scanning the arena.

Everyone's doppelgänger had found their counterpart....

So where was Kara's?

"Watch out, Aru!" screamed Kara.

Almost too late, Aru saw Other Aru's lightning spear careening toward her. Aru sidestepped it neatly, then flung out Vajra like a net. It caught Other Aru around the ankles, knocking her to the ground. Aru almost smiled before she heard something whistling in the air just behind her. Other Aru's lightning bolt had flattened into a discus and slammed into her back, sending her sprawling across the stone floor.

Aru rolled to her side, glancing up just as Other Aru's lightning bolt transformed into a spear aimed straight for her heart. Aru scrambled for her own Vajra, but then violet light burst around her. Mini had cast a shield, and Other Aru's lightning bolt had bounced off it.

"I got you, Aru—" Mini started to say.

But the battle changed then. It was as if the moment Mini decided to protect someone other than herself, a switch was flipped inside the doppelgängers' heads. Until that second, they had only attacked their own counterparts. Brynne and Other Brynne had stood locked in their own hurricane. Aiden and Other Aiden were still meeting blade with blade.

Now they exchanged looks with their comrades, and chaos reigned.

Other Brynne transformed into a panther and lunged toward Mini's throat. Violet light shimmered around Mini, who went invisible on the spot. Other Brynne skidded to a halt before—BAM!—Mini's force field bounced her backward.

Brynne whooped out, "YEAH! GET ME, MINI!"

But her grin quickly fell when Other Mini winked out of sight.

"Uh-oh," Brynne said.

Brynne threw up her cyclones. Blue and purple sparks clashed together, enveloping the fighting Brynnes and Minis. Aru grabbed Kara's hand and swung her around until they were back-to-back.

"I got your back, if you got mine," she said.

Kara beamed.

Not ten feet away, Aiden shoved Other Aiden backward, then sprinted toward them. "Okay, what now?" he asked.

Other Aiden and Other Aru prowled closer. Kara threw her trident, knocking Other Aiden's scimitar to the floor. Aru expected that he and Other Aru would lunge or strike again, but instead, the two doppelgängers stood still. Aru, Kara, and Aiden moved closer together, their weapons out and shining.

Slowly, Other Aiden reached for his fallen scimitar and then started to laugh. "Oh, Aiden. You know the worst thing about being you?"

Aiden adjusted his grip on his scimitars. "The fact that I'm not a morning person?"

Other Aiden smiled, straightened up, then looked between Aru and Kara.

"No, it's the fact that you're haunted," said Other Aiden. "You know you're going to end up like Mom or Dad. You'll either be sad and left behind, or realize you made the wrong choice and set your life on fire. Let me take the guessing out of it and put you out of your misery."

Beside Aru, Aiden's face paled.

"WAIT!" she called out.

But Aiden sprang forward, charging at his doppelgänger with vicious speed. Other Aiden brought up his scimitars, and they were once more lost in a fight. Aru didn't even have a second to wonder what Other Aiden was talking about before Other Aru started stalking toward her and Kara.

"One of us has to pin her in place, and then the other can grab the eye," said Aru.

"I hope I don't confuse—" started Kara, but Aru didn't hear the rest of her sentence, because Other Aru threw her spear. Kara and Aru sprang apart. Now Other Aru stood neatly between them, rotating slowly on the spot with her lightning bolt held over her head.

"Catch her!" screamed Aru.

Kara hurled her trident, knocking Other Aru to the ground and neatly restraining her by the neck. Aru darted forward and kicked away her lightning bolt.

Other Aru thrashed angrily, trying to pull up the trident.

"You're not one of us!" she screamed at Kara. "You never will be!"

"Ignore her!" yelled Aru.

Kara's face was a mask of concentration as she grabbed her trident's handle and held it firmly in place. "Go, Aru. *Now…*"

Aru stumbled forward, narrowly missing the Aidens, who were still slashing their scimitars at each other. Not ten feet away, the blue lotus hovered in its pillar of light. The eye, floating over it, slowly rotated to face her. She stretched out her hand, blinking back tears as wind from Brynne and Mini's battle threw dust into her eyes.

Her fingers had almost reached the edge of the eye when Kara screamed, "WATCH OUT!"

Aru spun around to see the Other Aru charging toward her. How had she gotten free? Aru extended Vajra like a sword and their lightning bolts clashed. Electricity sparked and flew around them. Then Other Aru let loose her bolt...but not at Aru—at *Vajra*. The weapon went spinning out of her hands.

"Vajra!" cried Aru.

She stretched out her hands for her lightning bolt to return, but on its way back, Other Aru hit it with another lightning strike and Vajra went soaring toward the opposite wall. Aru tried to stand up, but her foot slipped on the stone pavement and she fell.

"When you think about it," said Other Aru, "it's really your own fault."

Other Aru lifted her javelin. Sparks flew from it and rained down on Aru, burning her flesh.

"NO!" yelled Kara.

"My blade is revenge, and my aim is true," whispered Other Aru.

Kara flung herself in front of Aru. Light spangled across Aru's vision. Too late, she felt the familiar electric purr of Vajra back in her outstretched hand. Too late, she found her footing and managed to stand up.

Kara was splayed out on the floor between Aru and Other Aru, her golden eyes staring blankly at the ceiling.

TWENTY-SEVEN

You Seem a Decent Fellow; I Hate to Kill You

Aru couldn't make herself move. She stared and stared at Kara's motionless body on the floor. Maybe if Aru just looked hard enough, the scene would change. But it didn't. If anything, the world broke faster around her.

Wind, dust, and violet light swirled through the area. Aiden and Other Aiden growled and thrashed, their scimitars now dented and lightning flashing between them. Behind the Other Aru, the blue lotus glowed brighter.

Aru finally bent down to reach Kara only for Other Aru to block her with a lightning sword.

"You can't help her," her clone said. "Now she's just another person you ended up destroying. Pretty familiar pattern, to be honest."

Aru stood up and Vajra turned into a sword to match her opponent's.

"You were too weak—that's why Boo turned on us!" Other Aru screamed, waving her lightning bolt. "You couldn't finish the Sleeper when you had the chance!"

Every terrible thought that had lurked in Aru's brain now found voice in this hateful person. And yet, no matter what insults her replica flung at her, Aru's gaze kept returning to one person: Kara.

Was she dead? Or just wounded? What could Aru *do*?

Aru dodged blow after blow. She grew tired and weak, and her footing became clumsy. Her arms felt heavy, her eyelids even heavier.

Eventually, she slipped and fell. Aru scrambled to get up, but Other Aru was faster. In a flash, she had cast out her lightning bolt as a net, pinning Aru to the wall. Vajra thrashed furiously, hurtling itself at the imposter lightning bolt, but it made no difference.

"My blade is revenge and my aim is true," said Other Aru.

A blade of revenge, thought Aru. It was the same thing Other Aru had whispered right before she got to Kara. And when Aru heard *revenge,* it triggered a memory of Boo quoting Confucius: *"If you seek revenge, you should dig two graves."*

Aru didn't want to destroy herself, and yet that was exactly what was happening.

So how could she stop it?

Maybe it was her tired mind jumbling voices together—the voices of so many people who had tried to teach her—but Aru also remembered Uttanka's gentle words: *We are all our own beginnings and our own ends. . . .*

Aru felt as if her whole soul had exhaled a sigh. She understood now.

Other Aru pulled back the lightning net. Vajra stretched into spear form, crackling proudly, but Aru made no move to throw her weapon.

"I knew you were weak," said Other Aru.

On the other side of the arena, the dust settled long enough for Aru to see Brynne and Mini standing back-to-back. Brynne was sporting a black eye. Their counterparts faced them, breathing heavily and looking just as scuffed. A few feet away, Aiden had thrown off Other Aiden's scimitars and kicked them across the room. He looked victorious for exactly one second before Other Aiden rushed at him with his bare hands and they tumbled to the floor.

This has to stop now, thought Aru.

Mini saw Kara sprawled out on the floor. She looked quickly between Aru and Other Aru, her eyes widening.

I don't like that look on your face, Aru. We have to keep fighting to save Kara.

No, thought back Aru. *We don't.*

She could hear Mini's panic like a thrumming string stretching between them, but she ignored it, focusing instead on her opponent.

"You've caused so much destruction," said Other Aru.

It stung, but Aru pushed it aside. "True," she said. "But I can't fix it if I get destroyed, too."

Other Aru scoffed, lifting her golden blade. "Any last words to yourself?"

Aru scowled. "Well, that's how I know you're a fake. I'd be quoting *Princess Bride* and be like 'You seem a decent fellow; I hate to kill you,' and then you'd say—"

"AHH!" screamed Other Aru, charging forward.

"Okay, not what I had in mind."

Aru braced herself. Her hands tightened into fists, but she kept them clenched at her side. She'd drawn Vajra back down to the form of a bracelet. Her lightning bolt frantically zapped at her wrist, as if pleading to fight, but Aru resisted. She held tight to Uttanka's words. She was the beginning and the end, and this was going to end with her.

"SHAH, WHAT ARE YOU DOING?" screamed Aiden.

"No, Aru! Keep fighting!" shouted Brynne. "Don't give up!"

"I'm not giving up," said Aru, closing her eyes. "I'm letting go."

Up until that moment, Aru hadn't considered how those painful memories of Boo, her mom, the Council, and the Sleeper were like claws sinking through her skin and into her soul. She only noticed it now because she released her anger as the Other Aru rushed at her. Aru felt *so* much lighter without all that resentment.

But she couldn't even appreciate it, because, the next moment, darkness exploded behind her eyes as she fell backward and her head hit stone.

TWENTY-EIGHT

The Mitochondria Is the Powerhouse of the Cell

The first thing Aru noticed was someone running their fingers along her skull. It felt kind of nice, actually, but then the person took their hand away.

"Well, no noticeable contusions," said Mini.

"What's that mean?" asked Brynne.

"It means Aru's got an exceptionally hard skull."

"Surprise, surprise," said Aiden.

Aru grumbled. Her mouth felt dry and her throat was scratchy as she said, "Stop talking about me behind my back."

"Don't worry, Shah, we're right in front of you," said Aiden.

Aru could practically hear the smirk in his voice. She opened her eyes to see her friends crouched around her and looking anxious. Mini squealed happily as she lifted Aru slightly to give her a hug.

"Ow... careful!" said Aru.

"Sorry, sorry," said Mini.

Around them, the chamber no longer looked like an arena. The walls had slid back to form a small room, the floor strewn with dust and debris. The doppelgängers had vanished, but the blue lotus remained in its column of light, rotating slowly. Just behind it, Kubera's eye blinked. Aru almost thought she'd imagined the whole battle...until she saw a familiar shape lying just beyond the group.

Kara.

Someone had crossed her arms over her chest. Her trident lay tucked in one elbow, its glow ebbing and flowing as if it were snoring. Brynne kept a stream of wind directed at her, which both lifted Kara off the dusty ground and caused her long hair to ribbon around her. Her small backpack had been placed over her belly, and through the half-closed zipper Aru saw the little blue book of poems Kara kept with her.

"She's not dead," said Mini. "And she doesn't seem to be in any pain, but we can't wake her up. It must be magic—an ordinary weapon wouldn't do this."

Aru frowned. "The doppelgänger said her blade was 'revenge,' but I didn't think she meant it literally.... I mean, that's not really possible, is it?"

"Getting attacked by doppelgängers shouldn't be possible, either," said Aiden. He looked suspiciously at the blue lotus some twenty feet away. "The moment you decided to let down your guard, the lotus looked like it caught fire. And then all our doubles disappeared on the spot. That perfume—I don't know what else to call it—also went away. Our eye colors changed back, too."

Aru looked into Aiden's eyes. They were once again the velvety darkness of a night sky. His eyes had a curious celestial quality that made you think you could actually fall into them.

"Shah?" asked Aiden, waving a hand in front of her face. "You look lost."

In your eyes, thought Aru.

"Wait—what?" asked Aiden. "What's in my eyes?"

You did that thing again where your inside voice became your outside voice, Mini pointed out unhelpfully.

"Nothing! I'm still... What's the word—?"

"Failing?" suggested Brynne.

I hate you, thought Aru.

Brynne grinned.

"Disoriented," said Mini, pulling Aru to her feet. "How do you feel, though? Honestly."

Kubera's eye swiveled toward Aru, as if waiting for her answer, too.

"Honestly? *Lighter,*" she said.

All those memories that had made her crave vengeance hadn't gone away, but for the first time Aru felt bigger than the moments that had hurt her. If all she did was focus on the bad things, she'd never find the strength to fix them.

The eye's lid drooped, as if it was getting sleepy.

"Why didn't you guys grab the eye while I was out?" asked Aru.

"We couldn't," said Brynne. "You were the one who made the doppelgängers disappear, so I'm guessing you have to be the one to catch it."

"We're kinda hoping that once you get it, Kara will wake up, too..." said Aiden, kneeling by Kara's side.

"Here goes," said Aru, taking a deep breath.

She walked over to the eye, her hand outstretched. On her wrist, Vajra snoozed away like a napping cat, electricity purring off the bracelet. Aru was ten feet away from the eye... then seven... then five. Directly in front of it, the blue lotus had stopped rotating, but it was still suspended in place as if guarding the eye. Aru felt a chill run up and down her spine.

Enough of this, Shah, she told herself.

She lunged and grabbed the blue lotus. She had only intended to shove it aside, but she found herself holding on. The petals felt like cold, starched silk against her palm. Its heady perfume of revenge gave way to a fragrance that filled Aru with a sinking feeling she knew all too well. It was the sensation that came from spending a beautiful sunny day indoors, convinced that she could go out tomorrow instead, only to find the next day soggy and gray. It was how she felt after a fight with her mom, when Aru had just slammed the door behind her, leaving all the ugly words she'd said on the other side.

The scent was regret.

It was so dizzying that Aru almost didn't see the long fingers reaching out from the center of the lotus blossom.

Almost.

Aru shrieked and jumped back, but not before the hand had grabbed hold of her wrist.

"Get off me!" screamed Aru.

Vajra sprang to life, and the others reached for their weapons. A flash of light haloed the lotus, and the next moment, Aru saw that the hand around her belonged to a tall young man now standing where the flower had been. He looked like a prince from ancient times. His silk jacket and trousers were dyed a rich purple that stood out against the soft brown of his skin. A circlet of pearls held back his black curls. He had shockingly blue eyes the precise color of the lotus petals.

Oh no, thought Aru. *You are* very *good looking.*

Eh, too pretty for me, came Brynne's mind-link message.

OR IT'S JUST CAMOUFLAGE AND HE'S A PRETTY MAN-EATING FLOWER-MAN! added Mini.

Stab or smile?! thought Aru, privately torn and ignoring her sisters' messages. *What do?!*

The war in her head lasted approximately three seconds before the lotus dude spoke.

"I suppose I should let go of your hand," he said.

It's honestly fine? Aru wanted to say, but she couldn't get the words out. He dropped her hand.

Normally, Vajra would be pulsing and sparking by now, without any encouragement from Aru. But her weapon seemed just as confused about the lotus dude as she was. Electricity spangled the air in short bursts, like an animal warily sniffing the air.

"Who are you?" demanded Aru.

"A guardian of sorts," said the man.

Behind him, Kubera's eye hovered just out of reach.

"A guardian?" asked Aiden, scowling. He pointed at the unconscious Kara floating in the air. "Who exactly were you guarding if this is what ends up happening?"

"I am the guardian of revenge and regret, two sides of a single coin."

Rage flashed through Aru. "Did you do this to her?"

"I did nothing," said the man. "It was you—or, at least, an aspect of you—that let her get hurt. There are always innocent casualties when it comes to vengeance."

"Can you...Can you fix her?" asked Mini.

"I'm afraid not, though I can assure you that she is in no pain," he said. "Revenge is a dark blade, and as with any dark wound, only light can fix it."

Huh? thought Aru.

"What kind of light?" asked Mini thoughtfully. "They've done studies about wavelengths and using visible red light as an anti-inflammatory measure by working on mitochondria—"

Brynne elbowed Mini, who stopped talking.

But the man looked confused. "Mitochondria?" he asked.

"It's the powerhouse of the cell," said Aru.

That was about the only thing she remembered from science.

"I do not know whether this...Lord Mitochondria can help you," said the man uncertainly. "All I know is that light can heal. My only role in this exercise was to test you, as I have done."

"Lord Kubera wanted to see what we would do if we got attacked by doppelgängers?" asked Brynne. "I thought the whole thing was about the 'sea testing our might'?"

"And it did," said the man, touching the blue lotus pinned to the front of his jacket. "Each petal of this flower was carved from the depths of the sea. The sea tested you as you fought against the greatest enemy you would ever face...and the sea watched you win."

Their greatest enemy, thought Aru. Not the Sleeper. Not the horde of demons...Just themselves. Aru waited for him to hand over Kubera's eye, but he didn't.

"So...if we won, why won't you give us the eye?"

"Because I do not think you truly understand what the Lord of Wealth wished you to know, children of the gods. If you are willing, there is a tale I would tell you."

Aru looked to her sisters.

We're running out of time! said Brynne.

But what if this is part of the test? sent back Aru.

When Brynne could do nothing but grumble, Aru turned to the man. "Tell us."

"Very well," said the princely-looking man, bowing his head. "My name is Shikhandi, and I was born to bring about the death of another."

TWENTY-NINE

The Tale of Shikhandi

When Aru closed her eyes, images bloomed.

She saw an ancient kingdom overlooking a vast river, and three princesses walking hand in hand through a garden. Shikhandi's voice echoed through the image, freezing it in place so it looked like a painting.

"In one of my lives, I was born Amba, Princess of the Kingdom of Kashi," said Shikhandi. "I was betrothed to the son of a neighboring king, and I thought...I thought I would be happy."

The images now blurred through Aru's head.

She watched as the three princesses struggled to break free of a man's grip, but he was too strong, and before long he had secured them all on a golden chariot. The horse-drawn vehicle sped through the dusty terrain of a desert kingdom before arriving at a new palace surrounded by mango and guava trees. Once the three princesses were taken inside, a handsome young king with light brown skin and coffee-dark eyes bowed to them in greeting.

"*I am in need of wives,*" he said.

"Hold up!" said Brynne loudly.

Aru's eyes shot open, and the vision of the palace vanished, replaced with the concrete walls of the chamber beneath the sea.

"So this dude's version of a proposal was straight up kidnapping?" demanded Brynne.

"Is that no longer a courtship practice in your lands?" asked Shikhandi mildly.

"Depends on how much you like prison," said Aiden.

"But . . . *who* kidnapped you and your sisters?" asked Aru.

"Bhishma," said Shikhandi softly. It looked like even saying the person's name felt like a knife being wrenched into him.

Aru knew that name. "Wasn't Bhishma a powerful prince who swore he'd never get married?"

Shikhandi nodded. "A fateful decision, in my case. . . . My sisters, however, found happiness. They accepted the king's hand in marriage. . . . I did not. I was betrothed to someone else, and I went back to him. But it did not go as I imagined."

Shikhandi waved his hand, and Aru saw Princess Amba standing in front of a different king. He was tall and broad-shouldered, dark-skinned, and had small eyes that reminded Aru of a rat.

"*You expect me to still accept you?*" said the king in the vision. "*You're nothing more than spoiled goods. You have spent time in the home of another man. I will not take you as my bride.*"

Amba looked stricken. Her shoulders hunched, like she was trying to make herself smaller.

"*Bhishma was the one who took you,*" said the king with a dismissive flip of his hand. "*Make him marry you.*"

The images churned again, this time showing Princess Amba standing before Bhishma in a forest at dusk. Amba was thin and had dark circles under her eyes. Bhishma was tall and muscular, his black hair held back by a simple diamond circlet. His facial features seemed carved, somehow. His nose was sharp, his cheek-bones sharper, but he didn't look cruel....

Just sad.

"I cannot give you what you wish, Princess," he said. *"I swore an oath to my father that I would take no bride, and I cannot go back on it."*

"You . . . You ruined my life," said Amba. *"My father's kingdom will no longer accept me. My betrothed threw me out. Not even my sisters' husband, for whom you kidnapped myself and my sisters, will accept me as a bride, because I rejected him for another king. No one will avenge my ruined pride and take up my cause, for they know they cannot win a fight against you!"*

Bhishma was quiet, but his cheeks turned red with embarrassment.

"And now you, the source of all my pain, will not accept me, either," said Amba. *"You destroyed every happiness for me. I have nowhere to go. Because of you, I am forever an outcast."*

"I am sorry," said Bhishma, stepping away from her. *"But there is nothing I can do to help you."*

Amba watched him go, a dangerous light entering her eyes. *"You are not sorry,"* she said. *"Not yet."*

Aru watched, horror creeping through her as the years blurred past in the images Shikhandi conjured. Amba's long black hair became matted. Her bones became visible under her skin. She stopped eating, drinking, and sleeping. She stood for years with her hands pressed together, the forest growing over her, and a chant to the gods forever on her lips: *"Let me be the one to destroy Bhishma."*

A white light exploded over the images of Amba, and the

images changed...this time showing Prince Shikhandi as the Potatoes knew him: tall and handsome, wearing a strange garland of blue lotuses. Scenes of war flashed through Aru's head until it was time for the final battle. The sunset looked like a bloodstain. Broken bodies covered the ground. Among the active warriors, Aru recognized the silhouettes of the Pandava brothers, as unlike Aru and her sisters as they could be. Shikhandi aimed a bow and arrow directly at Bhishma, who looked old and gray and impossibly tired.

The moment Bhishma saw Shikhandi, he lowered his own bow and arrow. *"I see you for who you once were,"* said Bhishma. *"I will not fight a woman."*

Pain flashed across the other man's face. *"I am no woman.... I am Shikhandi."* He let loose his arrow....

And the vision went dark.

Aru shook herself, staring around her. Beside her, Mini scrubbed at her eyes and Brynne looked disgusted. Aiden's face was twisted with pity.

"I have been born many times, but never once have I lived," said Shikhandi. "Even when I got the very thing I asked for, Bhishma refused to see me as I was. I have found peace now, but I might have had it sooner, had I not sought the destruction of another."

"*I* don't blame you," said Brynne angrily. "I would fight!"

Shikhandi smiled. "Ah, but this test was not about whether or not you could fight...but whether or not you knew when to *stop.*"

Shikhandi reached for Kubera's eye and held it out to Aru. "Remember what it felt like to let go of your fury," he said. "Remember the freedom in it, daughter of the gods."

With that, Shikhandi dropped the eye into her palm. "Now

go," he said. "For you still have one more trial, and the army of the Sleeper inches ever closer to Lanka."

Aru closed her fingers around the eye, but couldn't stop herself from asking one last question. "Why don't you fight with us?"

Shikhandi eyed her solemnly. "As I have learned over my many lives, sometimes the best way to win is to walk away. My fighting days are over. It is your battle, Pandavas, but it will not be mine."

The back wall of the small concrete room melted into a glass tunnel lined with glowing silver filaments. The passage stretched far across the dark seafloor. Aru turned to say goodbye to Shikhandi, but the prince had disappeared.

In the place where he had stood lay a single blue petal. Aru picked it up carefully, remembering both the stiff-silk sensation of the lotus and the way it had felt to let go of her anger. She didn't know when she'd need to summon that feeling again, but she wanted to keep the petal close just in case.

The Pandavas stood at the tunnel entrance, Kara floating a few feet away from them.

"What's next?" asked Brynne.

Aru looked at Kara guiltily. The other girl had dove in front of Aru to protect her. "We can't just leave Kara like this."

"Shikhandi said that light will heal her," said Mini. "What about *our* light? Or even Kara's? Sunny is literally a beam of sunlight."

The trident lay across Kara's chest, its glow softly flickering with the rise and fall of her breathing. Brynne tried to tug on the handle so she could shine the weapon's light more directly on Kara, but it wouldn't budge. Maybe no one but Kara could touch it, Aru thought.

Aru called to Vajra and it coiled down her arm, stretching toward Kara's hand. *Gently,* said Aru. Her lightning bolt gave a little sizzle, like the sound that came from walking over a carpet in socks and then touching a doorknob.

But that bolt of electricity didn't affect Kara in the slightest.

"My turn!" said Mini, touching the tip of Kara's nose with her Death Danda. A faint violet *pop!* lit up the air, but Kara still didn't move.

"Should I try a little fire?" asked Brynne, hoisting her wind mace.

Mini leaped in front of Kara, her arms out wide. "I *really* don't think that's a good idea!"

"The whole point is to revive her," said Aru. "Not accidentally burn her to a crisp."

"I was just trying to help!" grumbled Brynne.

"Maybe we'll find the right light in the third trial?" said Aiden. "I mean, it is *literally* in the sky."

Aru hadn't thought of that. She replayed Kubera's rhyme in her head:

Three trials I grant you, one for each day!
To start, the land shall test your heart!
Next, the sea shall try your might!
Last, the sky shall judge your sight!
All three things you need to wield such power.
Wisdom must prevail for peace to flower.

"There's something wrong with the eye," said Mini, cutting through her thoughts.

"Huh?" asked Aru, looking down.

The eye, which previously had glowed brightly when serving as a portal from one trial to the next, looked noticeably dimmer.

"Is it broken?" asked Mini, moving closer.

"It doesn't look broken..." said Aru, holding it up.

"Maybe it's getting bad questing reception in here," suggested Brynne, "and we need to move to the end of the tunnel?"

"Or maybe it's just going to sit back and see what happens next," said Aiden. "Kubera wasn't sure he was going to let us use it as a portal the whole time."

"So what, he's just watching us fail?" asked Aru. She waved her hand in front of the eye. "Helloooo?"

It blinked lazily.

"What are we going to do?" asked Brynne. "We need to get to the next trial *and* find some way to bring Kara back."

"Maybe there's a portal at the end of the tunnel?" suggested Mini.

They continued walking, each lost in their own thoughts. Aru kept glancing at the eye floating serenely beside them. Was it just her imagination, or did one of its faster blinks look a whole lot like a wink?

As they walked, a strand of hair blew across Kara's face. Aiden reached forward and brushed it off her forehead. It was a tiny movement. It hardly lasted a second....

So why did it make Aru feel it as if a rug had been ripped out from beneath her?

Aiden had never touched *her* hair. On the one hand, Aru was grateful for that. If he ever did, she'd probably end up electrocuting him by accident. But still...it would've been nice if he'd tried? It would've *meant* something. The thought made Aru go cold inside. Did Aiden like Kara?

"Stop," called out Brynne, throwing out her arm. "There's someone at the other end."

Far away, a murky shadow stretched across the wall....

"Another demon?" asked Aru. She flicked her wrist and Vajra turned into a javelin.

"Let's hope it's just one," said Mini, twirling her Death Danda. "I'm making us invisible."

Brynne raised her wind mace. "I'll keep us silent."

Keeping one gust of air under Kara, Brynne directed a different vortex to swirl around the group. Mini whispered something under her breath, and a twinkling violet invisibility sheet stretched over them.

"Best to ambush, I think," said Aru. "They won't know what hit them."

"Agreed," said Aiden. He fell into step shoulder to shoulder with Aru.

"Uh, you've got something on your face," said Aiden, pointing to his own cheek.

"If it's a hair, you could just brush it off," said Aru, angling her face a little toward his.

"I think it's blood?" said Aiden, recoiling slightly.

"WHAT?!"

"Now!" yelled Brynne as they got within a few feet of the figure in the darkness.

Brynne aimed a cloud of steam at the being just as Mini threw off the invisibility sheet. Aru cast her lightning-bolt net. There was a sizzling crack and a howl of pain before a familiar voice shouted, "Again with the demented rope? Really, Shah?"

The Potatoes raced forward, and when the fog from Brynne's attack cleared, Aru spied a garish tie-dyed denim jacket, blinding-white sneakers, and a familiar smirk. Pinned beneath Aru's net, Prince Rudra of Naga-Loka managed a weak wave.

"Sup, fellow Potatoes?" said Rudy.

THIRTY

Inconceivable!

"Rudy, *what* are you doing here?" asked Aiden.

He bent down to hoist the naga off the ground, but Rudy batted away his hand and leaped up, dusting the shoulders of his jacket and pretending like nothing had happened.

"That's a nice way to greet your closest living relative," said Rudy.

"You're not my only cousin, Rudy," pointed out Aiden.

"I'm the only one who *matters*."

Aiden groaned and pinched the bridge of his nose, which he did a lot whenever he was with Rudy.

"Who's the cute unconscious girl?" asked Rudy, craning his head to look at Kara.

"She's the Sleeper's daughter," said Brynne.

Other daughter, Aru wanted to say. But she didn't.

"She single?" asked Rudy.

"Me?" asked Mini.

"Huh?" said Rudy, looking at Mini as if he'd just noticed her standing there. "I meant the unconscious chick."

"*That's* your first question about her?" demanded Aiden.

"I mean, I figured I'm missing some info, but you guys will just fill me in later."

"Info, along with brain cells," muttered Aiden.

"She's not a *chick*," said Aru. "A *chick* is a flightless baby bird, and Kara's got a sunlight trident...."

"And she's smart and has a ridiculous vocabulary," said Mini.

"And exceptional fighting skills," added Brynne grudgingly.

Rudy frowned. "I wasn't calling her a bird. I was calling her a *chick*, like, '*Cute or Handsome being of Indeterminate origin who might Consider Killing you.*' You know. A chick."

The Potatoes stared at him.

"So, what's this chick's name?" asked Rudy.

"You keep using that word..." said Aru. "I do not think it means what you think it means."

"Her name is Kara," said Mini.

"Cool," said Rudy. "So, do you want to keep talking in this tunnel, or do you want to come back to my palace?"

"I hate that you just said that sentence," said Aiden.

Rudy ignored him.

"That could be...interesting," said Mini.

Aru scrutinized her sister's face, wondering if Mini still had a crush on the naga.

"I can't believe we ran into you," Aiden said to Rudy, shaking his head.

"I can," said Aru.

The last time she'd seen Sheela, the prophetic girl had told her *Two friends will return. One you will welcome, the other you'll spurn.*

Though Aru frequently wanted to kick Rudy, she had no

desire to spurn him. Which meant he was the welcome friend. Who was the other one?

"How did you find us?" asked Brynne.

"I mean, technically, you guys are on *my* property. This tunnel is part of my parents' royal naga territory. I heard a weird crashing sound and came out to investigate."

"You must have heard our battle," said Mini, eager to talk to him. "We were fighting our doubles, and Aru—"

"See that?" Rudy talked over her, puffing out his chest a bit. "*I'm* officially on guard duty, which proves that my family thinks I deserved an upgrade in responsibility. I mean, even *I* lost count of how many times I saved your lives on the last quest. My parents are calling me by my full title now: Prince Rudra of Naga-Loka, Heir of the Jewel-Strewn Seas. And I even have facial hair."

Rudy angled his face up and Aru saw a single sad hair beneath his nose.

"Last time I saw you, your mom called you 'Baby Snekky-Snake' and carried you into a fountain," said Mini with a little edge to her voice.

Aru snickered.

"Also, that is *a* hair," said Aiden.

"That's because I had to shave the rest! It was getting unruly!" Rudy scowled. "And my mom was using my DJ name then...."

"DJ Baby Snekky-Snake?" asked Aiden.

"The music industry is crowded—I need to distinguish myself," grumbled Rudy.

"How far is your place?" asked Brynne. "I could use a break."

"C'mon. I'll take you back to the palace, and you guys can shower." Rudy paused, sniffing the air and frowning. "On second thought, you *have* to shower. You smell like rancid potatoes. And you look—"

One glare from Aiden and Rudy coughed loudly. *"Tired,"* he continued. "I'll feed you and you can rest and change and whatever."

"Food?" Brynne perked up. "What kind of food?"

"Whatever you want!" said Rudy. "Then we can figure out what to do next. Fair warning: It's my parents' summer shack, so it's tiny."

Tiny the palace was not.

It was roughly the size of a celebrity compound, its mother-of-pearl exterior sprawling across the ocean bed. Inside, the walls were made of enchanted aquamarine stone, and floating moon-jellyfish chandeliers patiently bobbed in the water. Everywhere Aru looked, piles of treasures met her eye—huge statues, odds and ends from shipwrecks, rubies and emeralds the size of her head.

As Rudy led them through the opulent halls of his "summer shack," the Potatoes filled him in on Kubera's trials, the doppelgängers' attack, and now, Kubera's weirdly defunct eye, which had gone dim instead of transporting them to their next trial. On top of that, the only thing that would cure Kara was *light*, and they were thousands of miles beneath an enchanted sea.

"Makes sense," said Rudy. "Lord Kubera happens to be pretty good friends with my parents, and I know for a fact, he *loves* his games. My mom doesn't actually like going to dinner at his palace because one party lasts almost a week, and she gets bored. But as for the light situation...My parents have this one treasure that might work, but I dunno how to use it."

"But *why* is Kubera playing games with us?" demanded Aru. "We've only got *one* day left before the Sleeper's army is supposed to attack!"

"I know," said Rudy quietly.

It was only then that Aru realized the palace was empty, which was strange, because Rudy came from a big family. "Where is everyone?"

"Off training the troops," said Rudy. For the first time, his confident smile faltered. "No one really knows what's going on with Lanka, and if Lord Kubera withholds his Nairrata army, then the rest of us have to be prepared to fight."

Aru felt a cold knot rising in her throat. She and her sisters were all that stood between the Otherworld and the Sleeper's approaching army. They *had* to win the Nairrata.

"But no worries!" said Rudy, grinning at Aru. "I'm sure you'll figure something out."

"Yeah," said Aru weakly. "No pressure."

An hour later, the cleaned-up Potatoes sat around a giant feast Brynne had casually whipped up. There were fluffy scrambled eggs—Rudy had assured her that they were from chickens and not snakes—custardy French toast drenched in cinnamon and powdered sugar, fresh fruit carved into elaborate animal shapes, a stack of blueberry pancakes, and miniature quiches.

"I call it BRYNNER time," said Brynne. "Breakfast for dinner, made by *moi.*"

Aru dug in, occasionally looking over at the nearby couch on which Kara lay. Even though Shikhandi had said Kara wasn't in any pain, Aru still felt a twinge of guilt looking at her. It was her fault Kara had ended up like this.

"What if Kubera won't let us continue with the trials until Kara is back to normal?" Aru wondered aloud.

Brynne, who was midway through her second stack of pancakes, paused. "Why would he care about that? She's not a Pandava."

"True..." said Aru. "But she *is* a Potato."

"And she's been with us every step of the way," said Mini. "We need to bring her out of this coma. It can't be good for her."

"I'm with Mini," said Aiden, glancing at Kara. "We need her. Kara seems...special."

Special.

The word reverberated through Aru's skull.

"I think I've got something that might help....Come with me." Rudy pushed away from the dining table.

The Potatoes followed him to a chamber that was the size of a two-car garage. Unlike the other rooms they'd seen, which had aquamarine walls with glass windows that looked out into the sea, this one reminded her of a sunken pirate ship. On the wood-plank walls, driftwood shelves were crammed with an array of odd treasures: jars full of old coins, a handful of statue busts, a plane propeller, and even a couple of paintings that sparkled with enchantments. A chandelier made of shark jawbones rotated above them. At the center of the large room was a ten-foot-high rectangular box made of fused metal patches.

"This is the fastest way to get to the surface," said Rudy, patting the side of the container. "It's an Anywhere Elevator. You go in, tell it everything you're looking for, and it will take you to the right place. It doesn't get used very often, though, so give your directions carefully or things could go...bad."

"What do you mean 'tell it everything you're looking for'?" asked Aru.

"It just knows stuff," said Rudy, shrugging. "When my parents go on their annual honeymoon—"

"No such thing as an annual honeymoon," said Aiden.

"There is for *my* parents," said Rudy, wrinkling his nose in disgust. "Last time they used it, my mom asked to go 'somewhere that focuses on wellness and has a rugged but not primitive landscape' and also 'great photo opportunities that will look more cultured than obnoxious on social media.' My dad just asked for a place that had a bar."

"So, technically, we could walk into the Anywhere Elevator and ask it to take us to the place where we could heal Kara *and* complete Kubera's third trial?" asked Aru.

"Yeah!" said Rudy. "The only problem is . . . I don't know how to get inside."

Aru studied the Anywhere Elevator. It didn't have a door panel or even any seams. Floating beside the cube was a glass prism containing a strange object. It looked like some kind of tool, but it shimmered, almost as if . . .

"It's a key," said Rudy. "It summons water, and it can also turn into other forms of water, like vapor or ice."

"And that's the key you use to open the elevator?" asked Aiden. Rudy nodded.

"Well, that's useless," said Brynne. "Can't we just smash a hole in the elevator and step inside?"

"Won't work," said Rudy.

"Yeah, right," said Brynne. "I can *totally* open this thing."

THIRTY-ONE

Brynne Cannot Open the Thing

Ten minutes, five broken vases, three ruined chairs, and one completely unchanged Anywhere Elevator later... Brynne conceded defeat.

"Okay," she said, panting. "I can't open that thing."

"See?" said Rudy. "Told ya."

"Could we ask your parents?" asked Aiden.

"No way," said Rudy. "They don't want anyone down here."

"What about your brothers?" asked Brynne.

Rudy made a face.

"I think I might have an idea—" started Mini, but Rudy interrupted as if he hadn't heard her.

"Maybe there's a button on it?" tried Rudy.

Mini cleared her throat and said in a near-whisper: "I, um, I said I had an idea—"

"Aru?" said Rudy. "Any ideas?"

Hurt flashed across Mini's face.

Aru looked pointedly at her sister and said through their mind link, *You are the daughter of the god of death.*

Let him know, added Brynne.

Mini's expression changed to one of cold determination. A flash of violet light burst around her.

"I *said* I had an idea," said Mini, holding up her Death Danda.

Rudy looked up, stunned. The purple glow highlighted the straight, glossy black strands of Mini's hair and her wide chocolate-brown eyes. He blinked.

"Gimme the key," she said, holding out her hand.

Rudy, still struck dumb, nodded and handed it over.

Mini examined the prism in her palm. "The reason no one knows what to do with this is that it demands human ingenuity," she said. "Not *magic*."

"Human ingenuity?" scoffed Rudy.

"Human *science*," said Mini, walking past him. "You said the key can turn into three states: ice, liquid, and gas. That means *water* is the answer."

Mini seemed to know instinctively what to do. She twirled the prism, and water rushed out from one end in a stream, as if it were a hose. Mini sprayed down the entire structure, then flipped the key in her hand, concentrating as she mouthed the word *ice*. Frost climbed up the Anywhere Elevator, until it looked like it was laced over in silver.

"My great-great-great-grandfather was a historian and my great-great-great-grandmother was an engineer, and there's this story in my family about how they worked together to break open a safe by pouring water over the metal cracks and then freezing it," said Mini. "When the whole thing froze over"—loud crackling sounds started popping in the air—"the expansion of the water molecules made it burst open."

The Anywhere Elevator fractured, the metal panes clattering to the ground and revealing a glass elevator within, complete with six huge armchairs and matching pillows. The top of the elevator seemed to dissolve into the air, so that it looked like a half-finished crystal cube that could end up, well, *anywhere*.

The Potatoes stared at Mini in silence. Mini held herself utterly still, then stepped forward and dropped the key in Rudy's hand.

YES, blasted Brynne through the mind link.

Aru started clapping.

"One, that was awesome," said Brynne. "But two... Why would your great-great-great-grandparents need to break into a safe?"

Mini shrugged. "I have *no* idea."

Aru wanted to ask more about Mini's interesting ancestors, but the Anywhere Elevator beckoned. Brynne and Aiden entered first, with an unconscious Kara floating beside them. Rudy went to the elevator and blocked Mini and Aru from entering.

"I... I was hoping I could come and help out?" said Rudy, looking straight at Mini. "Seriously. Tell me what to do!"

"You can start by getting out of my way," said Mini, bored.

"I mean, yeah, sure, but what else?" said Rudy, staying put. "I'm a prince...."

Mini raised an eyebrow, as if saying *So?*

"And my parents are good friends with Lord Kubera! If something goes wrong, I can totally help smooth it out! And I know you're down one person because of the unconscious girl, so I can fight in her place. Or I could just watch over her and make sure she's safe while *you guys* fight?"

Honestly, Aru thought it couldn't hurt. Rudy *did* know a lot of people in the Otherworld, and it wasn't like they had any idea where they were going to end up next. Although she did have major concerns about Rudy's fighting techniques. Or rather, the lack thereof.

Mini looked at Brynne, who said through their mind link, *Up to you. That said, literally* no one *is worthy of you. Especially some dumb prince who does not respect YOUR POWER.*

Then Mini glanced at Aru through the glass wall of the Anywhere Elevator. Aru raised an eyebrow and said, *You're the daughter of the god of death. Act like it.*

Aiden looked away, fiddling with Shadowfax.

"Fine. You can come with us," said Mini, flipping her hair and pushing past Rudy. "But while you may be a prince, I'm a demigod. So let's just remember who's the boss."

THIRTY-TWO

I Love a Good Ole Deadly Family Reunion

Aru blinked rapidly against the terrible brightness of wherever it was the Anywhere Elevator had taken them. The air was searing, and her skin felt sunburned within seconds.

"Hold on," said Mini. "I can help."

A burst of cool violet light spread over Aru. Huddled under Mini's shield, the Potatoes could finally see around them.

When Mini had asked the Anywhere Elevator to take them to the place where they could restore Kara *and* complete Kubera's third trial, about all Aru had imagined was that it would get them out of the water.

Maybe put them on a rooftop somewhere.

Or a cliff.

Someplace where the sky was visible. After all, the only hint they had about the third trial was *Last, the sky shall judge your sight.*

She'd never expected *this*. . . .

Above them, stars winked against the velvety-black expanse of space. Beneath them wound a familiar star-paved road studded with huge palaces. Aru recognized it as Navagraha Avenue, the boulevard of planetary gods and mansions.

So far, Aru had learned where many of the gods lived...but not three particular deities and their equally powerful consorts.

Boo called these three the greatest of the gods. There was Vishnu, the preserver; Shiva, the destroyer; and Brahma, the creator. And then their wives...Lakshmi, the goddess of fortune; Parvati, the Mother Goddess; and Saraswati, the goddess of knowledge. They stayed far out of sight, even to the Otherworld.

"Why don't *they* just stop the war?" Aru had once asked.

Boo had laughed. "Oh, child. We are not even a blink in their eyes. We can hope they have a plan, but there's no way we could understand it."

Now, Aru stared up at the stars, wondering if she could poke the universe. *Am I... doing this whole plan thing right?*

But the universe didn't answer, and a moment later, Aru turned back to face the glittering palace where the Anywhere Elevator had dropped them off. Its walls shone so brightly they looked like slabs of pure sunlight.

"So, Mini brought us to...the sun," said Aiden.

"*I* didn't pick the sun! The Anywhere Elevator did."

Beside Aru, Kubera's eye, which had been following them listlessly, now brightened. It knocked against Mini's shield as if eager to be let out.

"Looks like we're in the right place," said Brynne.

"*Wrong,*" murmured Rudy, whipping on a pair of shades. He flipped up the collar of his jacket. "There's nothing *right* about this climate for my skin. I could shrivel up here. Look! My scales are dulling already!"

"You'll be fine. I'm pretty sure Dee Dee offers both UVA and UVB protection," said Mini with a fond glance at her Death Danda.

"Now what do we do?" asked Brynne. "I bet the second we remove the shield, the eye will go straight for the House of the Sun, and we don't know what will happen."

"My mustache..." groaned Rudy. He patted the single lonely hair on his upper lip. "It's wilting."

"Here, lemme see?" asked Aiden.

Rudy turned to him. "Oh good, you can help me, though I don't know how, considering there's nothing on your face except—"

Quick as a flash, Aiden grabbed Rudy's mustache hair and yanked it out.

"OW!" said Rudy, clapping his hand over his mouth. *"What did you do?"*

"I put it out of its misery," said Aiden. "And maybe now I can say the same thing for us."

Rudy glared at him. "You're a monster!"

Just then, a bright light flared inside the bubble.

"Whoa, what's happening to Kara?" asked Mini.

Aru looked down to see that the trident, Sunny, had brightened, and glimmering gold strands were racing through Kara's hair.

"Maybe she's waking up!" said Mini.

The eye knocked again at the shield. Ahead of them, the door to the House of the Sun swung open. Sunlight spilled out onto the grassy lawn.

"Someone knows we're here," said Aru.

Her heart raced a little faster. How would the god of the sun test them? And how long would it take?

She tapped Vajra twice, and her lightning bolt twisted up her arm like a sparkling rope. "Let's go," she said.

Aru didn't know what they would find inside the House of the Sun. A lot of air-conditioning? Floor tiles made from crushed-up sunglasses? Instead, there was ... nothing. Well, almost nothing. The palace was full of floating clouds.

It was eerily quiet. Soft, warm sunlight—the cozy kind that belongs to lazy Sunday afternoons—radiated off the polished gold floor. Low-lying clouds serenely glided through the pillared entry hall, and the vaulted ceiling overhead had skylights that opened to a fathomless, star-strewn space. The eye, which had zoomed through the front door, now hovered in the middle of the chamber as if waiting for something.

"Hello?" called Mini.

Aru looked at Kara, still being held aloft by Gogo's gentle wind. Kara appeared brighter here, but she still hadn't woken up.

"What if we just, I dunno, slowly rotate her?" asked Aru. "I mean, the walls have lots of sunlight.... Maybe she just has to soak up enough of it...."

"She's not a *marshmallow*, Shah," said Brynne. "I don't think it works that way."

Rudy fell backward onto one of the clouds and flapped his arms as if trying to make a snow angel.

"*Very* nice quality," he said. "At least twelve-hundred-cloud count. I wonder where they got this. I heard only Airavata can make clouds this soft, but he's very particular about who gets his product."

Airavata was one of the vahanas, or mounts, of Lord Indra.

But Aru didn't know that the white elephant knitted clouds. How could he do that without thumbs?

"Maybe it's a knockoff," said Rudy haughtily.

"It's not," said an unfamiliar voice.

A pair of goddesses descended through the clouds. They both had beautiful dark skin and glowing amber eyes, and each wore a crown that looked like shards of sunlight. One of them was draped in a gown of shadows. The other wore a gown of evening clouds that billowed out behind her. The goddess in the cloud dress had Kubera's eye clutched in her hand. Aru tensed. Was this the test? Were they supposed to snatch it from her hands or something?

Rudy scrambled so fast to get out of the cloud that he fell on the floor.

"Hello, granddaughter," said the goddess in the cloud dress as she gazed down at Mini. Then her eyes roved to Kara.

Was it Aru's imagination, or did the goddess inhale sharply? Something flickered in her eyes—a sheen of silver, like how Sheela's eyes shifted color when she saw something far in the future.

"How intriguing..." said the goddess. Her voice was so relaxing Aru suspected she could take a nap on the pure sound of it.

"Granddaughter?" asked Mini.

"You are the daughter of the Lord of Death, are you not, child?" asked the goddess.

"I am," said Mini.

"Then you alone may address me with your request," said the goddess loftily.

Mini's eyes widened. "Um... We come here to humbly ask for your help in reviving our friend... and, uh, we also need the eye in your hand? You see, there's a war coming to Lanka, and we need to finish this trial today to earn Lord Kubera's army. Could you please help us?"

Mini swallowed hard and then gestured to the rest of them. They each bent over to touch the ground in respect. Aru looked up to see the twin goddesses studying them coolly. To Rudy, the cloud-dressed goddess gave a small bow. To Brynne and Aiden, she granted a smile.

When it came to Aru, she . . .

. . . scowled.

"*You*," she said, and this time her voice was not so kind.

"I was wondering when you'd notice that one," said the goddess wearing shadows. She'd been silent the whole time, but now she rubbed her hands together a touch too gleefully.

The cloud goddess ignored her twin and stepped toward Aru. "Do you know who I am?"

"Mini's grandmother?" asked Aru. "And so, therefore, kinda adjacent-related to . . . me?"

"Nice try," muttered Aiden.

"I am Saranyu, goddess of clouds and chief queen of the Sun Lord, Surya," she said, drawing herself up. "Mother of Yama, the Lord of Death, and Yamuna, the river goddess, and the Ashvin twins, Lords of Health and Medicine and Sunrise and Sunset, and Revanta, Lord of Horses."

Aru stared at her. Was she supposed to clap or something? Ask to see a résumé? Tell her that sounded a lot cooler than Mother of Dragons?

"That's . . . good?" said Aru.

"And *you* are the daughter of the god of thunder," spat Saranyu. "The god responsible for the death of my brother."

"That's . . . not good," said Aru. She took a step back, raising her hands and hoping Vajra decided to stay in its very humble bracelet form.

"Maybe it was an accident?" ventured Aru.

"Your father, Indra, cut off his *head*."

"Oh," said Aru, in a smaller voice. "Yeah, that sounds kinda intentional."

"And then he hired a carpenter to carve off each of my brother's other three heads, and he threw them across the earth so my poor Tsiras could never be revived!"

"Well, that just sounds like overkill and paranoia to me," said Aru.

"And now you dare to make demands of me?" asked Saranyu. The clouds around her bubbled up.

"Technically, *I* am making the demand?" said Mini, raising her hand. "If that helps?"

"And you stroll into *my* home?" continued Saranyu, as if she hadn't heard Mini at all.

"*Our* home," said the shadow goddess.

At her twin's words, Saranyu's face darkened. "Not by choice."

"Oh really? So you didn't choose to leave the splendid halls of the House of the Sun?" The shadow-gowned goddess tossed her hair. "If you don't like being here, you can leave again, and like last time, I'm sure no one will notice."

Aiden looked alarmed. He muttered to Brynne, "I thought they're sisters?"

Brynne smirked, her gaze flicking to Aru. "Sometimes sisters fight."

True, thought Aru. But not like that. Not like every word was a knife shaped out of ice.

"We're *not* sisters," said Saranyu viciously.

Aru frowned. If they weren't sisters, then how come they had the same face?

"You look identical, though?" said Rudy.

Saranyu snorted. "Merely because she is my shadow."

The goddess in shadows scowled. "Perhaps I began that way, yes."

"If you're just her shadow, then—" started Brynne.

The goddess whirled around, her face contorted in fury. "*Just* her shadow?" she spat, darkness pooling underneath her. "I am Chhaya, goddess of shadows and second queen to the Sun Lord, Surya. I am the Mother of Shani, Lord of the House of Saturn, and Tapti, the incomparably beautiful river goddess."

Shani! Aru remembered meeting the Lord of Saturn on their last quest. He probably would've been pleasant to be around if not for the burning-gaze-that-incinerated-everything-in-its-path thing.

"But how did you...?" Mini started. "No offense, but..." She trailed off.

"How did I go from being a reflection to being a queen?" asked Chhaya, lifting an eyebrow.

"You mean how did she go from a temporary replacement to a usurper?" demanded Saranyu, crossing her arms.

"Um..." said Mini. "Sure?"

"Like this..." said Saranyu.

She swept aside a swath of clouds and stomped on the gold floor. Images shimmered on the ground, showing Saranyu standing beside Surya, the god of the sun. Aru squinted. It was like catching the sun's reflection in a mirror. In the images, Saranyu looked as if she was always wincing and rubbing her eyes.

"My husband was so resplendent he radiated an eternal source of heat," said Saranyu. "He was, in truth, too hot to bear."

Aru waited one second...two seconds...and then started choke-laughing, which is what happens when one tries not to laugh but the laugh wriggles out your throat anyway.

"I understand that," said Rudy solemnly. "At least, I *did*, before someone ripped off my mustache out of jealousy."

"It was *a* hair," Aiden said with a sigh.

"There would've been more!" said Rudy. "Eventually."

Brynne swatted both of them.

"I had to leave or I'd burn up," said Saranyu. "But I didn't want him to notice. And so I left behind a decoy."

She swiped her hand in the air and the images in the floor changed, now showing Saranyu staring at her shadow and making some complicated gestures over the shape. The outline of the shadow quivered before peeling off the ground. It shook itself once and then crumbled, revealing Chhaya beneath. Afterward, Saranyu stole out of the palace with nothing but the cloak she was wearing.

"It worked for a time," said Saranyu, sighing. "But eventually I was found out."

"My fault," said Chhaya, raising her hand. "Saranyu is allergic to chickpeas. How was I supposed to know? It was the chickpeas that gave it away, not my face. He found me quite pleasing to look at."

"You are a mere imitation of me," said Saranyu dismissively. "And so, Surya brought me back home and I promised to wear sunglasses more often."

Chhaya reached up and adjusted the crown on her head. "Worked out quite nicely for me, too. I got to be royalty."

"Hmpf," said Saranyu. "It does not change the fact that I am the more beautiful one between us."

"Lies!" spat Chhaya. She considered the Pandavas for a moment, and then a catlike grin slowly formed on her face. "Perhaps we might put it to the children to decide?"

"Very well," said Saranyu, raising an eyebrow. "Should you find me the more beautiful one, I will restore your friend to good health."

"Should you find *me* the lovelier, *I* shall send you to wherever you need to go next," said Chhaya.

Easy pick, said Brynne through their mind link. *Kubera said his eye was like a portal, so—*

"You cannot leave the House of the Sun without our express permission," Chhaya added.

Mini turned to Saranyu. "But . . . But I'm your granddaughter. *You'd* let us go, right?"

Saranyu looked fondly at Mini and said, "No."

"What? B-but we told you there's a war coming! And the gods want us to fight—"

"Is that so?" asked Chhaya softly. "Do you really have the favor of the heavens? Or are you just an annoyance to them?"

Aru shifted on the spot. Ever since that disastrous publicity stunt with Opal and the rest of the Otherworld, Aru knew she hadn't exactly earned the devas' trust. Which was why the Pandavas were being forced to go through these trials for Kubera's army instead of just being granted control of it.

But did that mean even the devas weren't on their side?

Aru shuddered. She didn't want to find out.

"The war is not on my land," said Saranyu. "So it is not my

problem. I would rather see the truth about the two of us made manifest by your decision. Make your choice. As for me, I claim my granddaughter's vote by blood."

At this, Chhaya smiled sharply, tendrils of smoke wrapping around her.

Aru didn't really care for Saranyu. What kind of grandma didn't want to help her grandkid? Besides, even if Saranyu could wake up Kara, that wouldn't do much for them if they couldn't leave the House of the Sun.

As if sensing what Aru was thinking, Chhaya slid her foot across the floor, creating an image of what the sun itself beheld . . .

The Sleeper's troops were somehow walking in the air over the sea. Gleaming weapons hung from dark belts around their waists. They wore horned helmets, and they roared as one when the gleam of Lanka rose in the distance.

They were getting close.

"I say Chhaya," said Aru quickly.

"Me too," said Brynne.

Saranyu's smile fell a little. She snapped her fingers, and the images on the ground disappeared. She beckoned with her fingers, and Kara floated a little higher, her hair still streaming around her. "And what if you discover that your friend will never wake without my help?"

Aru felt her throat tighten. What had she done? Had she sacrificed Kara?

"Then I'm with Mini," said Rudy. Mini looked at him, surprised.

Saranyu's smile flickered back to life before both goddesses turned to Aiden. "And what about you? You who are not a demigod, but whose veins nonetheless run with starlight. Do you find me the most beautiful one? I could restore your lovely little friend, and I could give you more power...."

Aiden turned red. "I—I'm not really... I'm—"

"The deciding vote," said Chhaya. "I can sniff out your secrets, Aiden Acharya. You would not wish to throw your world into the hardship of war, would you? I can show you the things you wish to see....Now *decide*."

Aiden looked between the two goddesses, his hand resting on his camera.

Does Aiden even know how to pick a favorite? Mini asked through the mind link. *He's kinda...um...indecisive.*

Nope, thought Brynne. *We're screwed.*

Indecisive was a nice way to put it. Aiden Acharya was *the worst* when it came to making up his mind about anything. He was the bane of every Atlanta ice-cream store, because he'd ask for a million samples, conclude he didn't want ice cream anyway, and then feel guilty and hold up the line figuring how much to leave in the tip jar as an apology. And now, he was the one forced to choose between returning to Lanka or restoring Kara.

"My mom always says not to compare two women," said Aiden.

We are going to die here, thought Aru.

"But," said Aiden, drawing himself up, "I have to say that the goddess who shows mercy by letting us go *and* waking up Kara would be the more beautiful one to me."

Aru thought he'd be looking at Kara at that moment, but instead his eyes went to hers. He held Aru's gaze for a moment, the briefest smile on his face, before he turned back to the goddesses.

"Bro, that was superb," said Rudy.

Saranyu seemed pleased, whereas Chhaya looked distinctly annoyed.

"There is a rare optimism in the way you see the world," Saranyu said to Aiden.

Aru stared at him, shocked, before she replayed in her head the point of the third trial. *The sky shall judge your sight.* Aiden was definitely the most observant of all the Potatoes, and it turned out he saw more than she had imagined. His hand moved subtly to the camera at his side, and she remembered how he'd been watching her when they entered Lanka. *I see you, Shah.* She felt strangely warm. And not just because they were inside the House of the Sun.

"For that, you have my blessings for the girl," said Saranyu. "Though remember, the cousin of bliss is regret. And there is much left for you to see."

Aru frowned. What did that mean? But just then Saranyu opened her hand, and a burst of sunlight washed over Kara.

Kara stirred and Aru's hope returned. The other Potatoes grinned and clapped.

"She will fully awaken once you leave this realm," said Saranyu.

"And you *will* leave," said Chhaya, smiling sharply. "It is too late in the day for you to reach Lanka on our husband's rays, I'm afraid—he has already passed over the city. But you may exit this way." She gestured to an unassuming door behind her. "Beware: It leads to a place littered with the past and all the things the sun hides away. Touch nothing and try not to look, for the secrets stored there belong to the sun alone. No mortals are meant to witness them, for they can drive one insane with curiosity. Some secrets are meant to stay hidden... others, as well you know, only fester. Particularly in families."

Aru frowned. "What does that mean?"

Chhaya's smile only sharpened. "What, you don't know the secret that tore apart the Pandavas all those years ago? How strange that it should start with my husband, the very banisher of secrets."

Aru shook her head. She knew the Pandavas hadn't *always* gotten along, but that was true of any sibling relationship.

Saranyu waved her hand, and the semitransparent image of a heavily pregnant girl sprang up between them. The girl looked like she belonged to ancient times. She was richly dressed, decked out in gold, and seemed only a couple of years older than Aru.

"This is Kunti, mother of the three eldest Pandavas," said Chhaya. "You see, when she was not much older than you, she was given a boon to invoke any god of her choice to bless her with a divine child... but she did not believe such a rare boon would work. And so she tested it on Surya."

In the image, the girl's hand went to her belly. Regret flashed across her face, and the image changed to show Kunti lowering a newborn into a basket placed along the bank of a muddy river.

"But of course, she was young and unwed and would have destroyed her family's honor had she kept the child," said Saranyu. "And so she floated him down the river.... That baby grew up to be Karna, the greatest foe of Arjuna and the beloved friend of the Pandavas' greatest enemy. The Pandavas never knew he was their brother until the war started, and by then, their tragic fates were sealed."

The image of Kunti and baby Karna disappeared, leaving Aru

confused. Why bother showing them that story? Aru knew her friends. They didn't have any secrets from one another. Even her mom had gotten better about not hiding things.

"So sad," said Chhaya with a slow smile. "But what a *delicious* secret, is it not? Everyone's hiding something...."

The door beyond Chhaya glowed brighter.

"Off you go, little ones," she said, smiling.

A wave of unease went through Aru, but what choice did they have? The eye wouldn't work here—it seemed to understand that it had no power inside the House of the Sun.

"May your journey be bright but not blinding," said Saranyu.

Chhaya snapped her fingers and the door opened, leading to a hallway that looked pure white. Chhaya's voice was a cold shadow slipping into her skull. "Hasten to your war, daughters of the gods...."

THIRTY-
THREE

Hi. Can I Exchange This
Prophecy? No? Crap.

A couple of years earlier, Aru's mom and a bunch of other historians had been invited to a tombstone-symbolism tour in the Oakland Cemetery in Atlanta. Aru had gone along because 1) What if there were ghosts? and 2) WHAT IF THERE WERE GHOSTS? and 3) If there weren't ghosts, at least she could imitate the creepy statues.

Aru loved Oakland Cemetery. It was silent and peaceful, the air perfumed with blooming irises, and the shade cast by the glossy magnolia trees was cool and inviting. So inviting, in fact, that when the tour guide started droning on about the Civil War, Aru had tucked herself up under a tree that overlooked the unmarked graves of Civil War–era soldiers. She remembered her eyelids closing and her body getting sleep-heavy when a raspy voice had whispered in her ear, *Not all of us have found rest here, little girl. And a body burning with energy such as yours could feed our restlessness for years. . . .*

Aru had scrambled out of the shade and run to her mom, whom she wouldn't let go of until they were back in the car. Afterward, she'd told herself that the whole thing must have been a bad dream. But she'd never forgotten what it had felt like right before she heard that ghostly voice. It was if she had stumbled into a place she wasn't meant to see, a place where the world turned in on itself and the light ran too thin, and all the shadows came alive.

That was how it felt now, as they entered the hallway lined with things the sun god had seen and never shared. It was full of low murmuring and soft weeping, harsh whispers and music played for no one. The sounds raised goose bumps on Aru's arms. Dozens of pure white pillars as tall as ancient oak trees lined the passage, which stretched the length of a football field and then came to an abrupt stop, like a balcony with no rail. Beyond, there was nothing but the star-strewn expanse of space. Between each pillar stretched a long, cloudy mirror. The floor beneath them looked more like steel wool than clouds, definitely not the softness spun by the cloud-knitting elephant, Airavata.

"This place is *not* the vibe," declared Rudy, throwing up his hood.

"I kinda like it!" said Mini.

"Let's just get out of here," said Brynne gruffly. Beside her, Kara floated on a ribbon of cloud that Lady Saranyu had given them. Kara was still glowing, her hair billowing around her eerily and her trident gleaming like a ray of sunlight.

"I'll take the lead," said Aru. Vajra wound up her arm as a rope and then stayed still and wary. "Mini, can you guard the middle? That way you can cast a shield on either side."

Mini nodded, twirling Dee Dee with one hand.

"Can I hide behind, I mean *assist* Mini?" asked Rudy.

"Ask her, not me," retorted Aru.

Rudy grinned at Mini. For the briefest second, joy spread across Mini's face, but she quickly turned her smile into a glare.

"I guess so," she said.

"Me and Ammamma will take the rear," said Brynne.

Aiden rolled his eyes at the nickname, as usual, then tapped Shadowfax. The camera quickly folded up and turned into a watch on his wrist.

"What, no photos?" asked Aru.

He looked around the hall, his gaze narrowing. "Some things aren't for us to see, Shah."

Just then, something flashed in the corner of Aru's eye. In one of the mirrors, instead of her own reflection, Aru saw a teenaged girl with long hair moving out of sight, her hands clutching her pregnant belly.

I wish I could keep you with me. But it's better this way. I'm so sorry.

A chill stole through Aru. There was something familiar about the girl, but Aru couldn't get a good look at her face. One moment she was there, and the next, she'd been swallowed up by the mirror's mist.

"Let's . . . Let's get moving," said Aru, trying to keep the tremble out of her voice.

She turned Vajra into a sword and kept a tight grip on it as they marched down the hall. Even though the space was open and light-filled, the air smelled musty, like the basement of an abandoned house. Aru tried to keep her eyes focused straight ahead, but small flashes of movement to her left and right kept stealing her attention.

Don't look, she told herself.

To avoid glancing anywhere else, Aru started reading what was written on the pillars surrounding them. She discovered they weren't just columns, but slender storage units labeled with rare things Surya had seen or heard on his travels.

One held:

BLACKBIRD LULLABIES

A BABY'S FOURTH YAWN

Another held:

A POLITICIAN TELLING A TRUTH

THE LAST WORDS OF THE DECEASED

Aru read the labels aloud, forcing one foot in front of the other. Up ahead was a pillar that looked slimmer than the rest....

PROPHECIES UNHEARD AND UNWANTED

Yikes, thought Aru, giving that one a wide berth. She'd had her fill of prophecies.

Just a few yards past it was the end of Surya's long hall. *Nearly there*, thought Aru, adjusting her hold on Vajra.

That was when Aru heard her name being called.

It wasn't one of them, but someone beyond the pillar of Prophecies Unheard and Unwanted.

Aru?

She froze. She knew that voice—it was her mother's! Mini and Brynne had said that Krithika had disappeared, but no one could hide from the sun. Aru remembered Chhaya's warning: *No mortals are meant to witness them....* But what if Surya had seen that her mother was trapped somewhere? Or wounded? If Aru looked, then maybe she could rescue her mom!

"HEY!" Mini shouted from behind her. "Why are you slowing down?"

"Not because something's after us, right?" asked Rudy. *"RIGHT, ARU?"*

She turned. In the mirror's reflection, she saw her mother waving her hands to get Aru's attention. Her clothes and hair looked wet, and droplets of gold clung to her skin. Aru noticed that her face was gaunt, as if she hadn't eaten in days, and there were dark smudges of sleeplessness under her eyes.

Help! Krithika Shah croaked out.

"Mom!" cried Aru.

In that second, everything else in the hall fell away. It was as if Krithika were no longer trapped in the mirror but standing right before Aru, shivering with cold, her hands outstretched...

Aru, come back to me. . . .

Then Krithika's eyes widened. She seemed to be gaping at something vast and terrifying right over Aru's shoulder. Aru jumped into action, spinning Vajra out to full length and whirling around, her lightning bolt clashing against something heavy.

"It's me, Shah!"

Aru blinked. She looked up to see Aiden glaring down at her, his scimitar raised to eye level and Vajra angrily pulsing against it. Shock rippled through Aru, and she turned to check the mirror again. The image of Krithika was gone. What had happened to her mom? What had she seen behind Aru?

"This place is playing tricks on you, Shah," said Aiden, grabbing her shoulder. "Focus on me. *Look at me.*"

Aiden was using that hypnotic voice on her, the one inherited from his apsara mother. Aru could feel it working its way through her brain. She felt herself getting lost in the fathomless dark of Aiden's eyes.

"It's going to be okay, Shah. I know you're scared, but we're here for you. We've got you, and we'll fix this . . . together. But first we have to get out."

It felt like her soul was warming itself by a nice fire. Aru's senses began flowing back to her.

Maybe Surya's hall noticed, too.

Because, just then, Krithika Shah's bony face once again loomed in front of her. Her smile was a rictus. Aru lurched backward and pushed up with Vajra just as Aiden brought his scimitar down defensively.

"Stop, Shah! You don't know what you're doing!"

The problem was, she thought she did.

Worry for her mom bubbled in her veins and coursed through her lightning bolt, making Vajra glow with a strange new radiance and fury. The force of her uppercut shattered Aiden's scimitar and threw him backward. A flash of violet light fell over Aru, and she looked up just as the last drop of the Krithika illusion faded from sight.

"Aru . . . what did you do?" asked Mini, breathing heavily while holding out her Death Danda.

Aru realized that the shield wasn't to protect Aru from some unseen force . . . it was to protect the rest of them from Aru. Mini lowered the shield, and Aru looked to her right, horror rising inside her.

Aiden.

She'd thrown him against the pillar of Prophecies Unheard and Unwanted. He groaned, shaking his head and forcing himself upright while clutching the only scimitar he had left.

Aru had never made her lightning bolt so powerful before. Boo had taught them that, as they grew and learned, so would their weapons, but Vajra had never done *anything* like this.

Aiden looked shocked . . . and then furious as he walked back to them.

"Didn't the shadow lady say not to touch anything?" whispered Rudy.

Brynne swatted him upside the head. "Real helpful, Rudy."

"Ow!"

"I'm so sorry," said Aru quickly. "I saw my mom, and I just forgot about everything else—"

"She told you *not* to look!" yelled Aiden.

"I said I'm sorry!" said Aru.

"Why don't you ever listen to anyone?" said Aiden.

"I *do*!" retorted Aru, her face growing hot. "You would've looked too if you saw what I did!"

"No, I wouldn't have, because *I* know what we could lose," said Aiden.

"Uh . . . guys?" said Rudy.

Aiden batted at the air. "Not now, Rudy—"

"*Lose?*" Aru barked out a scornful laugh. "What do you know about loss?"

"Plenty," snarled Aiden.

"Um, guys?" said Brynne.

Aiden and Aru ignored her.

"How about losing your dad because he tried to avoid his terrible destiny?" shot back Aru. "Or losing your mom because she disappeared when you needed her most and now you have no idea where she is? Or losing all your *trust* in people, because they keep failing you!"

Aiden, still furious, closed and opened his mouth for a few seconds before speaking. "I know all that, and I'm sorry for you, but what we could lose if we don't get back to Lanka in time is even worse, Shah," he said, staring at her. "We'd lose *hope*. We'd lose hope that any of it could change, or that any of this awful stuff happened for a reason."

"Guys!" shouted Mini. "Enough! We have to move—now!"

Aru spun around and stopped short. A tiny seam was now visible in the pillar of Prophecies Unheard and Unwanted. Smoky wisps snaked out of it, forming words that were spoken by a disembodied voice:

Those whom it does not concern shall not hear.... Who will hear us hear us hear ussssss...?

A giant *crack!* ripped through the air, and the pillar split open like an egg, exhaling a few more prophecies like a grievous sigh. One of the smoky ribbons coiled toward Aiden, growing brighter as if it recognized him.

Aiden Acharya... it said.

And then, at once, all the prophecies spilled out. A wave of them crashed into a nearby pillar, unleashing strange birdsongs. Another wave crashed into the pillar of politicians' truths, and the voices of men and women clamored in the air.

"Run!" yelled Aru.

The Potatoes sprinted forward, Kubera's eye zooming along with them. Brynne hauled Kara off the slow-moving cloud and carried her over the shoulder. Aru panted as the end of the hallway drew closer. She thought there'd be a hidden staircase there, or maybe a door would magically appear, but no. They stopped short at a sharp drop into nothing.

"Where do we go?" screamed Brynne.

Aru panicked. Even if she turned her lightning bolt into a hoverboard, they'd never make it back down to Lanka in time.

Right on their heels, the avalanche of prophecies swarmed

toward them. Aru grabbed Kubera's eye and shook it. "C'MON!" she yelled. "Help us! We've done everything you asked!"

But when she released the eye, it seemed to do nothing but glare at her.

"Chhaya!" said Mini, her eyes widening.

Aru turned to see the goddess of shadows smiling at them.

"Oops. Seems I forgot to tell you that only those who have the gods' favor can get anywhere with this route." Chhaya chuckled. "You want to know whether the gods are smiling upon your journey? Well, here's one way to find out."

Chhaya flicked her wrist. Shadows shot out from her fingertips and grabbed Aru and the others around their ankles.

"WHAT ARE YOU DOING?" yelled Aru.

"My father will hear about this!" shouted Rudy.

Chhaya shrugged, then yanked. The group dangled over the edge of the room, barely held in place by the goddess's ropy shadows.

"Wouldn't want to be rude," said Chhaya. "Looks like someone wants a word with you, boy."

Aru craned her neck to see one prophetic ribbon of smoke wind its way to Aiden. It grew thicker and more solid, forming the barest suggestion of a woman's face. Aiden's eyes flew wide open.

"Beware, Aiden Acharya. . . . The girl you love will be the death of you."

"Ooh . . . ominous," said Chhaya.

Aru had barely wrapped her head around what she'd heard and all that had happened when Chhaya let go.

"Oops again."

The Potatoes plummeted through the darkness of space.

THIRTY-FOUR

Are You There, God-Dad?
It's Me, Aru.

The Potatoes careened through the dark, stars swirling all around them.

"I! HATE! THIS!" yelled Rudy.

Brynne tried to drag out her wind mace, but they were falling so fast the magic wouldn't catch. Vajra couldn't hold the shape of a hoverboard. Mini cast out shields only for them to fizzle and blip out. On Aru's left, Kara fell gracefully, blissfully unaware, while Aiden grasped uselessly at the inky clouds. He didn't look at Aru. In the back of her head, Aru could still hear the rasping prophetic voice: *Aiden Acharya. . . . The girl you love will be the death of you.*

What did that mean?

And who was the girl?

"What do we do?" yelled Mini.

It snapped Aru's thoughts back to their current situation. Technically, they could keep falling until the end of time. Boo had once told them that the Otherworld's space was not like human space. Distance didn't work the same way. Aru glanced up. In her head, they'd been tumbling for maybe ten seconds. But the House of the Sun looked miles away, like a match struck in the distance.

They might fall right into Lanka, or they could end up someplace else entirely....

Chhaya's voice moved through Aru's thoughts. *You want to know whether the gods are smiling upon your journey? Well, here's one way to find out.*

"We need the gods' favor!" said Aru loudly.

"DEAR GODS, I PROMISE I'LL DONATE ALL OF— I MEAN, MOST ... WELL, DEFINITELY *SOME* OF MY TREASURE!" hollered Rudy.

"What a sacrifice!" snarked Brynne.

"We're not going to get their attention by yelling at them!" said Mini.

Something shifted in the space around them. The stars drew into sharper relief against the dark nothingness. Far below them, a huge bank of sunset clouds in every hue of pink and orange appeared. And on top of the clouds sat the glittering heavenly city of Amaravati, home of Lord Indra himself. Aru's heart leaped at the sight.

"HEY!" she hollered, waving her arms. "ARE YOU THERE, GOD-DAD? IT'S ME, ARU!"

But nothing changed.

"*Focus*, Aru!" called Mini.

Why was her voice coming from above Aru?

Aru looked up and saw that Mini had slowed her own fall. Her legs were crisscrossed and her eyes were closed. A faint purple glow enveloped her body.

A bright light stole Aru's attention, and the city of Amaravati came and went in a flash. Now the sunset cloud bank hovered at eye level. The clouds looked like mountains of whipped cream, pulled into shapes that were almost recognizable. One mound kind of reminded Aru of an elephant.

"If we don't get the gods' attention now, we're *never* going to make it to Lanka!" yelled Brynne.

"I don't want to fall to my death!" moaned Rudy.

"Probably impossible, since this is the fall that won't end," said Mini serenely. "You're much more likely to die of dehydration or starvation. Or you might get hypothermia and freeze to death."

"WHAT?!" screamed Rudy.

Aru clapped her hands over her ears and squeezed her eyes shut. Mini was right—she needed to focus. Aru tuned out her arguing friends. She tuned out Chhaya's laughter, the mirage of her mother's haunted face, and the prophetic voice that had whispered to Aiden. None of it would matter anyway, if they couldn't get back to Lanka.

Please, please, please, thought Aru. And then, quietly—so quietly she could hardly acknowledge it to herself—Aru asked, *Do you even think I'm doing a good job?*

It was a thought she had come to dread.

Aru hadn't forgotten that the Otherworld had turned on her. Some people blamed her for bringing about this war. Many had lost faith in the Pandavas. Every now and then Aru wondered if that was a sign that their soul dads were just as disappointed in them.

I believe in us, thought Aru fiercely. *And if you do, too, then give us a sign.*

Aru opened her eyes. Now Amaravati was far above them. Disappointment stole her breath.

This was it. They'd really failed.

Chhaya had been right to laugh. They'd never had the gods' favor.

What was happening right now in Lanka? Was the Sleeper's army already there? Was Kubera squealing with delight in his throne? Or—

"What is *that?*" asked Aiden loudly.

Aru looked up. It seemed a piece of the Amaravati cloud bank had broken off and was now drifting toward them. An enormous puffy thing as pale as bone, with a tufted cloud on each side and a curved tail that made it look a lot like . . .

"That's an elephant!" said Brynne.

The cloud elephant drew closer, and Aru could see that it was huge, at least three times the size of an animal she'd see at a zoo. Its skin was pure white, and its deep brown eyes regarded them warmly. Silken cords were stretched between its two curved tusks like an unfinished weaving on a loom.

"Airavata!" shouted Rudy.

Aru's eyes widened. Airavata wasn't just the elephant that spun clouds. He was also a mount of Lord Indra himself. At the realization, Aru felt Vajra squeeze warmly around her wrist. This was the best fatherly pat on the back she could have hoped for.

Airavata trumpeted loudly, then dove under Aru and soared back up to catch her in mid-fall. Aru felt her stomach swoop as she landed squarely on Airavata's back. Mini, Brynne, Kara, Rudy, and Aiden tumbled on after her.

Airavata trumpeted in triumph, then wove between the stars, his giant white ears spreading out like wings. The moment the elephant sounded off, Aru felt her skin prickle all over. It was the same sensation she got whenever she crossed through portals in the Otherworld. Aru blinked, and it was as if they had entered another dimension. Instead of the darkness of Otherworld space, they were now soaring across a dusky evening sky, and instead of endless stars, there was a vast, dark ocean beneath them. Airavata's shadow stretched over the waves. Salt and wind tangled in Aru's hair, and she breathed deeply, feeling her lungs expanding.

"There's Lanka!" said Mini, pointing.

Aru's heart rate kicked up as the city drew into focus. Atop Airavata's back, Kubera's eye bounced happily. Had they done it? thought Aru cautiously. Had they really made it back in time and won Kubera's army *and* the powerful astra?

Within moments, Airavata had crossed the ocean and made it to Lanka's center. Aru tried to see if people were running around and screaming, but for all its flashing lights, the area seemed completely *empty*.

Airavata alighted in Kubera's private courtyard with a loud *whumpf!* that rattled Aru's teeth. Brynne hopped off first. Aru glanced at the palace. It looked just as it had when they left: a line of golden stairs leading to a platform with a single unbroken wall of gold. Doubts and worries flared inside Aru like fireworks. Had they come too late? Would Kubera let them in?

But as soon as Aru's feet met the ground, the wall of gold instantly melted to reveal an archway waiting for them. In the distance, Aru thought she heard the echoes of clashing weapons. Her lungs constricted.

Brynne swiveled her wind mace, and a soft breeze carried Kara to the courtyard floor. The moment Kara's body touched it, she opened her eyes and gulped in air. Saranyu had kept her promise.

Kara sat up and looked around her. Sunny the trident glowed

brightly on her lap. Then she leaped to her feet, staring around at the Potatoes.

Aru felt awkward. What if Kara blamed them for getting her hurt? Or what if she didn't remember them at all and hurled Sunny at them? Or . . .

Kara ran straight at the Potatoes, her arms wide, catching Aru, Brynne, and Mini in a group hug.

"No touchy!" Mini tried to say as Kara threw an arm around her. "Elbow bumps only. Oh, never mind. . . ."

Aru felt a rush of warmth.

"Thank you for saving me," said Kara, pulling back. "We did it! We got back in time!"

"Maybe . . ." said Aru, looking at the door. "We have to hurry. Aiden? Rudy?"

Aiden stood off to the side, his face sullen and drawn. "Glad you're back, Kara," he said stiffly.

Aru noticed that he was holding his wrist a little strangely. Had he hurt it?

"You okay?" asked Aru, moving toward him.

Aiden stepped back quickly, not looking at her. "I'm fine, Shah."

Stung, Aru let her arms drop to her sides just as Brynne went to him and shook him lightly.

"Hey," she said. "Stop that."

Aiden scowled. "I'm not—"

"Prophecies are weird, and they'll eat up your brain," said Brynne. "I mean, for all you know, you could die by eating some weird flower called the Girl You Love."

"Super reassuring, thanks."

"If it helps, I *am* the daughter of the god of death," said Mini. "We're not going to let anything happen to you, Wifey."

Aiden smiled, but it didn't reach his eyes. "I know."

"What prophecy?" asked Kara.

"It's nothing," said Aiden.

"Yeah, it's nothing," said Brynne, clapping him on the back. "Just the end of all his romantic aspirations."

"I didn't know you had any," said Aru.

Aiden glanced at her, then looked away. "I don't. Let's go."

He walked to the stairs. Brynne tried to muster a smile, but Aru caught the strained line of worry pulling at her mouth. Even Mini looked faintly disturbed.

A loud trumpeting caught their attention, and Aru turned to see Rudy standing in front of Airavata. The naga was draped in clouds, and it kind of looked like Airavata had knitted him into a giant meringue. Airavata made a happy rumbling sound, then patted the top of Rudy's head with his trunk.

"Look upon me and despair, mortals!" he said. "I'm *ready* to fight in my new cloud armor."

Mini giggled.

Brynne glared at him. "You look like a deranged cake topper."

Rudy ignored her, and swept a bow in Kara's direction. "Hi, I don't know if you know this, but I'm a prince—"

Kara frowned, looking confused.

"Kara, Rudy, Rudy, Kara," said Brynne tersely. "Kara, ignore Rudy."

Rudy scowled.

Overhead, the archway glinted, beckoning to them. Aru walked over to Airavata. The cloud elephant regarded her solemnly.

"Any chance you want to ride into battle with us?" asked Aru hopefully. "I'd probably look ten times fiercer with you."

Airavata snorted.

"Gonna take that as a no," said Aru. "Will you... Will you tell him I said thank you?"

Airavata flapped his large white ears. With his trunk, he tugged at the silken cord between his tusks, and a soft thundercloud the size of Aru's hand knitted itself before her eyes. It drifted gently over to her and she touched it gingerly, only to have it burst apart. The air was filled with the scent of the world after a thunderstorm... the smell of rain-soaked stone steps and the faint metallic fizz in the air that she imagined she could taste on her tongue. It felt like the kind of hard won-peace that always follows a tempest. Aru closed her eyes and breathed it in.

"Thanks," she said.

But when she looked up, Airavata was gone.

There was nothing left for her to do but face Kubera. As Aru followed the others through the doorway, she could hear the sound of marching soldiers getting closer and closer. Thunder churned inside her, and on her arm, Vajra glowed fiercely. Everything Kubera had asked, they had done.

He had to give them the Nairrata army.

Aru held on to that hope as the Potatoes crossed the threshold and entered Kubera's throne room.

The chamber had completely changed. It looked nothing like the place they had first entered days ago....

On the other side of the threshold, they stepped out onto a huge golden pier, as long as an aircraft carrier, jutting into the dark blue ocean. There was no sign of the god of treasures except the eye that had accompanied them all this time, which was wide and unblinking.

Then Aiden called out, "Lanka—it's gone!"

Aru whirled around. The pointy city skyline had disappeared completely. The pier was now floating in the middle of the sea. The sun bore down on their heads, and the gold beneath their shoes radiated heat.

Where had everyone gone?

Where was the Sleeper's army?

A loud *bang!* went off in the middle of their circle. There was a flash of light and a puff of smoke, reminding Aru of the mongoose show.

"Oh my gods," said Mini when the air cleared.

There, standing in all their finery, were Hanuman and Urvashi.

THIRTY-FIVE

I Really Need a Hug

Brynne ran to her half brother and flung her arms around his neck. Hanuman, the monkey-faced demigod and Lord of Strength, picked up Brynne in a ginormous hug. Urvashi opened her arms to Aiden, her nephew, and he embraced her.

Rudy, who looked starstruck by the sight of Urvashi, followed him. "Uh, I'm related to Aiden. . . . Can I have a hug, too?"

Mini and Kara hung back with Aru.

Kara looked nervous. "What do I tell them?"

"Tell them you're with us," said Mini. "They'll understand, trust me."

Brynne beckoned Kara. With one last panicked look at Aru and Mini, Kara walked toward Brynne and Hanuman, her ring glowing brighter on her hand. Part of Aru yearned to join them. She felt like bothering Hanuman, who for some reason was dressed in a gold tuxedo and had a coin dangling from his left ear. She itched to check on Urvashi, who, in her gold sari, looked like she'd been wrapped in sunlight. She wanted to make sure both of them were okay and hadn't been hurt...and at the same time, she wanted to yell at them.

I know this is my fault, but it's yours, *too!*

Just then, Hanuman and Urvashi caught her eye. She didn't move. Beside her, Mini coughed lightly, and Aru glanced over to see her sister staring at her with a worried expression.

"Are you going to be okay talking to them by yourself?" she asked. "I can go with you...."

Aru would've squeezed Mini's hand, but she didn't need a lecture about germs just then. "I'll be okay," she said, smiling. "But thanks."

Mini nodded, then frowned at the sky. "There's something weird about this whole thing, isn't there?"

Aru shivered as Hanuman and Urvashi turned fully in her direction. She couldn't shake the feeling that someone was watching all of them. Perhaps it was just Kubera's golden eye, floating through the space, its lid open wide.

"Kubera said he would only return Hanuman and Urvashi if we got past the first three trials," said Mini. "I *think* we did? But he's not here, and neither is the Nairrata army. And where's the astra he promised us? At least Hanuman and Urvashi are safe...."

For some reason, Aru's gaze kept returning to the storm clouds on the horizon. They seemed to be moving closer, but Aru hadn't heard any telltale sounds of thunder rippling across the sky.

Awkward convo incoming, warned Brynne as Hanuman and Urvashi made their way to Aru. *And no news about Kubera. They were trapped, and then all of a sudden they weren't.*

Aru frowned. That didn't seem right.

Keep an eye on those clouds, she warned Mini and Brynne.

Mini shot Aru one last smile, then headed off to give her some privacy.

When Hanuman and Urvashi reached her, Aru opened and closed her mouth. For the longest time, she'd imagined exactly what she would say to them. But when it came down to reality, she was tongue-tied. Aru thought of Shikhandi and how he'd cycled through pain and vengeance and only ended up exhausted.

"I know what you said to my mom," she finally blurted out. "I saw it and…"

Aru couldn't keep going. She was angry, yes, but also tired. Tired of being so angry. Tired of being so worried. And now, when they had burst in ready for one last fight, she couldn't even have that. It took Aru a few moments to realize she was shaking. It took another few moments to realize there were tears running down her face.

"Oh, child," said Urvashi, swooping down to hug her. "I'm so sorry."

"This may not be what you wish to hear, but please believe us when we tell you we were trying to do what we thought was right," said Hanuman in his rumbling voice. "Sometimes there are no easy answers. All we can do is try our best to perform our duty to ourselves and the people we care about and hope everything will work out. And when something comes to a bad end, we need to ask ourselves: Is this really the end, or just an ugly middle?"

Hanuman laid his hand on top of Aru's head. His palm was warm and heavy, and Aru was fiercely reminded of Subala. Boo should be here, sitting on her shoulder or hopping around on her head. Their pigeon mentor had tried to do just what Hanuman said: perform his duty. Boo had thought he could protect the

Pandavas by betraying them. As for the ugly things he'd allegedly said about them afterward, Aru wasn't sure she believed Kubera... though it was much easier to be angry than to be hurt.

"Guys..." called Brynne.

Aru swiped at her tears, stepping away from Hanuman and Urvashi. Maybe later there would be more for her to say, but for right now she turned, following Brynne's pointed finger, and fear pulsed through her veins.

Or maybe there would never be another time.

What she'd mistaken for storm clouds were worse. Much worse. As the shapes drew nearer, icy fear dripped through Aru's veins when she recognized the Sleeper's army fast approaching, closing around them like a giant fishing net.

The Potatoes rushed over to her.

"What do we do?" asked Mini nervously.

"What about the Nairrata army?" asked Brynne.

"Or the astra?" asked Kara.

"Or Kubera?" asked Aiden.

Rudy raised his hand. "Um, can I leave now?"

"NO!" said everyone at the same time.

Aru could feel her friends looking at her. She glanced down and saw that Vajra had formed a trellis of electricity that ran up and down her arm. It kinda made her feel like Iron Man. Except Iron Man would have the entire Avengers to wreak havoc on the Sleeper's army.

Well, she had the Potatoes.

"What's your decision, Pandavas?" asked Hanuman.

"We fight," said Aru simply.

"Without all the other stuff?" asked Brynne.

"We fight," Aru repeated.

It was the only answer that made any sense. All she could do was try her best to perform her duty. And for a Pandava, that meant protecting the people she loved.

With that realization, Aru felt a strange sense of calm seep through her. It told her this was exactly where she needed to be. She glanced up at Urvashi and Hanuman for confirmation, and they nodded curtly. A grim look of understanding flashed across their faces.

The Sleeper's massive army drew closer—rows of demons marching over the sea, each lumbering footstep sending waves crashing over Kubera's golden throne.

"Fall into formation," said Aru.

Brynne stood right behind Aru. Mini and Rudy paired up on the right, and Aiden and Kara took the left.

Hanuman leaped into the water, clapped once, and instantly shot up as tall as a skyscraper. He let out a roar so loud the breakers reared backward, revealing the pale sandy belly of the seafloor. Their opponents hesitated for a moment and then surged forward.

Urvashi rose into the air, her limbs held out in graceful stillness. She snapped her fingers, and music filled the air. Next she began to dance, her legs blurring beneath her. With each movement of her hands, the sky was imprinted with small stars that flashed mirror bright to confuse the enemy. The demons covered their eyes and carried on.

Aru scanned the approaching army. They numbered in the thousands, while there were exactly...eight...on her side.

"I *still* don't know what a microwave does," said Rudy mournfully. "And now I'm going to die not knowing...."

"Well, there's always reincarnation," said Mini brightly.

Rudy whimpered.

"I'm not afraid," said Brynne, adjusting her grip on her wind mace. She bared her teeth at the vicious troops as their knives and blades and spears cut through the water.

Kara looked at Aru, and Aru smiled. Nothing was going to throw her off.

She closed her eyes. *I'm ready*, she thought. Against her skin, Vajra burned brighter, grew larger.

"Shah, I need to tell you something," said Aiden quickly. "I think, I mean, I know that—"

Just then, it started to rain. But it wasn't an ordinary rain. The heavens opened up and fat droplets of pure gold hit the floor with a sharp *ding!* The gold fell everywhere—on them, between them, and on the sea. Aru instinctively cowered, but it didn't hurt like she'd thought it would.

Then, over the sound of the miraculous shower, Aru heard the deep rumble of Kubera's laughter.

"Well, color me entertained . . . and impressed. As you have asked, you shall receive, for I always pay my debts."

Aru watched, wide-eyed, as the golden droplets began to tremble, expand, and change shape. In a matter of seconds, each one stretched into a six-foot-high pillar. Then, in a blink, they morphed from pillars into *soldiers*. Each wore a helmet of gold that covered their face. Their muscled golden bodies were covered in armor etched in filigree, and their powerful hands held shining swords and shields.

The Nairrata army had arrived.

THIRTY-SIX

Big Mistake. Huge.

Aru felt the world holding its breath.

The Sleeper's army was rushing toward them, but everything happened so slowly it seemed like time was melting. Aru thought she could hear the water parting around his soldiers' knees. She could smell the sun-warmed metal of her golden army's shining armor as they stood next to her. The two sides were hundreds of feet apart, but that space would be closed in a matter of minutes.

Energy surged through Aru. In her hand, Vajra twisted with a new feral strength...the same kind it had demonstrated against Aiden in Surya's storage hallway. Aru felt her hair lift off her shoulders. She blinked. Her vision had changed, turning diamond sharp, and she was able to pick out electrical currents in the air, like threads in a powerful tapestry. All she had to do was *reach* for them.

"I feel...kinda funny," said Mini.

Aru turned to look at her. Purple flashed in the depths of Mini's eyes and violet-tinged shadows poured out of her Death Danda.

"Bad funny?"

Mini grinned. Her teeth looked pointier. "*Intense* funny."

Beside Aru, Kara's trident turned so bright, Aru could barely look at it. Brynne was changing, too. Her eyes looked ocean-tinted. In a matter of seconds, she blurred through a dozen menacing shapes—a growling panther, an azure bear, a sharp-clawed wolverine, and even a massive saltwater crocodile. Crocodile-Brynne snapped, and a cold wind blew around them.

"Uh, what's going on with you guys?" asked Aiden.

"Is it puberty?" whispered Rudy nervously.

Aiden swatted him.

Brynne turned back into herself and smacked her lips. "Nope. It's Pandava power."

One of the Nairrata troops turned to study Aiden, who held a single scimitar instead of his usual two. The soldier swiveled its head to look at the golden sword in its own fist, then back at Aiden's empty hand. With a nod, the warrior tossed the sword to Aiden, who caught it one-handed

"Shah?" he asked, glancing at Aru.

Wordlessly, Aru touched her lightning bolt to his blades and a jagged burst of electricity clambered up the metal.

"Okay, what about *my* glow-up?" demanded Rudy, holding out a pocketknife. "HELLO?"

The Nairrata army banged their swords against their shields as the first row of the Sleeper's army neared the golden platform. As one, the soldiers turned to face the Pandavas, and Aru could feel them waiting for her command.

Her mind whirled through the tactics Hanuman and Boo had taught them over the years.

The enemy was coming in from three sides. Their position

was too dangerous. Aru wanted to keep the Sleeper's army in her line of sight, and there was only one way to do that.

Brynne met her gaze, and they exchanged a silent understanding.

"That'll be messy," said Mini, reading Aru's thoughts.

"What will be messy?" asked Kara.

"You'll see," said Aru. "Brynne, tell Hanuman and Urvashi. Then get ready."

In a flash of blue light, Brynne transformed into an eagle. She winged up to Urvashi, then soared down to whisper in Hanuman's ear. He turned to Aru and nodded in approval.

Aru raised her lightning bolt high over her head. *Let them come,* she thought.

"Now?" asked Brynne.

"Hold…"

This close up, Aru could make out the details of individual soldiers coming their way. She saw the thick scar twisting across the face of a lion-headed rakshasa. A stunning dark-skinned yakshini smiled wide, revealing broken teeth.

The Sleeper's army was composed of beings both monstrous and beautiful, all of them united under his promise to "end the tyranny of fate." For the longest time, Aru had thought that her pity for these people meant that she had no right to fight them. But then Aru pictured the families in the Otherworld cowering in corners of the Night Bazaar, living under a state of emergency that had ruined their lives and terrorized their every thought.

Aru may have understood what the Sleeper was fighting for, but she didn't like *how* he was doing it, and *that* determined the side she stood on.

"Now!" yelled Aru.

Mini lunged, casting her Death Danda directly in front of Aru. Purple light surged across the golden floor and extended into the sea. The Sleeper's troops cried out as it shot a direct line through their battalion, forcing them to scatter as water sprayed up in fifty-foot-high sheets. Hanuman roared as he bent down and gathered up soldiers in his arms, flinging them to one side of the ocean. Brynne charged forward as an elephant, herding other warriors into the same area. She trumpeted loudly, and a third of the Nairrata swarmed after her.

Golden swords clashed against spears and shields. The combatants' feet glowed with a fuzzy enchantment to keep them from sinking into the water, and the nearer they got to Aru, the louder their footsteps sounded, until it was as if someone had unstoppered a thunderstorm right next to her ears.

"I need some kind of sound blast," Aru shouted to Rudy over the din. "Something that will knock the enemy back!"

"I got'chu, Aru," said Rudy. He rummaged through his backpack, then hauled out five bright orange crystals and hurled them into the sea. Noise like the buzzing of a thousand insects filled the air. The Sleeper's soldiers ducked, flailed, covered their heads, and ran from the sound, leaving one section of the ocean empty and calm.

"Good work, Rudy!" said Aru.

He grinned. "I'll stay on noise control!" Rudy shouted. In a blink, he morphed into his naga form and slithered into the water.

Now the Sleeper's army was gathered on one side of the sea, like a hand fan slowly closing.

Step one complete, thought Aru. *Make sure we're not surrounded.*

In the sky above, Urvashi began to beat a new rhythm, knitting up the ocean to shield them from rear attacks. Aru thrust

Vajra upward, and lightning crackled around her, illuminating the chopping waves. At her gesture, the Nairrata army surged forward, grappling with the Sleeper's troops.

Aru scanned the melee, steeling herself for the sight of the Sleeper's silhouette weaving in and out of his army, or the unmistakable sound of Boo's flapping wings. But neither materialized. That was for the best, thought Aru. Now she could take her next step without distraction.

Step two, surround them.

Aru heard the clip-clop of hooves as Brynne, in horse form, galloped up to Aiden and nudged him. He climbed astride her back and, with one backward glance at Aru, Brynne ran and leaped off the side of the platform, springing into the throng of soldiers. Aiden brandished his glowing scimitar and sword, beating back the soldiers. In all the spray around them, Aru almost didn't see the yaksha shimmering beneath the water's surface. Its long blue arm stretched out—

"AIDEN!" she yelled.

He lurched back, saw the enemy, and sliced down with his scimitar, neatly removing the soldier's hand. The yaksha howled before disappearing under the water.

"They're climbing up!" called Mini, pulling Aru's attention away from Aiden and Brynne.

Aru saw that chunks of the Sleeper's army had broken off and were clambering onto the golden platform. Two dozen troops charged across the space. Aru aimed her lightning bolt, but Kara darted in front of her.

"Let me, Aru," said Kara. She leaned at an angle, curving her arm back before aiming the trident. In a flash, the bright weapon spun out in an arc, shattering the soldiers' shields.

Mini's eyes glowed purple, and shadows erupted from the end of her Death Danda. The shapes reared up like massive cobras, striking down the enemy.

Aru's jaw dropped.

"Huh, shadow magic," said Mini with surprise when a row of soldiers fell unconscious into the water. *"Nice."*

"Not for those guys," said Aru, as the next line of offense backed away from Mini in terror.

"Fun fact!" said Kara. "The word for 'fear of shadows' is *sciophobia!*"

"Well—" started Aru.

"Pandavas, look out!" yelled Urvashi from far above.

Whereas a second ago Aru had been able to see the Nairrata army enclosing the Sleeper's soldiers as Brynne, Aiden, and Hanuman herded the attackers into place, now her view was completely obscured by mist. She detected a faint hissing, and it made her blood run cold.

Something was coming for them.... But what?

Out of the mist flew a hundred arrows. Too late, Aru twirled Vajra, knocking away a few of the deadly projectiles, but one got through and grazed her arm. Pain flashed through her.

Purple light burst across Aru's vision as Mini brought up a violet shield. One arrow got caught in it, sinking up to its fletching. Its razor-sharp tip was *inches* from Kara's nose. She stumbled back, trembling.

The mist cleared just enough for Aru to see two dozen of the Sleeper's archers crawling onto the golden platform, scowling in determination.

On the one hand, this was not good.

The Nairrata fighters were barely keeping up. If they couldn't surround the foe and concentrate their attack, they'd lose this battle.

On the other hand, Aru felt Vajra lengthening and bristling with electricity. Once again a surge of power coursed through her, zipping up her spine, filling her blood with lightning. Mini caught the look in Aru's eye, and lowered her shield.

The Sleeper's soldiers roared, rushing at her.

"Big mistake," Aru said. "Huge."

She grinned—mostly because she'd always wanted to say that line—and then Aru Shah let loose her lightning bolt.

BOOM!

Vajra exploded on the golden deck.

In the past, Vajra could probably clear, like, maybe three demons in one go.

This was not the past.

Aru watched her lightning bolt blur across the floor. Throughout the air, Aru could detect a lace of electricity, sleeping threads of energy. In her mind, she urged Vajra to gather those threads and enhance their sizzle.

Vajra paused just before it reached the archers, as if waiting for one final nudge from Aru.

"Get 'em," she said.

The lightning bolt crackled its way down the front line of soldiers, knocking them back into the water. Then it zipped across the next row and a few more after that before zooming back into Aru's hand. The force of Vajra's newfound power left a streak of smoke curling on the platform.

"Whoa," said Mini, looking at Aru in awe.

THAT WAS SICK! hollered Brynne through their mind link.

The battle halted around them. Aru could hear the din of

soldiers complaining about not being able to see. Fog rolled across the golden floor and something winged out of the mist....

A pit opened in Aru's stomach as a familiar form took shape, heading straight for her.

Boo.

THIRTY-SEVEN

The Worst Wish

Aru's first thought upon seeing Boo was not what she'd imagined it would be.

She'd expected to be incredibly angry at him for all the hurt he had caused them.

Instead, Aru just wondered if Mini had saved him an Oreo.

It was such a disconnected thought in the middle of a battle. But it vanished with the mist and Boo's screech.

"What are you doing here?" he demanded, swooping toward them. "I told Kubera to keep you out of this!"

Rage bristled through Aru. Oh, she had heard exactly how Boo had instructed Kubera. His poisonous words rose in Aru's head like ghosts:

Don't bother with them!

They're nothing more than weak children, not worthy of anyone's time or attention.

The lines echoed through Aru's skull. Beside her, Aru could see resentment flashing across Mini's face, too.

"You're not supposed to be here!" shouted Boo. "Get out! *Go!*"

"We're not going anywhere," said Aru, planting her feet firmly on the floor.

"You were wrong about us," said Mini. "We *are* worth it."

"Worth it? What are you talking about?" shouted Boo. He looked confused. Then something in him changed. His beak dropped open in shock. "You *heard* what I said to Lord Kubera?"

"EVERY WORD!" shouted Brynne, stomping toward him in the form of a bear.

By then, Aru's plan had come to fruition. They had beaten back the Sleeper's army, which was now huddled in a tight knot and hemmed in by golden soldiers who had followed Aru's every command. Overhead, Urvashi was weaving a spell through dance to prevent the enemy from escaping. Rudy was warding the new boundaries with his musical enchantments while Hanuman and Aiden beat back any stragglers, keeping them away from the deck where Aru, Mini, Bear-Brynne, and Kara stood glaring up at Boo.

"Girls and—" Boo paused, glaring at Kara. "Who are you?"

She raised her trident menacingly. "You don't want to find out."

Ooh, good line, thought Aru.

As if she'd heard her, Kara grinned.

"Listen to me—you all have to leave *this* instant!" shouted Boo.

"You're not our teacher anymore!" shot back Aru. "You left that behind when you betrayed us to the Sleeper."

"I did what I had to do to protect you!" pleaded Boo. "I will *always* try to protect—"

Raw fury zipped through Aru. She was sick of people lying to them and going behind their backs. She didn't know exactly what to believe anymore, but there was one thing she knew for certain: she didn't believe Boo.

Aru raised Vajra high over her head. "I'm giving you one chance to get lost," she snarled.

A wounded expression flitted over the pigeon's face. He cocked his head to one side and squinted.

"You will always be my Pandavas," he said. "I can explain. I would never—"

No! thought Aru violently. "Enough!" she screamed.

Vajra shot up in height, towering nearly eight feet in the air. The lightning bolt cast a harsh glow over the platform.

"I wish you would just get out of our lives!"

Ugly words have a tendency to burn the mouth, and as Aru spoke, she felt scalded. Even more so when the words seemed to hang in the air between her and Boo.

The pigeon's wings drooped, and he fell a couple of inches in the air. But the next moment, he seemed to recall something. With a burst of effort, he dove toward them, squawking, "I'll get out of your lives the moment I know *yours* are safe!"

Aru was so stunned that she lurched backward. Boo batted at them with his wings, expertly weaving in and out between their weapons, forcing them back step by step.

"What—are—you—doing?" demanded Bear-Brynne.

"It's a—" Boo started to say.

But at that moment, the golden platform was ripped apart by an explosion. Huge slabs of gold suddenly jutted up like icebergs. The force of it threw Aru onto her back. She scrambled to sit up just as fragments flew at her head. Aru couldn't perceive any sound beyond the ringing in her ears, but she didn't have to hear

Boo finish his sentence to understand what he'd been trying to tell them.

Trap.

It's a trap.

Aru felt like all her movements were slow, like she was swimming in a tank of honey. She fumbled for her lightning bolt, but she couldn't do anything to stop a hunk of gold the size of a couch from heading straight for them. Dimly, she could hear Boo shouting for them to dive into the waves. Aru wanted to do something, *anything*, but she was too sluggish. She braced herself, squeezing her eyes shut, and...

BAM!

Aru looked up to see the huge piece of gold bounce off Mini's violet shield. Mini panted, red-faced with effort. Her shields had never been this strong before. This one was like an impenetrable shell around Kara, Bear-Brynne, and Aru as they stood in a hole in the destroyed floor, knee-deep in the seawater, waves sloshing up the side of the shield.

Aru watched, helpless, as the remains of the floor drifted away. She could now see that bright golden shards had lodged themselves in the joints of the Nairrata soldiers' armor, inhibiting their movements. As the golden army slowed down, the Sleeper's army gained momentum, and Hanuman and Aiden fought furiously to contain them.

"What are we going to do?" asked Mini. "Maybe Boo can—"

"No," groaned Brynne, dropping her bear guise. "No!"

Aru turned. Something in her broke even before she saw her worst fears confirmed. There, bobbing on top of the waves a few feet away, lay Boo. His eyes were open. The force of the explosion had blown off some of his plumage, and as Aru stretched out her hand to scoop him up, a single gray feather sifted down from the sky and landed in her palm.

I didn't mean it! she thought wildly. *I take back what I said!*

But it was too late. Or rather, it didn't make a difference.

Boo was gone.

Forever.

THIRTY-EIGHT

Ugly Applause

Aru went numb as she watched the Sleeper's troops lurch toward them, shoving aside chunks of gold in their path.

Out of the corner of her eye, Aru could see Hanuman and Aiden struggling—and failing—to beat back the swarming army. Rudy was still launching jewels into the sea, and though they erupted into noise that made many of the soldiers stagger backward, it wasn't enough. Above them, floating gold dust disrupted Urvashi's enchantments and illusions.

Aru could see all this, but she couldn't make herself move. Grief had frozen her in place.

Boo was *gone*.

When Aru thought of the last words she'd screamed at him, all she wanted to do was disappear.

A yaksha with an evil grin stood over her. "There's nowhere for you to hide," he said. "You thought your golden army could protect you, but the Sleeper has a plan for everything . . . even *you*."

Around them, the Nairrata army struggled to remove the gold nuggets that had gotten trapped in their joints.

"You thought your army was indestructible, and they are . . . to everything except Lanka gold," sneered a rakshasa. "The Sleeper knew that Kubera wouldn't be able to resist getting involved in a fight."

A group of about forty soldiers closed in on Kara, Brynne, Mini, and Aru. Mini kept her Death Danda raised high, but Aru noticed a sheen of sweat breaking out across her forehead. Even with her enhanced powers, Mini wouldn't be able to shield them forever.

What are we going to do? asked Brynne via the mind link.

Aru's thoughts raced through the possibilities. Without the Nairrata army, it was just them against the Sleeper's troops. True, they'd brought down many of them, but definitely not enough to make it a fair fight.

Aru was still thinking when one of the asuras started laughing and spat out, "Not even that stupid, feathery traitor could help you, and he died trying to do it!"

Aru went cold.

Boo wasn't some "stupid, feathery traitor." He was their teacher. He was their protector . . . for better or for worse. And they were his Pandavas.

The answer came to her in a frosty fury. "We show them *exactly* who we are . . . *Pandavas*."

Aru could sense energy rippling through Mini and Brynne. Even Kara, who hadn't known Boo, picked up on their rage. Ice crept across Mini's shield. Kara's trident flushed blue at the bottom of the tines, like a flame. Brynne's fur looked tinged with silver as she transformed into a huge boar. And Aru?

Her lightning bolt turned iridescent, flashing with all the colors of a rainbow.

Three, two . . .

Mini lowered the shield, and the Pandavas plunged forward through the water. Brynne charged into the ranks of the Sleeper's army, tossing soldiers into the air with her tusks. Kara spun around, loosing her trident and catching enemies across their guts. Brynne transformed back into a human and rotated her mace so sharply that a savage wind whipped a dozen foes into a cyclone that left them spinning in midair. Then she slammed down her weapon and they crashed onto the jagged golden shards sticking out of the sea.

As a group of warriors rushed Mini, she flashed an eerie smile. One moment she was there, and the next, she had winked out. She reappeared behind the line of soldiers and tapped one on the shoulder. When he turned around, she waved, then knocked out three of them with an expert swipe of her Death Danda.

Aru blasted through the horde, darting and weaving while swinging Vajra like a scythe. Her movements were cold and precise, her rhythm in perfect tandem with her sisters. Every thought in her head narrowed down to one command:

Fight.

Fight.

Fight!

Eventually, Mini's voice reached her: *Aru . . . Aru, it's done. It's finished.*

Aru bent over, trying to catch her breath. Her hair fell in damp hanks around her face. Her lungs ached.

At last she'd recovered enough to peek around her. The Sleeper's army had dispersed. Some were floating unconscious in the swells; others were clinging to pieces of broken floor.

The Potatoes came together slowly. They looked as battered

and exhausted as Aru felt. Their skin was sunburned and their hair encrusted with sea salt.

Hanuman let out a roar that shook the waves: "VICTORY FOR THE DEVAS!"

Urvashi floated down toward them and hovered over the water.

Aru swiveled around, dazed. Was this victory? She squinted, trying to find the exact slab on which she had carefully placed Boo. She needed to go to him. Maybe he wasn't really dead.... Maybe he was just injured....

You know what you saw, whispered a sad voice in her heart.

Aru stifled that thought. She didn't want it to be true.

No matter how she looked at it, this didn't feel like a victory. Something was wrong. And it wasn't just Boo's death that made her feel that way.

"No!" Aru heard Urvashi scream. It sounded like it was coming from someplace far away.

Beside Aru, Kara winced sharply. Her hand flew to the back of her neck, where a dime-size glow of light flashed like a beacon. Aru's heart seized. Kara's ward allowed her to feel when the Sleeper was near....

"Run!" Aru yelled.

But the second she turned, a shadowy sphere curled over her. Too late. The Sleeper had trapped her and her friends.

He stood before them, as tall and handsome as a king, but far too gaunt. His cheekbones looked carved, and his mismatched blue and brown eyes were intense and obsessive. When he saw Kara, surprise—and a slight frown—flitted across his face.

He barely spared a glance at the others, and instead addressed Kara and Aru. "Daughters," he said in his smooth, dark voice. "I am impressed by your battle prowess, but family does not fight family. What on earth do you think you're doing here? And Kara...My dear, I expected so much better of you."

Aru's face burned, and Kara made herself small.

The two of them had come so far together. They had busted out of the Sleeper's lair, risked their lives in a series of trials, and faced overwhelming odds in combat. And now, after everything, he was talking to them like a *disappointed parent*?

"I'm...I'm doing what's right," said Kara.

"What's *right* is rejoining your family," said the Sleeper calmly. "You both must come back with me at once. If you do not, there will be consequences."

A shadow glided from his fingertips and snaked toward Rudy, Brynne, and Aiden....

"No!" said Kara, slamming down her trident. Sunlight radiated around her, bleaching the shadows gray. "We're not going back with you. I—I'm sorry, Dad. But what you're doing is wrong. It's evil."

Sunny glowed even brighter with those words. The Sleeper looked at it intently, his eyes flashing between Aru and Kara. Around them, Aru noticed Aiden had raised his swords and Brynne had hoisted her wind mace. Mini lifted her Death Danda high over her head, and Rudy—still in his full naga form—reared taller on his coils.

"All of you would fight me?" asked the Sleeper quietly.

"I've known this chick for exactly twelve hours," announced Rudy, gesturing at Kara, "but I will happily *destroy* something on her behalf."

Kara scowled. *"Chick?"*

"Don't worry, it doesn't mean what you think it does," muttered Aru.

The Sleeper didn't seem amused. His eyes widened slightly as he took in their weapons ... as if he was just now seeing how much more powerful they had become. On the one hand, it made Aru feel hopeful. On the other hand, if this was the first time he was noticing, that meant he hadn't been watching the battle.

So where had he been?

The Sleeper's gaze scanned his fallen army. "You performed well in my little test today."

"Test?!" Aru screamed in outrage. "People got killed—"

He held up a hand to silence her. "Don't you see? Every time we meet, you realize more of your potential. Without me, what is a Pandava? Just a child with a fancy toy it does not understand."

"Better that than spreading lies and hurting people," said Kara, her chin high.

The Sleeper leaned forward and stroked her cheek. "One day, my lovelies, you will recognize what I have done for you, and on that day, you will join me." He stood up. "That day will come sooner than you think."

He spread his arms wide, throwing open the shadowy sphere he'd pulled down around them. The force of his gesture tossed Hanuman and Urvashi backward.

Power surged from the Sleeper's fingertips. With a scoop of his hand, each of his soldiers was wrapped in a veil of mist and lifted into the air. He twirled a finger and several eddies appeared in the sea. One by one, he deposited his troops into the whirlpools, which Aru guessed were portals back to his headquarters, wherever that was.

When the army was gone, the Sleeper wiped his hands together, causing giant waves to rise and break near their feet, cloaking them in sea foam. Then he looked straight at Aru. His hand went to the necklace of memories around his throat.

"I am deeply grateful for this gift, Aru," he said. "For now I know, beyond a shadow of a doubt, that I am on the right path. I will *still* do anything for my family. And thanks to this wonderfully diverting battle, I know exactly where to start."

Start? thought Aru. *Start what?* And by *diverting*, did he mean amusing, or distracting? Was he trying to divert the devas' attention from something more important, like the location of the nectar of immortality? It was impossible that he had found it.... Right?

She didn't have a chance to learn more, because, with a final crash of waves, the Sleeper disappeared. Aru coughed, spitting out seawater. She dragged her hand across her mouth. Her heart was pounding, and her ears were ringing with...

Applause?

As the sea mist cleared, and the Potatoes drew closer to one another, new shapes took form around them.

"Well," said Aiden over the din of happy shouts and whistles, "now we know what happened to the entirety of Lanka...."

A massive amphitheater made of gold flickered into visibility around the Pandavas, the stands full of the cheering citizens of Lanka. In the air above it, several floating screens flared to life, showing what appeared to be live feeds from all around the Otherworld: people celebrating in the Night Bazaar, apsaras and yakshas dancing for joy in the jewel-studded corridors of the heavens, nagas and naginis reveling in halls of sapphire. Everyone chanted one word:

"PAN-DA-VAS! PAN-DA-VAS! PAN-DA-VAS!"

THIRTY-NINE

ARE YOU NOT ENTERTAINED?

Aru had lost track of time. Everything seemed to blur together. The exploding floor, Boo's body floating on top of the waves, the burst of light from Vajra, the Sleeper's shadows, and now the thunderous applause from the whole population of Lanka. Her eyes burned from the screens flashing overhead, and her ears buzzed from people shouting their names.

"ARU! ARU, I'M YOUR NUMBER ONE FAN!" someone screamed from the stands.

"Ooh," said Rudy, holding up his phone to show the Potatoes his screen. "Hashtag-IStandWithThePandavas is trending number one on Chatter!"

"What's Chatter?" asked Aru.

She wasn't actually curious. She just wanted to keep up the pretense of conversation so she wouldn't be alone with her thoughts.

That day will come sooner than you think, the Sleeper had said.

"It's like Twitter for the Otherworld," said Aiden.

"What's Twitter?" asked Rudy.

"A cesspit," said Brynne darkly.

The amphitheater slid toward them slowly. Aru stumbled back nervously as the crowd began to rise from their seats, shouting the Pandavas' names.

Aru looked around anxiously for an escape route. To her right, a hallway made of glass and gold sprouted from the ocean and grew like an enchanted vine, wending its way over the water and far away from the crowd that was now spilling out into the ocean, waving their phones and pens and paper.

Aru didn't know who had commanded it—maybe Brynne?— but the Nairrata army instantly encircled the group, raising their golden weapons to ward off anyone who tried to chase them.

"This way!" Hanuman called, motioning them down the enchanted hall.

"Where does this lead?" asked Aiden.

"Back to Kubera's palace," said Urvashi, ushering them away from the crowds. "When we're there, you can call off your army."

My army, thought Aru, looking at the hulking metal soldiers. She noticed that the troops were now free of the shards that had clogged their joints. How ironic that gold was the one thing that could stop the Nairrata.

She didn't want to meet up with Kubera again. The whole time, he'd known this was an arena. And he hadn't lifted a finger to help them . . . or save Boo.

Aru put her hand in her jeans pocket and stroked the feather inside. It was the only thing she had left of the pigeon. Aru's chest felt tight. It didn't feel right to leave his body behind. Maybe after this meeting they could go back to the ocean and find it.

Brynne looked back over her shoulder at the crowd and her stunned expression melted into one of disgust. "So much has changed in, like, *days,*" she said. "Last week, they hated us."

"Now we're their saviors, and they're our number one fans," said Aiden.

The thought sat uncomfortably inside Aru. Everyone had been staring down at them, watching them struggle and fight... watching Boo die to save them.

None of them had tried to help.

Before, people applauding her would've been a dream come true. Now it just annoyed her.

"Aru?" asked Kara. "I wasn't sure if, um, it was okay to ask you, but—"

Aru could guess what Kara wanted to know. "You could have gone with the Sleeper," she said.

"No, I—"

"But you didn't," Aru cut in. "So you're stuck with us now. And that's that."

Kara beamed. "Really?"

"Really," said Aru, flashing a true smile.

"Really!" chimed in Mini.

"Really," added Brynne.

Kara looked happy, but her hand fluttered to her chest anyway, as if she were hurting. Aru knew how she felt. They'd won, but not forever, and not without losing something dear. What was the word Kara had used for situations like this? *Pyrrhic.* The victory had cost too much for all of them.

Except maybe Rudy.

He seemed delighted with all the new attention. He walked

backward, blowing kisses to the crowd through the glass walls of the hallway. People threw flowers on top of the tunnel.

"THANK YOU! THANK YOU! FOLLOW ME ON SOCIAL MEDIA! MY INSTAGRAM HANDLE IS—"

Mini sighed, grabbing Rudy's arm and hauling him forward.

At the end of the tunnel was a semi-dark room adorned with soft silken pillows and floating candles. Brynne's eyes went immediately to the single platter of samosas on the low-lying table.

"Kubera wants you to wait for him here," said Hanuman.

"The two of us must go back to the Otherworld," said Urvashi. "We have left it unprotected for too long."

They hugged each of the Pandavas.

"What you did today was truly a feat worthy of legends," Urvashi said warmly. "The heavens will not forget your bravery."

"And neither will the Otherworld," Hanuman added, patting their backs.

"What about Boo?" asked Mini. "He...He died trying to protect us."

Hanuman bowed his head. "We shall make sure his sacrifice is not forgotten, either."

"But where is he?" asked Aru. She didn't want to say *body* out loud. It didn't feel right.

Hanuman and Urvashi exchanged a glance.

"*No,*" said Aru firmly. "Not that again. Don't hide things from us anymore—"

"Peace, Aru," said Hanuman, holding out his hands. "Kubera found something, and he wants to give it to you himself. He says it's good news."

Aru almost laughed. Good news from Kubera? It had to be a trick.

"He will explain," said Hanuman.

"We must go," said Urvashi urgently. "We have to make sure boundaries are secure. The Sleeper will try one last time...."

"And, with your help, we will be ready," said Hanuman, looking proudly at them.

With that, they disappeared, leaving only a faint trail of music behind them. The Potatoes stared around at one another.

"I'm too sad to eat, but I'm too restless *not* to eat," said Brynne, studying the table. A moment later, she dragged the entire platter of samosas toward her. Brynne was about to take a giant bite when Kubera materialized in the room with a loud *pop!*

"AHHH!" screamed Brynne, reeling backward.

The platter fell to the floor, and the samosas split open, dribbling out spiced potatoes and peas. All except one. Biju the mongoose hopped out of Kubera's lap and ran to the intact samosa just as Brynne reached out to snatch it. Biju got there first and gobbled it on the spot.

"Dumb weasel," muttered Brynne.

Biju burped, then hissed at her. Two amethysts fell from its mouth.

Brynne looked ready to clobber the mongoose when Kubera cleared his throat loudly. Aru noticed that the Lord of Wealth had changed his whole look since they'd last seen him. Now he was dressed head to toe in a pearlescent suit. White gold winked at his ears and throat. Huge pearl rings covered his fingers, and he'd even swapped out his golden eye patch for one of white silk.

"Thanks for all your *help* on the battlefield," Aru couldn't help saying straight off.

"You're welcome," said Kubera in his deep, rumbling voice. "Before this whole showdown shenanigan started, I was thinking to myself that war is so... boring. Why not add a little *pizzazz* to your doom? Set the stage a little, add some good seating."

"Reminded me of the movie *Gladiator*," said Aru, "what with all the passive watching when it comes to fatal combat."

Come to think of it, she really should've shouted *ARE YOU NOT ENTERTAINED?* at the end of the whole thing, but she'd been too sad. Now that sadness was turning into anger all over again.

"Really?" said Kubera, clapping once. "How delightful!"

Careful, Shah, came Brynne's mind message.

Aru bit her tongue to avoid saying anything more.

"By now you've seen that you can wield the Nairrata army to do your bidding," said Kubera. "Well, not all of you. Only those in the possession of a god-given weapon may command it." He gestured vaguely at only Rudy and Aiden, even though Kara was sitting next to Aru. "It's *super* fun to have an army. Very imposing. Plus, a great driver of tourism if you're thinking about opening up an island resort or some such."

"Ooh!" said Rudy, perking up.

"Yeah... That's not exactly a priority at the moment?" said Aru.

Rudy deflated.

"Excuse me, but what exactly are we supposed to *do* with the army?" cut in Mini.

Aru hadn't thought of that. If you suddenly owned a ginormous army, did they accompany you everywhere? For a moment, Aru pictured walking into her first day of high school with golden soldiers at her back.

That wouldn't be so bad....

"Oh yes," grumbled Kubera. "Your *guardians* had something to say about all that. Something about how, for your own safety, you should command the Nairrata army to stay in the heavens until summoned."

"Oh."

"I know," said Kubera, sighing. "It *reeks* of responsibility. But do you agree?"

Aru, Brynne, and Mini looked at one another and nodded. In Aru's head, as clear and bright as if it were a mind message sent from her sisters, Aru saw the golden army transform. Their mechanical arms and legs shot into their sockets, their helmeted heads popped down into their necks, and their torsos shrank into raindrops that zoomed upward and disappeared into the sky.

"They're very communicative," said Kubera.

Aru shook her head a little. She could see *her* army...in her brain. That was both awesome and unsettling.

"Well, I guess that settles that!" said Kubera, stretching.

"No," said Aiden. "The astra. It belongs to us now. Like you promised."

Kubera stopped in mid-yawn. A shrewd look crept into his gaze. With a sigh, he removed the white-gold necklace from around his throat and held it out in front of them.

"As you so desire," he grumbled. "But I don't envy you the price of having to wear such a powerful thing. In fact, conveniently forgetting about that part of the bargain was my gift to you."

According to Kara, this item was capable of destroying the weapons of the gods. Aru hadn't forgotten what had happened when they'd said the weapon's full name aloud. It had been like watching the wind, sky, and earth tremble with fear. But it didn't *look* particularly scary. It was nothing more than a thumbnail-size piece of gold hanging from a thin gold chain.

"Take it," said Kubera, offering it to Aru.

She extended her hand. The moment the necklace dropped into her palm, Aru felt an instant *hollowing* sensation. It was strong, and yet it was the exact opposite of power. Whereas power amplified, the astra erased. It was the kind of negative power that could strip a stately leafy oak into a twig in a manner of seconds. Vajra spooked, transforming from a bracelet to a pure electrical charge that raced up her arms and neck. Aru almost dropped the astra necklace onto the ground.

"*Careful*, careful!" chided Kubera. "It's terrible, isn't it? I tried to make it, I don't know, less horrible. Sorta like 'deadly, but make it fashion,' though it still feels rather...deadly and, if I'm being quite honest, it's *not* very fashionable. Very early 2000s. I hate it."

"We have to *wear* it?" asked Aru, holding the weapon at arm's length.

"Like jewelry!" said Kubera brightly.

Aru shuddered. This thing wasn't a necklace—it was a noose.

"It's safest when worn on one's person, yes. After the initial shock, it's not so bad," said Kubera. "But you may take turns with it."

"Like a Horcrux..." Rudy whispered under his breath. "Why do we always end up with Horcruxes?"

"No one's asking *you* to wear it," said Aiden.

"Oh, thank gods," said Rudy, letting out a breath. "That chain would clash with all my outfits."

"Who wants to go first?" asked Aru.

At the same time, Mini hollered, "NOSE GOES!"

Brynne and Mini clapped their hands over their noses. Aru scowled, then put the chain around her neck. When the golden shard of the astra hit her skin, she felt like she'd been thrown into a snowbank. A minute later, though, the feeling passed.

"Uncomfortable, yes," said Kubera. "But a necessary precaution. Now all you must do is declare those who are allowed to take it from you. No one else will be able to."

"But... But if that's true, then how could the Sleeper have taken it from you?" asked Aru.

Kubera sighed. "Through a loophole. Ages ago, only a few of the gods could remember the weapon's true name, and we did not know who might need it again and why. So we decided that only those gods who knew the weapon's full name could ask for it. But we also allowed for some discretion on the gods' part so it wouldn't be denied from worthy mortal heroes."

"Or heroines," said Aru.

"Or *heroines*," conceded Kubera. "*You* were the first people to ask for the weapon by the correct name in, oh, I don't know, three thousand years? Give or take? You reached me before the Sleeper did, and I have deemed you worthy of wielding it. So now it's your turn. Speak now, Pandava."

"Uh," said Aru, panicking for a second.

She definitely didn't want the Sleeper to take it. Or the gods. Or demons. Or, honestly, anyone who wasn't—

"No one except another Pandava sister can take the astra from me," said Aru, glancing at Brynne and Mini.

They bowed their heads. Beside Aru, Kara nodded encouragingly. But when Aru looked at Kubera, he closed his eye and frowned for a moment. Annoyance prickled at Aru. Why did he seem regretful suddenly? Had she said something wrong?

"Very well," he said. "On to our next, and last, order of business. Biju?"

The mongoose, who had been greedily—and somewhat smugly—eating all the broken samosas in front of Brynne, looked up. It chirped, and a bright peridot gem clattered to the ground. Biju scampered up to Kubera's throne, disappeared behind it, and then emerged a couple of moments later carrying something in its mouth. The object's color was beautiful, like flames glimpsed through a ruby. But it was too round and smooth to be a precious stone. It looked a lot like ...

"Is that an egg?" asked Mini.

"Yes," said Kubera. "Biju was most excited upon finding it. Mongooses love eggs, you know. I myself can't *stand* the texture. But Biju brought it to me when he figured out what it was. Or rather, *who* it is."

The animal laid the deep red egg on the ground before Mini.

She picked it up and gasped. "It feels ... familiar," she said, weighing it in her hand. "I don't know how to explain it."

Mini passed it to Brynne, who also looked stunned.

"I mean, that's impossible, right?" asked Mini.

Brynne handed it to Aiden. A slow smile spread across his face as he placed the egg gently into Aru's palm. The moment Aru touched it, a memory flared inside her skull: a pigeon preening its feathers and tucking its head under its wing to sleep.

"Wait," she said. "This ... This is *Boo*?"

"Well, he—or she or they; one can never tell what souls want to be—may want a different name once it hatches," said Kubera. "You were the ones who freed Subala, after all. Perhaps he will want nothing to do with the life he previously had."

"Freed him?" repeated Aru, shocked. "But he was cursed!

Only a wish could free him...." Aru trailed off, as the exact words she'd said floated back to her: *I wish you would just get out of our lives.*

The words had been so ugly that Aru had felt nothing but guilt over what she'd said. She hadn't even considered that it was the first time she'd said *I wish* to Boo. It was a cruel twist to his curse.

If she'd known that was all it would take, she could've freed Boo ages ago. Maybe all she'd needed to say was: *I wish you were free.* But she'd never thought of that, and Boo, panicked and trapped, had ended up going to the worst lengths imaginable to try to save them.

"Whatever hatches from that egg will no longer be Subala," said Kubera. "But it will contain his soul. And a new chance."

Biju crept a little closer to Aru, as if stalking the egg.

"Stop that!" snapped Kubera.

Biju scowled.

"We don't eat our friends!"

Biju huffed, and a round opal fell from its mouth.

"Unless they become enemies...in which case, fair is fair," said Kubera, shrugging.

Mini looked horrified, and Kara giggled at her expression. Brynne stared hungrily at the empty platter while Rudy kept trying to snatch up the little gemstones Biju dropped whenever he opened his mouth.

Aru caught Aiden glancing at her. For the first time since the nightmare of everything that had happened in the House of the Sun, he smiled. She smiled back, then peered down at the flame-and-ruby-swirled egg in her hands. She pulled it a little closer to her belly, and the knot of guilt inside her loosened.

Aru never thought she'd think this way, but she'd had her fill of gold and jewels. She'd seen enough of both to last several lifetimes, and in the end, neither compared to the rare treasure in her hand. A golden army might be precious, but a second chance with someone she loved?

That was priceless.

FORTY

I Have a Boyfriend in Canada

After their meeting with Kubera, Rudy decided to return to his parents' palace. First he gave the Potatoes multiple, though somewhat unwanted, assurances that he'd find a way to see them every week.

"I'm *literally* a hero," said Rudy. "*And* I'm a prince. Who's going to say no to me now?"

He winked. Aru noticed that this time he wasn't looking at her . . . but at Mini. Who didn't seem to notice. Or, if she did, she acted like it didn't matter.

Mini, Brynne, and Aiden were able to get ahold of their families . . . but there was still no word from Krithika Shah.

"What if she hasn't come back yet?" asked Aru.

Kara squeezed her hand. "She will."

Together, the five of them returned through the newly reopened portals to Atlanta. On one side of the street stood the Museum of Ancient Indian Art and Culture. On the other side stood the elegant home that belonged to Aiden and his mom.

"Do you want me to come with you?" asked Aiden.

"That's okay," she said. "Your mom is probably waiting for you."

Aiden nodded. He looked like he wanted to say something else, but he turned and left.

"Is he okay?" asked Kara.

Brynne shrugged. "Are any of us?"

Normally that sentence would've made Aru sad, but it didn't really hit the same way when Brynne was in the form of a rather large blue chicken. Across her feathered back was a makeshift nest containing a bright-red egg swaddled in scraps of silk.

When Kubera had given them the egg, none of them had been exactly sure what to do with it.

The conversation had gone like this:

Mini (cradling the egg): Do we keep it in a warm place? Does it want blankets? Feathers?

Aru: Does this make us mother hens?

Aiden: I don't think whatever's inside that egg is a chicken.

Aru: Too bad *we* can't be chickens . . . (turning to Brynne) Oh my god, wait—

Brynne: No.

Aru: You have to.

Brynne: No—

Kara (interrupting): Chickens are living descendants of dinosaurs, if that makes you feel any better?

Brynne: Cool! But *no*.

Aru: Do it.

Brynne: Shah, I swear—

Mini (holding up the Boo egg): Please? Do it for the children.

Brynne: I hate you guys.

Brynne had turned herself into a blue chicken the size of a rottweiler. It was a little...unsettling. But the larger forms she could now assume seemed to be a consequence of her expanded powers—powers that had kicked in at the start of the battle and hadn't left any of them. So. That was cool. But terrifying. Even Aiden had refused to take a picture.

"Some horrors need not be documented," he'd said solemnly.

Brynne had squawked at him.

Now Aru and her sisters (and chicken sister) crossed the steps of the museum. It was late June, and the air was stiflingly hot. Even the crickets in the myrtle trees had fallen asleep. Aru pushed open the double doors, her whole heart full of waiting. It was cool and dark inside. That was a good sign, thought Aru. *Someone* had to be home to control the thermostat.

"Mom?" Aru called.

Upstairs, Aru heard a faint rustling. Painful hope burst through her lungs. She charged up the stairs, taking the steps two or three at a time.

"MOM!" called Aru.

Aru was at the top of the landing when she saw it: a tiny bird trapped between the open screen and the glass in the hall window. When the bird saw Aru, it spooked and freed itself, disappearing in the branches of the linden tree outside.

"Mom..." said Aru quietly.

She should've known her mother wouldn't be there. When Aru peered over the banister, she saw a fine layer of dust coating the floors and exhibits. She sighed and walked into the small apartment. Normally, she would smell ink and old papers, a whiff of chai from her mother's mug, and beneath it all, the soft hint of her perfume. But the apartment was as bare and odorless as a stone. Aru stood in the middle of the living room for what felt like an eternity until she heard footsteps behind her. Her sisters stood in the doorway.

"We'll find her, Shah," said Brynne, who had transformed back into her regular form and was now holding the Boo egg in her hand.

"We'll figure something out," said Mini fiercely. "We promise."

Together, Aru and her sisters made a nest of soft sweaters for the Boo egg and carefully placed it in a little alcove by the door that led to the stairs. Afterward, Brynne and Mini said it was time to send an update to the Otherworld.

"They've been dying to hear from us," said Brynne, patting the Boo egg good-bye.

"Do they know anything more about where the Sleeper went?" asked Aru.

Beside her, Kara stiffened.

"I don't know yet," said Brynne. "But he was looking for something while the battle was going on . . . and now that he can't get the astra, there's only one thing the Sleeper wants."

"The nectar of immortality," said Kara softly.

"It's not in the Ocean of Milk anymore, though," said Mini. "It's supposed to be hidden so well that no one can find it, not even the devas."

Kara looked nervous. "You don't know what he's capable of."

"True, but *we* have the astra *and* a giant golden army, so . . . I dunno. I'd say we're still winning," said Brynne.

"Definitely," said Mini. Then her smile faded and she looked sorrowfully between Aru and Kara. "You guys shouldn't stay here alone. We can go between houses now that the portals are open?"

"I call first sleepover at my house, because I *need* to try out some new recipes, and I don't believe in small serving sizes," announced Brynne.

"Done!" said Mini. "We'll come pick you up when we finish with Hanuman and Urvashi."

Aru nodded in agreement, but the whole time she felt like she was somewhere else. Of course she was worried about what the Sleeper was looking for, and what he might do next...but her mind kept drifting to her mom. Where was she? Why hadn't she come back yet? Aru was so lost in her musing that she didn't even notice Brynne and Mini had left until Kara touched her shoulder and jolted her out of her thoughts.

"You okay?" asked Kara.

"Yeah," mumbled Aru.

"I know how you feel," said Kara quietly. "I know what it's like to wait for someone to show up, to worry all the time about what's happened to them. It's like someone's eating you alive from the inside out."

Aru nodded. "So what do you do?"

Kara took a deep breath. "I remember that *'hope' is the thing with feathers.*"

Aru laughed. "What?"

"You know that book of poems I'm always carrying around?" asked Kara.

Aru remembered seeing it in Kara's lap and again in her backpack when she was unconscious: a thin blue volume of Emily Dickinson poems.

"In one of her poems, she calls hope the 'thing with feathers,' and I always think about that.... Maybe when we hope for something, the hope flies off to find whatever it is we're thinking about... and then it brings it back to us," said Kara. "And when there's nothing else we can do, at least we can hope. You know what I mean?"

Aru was silent for a moment.

"I think I do," she said after a while.

"Whatever happens, you're not alone," said Kara, bumping her shoulder.

Aru smiled. That was true. She had the Potatoes. And for now, she had to continue her training, and get stronger for her next encounter with the Sleeper. She had to keep going.

She had to keep hoping.

Over the next eight months, Aru found a new balance. Sheela and Nikita's family moved into the house beside Aiden's, and for the first time, all five Pandavas started training together. Brynne's uncles, Gunky and Funky, and Mini's parents, took turns housing Aru and Kara. The Boo egg—which still hadn't hatched but seemed to grow bigger little by little—traveled between the girls' houses every month. At first they'd thought it would hatch in three weeks, like most eggs... but Boo was taking his time.

"Definitely not going to be a normal bird," Mini had said, tapping the egg a little.

Each Pandava—except for Sheela and Nikita, whose parents had refused on the grounds that the twins hadn't even managed to keep a goldfish alive—had her own Boo egg house. Mini had spent hours researching birds' nesting patterns before building the egg an incubator, and Brynne had added an attachment to her constantly working oven so the egg would always be warm. Aru kept the nest of soft sweaters. Boo had always loved snuggling in them in the winter, and she wondered if whatever lay inside his egg now would feel the same way.

On Sundays, Aiden's mom threw dinner parties, and the house was full of joyful noise and delicious smells. On those nights, the Potatoes fought over what movie to watch. It was Aru's favorite day of the week.

Their friend Hira, the shape-shifting rakshasi, liked the X-Men and amused herself by turning into Mystique. Nikita liked reruns of *Project Runway*, while Sheela kept pushing for thrillers, which was somewhat frightening. Aiden usually tried to convince them to watch a documentary. Mini liked rom-coms, and Brynne either wanted a cooking show or an action movie, while Aru tended to pick out weirder films. Kara went along with pretty much everything. Last week was Aru's turn, so she'd made them watch *Snakes on a Plane*. By the end of it, Rudy was furious.

"This is the most disrespectful and inaccurate thing I've ever seen," he'd hissed. "We would *never* go on a commercial flight!"

"Yeah, that's definitely the biggest inaccuracy of the whole film," said Aiden.

Aru laughed. She might've felt sad over these past few months, but she'd never felt lonely. She had her sisters and friends. In the Otherworld, the Potatoes had never been more popular. Of course, some people—mainly Opal, who had made their lives a nightmare last year—had complained that the Pandavas had let the Sleeper get away yet *again*. But for the most part, people thought that the reincarnated warrior sisters had proven their heroism, and would be able to keep them safe.

In fact, all the attention on them got so overwhelming that Hanuman had to move their training sessions to a secret location accessible only through a portal that opened at his touch. On the other side was a spherical arena, bigger than two Olympic-size pools placed together. Sometimes, Hanuman transformed the whole place to look like a dense jungle, full of camouflaged pits and vines that could break without warning. Other times, he filled the whole thing with murky water full of vortices and sharp objects, and forced them to fight their way across it.

"You're more powerful now, Pandavas," Hanuman had said during one of their training sessions early on. "But that doesn't make the Sleeper any weaker. Wherever he is, he's gathering strength for his ultimate objective: finding the nectar of immortality."

It was just as her mom and Kara had said from the beginning, thought Aru.

"The devas learned of the Sleeper's mission when their army captured and interrogated one of his troops," Hanuman went on. "The soldier confirmed that, as the battle of Lanka raged, the Sleeper took advantage of the Otherworld's distractedness and moved even closer to his goal."

"We are scouring the seas, doing everything we can to find the amrita before he does, but you must remain on call," said Urvashi. "And we're increasing security around all your homes. No one should be able to get in."

"What if my mom tries to come home?" asked Aru, panicked.

Urvashi's sternness softened. "The museum will recognize her and let her through. Do not worry, Aru. Your mother is too clever by far to land herself in serious trouble."

At first, Aru had worried that the Sleeper would try to come after them again, but Kara calmed her.

"If he comes near us, I'll know," she said, tapping the gold circle on the back of her neck. Aru remembered the burst of light before the Sleeper had materialized in Lanka. "We'll be ready."

Ever since that assurance, Aru had noticed that Kara had a habit of rubbing the golden patch on her skin. Whenever they went on walks through the neighborhood or visited the Night Bazaar for shopping, Kara would reach up and touch the circle, as if waiting for something to happen.

One day, when Kara did it again during a run to the grocery store for one of Brynne's food experiments, Aru couldn't help asking, "Does that thing itch?"

"What? Oh...no," said Kara. Her cheeks turned red. "It, well, you know how it lights up when the Sleeper is nearby?"

"You think the Sleeper is here?" asked Aru, alarmed. She eyed the row of carrots and celery suspiciously.

"No!" said Kara hurriedly. "Not him! The ward isn't just for Dad.... He made it so it would work for my mom, too. I used to wonder if she'd come find me someday, but she's never tried. Or maybe she can't, who knows. But around here there's so many people, and I guess I just hoped that maybe one of them would be her."

Aru fell quiet for a moment. "What would you do if you saw her?"

Kara shrugged. "I don't know...I guess I'd just want to know why she left. Or if she ever thinks about me. It doesn't really matter anymore, though."

"Really?" asked Aru.

"Really," said Kara, smiling. "I used to dream about being

part of a big family. I wanted to fight over clothes with siblings and argue about who got to watch what…and now I do. So it's pretty great."

Barring the stuff out of her control, Aru had found more pockets of happiness than she'd expected to with her mom gone.

Minus the fact that Aru Shah was officially a high schooler.

Thanks to Hira, who posed as her mom, and Urvashi, who used delicate enchantments to sidestep school bureaucracy, Aru and Kara started ninth grade in September. Aru hadn't been sure how they were going to be able to afford the fancy new school's tuition, but then, sometime in July, a surprise came in the mail. When Aru opened the box, she found it filled to the brim with rare gems, a golden letter lying on top.

The other day I reminded Biju of how strange you and your mortal sisters are, and being the hilarious person that I am, this caused him to laugh uncontrollably. Or maybe he was choking. I have decided I'd rather not know. Anyway, it only seemed fair to give you what he coughed up, considering you were the ones who had made him laugh. If you call this "generosity," I will turn everyone you love into a golden statue.

Farewell!

"Thanks, mongoose," said Aru with a grin.

Ninth grade was predictably awful, and it didn't help that everyone still thought she had missed part of the last school year because she'd gotten mono from kissing someone. To make everyone stop guessing who it was, Aru eventually wound up telling people she had a boyfriend in Canada named…Bert.

"*Bert?*" repeated Kara, laughing.

By then, it was the beginning of February.

The world wore a thin coat of frost, and Aru's fifteenth birthday was two weeks away. The Potatoes had finished their evening training session, and Kara had just informed them about Aru's Canadian boyfriend.

"It was the only name I could come up with on short notice!" she grumbled.

"You could've just said someone coughed on you," said Mini. "Instead you came up with ... Bert."

"Bert is a *gentleman*," said Aru primly.

Kara and Mini had only laughed harder.

"Maybe you should invite *Bert* to your birthday party," joked Mini.

Honestly, Aru wasn't in the mood for a big party this year. It would be the first birthday without her mom. But the Potatoes insisted that she had to take her mind off stuff and had started planning the party for her.

"I have many ideas for your wardrobe," said Nikita. "I have decided you will have only three outfit changes. That's all I can manage on such short notice."

"Only *three*?" asked Aru, her jaw dropping. "Are you for real?"

Nikita, who was lazily conjuring thorny bloodred roses out of the ground, fixed Aru with a haughty stare. "I realize my fabulousness seems too good to be true, but I am *very* real and *very* serious."

"Your party will be one with unexpected guests," said Sheela in her singsong voice. Her eyes flashed silver with prophecy.

The Potatoes went still.

"What kind of unexpected guests?" asked Aru, her heart racing. "Like ... like my mom?"

"I couldn't see that clearly," said Sheela guiltily. "But...I know they will be important guests."

Guests.

So, more than one, thought Aru.

But who else?

"It's going to be *epic*," said Rudy. "Plus, I'm DJ-ing."

"I've got catering covered," said Brynne.

"I got the decorations!" said Mini happily.

"Now we just need a photographer," said Kara, glancing at Aiden.

Aru looked over at him. He was leaning against the wall, fiddling with Shadowfax. With his black hoodie and jeans, he blended into the dark background of the spherical arena. But when he looked up, Aru caught that eerie sparkle in his eyes that reminded her of stars and dusk. Aiden hardly acknowledged her these days, Aru thought, with a stinging feeling. He was fine in groups, but he never spoke to Aru one-on-one. Even when they were around other people, it seemed like he was talking to everyone except her.

"I guess that'll be me?" he said.

"You'll be great!" said Kara, beaming. With a blush, she added, "Like always."

Aiden smiled at her, then went back to his camera. Brynne and Mini snuck a glance at Aru, but she pretended not to notice. Aiden might not talk to Aru anymore, but he had no problem with Kara. Even though Kara had become just as close to her as her other sisters, Aru never brought up how she felt about Aiden.

First, because it would be weird.

Second, she was pretty sure Kara and Aiden liked each other, so how would Aru's feelings change anything?

And third, because Kara was super nice, and if she found out how Aru felt, she'd probably feel awful and stop talking to Aiden, and then everything would be weird and the Potato dynamic would go up in flames and she just could not deal.

So she said nothing.

It didn't matter, Aru told herself. Her birthday was coming up. She had an epic party to look forward to. And something deep in her heart told her that her mom was finally coming home.

FORTY-ONE

Happy Birthday, Aru Shah

Today, Aru Shah was fifteen years old.

She wasn't sure what she expected to happen. Magically glossy tresses? The sudden, inexplicable disappearance of unwanted facial hair? Waking up to birds and small animals doing her hair and bringing her clothes?

Would've been awesome, but...nope.

Instead, Aru had spent the day rewatching movies and eating whatever baked goods Brynne dropped off, because she was totally barred from leaving the upstairs apartment until the transformation of the downstairs was complete. All day, Aru could hear Rudy testing out the sound system and Mini yelling about disinfecting the decorations. She smelled Brynne's Extra-Amazing-All-Other-Cakes-Should-Quit Chocolate Cake, which had taken her awesome sister *three* days to make. When Aru had peeked—shortly before Brynne directed a powerful wind to force her back, because *they weren't done yet!*—she'd seen Kara carrying bundles of string lights and Aiden snapping photos, and Aru had been *almost* happy.

Almost.

Now, with just five minutes to go before she went downstairs, Aru glanced at the photo of her and her mom on the mantel.

"Yesterday, Urvashi said I was starting to look like you," said Aru to the photo.

Aru hadn't believed Urvashi, but now that she looked in the mirror, she saw that something about her *had* changed. Her skin was still darker than Krithika's, and Aru liked it that way. Her hair wasn't as curly and glossy, but it was thick and heavy and fell past her shoulders, and she was pleased with the fishtail side braid she had made for her party. Unlike her mom, who was endlessly fashionable, Aru would prefer to spend an entire day in pajamas. Tonight, though, she was wearing a two-piece dress made special for her by Nikita. The skirt was dark gold and high-waisted, with a pattern of gold-foil lightning bolts. The top was black velvet studded with gold pearls, and it had ballooned sleeves that cinched delicately at her wrists. Maybe that was it—she was now old enough to pull off this kind of look.

"What do you think?" Aru asked the picture.

Through the Pandava mind link, Aru heard Brynne's voice: *NOW you can come down!*

Aru grinned. "Wish me luck, Mom. Love you."

As Aru walked to the door to the stairs, she carefully tucked the astra necklace behind the neckline of her blouse. Ever since Kubera had given them the weapon as a pendant, the Pandava sisters had taken turns wearing it. Most of the time, Aru didn't mind it, but on some nights she could feel it like a heaviness lying over her heart.

"One of us can wear it on your birthday?" Mini had suggested the other day. "So you can be free?"

Brynne had nodded.

"It's fine," said Aru.

Honestly, she was kind of grateful for its sometimes-annoying presence. At least it kept her mind off the fact that Krithika still hadn't returned.

Once she had reached the alcove by the door, Aru checked on the Boo egg. It seemed to be getting warmer with each passing day, and now when Aru stroked it, it was like touching a too-hot glass straight out of the dishwasher.

"Be good," said Aru, giving it a kiss for luck.

The egg was silent.

Leaning against the wall beneath the nest was Aru's backpack. About two years ago, Kamadeva, the god of love, had given Aru a silver lipstick tube that was actually a celestial spotlight.

Use it when you feel like the world should see you in a different light.

Her fifteenth birthday seemed as good of a time as any?

Aru dug into the messy depths of her backpack. There, lying amid some candy wrappers, was the lipstick tube and something else she hadn't seen in a while....

It was a little gold coin, with the letters IO(F)U printed across it, for *Incendiary Offers of Future Use*. Agni, the god of fire, had given it to her ages ago. He'd said something rather strange when he did: *I have an arsenal of weapons that you will have need of, daughter of Indra. When that time comes, call on me.*

Aru frowned, grabbed the lipstick, and shut her bag. Then she untwisted the tube. Immediately, a beam of silvery light engulfed Aru. Her hair lifted a little off her back. On her wrist, Vajra sent curls of electric curiosity down her arm.

"Happy birthday to *me*," said Aru, throwing open the door and walking down the stairs.

Aru's birthday party started off *great*.

There was cake! And music! Plus, Mini and Kara had decorated the museum so that it looked like the inside of a fairy-tale carnival tent. Hira and Brynne—wearing matching chef hats—had made the food, which wrapped around the lobby in a delicious circle. Sheela sat in a corner, joyfully counting each string lightbulb, while Nikita stalked Aru's every move.

"Don't slouch!" Nikita scolded. "You're ruining the angle of the outfit! And stop doing that!"

"What?" asked Aru. "Breathing?"

"Do it more elegantly."

Aru responded by tweaking Nikita's nose.

Nikita was not amused.

Security was still too tight for Kara and Aru to have invited their human friends from high school, but the museum was plenty full, with classmates from the Otherworld, Rudy's "posse" of naga friends—who kept getting distracted by products of human ingenuity, like staplers—and a few adults. Gunky and Funky, plus Sheela and Nikita's parents, had insisted on "monitoring" them, which Aru thought was a little rude, but fine.

Honestly, things were going pretty well until Aru saw Kara tap Aiden on the shoulder. Aiden was the only one who hadn't wished Aru a happy birthday yet. Sure, he'd sung the song and clapped along with everyone else, but that was the bare minimum anyone had to do at a birthday party! Aru was *sure* he was going to say something to her. When she'd walked down the stairs, she could've sworn that he looked a little stunned for a moment.

Apparently, she was wrong.

Aiden bent down so Kara could whisper something in his ear. After a moment, he nodded toward the Hall of the Gods exhibit, which was supposed to be off-limits for guests....

Aru watched them leave, her stomach flipping.

Let them go, said part of her.

FOLLOW THEM AND FIND OUT WHAT'S HAPPENING! screamed the other part.

Aru swayed a bit, and then, with a loud huff, she wove in and out between her guests and silently followed Aiden and Kara.

She crouched behind a pillar near a mural showing the Pandava brothers in mid-battle. Aru had never liked looking at the painting—it was kinda gory, and Arjuna was super muscly and Aru was decidedly *not*—but now she didn't have a choice. She found herself face-to-face with Karna, the half brother of the Pandavas, and the sworn enemy of Arjuna.

She pushed the mural out of her thoughts as she strained to hear Aiden and Kara's conversation over the pulsing sounds of Rudy's music. Here and there, she caught bits and pieces...small talk about the weather and the party.

Boringggg, thought Aru, followed by *What about me?*

One of the nearby statues, a depiction of the god Krishna playing his lute, seemed to cast a scolding look at her.

Oh, c'mon, thought Aru. *You'd want to know, too.*

Maybe it was Aru's imagination, but the statue looked at her a little huffily, as if saying, *Would not!*

"I like you," said Kara, laughing a little. "I don't like keeping secrets or holding stuff in, and so I...I wanted to tell you."

Aru's stomach twisted. There it was. The thing she always knew, and now she'd made herself hear it. What was she doing here, lurking among the statues? She should leave. She should get back to her own birthday party and steal the cake and—

"Oh," said Aiden. He sounded confused. "Kara...I've always thought of you as a friend. A *good* friend, you know? I don't want to ruin that—"

Wait, what? Aru tried to crane her neck, but she couldn't see beyond Krishna, who was blocking her with that stern *STOP SNOOPING!* Face. Aru caught another muffled exchange, a loud sniff, and then Kara stormed out of the hall. A pang of sorrow hit Aru. She felt bad that Kara had been hurt, but—and maybe this made her a little terrible—she also felt relieved that she wasn't the only person who had been rejected by Aiden I-Only-Like-My-Camera Acharya.

Time to go, thought Aru.

She scuttled like a crab from behind one of the statues. She'd made it a couple of feet when a shadow fell over her. Aru looked up to see Aiden standing there, peering down as if he couldn't decide if he should laugh or scowl.

"*What* are you doing?" asked Aiden.

"Nothing!" said Aru, shooting up to her feet.

"I can see that," said Aiden. A moment later, he backed away, that familiar coldness closing up his expression. He averted his eyes and mumbled "I gotta go..." as he moved past her.

That's it, thought Aru. She'd had enough.

"What's your problem lately?" she blurted.

Aiden froze. He turned around to face her, hands shoved in his pockets. "I don't have a problem."

"Yeah, you *do*. With *me*," said Aru. "Do you hate me or something?"

"What?" said Aiden. "Of course not."

"Well, you've been acting like it! Whenever I enter a room, you leave it. If I say something, you act like you didn't hear it. I thought maybe it's because you were grossed out that I..."

Say it, said one part of her.

Don't say it, said another part.

"That you what, Shah?" asked Aiden.

"That I *like* you," said Aru in a rush. "And I know you don't like me. And I didn't ask you to! And I didn't make it awkward! Or, at least, I tried not to make it *more* awkward than I usually do, which is really freaking hard, and I was okay with just being friends, but now we're barely even friends and it's awful and—"

"Slow down a second, Shah," said Aiden, taking a step closer.

Aiden had grown even taller over the past few months, which was annoying, because Aru had to look up to glare at him, so it probably didn't have the same effect. She was mad, and her stomach was all twisted up, and since she'd already started blabbering, she might as well keep going. *"And,"* she said, taking a deep breath, "you didn't even wish me happy birthday! Which is so *rude*—"

Something happened.

Aru had one of those weird out-of-body moments, as if her brain was processing things at a lag. Suddenly, Aiden's face was a lot closer than it had been seconds ago. And then...whatever space lay between them was cinched closed.

Aiden Acharya kissed her.

An actual, real life, this-is-truly-happening-what-was-the-last-thing-I-ate *kiss*.

Aru's eyes flew wide open. Her mind kept trying to snatch at sensations: Aiden's warm mouth, and how he smelled like clean laundry and cooking spices. A bizarre terror spiked through her thoughts: What was she supposed to do with her *hands*? Was it rude that they were just hanging by her side? Should she pat him on the back?

Do NOT *pat him on the back,* warned a voice in her head.

A second—or maybe an eternity—later, Aiden pulled back. His dusk-colored eyes looked wide and…stunned? But not in a bad way.

"Happy birthday, Aru," he said.

Sometimes people talk about *fireworks* when it comes to kisses. As if the whole world is supposed to explode in joy. That wasn't how she felt. She felt like one gigantic, dorky grin. Like someone had poured sunlight down her veins, because she was warm all over.

But maybe you couldn't choose when the fireworks happened.

Because just then, right down the hall, something exploded. Aiden and Aru sprang apart as dust and plaster rained down from the ceiling. In the Hall of the Gods, the statues violently trembled, shaking atop their pedestals. On Aru's wrist, Vajra glowed a warning shade of silver and gold.

"What was that?" asked Aiden.

He tapped his wrists together, and his golden scimitars—one that was on permanent loan from the Nairrata—slashed out. A deep rumbling sound rolled through the museum. If Aru had felt like there was sunshine in her veins earlier, frost had quickly replaced it.

Brynne's mind message blared through her skull: *Aru, you need to get over here NOW.*

FORTY-TWO

Wait...Who? What? HOW?

Aru ran into the museum lobby, Aiden close behind her. The moment they turned the corner, her heart juddered to a stop. Minutes ago, her birthday party had been in full swing. Now it was a nightmare.

The colorful lights that had been strung across the ceiling were drooping dangerously low. The cake had fallen to the floor. Greg the elephant statue had burst apart, and his stone trunk lay in the middle of the dust-strewn floor. Most of the lobby had been swallowed up by a huge, murky sphere. Shadows wriggled across its surface like snakes. On the other side of it, Aru could see her sisters and friends...*frozen.* Aiden gasped.

It was just like the moment when she'd unleashed the Sleeper—when she'd lit the lamp and her life had changed forever. Brynne's and Mini's eyes were wide and unfocused, staring into nothing. Rudy was in mid-scream. Hira was crouched behind Brynne, her eyes squeezed shut....

"Happy birthday, Arundhati."

The Sleeper stepped out of the sphere, draped in darkness. He made a vague gesture to the museum lying in rubble around them.

"I apologize for barging in like this, but I wouldn't miss my daughter's fifteenth birthday for anything," he said. "And if all goes according to plan, I will never have to miss your birthday ever again."

He smiled at her, and then he turned his blue and brown eyes to her friends in suspended animation. "A powerful spell, I must admit—one I haven't used since our meeting three years ago. It's quite a draining endeavor, even though this version is a less powerful one. It will allow for exactly eleven minutes of stillness—more than enough time to convince you to let me back into your life."

"You made your choices," said Aru. She hated the way her voice was shaking. "And I've made mine. There's *no way* I'm joining you."

Next to her, Aiden clanged his scimitars together. Aru raised her lightning bolt, fury threading through her....

"Nuh-uh-uh," said the Sleeper, wagging a finger at her. "I wouldn't do that."

He took one step to the left and revealed Kara standing there, trembling, her wrists bound. The ring on her hand looked dull. There was a faint glow behind her, and Aru knew the beacon must have gone off.

The Sleeper frowned at Aiden, tilting his head to the side as annoyance rippled across his face. "Who is *this*? Were you *alone* with him?" he demanded. Then he started to laugh. "Ah, so this is what parenting feels like. Well, that's easily settled."

The Sleeper snapped his fingers, and Aiden went limp, falling to the ground.

"No!" cried Kara.

"What have you done?" screamed Aru, dropping to her knees.

Aiden's eyes were wide open, his lips parted. He was breathing, but he wouldn't move.

"He'll be fine," said the Sleeper, annoyed. "Though, considering his last thought was about a certain *kiss*, I'm not so certain he deserves—"

Across the lobby, the entry doors burst open. For a moment, Aru couldn't make out the figure silhouetted in the threshold. But then the person stepped forward, and Aru's heart threatened to burst.

"Mom!"

She'd come back!

"Get away from them!" Krithika yelled at her husband.

She raced across the lobby, and Aru ran toward her, completely sidestepping the Sleeper. She'd take any risk to hug her mom again.

Krithika Shah caught her in an embrace. Aru breathed deeply, fighting back a sob. She caught a trace of her mother's perfume... but her mom's body didn't feel the same. It was too thin, and the arms around Aru seemed frail. Aru pulled back to look into her face. It was almost skeletal, and now Aru could see the grime on her clothes and the way her mother struggled to stand.

"What happened to—?" Aru started to say, when a bright light illuminated the room.

Aru spun around, lifting her lightning bolt high, only to lower it when she saw that the light had come not from the Sleeper, but Kara. Aru's half sister gasped at the much brighter glow that now surrounded her. Aru was stunned. That beacon was supposed to alert Kara to the presence of the Sleeper, and also to her mom.... Did that mean...?

Aru looked between Krithika and Kara, and the similarities in their faces melded as comprehension struck her in the gut.

She and Kara didn't just share a father....

"*You're* my mom?" asked Kara, looking straight at Krithika. "But...how?"

Krithika said nothing. She just leaned harder on Aru, as if she were about to faint any second.

"I thought you never came looking for me because you couldn't," said Kara softly. Her eyes moved to Aru. "But I guess it was because you had a daughter you wanted to keep instead."

"No," said Krithika, fighting to speak. "It's not what you think, I swear it. I—"

"Oh, my Kara," said the Sleeper, wrapping his arm around her. "I never meant for you to find out this way. Pay no mind to your mother. She doesn't know what a treasure you are."

Kara was shaking. Silent tears streamed down her face.

"I'm no one," she said.

"You couldn't be more wrong, child," said the Sleeper. "Your mother wanted to hide the truth from you. *I* always planned to tell you, but first I had to make sure I could give you all that you deserve and—"

"Stop it," said Krithika hoarsely. "Enough! I've been watching you, Suyodhana, I see what—"

The Sleeper flicked his wrist, and Krithika crumpled. Aru caught her before she fell to the floor. Her eyes were open and straining, as if she could hear everything but say nothing.

Aru's jaw clenched. She swiveled Vajra in her hand and lunged toward the Sleeper.

At the same moment, he reached for Kara's neck. "You are *not* no one," he said. "You just never learned your true identity, because the name was never spoken in your presence. So I shall say it now...."

Aru took another step closer, only for the Sleeper to snap his fingers at her. Shadows leaped out of the tile floor and wrapped around her wrists and ankles, rooting her in place. She thrashed, and the astra necklace swung out from the neckline of her dress. Aru hoped the Sleeper wouldn't know what it was.

She was on the verge of summoning the Nairrata army with her mind when the Sleeper said, "You too bear the soul of a Pandava, Kara."

Overhead, a hole opened in the roof the museum, the plaster, wood beams, and slate tiles slowly dissolving to reveal the sunny sky above. A ray of light struck Kara in the face. She glowed, radiant and lovely, as the beam lifted her into the air....

"You were Claimed the moment you were born, when a drop of sunlight fell into your hand and you clutched it tight. You are the reincarnation of Karna. You are the daughter of Surya, god of the sun."

FORTY-THREE

Keeping Promises

Aru felt light-headed in that second.

Kara was a demigod. And not just any demigod, but the reincarnation of Karna, the son born to Arjuna's mother long before she was wed. The brother who spent his whole life battling the Pandavas, not knowing until it was too late that he was fighting his own family.

All the signs had been there, but somehow Aru hadn't seen them. The way Kara glowed. The fact that her weapon, Sunny, was a drop of sunlight forged into a trident. How she'd *felt* like a true sister all this time.

Aru...

Aru looked up. The Sleeper's spell was fading. Brynne and Mini were the first to struggle against their bindings. Their weapons glowed blue and violet. On the floor nearby, Aiden stirred weakly.

At that moment, Kara dropped back down to earth. The shadow ropes around her wrists had vanished. Her hazel eyes sheened gold as she looked between Aru, Krithika, and the Sleeper.

"I know your deepest desire, Kara," said the Sleeper in a gentle, loving tone that Aru found very disturbing. "All you have ever wished for is a family to call your own. I can give you that, my daughter. Everything I've told you is true. I took you away and raised you as my own so *I* could be the one to guide you to your true potential. And now I have found the path that will lead us to what we both want: a new chance."

"Don't listen to him," said Aru, straining toward Kara.

But Kara's attention was fixed on the Sleeper. "What do you mean?" she asked softly.

"You possess the power of light, Kara," said the Sleeper. "Only you can guide us through the darkness of the ever-moving labyrinth and lead us to the nectar of immortality. Then we can be a family. Me, you, Aru...even your mother. We can change time, so we never have to experience such pain again....Do you trust me, child?"

Tears streamed down Kara's face. The shadow-covered sphere holding everyone else at bay began to thin and grow translucent.

"Kara!" yelled Mini. "Don't listen to him!"

"Kara, *no*," said Aru.

"It's the only way, daughter," said the Sleeper solemnly. "Who will you trust? The family that did not want you, or the father who has chosen you?"

Krithika twitched on the ground, fighting her enchanted paralysis. Aru strained to move, to reach out her hand to Kara.

"We'll deal with this *together*," said Aru. "We've been through so much...."

Kara took a step toward her, and the Sleeper *tsked* softly.

"Your sister needs to learn what the word *together* means, Kara," he said. "The Pandavas never saw you for who you were.

Or perhaps they didn't *want* to? They nearly left you behind and didn't allow you to explore the full extent of your powers. And when you confided to this boy, where was Aru? Hiding behind a statue, watching you get humiliated ... waiting to take what you thought might be yours—"

"That's not true!" said Aru loudly. She faltered. Some of it was. "I mean, it wasn't like that...."

Kara appeared wounded, like every one of the Sleeper's accusations had stabbed her in the heart. Her eyes flitted to Aiden, who was pushing himself up from the ground. His gaze went straight to Aru.

"When have I ever lied to you, Kara?" asked the Sleeper. He put his hands on her shoulders. "I'm the one who has taken care of you. I'm the one who rescued you from a terrible home. I'm the only one who truly loves you—"

"That right there is a lie!" yelled Aru. "*We* love you, Kara. You're one of us!"

Kara's gaze flew to Krithika, who was looking at Aru. Then Kara turned to Aru, tears flowing down her face. "Did you know?" she asked quietly. "Did you know she was my mom, too?"

"No," said Aru. "No, I swear it, Kara. She—"

"We can't always trust the ones we love," said the Sleeper in his silky voice. Kara glanced at Aiden, hurt tugging at her mouth. The Sleeper bent down and whispered something in Kara's ear. Her eyes went wide. Then he drew back and said, "Do you really want our family to fight?"

Kara shook her head.

"Then come with me," said the Sleeper, holding out his hand. He addressed Aru. "This goes for you too, daughter. Everything I do is in service of our family."

"Wait, Kara. Don't go!" pleaded Aru.

On her wrist, Vajra flickered through shapes: one moment a bracelet, the next a ribbon of electricity furiously running up and down Aru's arms and legs as it tried in vain to free her from her shadow bindings.

Once more, Kara took a step toward Aru.

Aru sagged in relief. At the same moment, the sphere of enchantment faded completely. Brynne and Mini leaped to Aru's side of the lobby. Mini conjured shadows that whipped through the museum and Brynne sent a tornado spinning toward the Sleeper. He whirled on the two of them, casting out his hands. Light burst around the room as they battled, but Aru focused only on Kara walking toward her.

"Aru," she said, a sad look in her eyes.

"Cut me loose!" said Aru. "We'll fight him together!"

Kara pulled her into a sharp hug. "Families shouldn't fight."

"I know, but—" Aru started to say.

A rush of cold air hit her neck as the astra necklace fell off. Aru looked at the ground, stunned. Had the chain broken? That should have been impossible. Then she looked up and saw the gold pendant dangling from Kara's hand.

Aru's heart beat fast. "What are you doing?"

"I'm sorry, Aru," said Kara. "Please believe me when I tell you I'm doing this because I love you guys. I don't want to see any of you get hurt. I...I want us to be a real family. I told you before that I want to do *good* in the world, and I think...I think I finally know how."

A second too late, Aru realized what Kara was going to do. Her mind went frantic. She had made the rule herself: No one but a sister could take that weapon-destroying necklace from her. Kara *was* her sister. And so, when Kara twirled the astra over her head, Aru had no one to blame but herself for what happened next.

Dust and debris churned around them as a powerful gale swept through the lobby. Aru's bindings dissolved. The roof of the museum blew off, and everyone was sent flying backward, hitting the walls. The wind howled in Aru's ears, but it was nothing compared to Brynne's scream.

"NO!"

Brynne looked like she was tugging on something that hovered above her. Her wind mace, Gogo, flashed in and out of visibility. It seemed torn—one moment it glowed blue, and the next it unraveled, dissolving into the wind that swept out of the room.

At the same time, shadows leaked out of the ground, pooling and bubbling on the floor like butter sizzling in a hot pan. Mini cried out in surprise, yanking on her Death Danda, which had dropped by her feet and seemed stuck there.

"Wait! No, no, no!"

Dee Dee melted into the tiles.

Panic seized Aru. Vajra was next.

Stay with me, she commanded it.

As if sensing her growing fear, her lightning bolt shimmered and twisted around her, like an anxious cat.

Fight with me, thought Aru.

She lifted Vajra and her lightning bolt lengthened to a spear. With one last burst of energy, Aru lunged toward Kara.

"What have you *done?*" snarled Aru, bringing down Vajra. She wanted to slice the astra necklace straight out of Kara's hands.

But Kara was too quick. She ducked and lashed out with her light trident.

"Get everyone out of here!" Aru shouted over the din to the others.

Brynne, Mini, and Aiden grabbed hold of Rudy, Hira, and the twins, and fled to the front door. Nearby, Krithika lay slumped against the wall, unconscious, while the Sleeper got to his feet and watched his daughters with keen interest.

As Vajra and Sunny clanged against each other, the sound was like someone had thrown wind chimes into the washing machine.

"It's for your own good!" yelled Kara, pushing Aru off her with the trident. The necklace still dangled from one fist.

Aru swiped out her hand, missing the necklace by inches. She charged forward once more as storm clouds gathered in the open ceiling overhead. Thunder and lightning shattered the sky.

Vajra twisted out of Aru's reach. The lightning bolt trembled as something elemental stole across it. It no longer seemed like *hers*, but just a random fork of lightning that had fallen to earth.

"Vajra?" whispered Aru.

The weapon contorted in the air, its shining zigzag shape facing her one last time. Aru reached out to grab it when a peal of thunder echoed in the room, stopping her hand. With one last shudder, Vajra shot up into the sky and lit up the clouds.

Brynne, Mini, and Aiden reentered the lobby, and shadow restraints immediately leaped out of the floor once more, tethering them in place. Brynne had her fists up. Mini was holding a stick she must have found outside. Aiden still had his scimitars, but without Vajra's electricity roping down them, they were nothing more than ordinary blades.

Only Kara's weapon was still intact and active. Aru wondered why. Maybe because Kara was the one who had used the astra?

In the middle of the room, the Sleeper sighed loudly. "Let there be no ill will between you two," he said, beckoning Kara. He patted her head. "Kara was only being a dutiful daughter. When the world is remade, we will all be together, as a family."

Kara looked horrified by what she had done. She clutched Sunny to her chest, staring at the floor. The astra necklace lay there, its now dull and lifeless pendant broken in half.

Behind Aru, Krithika tried to stand, only to fall to her knees. "Don't," she croaked, her eyes on the Sleeper. "You promised me...."

For a moment, something human flashed in the Sleeper's eyes. Pain and sorrow, and so much . . . *longing*.

"I promised that, if I had to, I would break the world in half to make our family whole and happy," he said roughly. "I intend to keep that promise, Krithika."

Without another word, he and Kara vanished on the spot. The shadowy restraints released and melted into the ruined floor of the museum as Krithika Shah collapsed on the ground.

FORTY-FOUR

A Game of Hot Potato

Krithika Shah had been sleeping on the couch for exactly nine hours and twelve minutes.

Aru knew because she had been watching her practically the entire time. Occasionally, Aru's hand reflexively moved to her wrist, where she expected her lightning bolt bracelet to be...but Vajra was gone. All of their weapons were *gone*, leaving them powerless.

How had everything ended up so... *wrong*?

One moment, Aiden Acharya had kissed her, and it had been amazing.

The next moment, all of that was shattered.

Aru felt too numb to cry, and maybe that was a good thing, because she was worried that if she started crying now, she wouldn't be able to stop.

Mini and Brynne had taken turns waiting beside her. Both of them were just as shell-shocked. Brynne's eyes were red from crying, and Mini had barely said a word.

After Kara and the Sleeper had left, everything had become a chaotic blur. The moment Brynne, Mini, and Aiden had shuttled them outside, Sheela and Nikita had fled with their parents and taken Hira with them for safety. Gunky and Funky had sounded the Otherworld alarms. Rudy had immediately gone back to the underwater kingdoms to warn the nagas.

"I should go to Hanuman and Urvashi," said Aiden. "What do I tell them about…you know…the weapons?"

Aru felt another sharp twist of loss deep in her stomach. *Vajra*. The lightning bolt had left, unraveling into its true elemental form and fleeing through the broken roof to join the storm clouds overhead.

"Don't mention the weapons," said Brynne. "If they find out we don't have them anymore *and* we've lost the astra, they'll panic."

"Maybe they *should* panic. We *don't* have our weapons," said Mini, her voice hollow. "We can't fight the Sleeper anymore. We don't have…anything."

"We need time to think," said Aru. "To figure something out—"

"There's nothing to figure out, Shah," said Brynne sadly. "I don't even think *you* can get us out of this one. All I want is to buy some time before we have to answer to everyone….I just want some peace and quiet before all of this ends."

Aiden nodded, his face bleak. He left without saying another word.

In the growing dark, Aru studied her mom's face. "What did you see?" she asked her quietly. "Where did you go? And why didn't you tell me about Kara?"

A weird thing about sleep is that sometimes you don't even notice when it happens. One moment you're awake, and the next…

Aru found herself at what might have been a tea party out of *Alice in Wonderland*. She stood before a long wooden table under the shade of swaying dream willow trees, whose branches were strung with lights. Floating in the air were fancy cakes of all shapes and sizes, porcelain cups full of sunset-colored tea, and a giant banner that read:

HAPPY BIRTHDAY, ARU!

But there were no hosts or guests. Aru's heart sank. "Sheela? Nikita? Where are you guys?"

There was a little *pop!* sound as Nikita appeared before her. She wore a shiny pink pantsuit with white boots, and her hair was accented with a garland of flowers whose blossoms changed colors as they weaved between her braids. Beside her appeared Sheela, wearing a plain denim dress, her braided hair pulled back with constellation clips.

Sheela flung her arms tightly around Aru. "Your birthday was ruined."

Aru hugged her back. "That's kinda the least of my problems right now."

"The untrue sister broke your heart," said Sheela quietly.

Aru stilled. *The untrue sister.* The words of the prophecy came crashing around her.

One sister shall turn out not to be true....

For the past year, that phrase had haunted her. Every day, Aru had wondered, was she the untrue sister? Did the fact that she was the Sleeper's daughter mean that, no matter what she did, she would always end up being the villain?

Instead, the prophecy had been about *Kara*. The other Pandava. Krithika and the Sleeper's secret daughter…

But it didn't make sense to Aru. If Kara was *their* daughter, why had the Sleeper only gone on his quest to change his fate when he knew Aru was about to be born?

There was something off about the whole thing.…

Nikita's voice broke into Aru's thoughts. "What Sheela means is, this whole setup was supposed to be waiting for you after your actual birthday, and now the surprise is ruined." She snapped her fingers and the tea party began to fold itself up. "My entire party-planning itinerary is a bust."

"I think there's a lot more at stake here," said Aru, but Nikita tutted and huffed.

"I even *tried* not to outshine you with my outfit today," she said, crossing her arms. "Do you understand the level of sacrifice that required?"

"It was a big sacrifice," whispered Sheela. "She was mad all morning."

"So, what are you going to do next, Shah?" asked Nikita. "We can help. We've been training, you know. Even Brynne was pretty impressed."

Aru frowned. "You still have your powers?"

Nikita and Sheela looked at each other and then nodded.

"But the astra necklace … It destroys all godly weapons," said Aru. "Our Pandava powers—"

"We're not weapons," said Sheela simply. "Are we?"

"Eh," said Nikita dismissively. "We're definitely more than our weapons."

Out of nowhere, Aru heard Boo's voice: *You are more than the things you fight with.*

Was that still true?

She couldn't even imagine being a Pandava without Vajra by her side.

Then again, a lot of things she hadn't imagined had come to pass.

"Do you foresee anything?" Aru asked, turning to Sheela. "Anything at all that could help?"

Worry flitted across Nikita's face as she turned to her twin. Sheela appeared nervous for a moment and then she concentrated, closing her eyes tight and furrowing her forehead. When Sheela's eyes flew open, they looked frosted over as she said, *"Look for the crack and the sparkle —one to welcome, the other to spend. And ahead lies something new. No way to avoid the fire and pain, but at least now you know that you are true."*

Aru's dream shifted abruptly, bleeding at the edges until Sheela and Nikita disappeared.

In her next dream, her mother was shaking her awake. The apartment was totally dark, and a little cold.

"Aru?" said Krithika. "Wake up, beta."

Aru blinked.

It wasn't a dream.

"Mom!" cried Aru.

Krithika wrapped her in a hug.

Aru had fallen asleep on the floor next to the couch. She sat up, her eyes adjusting to the light. It was a new day already, and the room was empty. "Where are Mini and Brynne?"

"I sent them home. They're just as distraught as you are, and besides, you and I need to talk," said Krithika. "I owe you an explanation."

"Yeah," said Aru, climbing onto the couch. "You do."

Krithika sighed. "Let me get some tea."

It seemed to take Krithika forever to go to the kitchen, fill the kettle with water, and light the burner under it.

"Start with Kara," said Aru.

Krithika rummaged in the cabinet for her box of tea. Finally, with her back to Aru, she began to talk.

"Before I met your father, and when I was much younger, I fell in love with someone who later died in a car accident. It was only afterward that I found out I was going to have Kara. I was young—too young, I felt, to handle a baby on my own," said Krithika. "I'd known before then that I was a *panchakanya*, destined to carry a future Pandava, but I wasn't expecting it at that time. I didn't know what that would mean for me or for... for Kara. In the end, I went to the edge of the Otherworld, where there are yakshas capable of keeping people frozen in a moment of time. I asked them to preserve Kara as a newborn until I could return, and they promised to hold her for ten years. If I didn't come back by then, they would place her with someone who would take care of her and raise her as their own."

The kettle whistled loudly. Krithika startled, then reached for a mug. She dropped in her tea bag, poured boiling water over it, then slowly and carefully made her way to the couch.

"I thought I'd easily be able to get back to her before my time was up," said Krithika, sitting beside Aru. "But then... so many things happened. I met Suyodhana. We learned of the prophecy... and then I found out I was going to have *you*. Suyodhana left, and when he returned, I... I trapped him in the lamp. When I finally had the chance to go back to the yakshas, it was too late. Kara had been adopted by a wonderful family in

California who loved her." Krithika stared into the steam rising from her tea. Her gaze looked faraway.

Aru was vibrating with rage. So the Sleeper *wasn't* Kara's father? And if she was with a loving family, then all that stuff about rescuing her from a bad situation was a *lie*. Kara had betrayed them for a lie. And maybe she never would have betrayed them at all if Krithika had just told Aru the truth about everything from the start.

"I went to visit Kara and her new family," Krithika continued. "I don't know what I thought I was going to do. Over a week's time, I never even summoned the nerve to knock on their front door. I ended up just watching them take walks and play with her outside."

"You mean you *stalked* them," said Aru. Her mother was surprising her more with every sentence.

Krithika winced. "What I did wasn't right, but at least I saw she could be happy there. I knew she'd have a chance at a normal life, one I couldn't give her."

Did that mean Aru's life was *abnormal*? Well, yeah, it was, pretty much.

"Kara said the Sleeper wiped her memories so she wouldn't have nightmares about that family," said Aru.

Krithika's grip on her tea mug turned white-knuckled and her lip trembled. "Don't listen to him, Aru. He may remember who he once was and what he once dreamed of, but he's gone over the edge. He'll say anything now, *do* anything to get what he wants."

Aru believed it. She remembered the look of pain that had crossed his face before he said, *I promised that, if I had to, I would break the world in half to make our family whole and happy.*

Aru thought back to the man he had once been, the man who'd traveled the world looking for a way just to be her dad....

That man was still inside the Sleeper, but he wasn't strong enough to come out.

Aru felt a fresh burst of pain—for herself, for her parents... and for her sister. All this time, Kara had only wanted a family. She'd actually had two—one adopted, and one biological. But the Sleeper had stolen both from her.

Krithika brought her shaking mug to her lips. "If I'd thought for an *instant* that my daughter was in an unsafe home, I would've done something."

"Did you know she was the reincarnation of Karna?" asked Aru.

Krithika shook her head. "No. I didn't think that was possible. I learned that the same moment you did, after I got home."

"From where?" asked Aru, her voice trembling. "We didn't see you for *months*, Mom...."

Krithika took a deep breath. "Every time you went away on a mission, I went on one of my own, to gather information. I knew the Sleeper was after the nectar of immortality, and I've been looking for clues about where it might be. The devas put it under a protective spell so the location of the labyrinth it's in changes with the moon. Most of *them* don't even know where it is at any given time." She lowered her voice. "According to a secret message I discovered, the only light that can reveal the path to it must come from the sun itself."

Understanding flooded through Aru.

"At first I thought that meant the amrita was far underground, or deep in the sea," Krithika said furtively. "But clearly he thinks Kara is the key to everything. After all, she came from the sun. If she has powers of light and truth, she might be able to see something that others cannot."

Aru felt like she was fighting for breath. With Kara by his side, the Sleeper had the capability not only to find the amrita, but also to make her summon the Nairrata army. Only those who wielded godly weapons could control the golden soldiers, and thanks to Kara, that no longer included Aru, Brynne, or Mini.

"So that's it, then," said Aru. "Everything we did to protect the Otherworld...It's just...gone. None of it mattered."

"I wasn't finished, beta," said Krithika, resting her hand against Aru's back. She continued in a whisper, even though no one was around to listen. "I think I know where the labyrinth is, and it will only be there until the full moon."

"So?"

"So...that's ten days from now," said Krithika. "We still have time to—"

"Time," repeated Aru dully. "What do you know about time, Mom? You were away *forever*."

Krithika averted her eyes, hurt. "When you get that far into the Otherworld, time moves differently—you've experienced the same thing. That's why I was gone for so long. But as soon as I realized what he was planning, I came back. The battle for Lanka was just the beginning. A test, I think, of both you and Kara."

Ten days.

Ten days to do *what*, exactly? wondered Aru.

Even if, by some bizarre stroke of luck, they actually got their celestial weapons back, how would they get to the amrita before the Sleeper? Besides, the only person who could help them find the nectar had left with him.

"Do you hate me, Aru?" asked her mother softly. "I haven't

been there for you enough, I know, and I tried to shelter you from the truth. But I never meant to hurt you. I thought I was doing—"

"The right thing?" finished Aru. The phrase reminded her of Kara.

Her mother nodded, silent tears running down her cheeks.

For a long time, Aru had been angry. Her fury was like a raging inferno, but eventually it had burned down to ashes, leaving her with nothing but pity. She pitied Boo, her dad, her mom, and Kara, and that pity made her calm.

Aru reached out and pulled Krithika into a hug. "I don't hate you, Mom."

I feel sorry for you, she thought, but didn't say aloud.

Krithika hugged her back tightly. "I'm not leaving you alone again, and I know how to help you this time."

"There's nothing to help with," said Aru, pulling back. "It's all over—"

A faint *cheep!* cut her off. *What was that?* Aru thought she'd imagined the sound when a louder, more insistent *cheep!* followed. It was coming from the sweater nest in the alcove by the door. Aru had given the egg a kiss and asked it for good luck right before entering her birthday party.

A flutter of nerves built up inside her chest as Aru crossed the room now. Sure enough, the Boo egg had begun to crack. Little bits of ruby-bright eggshell had fallen to the ground.

Cheep!

One piece of shell bounced off something shiny on the floor. Aru saw that her backpack had tipped over and spilled its contents: an empty packet of Twizzlers, a half-empty bottle of hand sanitizer, and that gold coin from Agni, the god of fire.

IO(F)U, it said on it (which Aru still thought sounded rude). Incendiary Offers for Future Use.

Aru bent down and picked it up, remembering Agni's words. *I have an arsenal of weapons that you will have need of.... When that time comes, call on me.*

Aru held her breath, staring around the room. What was it that Sheela had said? *Look for the crack and the sparkle.* Aru glanced at the Boo egg slowly breaking and the shiny coin in her hands.

She'd found both.

Ahead lies something new....

No way to avoid the fire and pain, but at least now you know that you are true....

Something new, thought Aru. In that second, it seemed like someone had opened a window, letting in light and fresh air.

Aru tapped into the Pandava mind link: *I'm calling an emergency meeting of the Potatoes. Come ASAP.*

FORTY-FIVE

I Don't Want to Be Frodo

The Potatoes assembled in the museum lobby within an hour. Greg was totally out of commission, but the front door still worked and so did the portal that Urvashi had installed in Aiden's house a couple of months back. A team of yakshas sent by Hanuman and Urvashi had just finished repairing the museum's broken ceiling and floors, leaving the Potatoes alone in the lobby. Their faces were downcast, their hands shoved in their pockets.

"Where are Sheela and Nikita?" asked Aru.

"We can't call the twins over without telling their parents," said Brynne, "and then they'd want to know why, and—"

"They'd find out we lost our weapons," finished Aru.

Brynne nodded, her fingers almost going to her neck, where she used to wear Gogo as a choker. She dropped her hand abruptly.

"Is this meeting about telling Hanuman and Urvashi what happened?" asked Mini. "We can't keep this a secret forever. If people are running around thinking we can protect them when we can't—"

"We *can*," said Aru. "I think we have other options. But before I tell you, I need to show you something. C'mon."

Aru led them upstairs. Krithika's bedroom door was shut so she could get some rest, but Aru had set up a surprise at the end of the hallway, on the windowsill.

Cheep!

Mini stopped short. "Is that...? Oh my god...Is it—?"

Brynne ran to the sweater nest.

"It's hatching!" said Aiden.

"Get your camera ready, Ammamma!"

Aiden lifted Shadowfax, but not before glancing at Aru. She pretended she didn't see him looking at her. They hadn't really spoken to each other since *the kiss*, and now Aru wasn't sure what to do. It's not like she could casually ask, *So...WHAT WAS THAT?* Could she?

One thing at a time, Shah, Aru told herself. *Starting with* this.

They all watched as larger pieces of the Boo egg fell away.

"Awww," said Rudy. "This looks just like my baby photos in the family album."

Everyone went silent. Rudy looked confused. "You guys weren't hatched in two hundred days?"

"No?" said Mini.

"Humans are weird."

Mini was about to argue with him, but just then the remains of the ruby egg caught fire. Aru jumped back and almost screamed before the blaze went out suddenly. There, in a smoldering pile of ashes, sat a baby bird no bigger than Aru's thumb. *Cheep!* The chick looked like a living flame, its fragile wings haloed with smoke. On top of its head wavered a burning blue crest.

"Boo?" said Mini, leaning closer.

Cheep!

"Is that really him?" asked Aiden.

"Well, we don't know if it's a him," said Brynne.

"Only one way to find out if it's got Boo's soul," said Aru.

She reached into her pocket, pulled out a packet of Oreos, and waved it in front of the baby bird's face. Immediately, it squawked and cheeped, flapping its wings until the end of the hall turned hotter than a furnace.

"Okay, okay, we believe you!" said Aru happily.

Baby Boo chirped again, then shook out his feathers. Mini held out her hand, and he hopped onto it, nestling happily in her palm. . . .

"Ow! Ow! Ow!" said Mini, doing a little jig. "Hot baby! Very hot—"

Brynne blew on Mini's hands, but that only made the flames around Baby Boo rise higher. He gave a delighted *chirp!*

"I got him," said Brynne, taking the chick. "*OWWW!* I do not got! Help!"

It was somehow the best and worst game of Hot Potato between the Potatoes. It ended with Aiden and Rudy fighting over who got to hold the chick longer.

"You already had your turn!" said Rudy, trying to wrench Baby Boo out of Aiden's hands. "Gimme!"

"You tried to feed him a diamond!" said Aiden.

"I was just showing it to him! Everyone loves shiny things!"

"It's *irresponsible*," said Aiden, bouncing Baby Boo in his hands.

"Why are you the worst?" grumbled Rudy. "He's going to like me more anyway when he grows up."

"I guess Boo left his pigeon form behind," said Aru, eyeing the chick's scarlet fluff.

"But what *is* he now? Some kind of . . . fire bird?" asked Mini. She looked worried. "How will we ever be able to tell if he has a fever? Are there veterinarians for magical creatures? What about food and—"

Cheep... zzz.

Boo had fallen asleep in Aiden's hands.

Mini smiled. She reached out to stroke his head, then yelped and blew on her burned finger. "I guess we can worry about it later."

"Speaking of later," said Aru, "there's something we need to do."

She pulled out the IO(F)U from Agni, then told them about what her mom had learned and Sheela's prophecy. Brynne's eyebrows shot up her forehead. Mini stared at the ticket, her mouth wide open.

"So...maybe we can get the weapons back?" asked Mini.

"I don't know for sure," said Aru. "But we only have ten days until the full moon, when the Sleeper and Kara can open the labyrinth. It's our only chance."

"Do you know how to find Agni?" asked Brynne.

"Nope."

"Do we have a backup plan?" asked Mini.

"Nope."

"Do we have... *any* plan?" asked Aiden.

"Nope," said Aru. "So, you with me, or no?"

"Yes, obviously," said Mini immediately.

Aru's heart lifted, and she grinned. "If you're really with me, you have to say the thing."

"Seriously, Aru?" sighed Brynne.

"Um, *yeah*," said Aru, crossing her arms. "Plus, I'm calling today an extension of my birthday. Deal. This is *it*, Potatoes. This is *the* last battle. So yeah, I want to hear you say the thing."

Mini took a deep breath. Then she sighed and said in her best Aragorn impression, "If by my life or death I can protect you, I will...."

Mini looked pointedly at Aiden.

"You have my sword," said Aiden.

Mini whispered to Rudy: "Say 'And you have my bow.'"

"But I don't have a bow?" whispered Rudy.

"Just say it. You know how Aru feels about *Lord of the Rings*."

"Can I have a bow after this?" asked Rudy. "No one else has one. I want my own weapon—"

"YES, Rudy, we will get you a bow," said Aiden. "Now just say the line."

"And you have my bow," said Rudy smugly.

The Potatoes turned to Brynne, who scowled.

"Why am I always Gimli in this scenario? I'm literally the tallest person here—"

Mini elbowed her.

"Ugh," said Brynne. *"And my ax."*

Boo sleepily lifted his head, adding, *Cheep.*

Aru smiled. It was kinda like what Kara had said days ago, when she was talking about that poem. Hope *was* the thing with feathers. It lifted the part of her that had been stomped in the dirt. Hope made her look out the window to the sun rising higher in the sky. Hope might be all that they had left, but it was something she needed to cling to, because it meant that even though things were awful...

They were far from over.

Glossary

MWA-HA-HA. I'VE LURED YOU HERE AGAIN. YAY ME! So, you know the drill by now, but indulge me anyway.... This glossary is by no means exhaustive or encapsulating of all the nuances of mythology. India is GINORMOUS, and these myths and legends vary from state to state. What you read here is merely a slice of what *I* understand from the stories *I* was told and the research *I* conducted. The wonderful thing about mythology is that its arms are wide enough to embrace many traditions from many regions. My hope is that this glossary gives you context for Aru's world, and perhaps nudges you to do some research of your own. ☺

Agni (UHG-nee) The Hindu god of fire.

Airavata (AY-rah-vat-uh) A white elephant! And no, not the terrible Christmas tradition where someone steals the present you were secretly excited about because they're actual Grinches. Airavata is said to be the king of the elephants, and he spends his time joyously knitting clouds. He supposedly arose out of the churning of the Ocean of Milk.

Amaravati (uh-MAR-uh-vah-tee) So, I have suffered the great misfortune of never being invited to/having visited this legendary city, but I hear it's, like, *amazing*. It has to be, considering it's the place where Lord Indra lives. It's overflowing with gold palaces and has celestial gardens full of a thousand marvels. I wonder what the flowers would smell like there. I imagine they smell like birthday cake, because it's basically heaven.

Ammamma (UH-muh-mah) *Grandmother* in Telugu, one of the many languages spoken in India, most commonly in the southern area.

Amrita (am-REE-tuh) The immortal drink of the gods. According to the legends, Sage Durvasa once cursed the gods to lose their immortality. To get it back, they had to churn the celestial Ocean of Milk. But in order to accomplish this feat, they had to seek assistance from the asuras, another semidivine race of beings who were constantly at war with the devas. In return for their help, the asuras demanded that the devas share a taste of the amrita. Which, you know, *fair*. But to gods, the word *fair* is just another word. So they tricked the asuras. The supreme god Vishnu, also known as the preserver, took on the form of Mohini, a beautiful enchantress. The asuras and devas lined up in two rows. While Mohini poured the amrita, the asuras were so mesmerized by her beauty that they didn't realize that she was giving *all* the immortality nectar to the gods and not them. Rude! By the way, I have no idea what amrita tastes like. Probably birthday cake.

Apsara (AHP-sah-rah) Apsaras are beautiful heavenly dancers who entertain in the Court of the Heavens. They're often the wives of heavenly musicians. In Hindu myths, apsaras are usually sent on errands by Lord Indra to break the meditation of sages who are getting a little too powerful. It's pretty hard to keep meditating when a celestial nymph starts dancing in front of you. And if you scorn her affection (as Arjuna did in the *Mahabharata*), she might just curse you. Just sayin'.

Aranyani (UH-rahn-YAH-nee) The Hindu goddess of forests and animals, who is married to the god of horsemanship, Revanta.

Ashvin Twins (ASH-vin) The gods of sunrise and sunset, and healing. They are the sons of the sun god, Surya, and fathers of the Pandava twins, Nakula and Sahadeva. They're considered the doctors of the gods and are often depicted with the faces of horses.

Astra (AH-struh) Supernatural weapons that are usually summoned into battle by a specific chant and are often paired to a specific deity. These days, I'm pretty sure it just means any weapon.

Asura (AH-soo-rah) A sometimes good, sometimes bad race of semidivine beings. They're most popularly known from the story about the churning of the Ocean of Milk.

Bhishma (BEE-shmah) One of the great warriors of the *Mahabharata*, who famously took a vow not to wed or sire any children. As the son of the river goddess, Ganga, he was nearly invincible and unmatched in battle. He was the eighth child of Ganga and King Shantanu, his seven brothers having been drowned one by one. Seems dramatic? You have no idea. You see, Bhishma was the reincarnation of one of the eight Vasus, or elemental deities. One day, his brothers saw a really cool-looking cow and stole it. BIG MISTAKE. The sage who owned the cow cursed them to become mortals on earth. Naturally, they were horrified. (Ugh! Cell phone plans? Human politicians? SPARE ME!) One of the Vasus agreed to take the full weight of the punishment and live a whole life on earth as Bhishma. And so when the other seven Vasus were reborn as mortals, they were allowed to escape mortality by dying and being reincarnated. Bhishma was, I guess, saved from drowning but doomed to live? Every tragedy or victory depends on how you look at it.

Brahma (BRUH-mah) The creator god in Hinduism, and part of the triumvirate represented by Lord Vishnu, the preserver, and Lord Shiva, the destroyer.

Brahmastra (BRUH-mah-struh) The most powerful weapon, created by Lord Brahma, god of creation, and capable of destroying the world.

Chhaya (CHAI-yuh) The goddess of shadows and wife of Surya, Lord of the Sun. Chhaya has a rather interesting origin story. Surya's first wife, Saranyu, could *not* stand her husband's heat, so she fled and left her shadow in her place. That shadow was Chhaya, who then had three children of her own with Surya. When he eventually figured out this was his wife's shadow, he reunited with Saranyu and they all lived together in what I'm sure was an extremely functional, not-awkward-at-all household.

Danda (DAHN-duh) A giant punishing rod that is often considered the symbol of the Dharma Raja, the god of the dead.

Devas (DEH-vahz) The Sanskrit term for the race of gods.

Dharma Raja (DAR-mah RAH-jah) The Lord of Death and Justice, also called Yama, and the father of the oldest Pandava brother, Yudhistira. His mount is a water buffalo.

Goloka (go-LOW-kuh) The realm of cows. Have I ever been able to find said planet? No. Does this upset me? Yes. I am envisioning lots of free ice cream.

Hanuman (HUH-noo-mahn) One of the main figures in the Indian epic the *Ramayana*, who was known for his devotion to the god king Rama and Rama's wife, Sita. Hanuman is the son of Vayu, the god of the wind, and Anjana, an apsara. He had lots of mischievous exploits as a kid, including mistaking the sun for a mango and trying to eat it. There are still temples and shrines dedicated to Hanuman, and he's often worshipped by wrestlers because of his incredible strength. He's the half brother of Bhima, the second-oldest Pandava brother.

Holi (HO-lee) A major Hindu festival, also known as the "festival of colors" or "festival of love," in which people feast and throw colored powders at one another. There are many different interpretations of the meaning of Holi and what the colors signify, depending on which region of India one's family is from. My family celebrates the triumph of good over evil, represented by the tale of Narasimha (see: **Narasimha**), who protected the devout son of a demon king.

Indra (IN-druh) The king of heaven, and the god of thunder and lightning. He is the father of Arjuna, the third-oldest Pandava brother. His main weapon is Vajra, a lightning bolt. He has two vahanas: Airavata, the white elephant who spins clouds, and Uchchaihshravas, the seven-headed white horse. I've got a pretty good guess what his favorite color is....

Kalpavriksha (kuhl-PUHV-rik-shaw) A divine wish-fulfilling tree. It is said to have roots of gold and silver, with boughs encased in costly jewels, and to reside in the paradise gardens of the god Indra. Sounds like a pretty useful thing to steal. Or protect. Just saying.

Kamadhenu (KAH-mah-DAY-new) The human-faced cow goddess, and goddess of plenty, for she provides milk and nourishment. She is also called the Mother of Cows, which to me seems way cooler than Mother of Dragons. All cows are considered sacred in Hinduism because they are manifestations of Kamadhenu.

Karna (CAR-nuh) Karna is the son of Surya and Queen Kunti, mother of the Pandavas. He is the archenemy of Arjuna. When Kunti found out that she could use a divine boon and ask any of the gods to give her a child, she didn't believe it. So . . . she tested it out on Surya, which resulted in Karna's birth. But Kunti was unmarried and a teenager. Out of fear, she abandoned Karna in a basket by the river, where he was found and raised by a kind charioteer. Karna became one of the most gifted and noble of warriors. He was a loyal friend of Duryodhana, the archenemy of the Pandavas. Karna was a rather tragic figure to me growing up. He's someone who was rejected a lot because of his perceived low birth, and yet he tried his best to honor and love the people who loved him back. Was he perfect? Nope. But I think he tried to do more good in the world than evil. And perhaps that's what matters most.

King Vali (VAH-lee) Vali, the son of Indra, was king of the vanaras and husband to Tara. He was blessed with the ability to take half his opponent's strength in any fight. He was killed by the god king Rama. While fighting against his brother, Rama hid behind a tree and shot him from behind.

Kishkinda (kish-KIN-duh): Home of the vanaras, the semi-monkey race.

Krishna (KRISH-nah) A major Hindu deity. He is worshipped as the eighth reincarnation of the god Vishnu and also as a supreme ruler in his own right. He is the god of compassion, tenderness, and love, and is popular for his charmingly mischievous personality.

Kubera (KOO-bear-uh) The god of riches and ruler of the legendary golden city of Lanka. He's often depicted as a dwarf adorned with jewels.

Kunti (KOON-tee) One of the panchakanya, or legendary women, and mother of the Pandavas. As a young woman, Kunti was given the boon to invoke any of the gods to bless her with a child. This resulted in the births of Karna, Yudhistira, Bhima, and Arjuna. Nakula and Sahadeva were the children of her co-queen, Madri, with whom she shared the blessing.

Lanka (LAHN-kuh) The legendary city of gold, sometimes ruled over by Kubera, sometimes ruled over by his demonic brother, Ravana. Lanka is a major setting in the epic poem the *Ramayana*.

Laxmana (LUCK-shmun) The younger brother of Rama and his aide in the Hindu epic the *Ramayana*. Sometimes he's considered a quarter of Lord Vishnu. Other times, he's considered the reincarnation of Shesha, the thousand-headed serpent and king of all nagas, devotee of Vishnu.

Mahabharata (MAH-hah-BAR-ah-tah) One of two Sanskrit epic poems of ancient India (the other being the *Ramayana*). It is an important source of information about the development of Hinduism between 400 BCE and 200 CE and tells the story of the struggle between two groups of cousins, the Kauravas and the Pandavas.

Maruts (MAH-roots) Minor storm deities often described as violent and aggressive and carrying lots of weapons. Legend says the Maruts once rode through the sky, splitting open clouds so that rain could fall on the earth.

Mohini (moe-HIH-nee) One of the avatars of Lord Vishnu, known as the goddess of enchantment. The gods and asuras banded together to churn the Ocean of Milk on the promise that the nectar of immortality would be shared among them. But the gods didn't want immortal demon counterparts, so Mohini tricked the asuras by pouring the nectar into the goblets of the gods while smiling over her shoulder at the demons.

Naga (**nagas**, pl.) (NAG-uh) A naga (male) or nagini (female) is one of a group of serpentine beings who are magical and, depending on the region in India, considered divine. Among the most famous nagas is Vasuki, one of the king serpents who was used as a rope when the gods and asuras churned the Ocean of Milk to get the elixir of life. Another is Uloopi, a nagini princess who fell in love with Arjuna, married him, and used a magical gem to save his life

Naga-Loka (NAG-uh-LOW-kuh) The abode of the naga people, or snake-people. It's said that Naga-Loka is a place strewn with precious jewels. Again, deeply disappointed to have received no invite.

Nairrata (NAY-rah-tuh) The vast army controlled by Kubera, Lord of Wealth and Treasure.

Nakula (nuh-KOO-luh) The most handsome Pandava brother, and a master of horses, swordsmanship, and healing. He is the twin of Sahadeva, and they are the children of the Ashvin twins.

Narasimha (NUHR-sihm-hah) A fearsome avatar of Lord Vishnu. Once, there was a demon king who was granted a boon. In typical tyrant fashion, he asked for invincibility, specifically: "I don't want to be killed at daytime or nighttime, indoors or outdoors, by man or by beast, or by any weapon." Then he was like "GOTCHA!" and proceeded to wreak havoc on the world. The only one who didn't fall in line with his plans was his son, Prahlad, who devoutly worshipped Lord Vishnu. To protect Prahlad and defeat the demon king, Vishnu appeared one day in the demon king's courtyard (not indoors or outdoors); at dusk (not daytime or nighttime); in the form of a man with the head of a lion (not by man or by beast) and then dragged the king onto his lap and ripped him apart with his claws (not a weapon)! And that, children, is why you should always have a lawyer review your wishes. Loopholes are persnickety things. Why the gods went to all that trouble is a mystery to me. After all, they could've just sent a girl. Bam! Riddle solved.

Navagraha (NUHV-grah-huh) The nine heavenly bodies (planets) that influence humans.

Pandava brothers (Arjuna, Yudhistira, Bhima, Nakula, and Sahadeva) (PAN-dah-vah, ar-JOO-nah, yoo-diss-TEE-ruh, BEE-muh, nuh-KOO-luh, saw-hah-DAY-vuh) Demigod warrior princes, and the heroes of the epic *Mahabharata* poem. Arjuna, Yudhistira, and Bhima were born to Queen Kunti, the first wife of King Pandu. Nakula and Sahadeva were born to Queen Madri, the second wife of King Pandu.

Queen Tara (TAH-ruh) The apsara wife and queen of King Vali of the vanaras. Tara is said to have placed a curse on the god king Rama out of grief when he slew her husband.

Rakshasa (RUCK-shaw-sah) A rakshasa (male) or rakshasi (female) is a mythological being, like a demigod. Sometimes good and sometimes bad, they are powerful sorcerers, and can change shape to take on any form.

Rama (RAH-mah) The hero of the epic poem the *Ramayana*. He was the seventh incarnation of the god Vishnu.

Ramayana (RAH-mah-YAWN-uh) One of the two great Sanskrit epic poems (the other being the *Mahabharata*), it describes how the god king Rama, aided by his brother and the monkey-faced demigod Hanuman, rescued his wife, Sita, from the ten-headed demon king, Ravana.

Ravana (RAH-vah-nah) A character in the Hindu epic the *Ramayana*, where he is depicted as the ten-headed demon king who stole Rama's wife, Sita. Ravana is described as having once been a follower of Shiva. He was also a great scholar, a capable ruler, a master of the *veena* (a musical instrument), and someone who wished to overpower the gods. He's one of my favorite antagonists, to be honest, because it just goes to show that the line between heroism and villainy can be a bit murky.

Revanta (REH-vahnt-ah) The god of horses, and the youngest son of Lord Surya. He is the consort of Aranyani, goddess of the forest.

Sahadeva (SAW-hah-DAY-vuh) The twin to Nakula, and the wisest of the Pandavas. He was known to be a great swordsman and also a brilliant astrologist, but he was cursed that if he should disclose events before they happened, his head would explode.

Salwar kameez (SAL-war KAH-meez) A traditional garment composed of a tunic and pants, often with a *dupatta* (scarf) to accent the piece.

Sanskrit (SAHN-skrit) An ancient language of India. Many Hindu scriptures and epic poems are written in Sanskrit.

Saranyu (SAW-rahn-yoo) The goddess of evening, and wife of Surya. She is the mother of Yama and Yamuna, and once fled her husband's home because it was too bright.

Shani (SHAH-nee) The Lord of Saturn and also the Lord of Justice. One day, his wife was super annoyed that he wasn't bothering to look at her (#relatable) and cursed him so that his gaze would be forever devastating, thus forcing his eyes always downward. But the curse was eventually lifted when, based on his karmic actions, he took on the title Lord of Justice.

Shikhandi (SHEE-kahn-DEE) Shikhandi is one of the heroes of the *Mahabharata*. In a previous life, he was Princess Amba, who swore revenge on Bhishma for ruining her life. Amba performed lots of penance to be the one to kill the invincible Bhishma, and did so in her reincarnation as Shikhandi.

Shiva (SHEE-vuh) One of the three main gods in the Hindu pantheon, often associated with destruction. He is also known as the Lord of Cosmic Dance. His consort is Parvati.

Sindhoor (SIN-door) A traditional mark of vermilion used to distinguish a married woman.

Sita (SEE-tuh) The reincarnation of Lakshmi, goddess of wealth and fortune, and consort of Lord Vishnu. Sita was the long-suffering wife of the god king Rama in the *Ramayana*. Her kidnapping by the demon king Ravana sparked an epic war.

Sugriva (SOO-gree-vuh) Brother of King Vali of the vanaras. Once, when the brothers fought a demon, Sugriva thought Vali was dead and returned to his kingdom and took his place as ruler of Kishkinda . . . and even married Vali's wife. When Vali eventually fought his way out, he was *not* pleased. He banished Sugriva, because he believed that he had intended to depose him the whole time. Eventually, Sugriva met Rama in the forest. Sugriva offered to help Rama win back Sita, and Rama offered to help him regain his lost status and wife, who had been vengefully taken as a second queen by Vali.

Surya (SOOR-yuh) The god of the sun, and father of many divine children and the demigod Karna.

Takshaka (TAHK-shah-kah) A naga king and former friend of Indra who once lived in the Khandava Forest before Arjuna helped burn it down, killing most of Takshaka's family. He swore vengeance on all the Pandavas ever since. Wonder why...

Tapti (TUP-tee) A river goddess of renowned beauty whose name means *the burning one*. She is the daughter of Surya and the mother of Kuru, the ancestral king who lent his name to Kurukshetra, another name for the war in the *Mahabharata*.

Urvashi (OOR-vah-shee) A famous apsara, considered the most beautiful of all the apsaras. Her name literally means *she who can control the hearts of others*.

Uttanka (ooh-TUHN-kuh) Uttanka was a revered sage who was granted the boon of being able to demand water whenever he wished. One day, Lord Krishna, wanting to honor his devotee, decided to give him amrita, the nectar of immortality. But Lord Indra devised a test. He appeared to Uttanka as a dirty, wandering hunter and offered him a waterskin that looked decidedly unhygienic. Uttanka, disgusted, refused what was offered and lost the chance to become immortal. Oof. Tough tomatoes.

Vanaras (VAH-nah-ruhs) A supernatural race of monkey-like people who lived in Kishkinda Kingdom. Most notably, they assisted the god king Rama in building a bridge across the sea that went from Kishkinda all the way to Lanka.

Vishnu (VISH-noo) The second god in the Hindu triumvirate (also known as the Trimurti). These three gods are responsible for the creation, upkeep, and destruction of the world. The other two gods are Brahma and Shiva. Brahma is the creator of the universe, and Shiva is the destroyer. Vishnu is worshipped as the preserver. He has taken many forms on earth in various avatars, most notably as Krishna, Mohini, and Rama.

Yaksha (YAHK-sha) A yaksha (male) or yakshini (female) is a supernatural being from Hindu, Buddhist, and Jain mythology. Yakshas are attendees of Kubera, the Hindu god of wealth.

Yama (YAH-muh) See: **Dharma Raja.**

Yamuna (yuh-MOO-nah) A highly worshipped river goddess and also the name of one of the largest tributary rivers in India. Yamuna is the daughter of the sun god, Surya, and sister to Yama, the god of death.

Coming in Spring 2022

ARU SHAH AND THE
NECTAR OF IMMORTALITY